D0829761

TRIBES of EDEN

OTHER TITLES BY WILLIAM H. THOMAS

In the Arms of Elders: A Parable of Wise Leadership and Community Building.
VanderWyk & Burnham, 2006

What Are Old People For?: How Elders Will Save the World.
VanderWyk & Burnham, 2004

Learning From Hannah.
VanderWyk & Burnham, 1999

Life Worth Living: How Someone You Love Can Still Enjoy Life in a Nursing Home: The Eden Alternative in Action.
VanderWyk & Burnham, 1996

The Eden Alternative: Nature, Hope and Nursing Homes.
University of Missouri Press, 1994

TRIBES of EDEN

a novel by

WILLIAM H. THOMAS

Sana Publications, Ithaca, NY

Sana Publications, Ithaca, NY
©2012 by William H. Thomas (Dr. Bill Thomas)
All rights reserved. Published 2012
Printed in the United States of America

No part of this book may be used or reproduced in any manner whatsoever without written permission except in the case of brief quotations embodied in critical articles and reviews.

ISBN: 978-0-615-57605-3
eISBN: 978-0-615-57604-6

[1. New World Oder, Resistance to—Fiction. 2. Post-apocalyptic—Fiction. 3. Dystopian Society—Fiction. 4. Coming of Age—Fiction. 5. Intergenerational Social Sustainability—Fiction. 6. Off-the-grid—Fiction. 7. Science Fiction] I. Title.

The text for this book is set in Chaparral Pro and Futura.

Publication Management and Editing by Right Livelihood
Cover Illustration by Jonas LaRance
Book Design by Melissa Brumer

For Diane.

PROLOGUE

The weight of the words pressed down on him, crushing him as if they were stones piled atop his chest. Habit made him tap the disconnect, but the line was already dead. The Chairman's judgment was final. The gleaming metal cocoon in which he sat was no longer his. Its shimmering liquid crystal light, the babble of its disembodied voices would, he knew, fade into mere memory. He closed his eyes, clenched them tight. He wanted to weep, but could not. Kallimos lay behind the coup. Kallimos was a tissue of lies. He knew that from the beginning.

He pulled himself heavily to his feet and smoothed the creases in his tailored jacket, running manicured hands over a vast belly. Even now, he registered a flicker of satisfaction. Smoked windows, backed by the night, mirrored his image. His thinning hair was cropped close and dyed jet black. The charcoal gray suit, cut from a luxury blend of nanofiber fabric, signaled his power. Senior officials, respected men, wore the same color because they knew he favored it. He looked down, the tips of his shoes peeked out from beneath his girth. The Chairman himself had commented on those shoes when they were new, had told him he liked them.

A pained sigh drew the compartment's stale air deep into his lungs. He shook his head. He needed to move, to get away. At the front of the vehicle, he thumbed the lock and watched the door swing slowly open. Outside air, damp and cool, rushed to greet him. He liked the way it felt on his skin. It was different. He stepped heavily down onto a corrugated metal step, then lowered himself to the ground. A cold drizzle peppered the metal awning overhead.

The sentry, who should have snapped to attention the moment he appeared, had abandoned his post. There was nothing left to guard. He turned and pushed the heavy door closed. He would miss its heavy metallic thunk. His gaze passed lovingly over the vehicle's armored exterior, as sleek and menacing as ever—but no longer his. He pushed the thought away. Nostalgia was weakness. Weakness invited death.

For the first time in a dozen years, he was alone outdoors in the night. He scanned his surroundings, but his eyes still favored the brightly lit interior. It didn't matter; there was nothing to see. Beyond the awning lay a monotony of forested hills and valleys. They stretched hundreds of kilometers in every direction. He reached instinctively for his cigarette case and produced it in a single fluid motion. Brushed titanium with jeweled hinges, it bore the inscription *Bonis Nocet Quisqus Malis Perpercit*. He looked for the words, but the light was dim and his vision wasn't as sharp as it had been when he was young. He grunted. He didn't need to see the words, he knew them by heart: *Whoever spares the bad injures the good*. It was the first lesson they taught him on his first day at the Department of Security and Justice's elite academy.

The cigarette case might prove valuable. He turned it over in his hand. With luck, he would be able to trade it for something useful. Three cigarettes remained. He selected one and lit it without thinking. The smoke felt good, like an old friend come to visit. He listened to the quiet. It was new. He pulled hard on the cigarette. His head buzzed. Somehow he missed the warning signs of treason in the making. He had been a fool. He had trusted.

The night's dank chill filtered into his clothing. Slowly, his body remembered how to shiver. He flicked the butt away. Should have saved it, he thought. Too late. The woods beyond the awning rustled. Hairs on the back of his neck rose. Someone or something was watching him. Watching him! The shame of it welled up inside of him. The desire to bang on the polished black door made him ache, made him raise his fist. Pride be damned, he would beg. He would fall on his knees and beg to be readmitted, beg for forgiveness, beg to bathe once more in the truth and the light of the GRID.

He stepped back and forced himself to look away from the vehicle. It was time to go. He ventured beyond the lip of the awning and discovered that the rain was much lighter than it sounded. His eyes, now accustomed to the dark, showed him a narrow footpath leading up and away from the compound. He remembered the way. He walked it many times when he was young. Now, in the hour of his greatest need, it would serve him again. Leafless trees stood straight and silent along its course. They dreamed of spring. The man who walked beneath them, however, was no longer entitled to dream. He'd been zeroed out.

The path curved to the left and then mounted the hillside in earnest. At the crest, he stopped to rest. His wheezing breath disturbed the night with the sound of a rusty bellows, too long neglected by its owner. Here, the footpath divided its course. The left-hand branch, he recalled, would return him to the Turnpike at a point just above the village of Bywater. From there, he could follow Mad Brook to the footbridge below the Rexford Falls. Across the bridge, an abandoned road descended into the valley. This was the route he had taken when he escaped the Shire all those years ago. What he would do when he reached the valley, he could not say—and did not want to imagine.

A gentle downhill grade lulled him falsely. Around him, hardwoods gave way to hemlocks. The trees, centenarians all, huddled close together. Beneath their spreading branches, he indulged in the sweetest of all fantasies: revenge. The Chairman would pay for what he had done. He'd make the man crawl before him, make him beg for mercy. But there would be no mercy. Those Kallimos addled fools would pay as well. The night sky would glow when he burned their villages. Soon, these hills would echo with their keening. The thought made him smile.

A stone, concealed by darkness, caught the point of his shoe. He fell hard. Fatigue and corpulence pinned him to the wet ground, forced him to lie still while he recovered his strength. He pulled himself up onto his hands and knees. Grieving the damage the earth was doing to his clothes, he crawled blindly forward, fumbling for a handhold. He slammed against the jagged bark of a tree. The pain brought him instantly to his feet. Warm liquid ran down his forehead. He wiped his brow, tasted his fingers—blood.

The terrain that had favored his progress now fell sharply away. A dozen careening steps plunged him into the knee-deep course of Mad Brook. In an instant, he knew he'd gone wrong. He was miles above the falls, and there was rough country in every direction. His heart pounding, he splashed his face with the icy water. He worked to clear his mind. The bastards had turned on him, but he was still a man of power, a man of action. He believed this about himself, even now. The mighty had trembled before him, and they would do so again. He scrambled to the stream bank and took hold of the tree roots that lay exposed there. A violent exertion brought him out of the rushing water and onto level ground. He leaned forward, hands braced against his knees, while he caught his wind. In the distance, he heard their song.

Wolves in the valley below the Shire were summoning each other to the hunt. He was upwind of them, and there was blood in the water—his blood.

The Death Song did what it was supposed to do, what it had done long before the first human being walked the Earth, what it would do long after the people were gone. It inspired a terror known only to the hunted. They sang while the man crashed blindly through a dense stand of thorn apples and climbed up and out of the valley. He emerged torn and bleeding. Still, he ran.

The Death Song echoed within the gorge, but his legs quivered with fatigue. He dropped into a fat man's awkward waddle. His pursuers fell back. Buoyed by hope, he turned toward the open ground on his right. He staggered forward, telling himself they lost his scent. Gradually, the ground beneath his feet softened. Clay clung to him, wet and sticky. He stopped. His breath came in heaving, ragged gasps.

They arrayed themselves in a half circle behind him. So close. They sang the Death Song once more. Panic whipped him, drove him forward. He ran as fast as the fear of death would carry him. The wolves veered away, giving him an opening to the left.

The muck deepened. He sloshed onward. Mud and water sucked the shoes off his feet. He did not care. Three more steps and the mire was shin deep. One more step and he was in up to his knees. The swamp's ancient scent of decay rose to greet him. He could go no farther. The pack understood this. They circled. The winter ahead would be long, and they were hungry for meat.

Then came his last human thought. *I, the hunter, was driven here, to this place, to my death.*

PART I

1
FLIGHT FROM CHICAGO
Fall, 2014

Kianna Wallace drummed her long thin fingers against the rim of the steering wheel and waited. She pulled the mirror down and checked her makeup. The light turned green, but the car in front of her did not move. She blared her horn. Chicago traffic was bad. Friday afternoon Chicago traffic was the worst. She spoke to the SUV's computer, "TRAFFIC REPORT." The radio came to life, *55 is backed up to the 294 interchange, 355 is a parking lot, north and south. Drivers are encouraged to use alternate routes...* She would be late, again. "RADIO OFF," then, "CALL JOHN." The earphone buzzed. "John? Hey honey, I'm still on Hanshaw. Can you believe it? Dean Ronch's meeting ran late. Kids home yet? I'll pick up Chinese. Should be home before seven. Love you."

"SMOOTH JAZZ." The music swelled, but it didn't help. She gritted her teeth as the traffic crept slowly forward. Thirteen years ago to the day, on September 12, 2001, John had rushed her to the hospital. Twins. Today, her babies became teenagers. It was just like her mother had said it would be. The years had passed in the blink of an eye. Kianna remembered her mother and father and wished they could have lived to see this day.

She was the beloved daughter and only child of James and Irene Dixon, legends of the political scene on Chicago's South Side. When she was a little girl, she'd climb into her father's lap and hear him rumble. People said he talked the way Muddy Waters sang. "Someday this little girl will be mayor, mayor of Chicago, then maybe even governor!" But it was not to be. With her parents' blessings, she would follow her own dreams and become a scientist, earning a PhD in Botany at Northwestern. Hands-in-the-dirt botany was what she loved best, but she let it go when the twins came. Running the university's plant genetics lab was more practical for a young mother. She thought of her own parents. In December, it would be seven years since she lost them. Drunk driver. Icy streets. She never forgot the ring of the phone in the night. Her heart still ached.

She snatched her order off the counter at the Golden Wok. Then it was left onto Graham for three blocks where a right delivered her to St. Joseph Street and she was home. "ENGINE OFF." She retrieved her purse, a valise that bulged with grant applications, and the sack of Chinese takeout. "LOCK DOORS." She stopped, looked up, and admired their home. It was a classic pre-war South Side bungalow. She loved its simple lines, the way its generous eaves sheltered the cozy front porch.

Kianna closed her eyes and pictured the way the autumn evening's sun would be warming its oak woodwork and flooring, making the house glow like a jeweled box. They paid cash for it, written the check with the life insurance money. It was the final gift from loving parents to their only child. She knew John missed them too. Kianna smiled at the memory of the first time she brought the mild-mannered, mathematically inclined, New England farm boy home to meet her parents. He was so soft and round—and white. Her mother lured her into the kitchen and asked if they loved each other. Kianna assured her that they did. Love was enough for her. Her father took a little longer to come around but, in time, embraced John as the son he'd never had, pocket protector and all.

She worked the key into the lock, stepped inside, and set down her packages. "John, Val, Eron, I'm home." The twins came tumbling down the staircase, all arms, legs, and happiness. They bounded into the entryway. Kianna received them into her open arms, held them tight, and wished them happy birthday.

"Where's Daddy?"

Val was tall, thin, and chocolate brown—just like her mother. She grumped, "Still in his office. He hasn't come out since we got home."

Kianna handed Eron the bag of Chinese takeout. He was his father's son. He was shorter than his sister but less serious too, with a winning smile and an easy, infectious laugh. "You two set the table and I'll go get him."

"Hey, it's our birthday!"

"Mine too," Kianna answered.

John Wallace was exactly where his wife knew he would be, surrounded by a bank of gleaming display screens in the tiny room he used as his office. She walked up behind him and laid her hands on his shoulders. "Good day?" His fingers made the keyboard chatter. She could see his pale, excited face reflected in the glass of the screen, his gray eyes danced with glee.

"Great day. Almost done." The tapping accelerated then stopped. He laughed then spun his chair around and faced Kianna. "I've got it right where I want it."

"Mmm hmm."

He was still wearing his favorite raggedy polo shirt. Soon, she'd make it
disappear. He would complain to her about it, but it was time.

"I mean, we know two spheres are simply connected. But what about
three spheres? Are they always simply connected?"

"You tell me."

"They are!"

"Time to eat. Bring the kids' presents down with you, OK?"

"Sure, babe." He stood and put his arms around her. "You smell nice."

Kianna laughed and pushed him away. "Later."

Eron called up to his parents, "Come on, you guys. Food's getting cold."

The four took their accustomed places at the round oak dinner table that
dominated the kitchen. Each of the Wallaces took a turn talking about the
day. Eron announced that he earned the top score on his math test.

"Oooh yeah," his father cooed, "Boolean algebra—gotta love it—gotta
love it!"

Val rolled her eyes with the exaggerated exasperation that only teenaged
daughters ever truly master. "Daaad," she complained.

John held out his hands, palms up, in mock disbelief. "What?"

Kianna jumped in, "Val, how did things go at lunch today?"

"Not good."

"Not well," her mother corrected her.

"Annie still won't even look at Kate, even though it wasn't Kate's fault."

"Ugh, just sit someplace else." Eron mumbled his advice through a
mouthful of General Tao's chicken.

Again, the eyes rolled.

Kianna reassured her daughter. "I know how hard it can be when friends
are fighting. Last semester, two of the students in my lab went through the
same thing."

"And they made up?"

Kianna nodded. The thought of reconciliation comforted Val.

"Do you think Anna and Kate will ever make up?"

"Sure," Kianna answered, "True friends find a way to forgive each other."

Because John's deepest passion involved mathematical descriptions
of complex three-dimensional objects, his family had learned to listen
respectfully to the long and highly animated descriptions of his work, even
though they had no idea what he was talking about. He concluded, "So if the
vectors cancel out, like I think they will—it's going to be huge, just huge."

Kianna retrieved the ice cream cake she had bought for the occasion. The store had written the twins' names on it with enamel green icing. She pushed thirteen candles into the cake and lit them. John switched off the lights. The day's fading light left the room dim but not dark. They sang "Happy Birthday". Then Val and Eron leaned forward, arm in arm, the soft glow of candlelight illuminating their cheerful, unlined faces.

John said, "Thirteen is a prime number, so it's got to be a good year. Make a wish!"

A whoosh of intermingled breath extinguished the candles.

Kianna served the cake while John presented the birthday gifts. Eron harrumphed, "Hers are always bigger than mine."

His father leaned comfortably back in his chair. "Now I would think a guy who'd just nailed his math test would understand that the size and value of birthday presents are independent variables."

Val went first. She carefully undid the wrapping paper and found a matching skirt and blouse. The skirt was pretty and short, though not so short her father would disapprove. The blouse went with her denim jacket. She smiled brightly, "Thanks, Mom. Thanks, Dad."

Eron's slim package held the console video game he wanted. "This is great!"

"As long as you remember," Kianna cautioned, "work before play."

"Sure, Mom."

John added, "I hear the graphics are fantastic. None of the old polygonal stuff, it's new. Really state of the art."

When the twins were in bed, John opened a bottle of wine. Kianna lit candles, and they settled onto the loveseat in the front room. It felt good to be together, to remember, together. They met, by chance, in the lobby of Northwestern's student union. Soon, they were studying together and playing footsie under the table. Kianna retold the story of the day John Wallace arrived on the doorstep of his Anglican family's New Hampshire stone farmhouse with his Chicago-born African American fiancée. His parents' sputtering dismay evaporated as soon as the discussion turned to the latest strategies for managing corn borer infestations. Kianna was welcomed fully into the Wallace family.

Between the wine, the candlelight, and the memories, they didn't even notice when the power failed. It was still off when they were ready for bed.

"It's probably a circuit breaker," John said.

Kianna searched for a flashlight, finally fishing one out of the back end of a cluttered kitchen drawer. It cast a pale yellow light just strong enough to guide John down the creaking wooden stairs and into the house's unfinished basement. The main circuit breaker panel was on the far wall. He inspected it carefully.

Kianna called down to him, "Can you fix it?"

"Power must be out. Everything's good here."

They were asleep in each other's arms when the electricity returned.

Two weeks later, September had nearly run its course. An unusually hot "Indian Summer" pushed the temperature over 100 degrees. Air—still, hot, and humid—clung to the earth and its people. On Saturday morning, the power failed again. This time, Kianna was prepared. She responded to the birthday blackout by shopping for fresh batteries, flashlights, and a wind-up radio. Now she cranked the handle and tuned in to WVON. Sonny Jones was on the air.

...never seen it so hot this late in the year. It's like the old song says, we're a 'city hotter than a match head.' Now I've got an e-mail right here on the screen in front of me. We've got the WVON back-up generators cranked up high, yes, sir. Now in this e-mail the mayor says the power failure was caused by a blown transformer somewhere in Ohio. And, get this, he 'urges the public to be patient.' Patient? In this heat? Get serious...

Monday morning arrived, and the grid was still down. School was cancelled. Like a million other families, the Wallaces celebrated the break in routine by emptying their freezer, firing up the propane grill, and feasting on meat and vegetables. On Wednesday, a cold front brought heavy rain and more seasonable temperatures. The world regained its balance.

By mid-October, Kianna was staying up late every night polishing her 2015 Department of Agriculture Grant application. John's hope for a quick mathematical victory over the connected spheres had faded, and he had re-submerged himself in the problem. Val was able to report, happily, on her lunchmates' reconciliation. Eron boasted he'd already reached the rank of "Doom Lord" in his new game.

As Halloween approached, the price of gasoline doubled. Reports of breakdowns, fires, and even sabotage at Gulf refineries spread swiftly. The talking heads on television speculated about all kinds of doomsday scenarios as fuel rationing began, but no one really knew how bad it could get. By mid-November, the electrical grid staggered from day to day. Coal shipments to midwestern power plants were inexplicably delayed. Schools couldn't hold classes, and students were dismissed until the New Year. The power in John's home office flicked on and off at odd intervals. When it was on, he searched the web for information about what was happening. Things were bad everywhere. Every sewage treatment plant in Los Angeles had failed on the same day, and eight million toilets overflowed. A prolonged brownout in Texas damaged refrigerators and freezers statewide.

The economy, sputtering all these years, finally went into tailspin, unravelling before John's eyes. The stock market crashed and trading was suspended indefinitely. Quick thinking led him to anticipate an electronic stampede on the banks. He managed to empty the family's checking and savings accounts just hours before the imposition of a national bank holiday. The system for calculating the unemployment rate broke down but everyone understood the reality: tens of millions of people were out of work. John joined them when the head of the company called and cancelled his contract.

Instead of providing calm reassurance, the government lurched and wobbled. Sunny optimism alternated crazily with vague but dire warnings. Elections, twice postponed to avoid "disenfranchising" voters, were cancelled outright. This was a great unraveling. The radio's tinny speaker barked out angry conspiracy theories, but no one could say for sure what the cause of the disruptions, the failures, or the breakdowns might be. North, south, east, and west—hard times lay upon the land. Nor was any group spared from what was happening. Rich or poor, young or old, black or white—all longed for a return to normal. For the time being, people still believed, still hoped, still found reason to believe. After all, the trucks that supplied the major grocery store chains continued to make their rounds, and the shelves remained stocked with the most basic necessities of life.

Kianna shared the mood of cautious confidence. She even found a patch of silver lining in the midst of the crisis. What had been an irksome hour-long commute was now a pleasant twenty minute drive down nearly empty streets. She worked under a federally funded grant and felt her job remained secure. They would get through.

As the days grew shorter, she gradually became aware of the knots of men who lurked in the dark, staring at her SUV as it passed, waiting. She did not like to imagine what they were waiting for.

By Thanksgiving, no one could get fuel oil delivered for any price. The grocery shelves began to run bare as panic and hoarding spread. Mid-December brought the first taste of winter to the city of Chicago, and behind the cold north wind came fear. Liquor store windows were of the first to go. Shards of broken glass littered the streets, but no one came to sweep them away. Kianna stopped going to work.

They huddled close to the radio.

WVON—*Everybody is asking 'Why? Why is this happening?' But it doesn't really matter why. Let's not do the blame game because that won't fix anything. Let's focus on keeping safe, keeping our families safe.* WGRB—*The people I'm talking to all say grocery stores will be restocked soon and there will be food on the shelves all winter. If people just sit tight, this will pass. The important thing is not to panic.* WGN—*Residents of Canaryville are advised to remain indoors. The area is considered to be dangerous, and police will be conducting operations directed against the criminal elements that are operating in that area.* WBEZ—*If those people come into my neighborhood, I'll tell you what—I am locked and loaded. I got plenty of ammo, and I'm gonna use it first chance I get. I'm not scared, not one bit. They're the ones that ought to be scared.*

The man who lived in the house across from them no longer seemed to be home, but they did not know when he had left or where he had gone. Cold and afraid, John and Kianna shivered under their blankets and considered the darkening future.

"I got a dial tone today." John murmured. "Mom answered, she and Dad are worried about us. They're afraid the city's going to explode."

Kianna nodded, she knew where John was going to take this.

"I've been thinking about making a run for the farm. It'd just be temporary. You know, until things settle down."

"Mmm hmm," Kianna agreed without enthusiasm.

"I've run the numbers. With the supplies we've got, we can get there in a straight shot. We won't need to stop for anything along the way."

"The house, John. We'll lose the house. You know we will." He knew she was right. People were being pushed, pushed hard, and they would not restrain themselves much longer. It wouldn't be long before an empty house would be an open invitation to break a window to get inside and take from what was left behind. If they stayed, they would have to fight to protect what was theirs. The farm seemed safer.

Tears welled in Kianna's eyes. John held her close.

She hated the idea of leaving Chicago, of abandoning their home to strangers, of running away.

"We have to get out, before the real trouble starts. Winter is going to be bad. People are going to die."

Kianna swallowed hard. "You're right," she said at last. "It'll be better for the kids to be on the farm." She touched his face. "Better for us, too."

"We will come back, Kianna. I promise you, when this is over, we'll came back home."

She bit her lip, then forced herself to speak. "It'll take some time to get the house ready...for winter."

"We'll tell the kids in the morning. They can help." John said.

They breakfasted their last quart of fresh milk and sliced bread with jam. Eron endorsed his father's plan. He was bored, even to the point of wishing to be back in school. Val took what she knew was her mother's side. "Let's just stay here, Dad. I don't want to leave. It scares me. The radio says people should just stay where they are."

John nodded gently. The fear he saw in Val's once so confident eyes pained him. A hank of thin light brown hair fell down across his forehead. He pushed it away and needlessly adjusted his glasses. "I know, honey. But the radio said the troubles would be over months ago. We can't just listen to the radio. We've got to think for ourselves, make our own decisions." He turned to Kianna, eager for her support.

"Dad's right," Kianna took her daughter's hand into hers, "We have to go."

Val looked away and nodded reluctantly. The decision was made.

The day of departure dawned crisp and cool. The grass on the front lawn was still green; the season's first snow still a week away. By mid-morning a tranquil blue vaulted above them. Jets no longer flew into or out of O'Hare. The quiet and the absence of long white contrails in the sky had the power to amaze.

John kept a wary watch on the street. His heart pounded as he stowed the luggage, containers of fuel, and crates of food and tools in their proper positions. It was all they had left. Kianna wandered through the house, their home. After she double-checked each window and door for the last time, she closed and locked the front door then climbed into the SUV, a dark blue Expedition, almost paid for. The twins sat in the back, seat belts buckled. They were anxious, but wanted to be brave.

John took Kianna's hand. "It's going to be OK." She nodded but did not answer. They backed out of the driveway onto an empty street. There was none of the chatter that usually filled the car at the start of the long drive to the Wallace family farm. Eron kept his nose pressed against the glass. The world had changed in the months he'd been kept at home. The stillness reminded him of the aftermath of a Chicago blizzard. The bustle, the fierce energy of the city was missing. He wondered where it had gone. The people he did see huddled in dense, anxious clumps. He could feel their fear and it made him afraid. Val took no interest in what lay outside her window, preferring to concentrate on her middle school's blue and gold 2013 yearbook. All of her friends were there, smiling at her from the comfort of its glossy pages, forever safe and happy. She wished they could be together again. She wished life could go back to the way it was.

Traffic in the city was light. They merged effortlessly onto I-90 east and passed the exit for South Bend at noon. Eron reached back and retrieved sandwiches and water from a cooler. Late afternoon brought a brisk north wind and a leaden sky. They'd crossed into Ohio and John maintained a mathematician's running commentary on the number of miles remaining. "Only 619 miles to go—a prime number for those of you keeping score at home."

Eron squirmed in his seat, "Mom, I've gotta go to the bathroom." He wasn't the only one.

John agreed, "Eron's right, we should stop. Tank's almost empty."

Kianna spoke, "REST AREA LOCATION." The screen flashed *Elyria Rest Stop: 19.4 miles ahead*. She turned to look at Eron. "Can you wait?" He nodded.

John slowed as they approached the pull off, alert for signs of danger. Rows of once proud digital gas pumps stood sheathed in plywood and plastic. The buildings remained in good repair. It seemed safe. John slid the SUV into a parking space adjacent to the restrooms, parking neatly between the empty lot's parallel yellow lines.

"Stay together," he said. "I'll go when you get back."

He watched Kianna, Eron, and Val hurry across the pavement. Just as they disappeared inside the rest stop, the rap of a ring against the driver's window startled him. A squat middle-aged man wearing a dark blue windbreaker and aviator-style mirrored sunglasses stood beside the car. He signaled authoritatively for John to roll the window down. With a day old beard, heavy gut, and burly shoulders, the man looked to John like an off-duty cop. Reluctantly, he pressed the window switch.

"Hey there, friend. I was wondering if you had any supplies in back there, anything you'd be willing to share?"

John fumbled for a polite response. "Sorry, really sorry. We've got just enough to get where we're going. I did the calculations myself."

"I'm afraid those calculations are going to have to change." The man pulled a dull gray handgun from beneath his jacket. "Out of the car. Now." John jerked his gaze back to the rest stop and saw his wife and children returning to the car, their arms raised, two men behind them. John got out of the car.

"Hands against the car, legs spread." Kianna and the twins soon joined him, hearts pounding as the men searched the interior.

Their leader maintained a steady self-justifying patter while the crime was committed. "We live here. You, you're just passing through. It's bad here. Real bad. We've got families to take care of."

Out of the corner of his eye, John could see the gunman's accomplices scurrying away with their gas cans, coolers, and luggage. When the car was empty, the gunman said, "Get into your car, start your engine, and keep on going wherever it is you're going."

John pleaded, "We're almost out of gas."

The thief lowered his weapon. A flicker of decency moved him to speak. "The radio's been saying a freighter's coming into Cleveland, due there any day. Check it out, maybe you can find what you need."

He raised the pistol again and waggled it at Kianna and the twins as he backed away. "I could kill you, but I won't. Just get the hell out of here." John, Kianna, Valerie, and Eron jumped into the SUV and slammed the doors. John punched the ignition, and the engine roared to life. He squealed the tires as he sped away from the rest stop and back onto I-90 east.

2
THE FLATS

Val reached for the seatbelt, pulled it around her, and clicked the buckle, hoping to be reassured by its embrace. She clutched the yearbook to her chest, afraid to speak or even move. Eron, his voice choked with grief, pleaded for forgiveness. "Dad, I'm really sorry I said I had to stop. I should've kept quiet. If I hadn't said anything, everything would still be OK."

John adjusted the rear view mirror so he could look his son in the eye. "I know what you're thinking Eron, and it's not true. This isn't your fault. We all had to stop. Mommy and I thought it was safe."

Kianna stared straight ahead, seething. When her anger was no longer incandescent, she spoke her thoughts aloud. "Those men keep it nice. It's bait for a trap."

John nodded. He could see it now. "What's done is done. We have to decide what to do next. We've got a couple of gallons in the tank. Enough to go thirty, maybe forty miles. The GPS says it's 606 miles to Keene. We need about..." He ran the numbers in his head. "About 40.7 gallons but I'd feel better if we had 42. One full tank would do the job."

Eager to help, Eron asked, "Dad, the man said we could get gas in Cleveland. We can get to Cleveland right?"

John said, "DISTANCE TO CLEVELAND." The answer flashed onto the screen, *36.4 Miles*. "It'll be close."

Kianna bristled, "He was lying. He just wanted to get rid of us."

Val leaned forward and touched her mother's arm. "I want to go home."

Kianna looked at John. Her eyes asked, *can we*? She wanted to go home too. She could accept whatever might come, if she was home.

John said, "CLEVELAND NEWS."

The SUV found WTAM and brought the radio to life.

...staying with the week's top story. City officials can neither confirm nor deny rumors of re-supply coming to the city via lake freighter as early as today. The most reliable, unofficial information available to this station suggests the first of the freighters will dock near the Flats this evening. Again, this is unofficial, but our sources say food, medicine, and fuel will all be available at Docks 20 and 22 beginning around 9:00 pm.

Kianna tried to punch this information into the GPS but fumbled with the on-screen keypad. Eron slid in between his parents. "Let me." His fingers flew across the screen. "Dad," he said. "It's 38.6 miles."

"It'll be close."

Kianna looked at her husband and children and said, "As long as we're together..."

"That's right," John agreed. "ROUTE TO THE FLATS."

It was dark when they entered the city. John exited I-90 as instructed then the GPS chimed, *turn left onto Frankfort Avenue.* He was thankful for assistance because this was a city transformed. Instead of threading his way through traffic, he guided the SUV along a deserted Frankfort Avenue. The upscale retail shops, store fronts he remembered from a visit a decade before, were shattered and empty. The headlamps made the thousands of shards of littered glass glitter like diamonds as they passed. He turned right onto W. Ninth Street, which delivered them into the heart of what had been the city's warehouse district. They rolled cautiously through empty intersections overhung by lifeless traffic signals. The aftermath of violence and eerie emptiness combined to remind him of a movie cliché. It was like the end of the world. He pushed the image away. They were just passing through. They would be alright.

At the corner of St. Claire and Tenth Street, the SUV coughed, sputtered, and died. John coasted to the shoulder. He rechecked the GPS. "The docks are just up ahead, maybe half a mile. We can walk," he looked at Kianna, "together." The idea of leaving the warm, safe interior of the SUV scared them all, but John put on a brave front. "Hey come on, everybody! Let's get some gas and maybe something to eat and get on out of here. Gran and Gramps are waiting for us!"

"Bundle up good," Kianna prodded Val and Eron. "It's gotten cold." Once they were assembled on the sidewalk, John punched the lock button on his key fob and slid it into his pocket. They crossed the street together and ducked into the alleyway connecting Tenth Street and Old River Road.

They emerged on the far side and found themselves standing, unexpectedly, on the bank of a flowing river of humanity. Yellow mercury vapor streetlights, running at half voltage, cast an eerie vintage glow over the scene. People, thousands of people, were shuffling in the same direction, driven by the same intention. They carried backpacks, pushed empty shopping carts, strollers, and wheelbarrows before them. All were eager to find what they needed, all of them wanted to believe their troubles were near an end.

John encouraged his wife and children, "This is great. The guy on the radio said this was the place. Look at all the people." He instinctively touched his belt as he spoke. Zippered inside was the last of their money. Kianna pulled Val and Eron close to her, held their hands as if they were, once again, small children. Comforted by John's strength she said, "We'll get what we need and be on our way. I'll bet we make it to Rochester before daylight."

The north wind gained strength, refused to be ignored. Eron studied the people around them as they edged forward. His console games had crowds, digital crowds; they cheered and booed as if they were just one person. This was a multitude of real people. He saw a young couple pushing a shopping cart that held a young boy, maybe five- or six-years-old. He was bundled so tightly against the weather that only his eyes could be seen. There was an old man limping along with the help of a shiny aluminum cane. So many people, so many different ages, sizes, and colors, all bundled against the weather. Each little cluster of humanity working and reworking the same calculus. Were the rumors true? Would they find what they needed? Should they continue or turn back? Was it safe?

The street was flanked by cinderblock warehouses, each a block wide, which made John nervous. As they approached the lake, he noticed that towering chain link gates blocked off the alleyways. They were marching along a narrow urban canyon. He suppressed his concern and offered a word of encouragement. "We're close. Not much farther now,"

"I can smell the lake," Eron agreed.

In the next instant, gunfire pierced the night, echoing among the closely spaced buildings and confusing the crowd. One, two, three, four shots rang out and, then, an unmistakable return volley. Up ahead, people screamed. The sounds shattered the brittle goodwill of those around them. Eron tugged on his father's sleeve, "Dad!" he looked up, into his father's face. John Wallace's lips moved wordlessly as he worked a complex mathematical incantation. "A wave," he barked the words, "there will be a wave!"

Ahead, out of sight, people were already turning their backs to the water. They abandoned reason and plunged into those who had been following them. The mob fell against itself like a cascade of demented dominoes. Those who hesitated, those who failed to instantly join the stampede, were knocked down—crushed to death.

John Wallace knew the wave would grow faster and stronger as it raced toward them. They had minutes, at most, to escape. He pulled his wife and children hard to the right and yelled, "Come on!" The general confusion created an opening for John to bull his way to the edge of the street. The crush was still two blocks away.

John pulled hard on a steel door. It was locked. The building's block wall towered over them, imprisoning them. Beside the door stood a dumpster heaped with rotted garbage. If they worked together, they could reach the roof from the top of the bin.

"Up—on there," he yelled. Kianna understood.

He boosted her up onto the dumpster's steel lid. Rats, alarmed by the banging, scurried up and out of the garbage. John boosted Val up into Kianna's arms. Eron was next.

Six hands reached for John Wallace as the human wave broke over him. The frenzied crush tore him from their grasp. Kianna screamed, "John!" And then he was gone.

Chaos ruled the world.

The mob hoped the dumpster might be their salvation as well, and they surged toward it. Anonymous hands clutched greedily at Kianna's legs. She kept the twins behind her, away from the desperate probing. She looked up and saw what John had seen, a sturdy downspout descending from the building's flat roof.

Val sobbed inconsolably. She sagged against her mother, clung to her. Eron scanned the sickening scene, searching for his father. He saw a shopping cart smashed nearly flat. The little boy was still inside, not moving, an orphan if he still lived. Gunfire echoed from the north and south. The mob cried out as if it was a wounded animal desperate to be put out of its misery.

Kianna seized Eron roughly by the shoulders. He pulled away. "Dad!" he cried. The boy tried to jump into the still seething crowd. Kianna pulled him back, forced him to look at her.

"No. No! You can't. I need you."

His mother's ferocity shocked him. He looked at her, focused on her face and willed himself to listen.

"Eron, you have to climb this pipe. I will help lift you. When you get to the roof reach down for Val."

"Mommy, I can't. I can't." he wailed.

Kianna shook him roughly. "Do it, now!" She pushed her son toward the pipe. A savage cocktail of fear and adrenaline drove him up and onto the roof. He lay down, shoulders hanging over the edge, and reached for Val. Kianna lifted his sister to him. He caught hold of her, brought her to safety.

With the twins safe above, Kianna swung her weight onto the pipe's brackets and reached up with her free hand. Val and Eron reached, and missed. On the second try, they took hold and started to pull their mother to safety. Others were now atop the dumpster. They too wanted to be rescued. A teenaged boy clawed at Kianna's legs, begging for help. She kicked at him, furiously and without mercy, and broke free. She scrambled up and onto the roof. Another round of gunfire brought another wave of panicked death. The boy who clung to Kianna was gone. Now, half a dozen men clung to the drainpipe. Without warning, their combined weight ripped the bolts from their anchors, and they all fell back into the mob. A moment later, they too disappeared.

Kianna and the twins stared numbly at the carnage. Tens of thousands lay dead on the street. Somewhere out there Kianna knew was the body of John Wallace. Husband. Father. Brother. Son. Hero.

She choked back her grief, turned to Val and Eron and said, "We've got to get away from here, now."

The twins stumbled awkwardly forward, moving only when their mother prodded them. The pea stone roofing ballast crunched under their feet. A light snow began to fall. The night sky all around them now glowed dull red. Cleveland was on fire. When they reached the far side of the roof, Kianna peered over the edge and found the street below bizarrely empty. The giant warehouse's street entrance was beneath them. They could jump down onto it and, from there, leap safely to the ground.

The screams of terror gradually faded. Kianna listened for sirens, but there were none. Untold thousands lay dying, and no one cared. Once they were on the street, Eron took hold of his mother's arm. "Mom, it's this way. Dad's back this way. We've got to go and find him." He pleaded with her—fearful, insistent.

Kianna looked away, unwilling to face her son, then lied, "Daddy will go back to the car. He'll meet us there." Eron swallowed hard, then slowly agreed to let his mother lead him. Val said nothing.

The sound of people moving echoed between the buildings. People were running for their lives. The chain link fences that spanned the narrow alleyways groaned and then gave way. People gushed through the openings, like water spurting from the end of a hose.

The roar of fear grew louder. Kianna said, "Run. We've got to run. Now."

Left, right, left again. The moonlit streets gave no clue as to where they were or where their car was parked. There were people behind them, and if those people caught up to them, they would die. That was all that mattered.

When Kianna and the twins stopped to catch their breath, the warehouses were gone, replaced by shabby wooden houses. She was about to speak when they heard men's voices barking at them. "Don't move! Get down!" They were instructed to lie face down on the cold ground arms and legs spread. Instead, they ran.

Mother and children plunged deep into the night. They crashed into a flimsy wooden gate, the force of their bodies tearing it from its rotted hinge post. Next came a waist-high chain link fence. They struggled over it and kept going. Their pursuers abandoned the chase.

It did not matter. They ran for their lives.

3
MAKENA AND KIKUYU

When they stopped running, Kianna, Val, and Eron found themselves in the cluttered backyard of a ramshackle house. It was quiet and they were alone. Kianna held her children close to her. They were wracked by silent sobs. Eron started to speak, but Kianna shushed him. She examined her children. Their neat suburban outerwear was torn and dirty, their faces caked with mud and tears but they were alive—and together. "Stay here," she whispered. "Don't move, don't make a sound."

Kianna crept up onto the back porch and peered through the window. The interior was dark. She tried the knob of the back door. It turned. She pushed it open. "Hello? Is anybody home?" She stood, heart pounding, on the threshold. She called again, raising her voice, hoping there would be no response. When a third query went unanswered, she felt confident enough to motion for the twins to follow her inside.

"There's no one home. We can hide in here."

Eron pulled the door closed behind him. The moon forced its way through dirty windows, granting enough light for them to see. The room was filled with jumbled heaps of newspapers, advertising circulars, magazines, and unopened junk mail. Mountains of paper buried the sink and stove. If there was a table, they could not see it. Kianna edged along the serpentine passage that ran from the backdoor into what might once have been a dining room. Val clung to her mother matching her every step. Eron hung back. All three stooped as they walked, trying to be small. Odd-sized pieces of cardboard were stacked nearly to the ceiling. The room reeked of mold.

The passage led the refugees to another door. It was closed. Kianna grasped the dull round knob and turned it slowly. She pushed gently, but the hinges still protested against the unexpected movement. She peered into the gap then jerked backward, knocking against Val who still huddled close behind her.

She stifled a cry of alarm then, in a whisper, "There's someone in there." Val and Eron trembled. Kianna forced herself to look again. This time she inched the door farther open. The flickering light of a single candle cast a shifting light onto the bare walls. An old woman sat on the floor in the middle of the room, cross-legged, eyes closed. She hummed softly to herself.

The tranquility of the scene eased her fear, and Kianna studied the woman closely. She looked to be in her late seventies, maybe her early eighties. She was very thin, with white skin so pale it seemed translucent. Her face was deeply etched. On closer inspection, Kianna could see that this was a woman who laughed easily and often. Silver hair, matted and snarled, ran riot across her scalp. She wore mismatched clothes that were hardly more than rags.

The old woman's eyes fluttered open, as if she had just returned from someplace far away. She saw Kianna and smiled. Then, in a voice so warm it could've melted butter, she said, "So, my dear Kikuyu, you've come home at last." Unsure of the meaning of these words but reassured by their tone, Kianna swung the door open and stood up straight. The old woman saw Val and Eron hiding behind their mother and clapped her hands with glee. "Kikuyu, you have children of your own—of course! You are all grown up now." Knobby fingers wiped her happy tears away.

"Thank you," was all Kianna could think to say.

"You've traveled such a long way. You must be tired."

"Yes, we are."

"Then rest, Kikuyu. We will talk later. You and the children should sleep." Kianna and the twins were immensely tired and the relief that came with her invitation magnified their fatigue. They huddled together on the mound of rags, sheets, towels, old clothes, and curtains that dominated the center of the room. Safe, they allowed sleep to overcome their grief.

When they woke, it was light and the old woman was gone. Together, they explored the remainder of the house. Every room, from the basement to the attic was crammed with cardboard boxes, each packed full of old newspapers, magazines, and scrap paper. The carless garage was, ironically, the least cluttered part of the house. In the kitchen, water still ran from the taps but the electrical outlets were dead. Outside, empty houses flanked a deserted street.

The pangs of hunger grew sharper as the morning wore on. Their last meal had been eaten in the car, with John, a time that now seemed to belong to another age, another world. Kianna searched the kitchen cabinets, but they were bare. Eron pawed through mounds of dusty newsprint. Hidden among the heaps he found a plain cardboard box sealed with gray adhesive tape. "Hey, Mom. Look at this." He brought it to her. "What do you think this is?"

Kianna inspected the package carefully. It seemed benign. "Go ahead," she said. Eron tore it open. Inside, arranged in rows, as neat as soldiers in formation, were metal foil packages of breakfast tarts, all of them strawberry flavored. Kianna thought of the old woman. Surely this food belonged to her. It was wrong to take it, but her children were hungry. She was hungry.

Eron pleaded, "Can we?"

"Yes."

They feasted where they stood, still wearing their jackets and boots, washing down dozens of the tarts with cool tap water drunk from chipped porcelain cups. Their hunger relieved, they returned to the living room and lay down on its heap of fabric. Eron said, "I'll bet Dad is OK. I'll bet he found a way out, even before we did. He probably went back to the car—he had the keys. He is probably looking for us now."

Kianna answered carefully, "I hope so."

Eron persisted, "Well how is he going to find us if we are in here? We should leave. We need to be looking for him."

"He'll find us if he can." She reached over and fussed with her son's kinky black hair.

"I miss him," Val said.

Kianna looked at her daughter and saw, in the sadness of her eyes, that she knew the truth. "I know you do, honey. So do I."

She held her children close, and they all cried hot tears until, at last, sleep came.

The smell of smoke woke Kianna. She sat up, tense. The movement roused Val, then Eron. Val sniffed the air. "I smell it too, Mom." Eron went to the window. On the street, people were running. Towering clouds of thick black smoke soared high overhead. He said, "There's a big fire somewhere. Everybody's running away."

Kianna and Val joined him at the window. Eron said, "See?"

His mother nodded. A stream of panicked people fled past their little house, but there was no one to help them, no one to reassure them, no one to tell them what to do.

Eron said, "We gotta get outta here, Mom."

"No." Kianna shook her head, "No. Check the house, make sure it's OK. We're safer in here than we would be out there."

An hour later, the street was empty. Darkness fell, and they slept.

"Kikuyu, it is time to get up."

Kianna startled awake. The woman from the night before had returned and was leaning over them, her face lit by the candle she held in her hand.

Her sudden reappearance frightened Kianna, who drew her children close to her.

"Where were you? We looked for you."

"I know."

There was an awkward pause.

"My name is Kianna. These are my children, Val and Eron. My husband John is...is missing."

"Oh I know all about it. People from the village told me everything I needed to know. Don't you worry, nothing more need be said. Your children, they are fine children, very fine children."

Reassured by this gentle response, Kianna smiled and asked, "What is your name?"

"You know my name, Kikuyu. I'm Makena. I'm the nurse, the nurse for Serewa."

"I'm sorry, Makena. It's just...we've...had a very hard time."

"Oh, I understand, darling one. No need to worry."

Kianna blushed in the darkness.

Makena remembered her duties as a host. "The children—they must be hungry. You too, Kikuyu. I have a treat for you!" As soon as Makena left the room, Kianna washed the jellied smudges from their faces with saliva and the sleeve of her own coat.

"Mommy?" Val asked, "What's wrong with her?"

Kianna answered, "I don't know, honey, but she seems nice. I am going to ask her if we can stay with her for a while."

"Til Dad comes?" asked Eron.

"That's right—just til Daddy comes for us."

The sound of a minor avalanche issued from the adjoining room. "No problem," Makena called cheerfully, "just a minute." When she reappeared she carried four strawberry Pop-Tarts, she held them out in front of her as if they were holy relics.

Eron opened his mouth but his mother spoke first, "Thank you so much. This is lovely." She looked at the twins, "Kids, what do you say to Makena?"

They thanked her in cautious unison.

"I wish I had githeri, mukimo, and a big cold pitcher of muratina, but..." Makena looked around helplessly, "but I'm afraid this is all I have."

"It is very fine food," Kianna reassured her.

Her confidence buoyed, Makena said, "Yes they are wonderful, aren't they? So fresh and tart. That's why they call them tarts."

When they finished eating, Kianna asked, "Do you live alone?"

"I think so. Sometimes it is hard..." She frowned, trying to remember, wanting to be helpful. "I can't say for sure." Then her countenance brightened. "But I've been waiting for you and the children for a very long time. At last Kikuyu and her children have come to stay. Now you are here, everything is as right as rain."

Kianna smiled weakly. She needed to be sure she understood, "Can we stay here with you for a while?"

Makena burst into laughter seemingly too big to have come from such a small body. "Of course, Kikuyu. I want you to stay."

Kianna allowed herself a deep sigh of relief. With a child tucked under each arm, she passed the night talking with Makena. As morning drew near, their host showed them where she slept. In the entrance hall beneath the stairs, there was a movable wooden panel that she slid to one side. Makena crawled into the opening, beckoned her guests to join her—and they did. Beneath the stairs was a perfectly warm, dark, soft hiding place. With a little bit of rustling and jostling, they each found a comfortable place. They slept together, safe in a nest of an old woman's making, safe to grieve their loss, eager to sleep without dreaming.

They soon found a comfortable routine. In the evening, they emerged from what Val called "the Burrow" and made ready for their day. Water no longer ran from the tap, so Kianna went outside to fill plastic buckets with clean snow. They made ten gallons a day for drinking and washing. Eron appointed himself watchman and patrolled window to window, though there was little to see. The neighborhood was deserted, and the unplowed streets, drifted deep with snow, remained empty.

One cold winter night Eron stumbled onto a small wooden box that contained a small bundle of documents. Together, they told the story of Makena's life. Her real name was Karen O'Malley. She was born in San Diego, had grown up there and then attended nursing school in Los Angeles. She graduated in 1962 and joined the Peace Corps in 1963. She had been the village nurse in Serewa, Kenya. She had married in 1968 and moved to Cleveland in 1980. Her husband died of liver cancer in 1998. The paper trail stopped there, sixteen years ago.

Kianna decided not to mention the papers to Makena.

Makena had entrusted Val with a small tin of wooden matches that fit snugly inside a handmade leather sack. The sack had been a gift from a friend of Makena's in Serewa and now it was Val's. She looped a string through its eyelet and was proud to wear it around her neck.

They all worked together to gather the fuel for the night's fire. Makena found this stressful and relied on Kianna and the twins for constant reassurance. "My, my, dear, dear, no, no. It's not right. I've been saving, saving for when I might need it…"

"We need it tonight Makena. Think of the children. We don't want the children to catch cold."

"That's right. That's right," Makena agreed hesitantly.

They built their fire in the metal drum which now occupied the center of the garage. Kianna had retrieved it from the cluttered backyard. The smoke escaped through the hole Eron had gleefully chopped into the roof above. They covered the windows to hide the firelight from prying eyes. When all was ready, Val solemnly struck a single match. The fire—being fed mainly with the enormous volume of newsprint and cardboard they had at their disposal—came on fast and hot. Yellow light filled the room and made their shadows dance happily across the walls. Makena always "made dinner" for them, presenting each of her guests with foil-wrapped strawberry Pop-Tarts.

Gradually, Kianna came to understand, Makena was living in another time. She could not remember the name of her street, nor did she care to do so. She did not remember the name of the doctor who had prescribed the "memory pills," which had done nothing more than upset her stomach. She could not remember the name of her husband, now long gone, whose death certificate they had found amid the clutter. For Makena, it was 1963, she was living in Serewa, and her beloved Kikuyu with her two fine children had come to stay.

After their meal, Makena entertained them with an inexhaustible supply of Kenyan riddles and songs.

"I have traveled with one who never tells me to rest. Who am I?"

"My shadow."

"I have a house without a door or a window. What am I?"

"An egg."

"I am an elephant with one ear. What am I?"

"A teacup."

They slept at dawn.

Inch by inch, the days grew longer. The rain came, melting the snow, preparing the earth for spring. Warmer weather also drew strangers into the neighborhood. Eron's obsession with watching, which had seemed childish in the depth of winter, now proved a wise precaution. He watched them, knew them by the way they stood, the way they walked. He called them the wanderers.

Late at night Eron called his mother to the window. "See them? Those two are new here. The tall one is the boss; he's always waving his arms around, like he's really angry. The short one started limping a couple of days ago. I don't know what happened to him. He always walks with his head down like he's sad." Eron pointed at the smaller man then glanced at his mother and saw the worry on her face. "It's OK, Mom," he reassured her. "They don't know we're here."

They were asleep in the Burrow when the sound of voices woke them. Strangers were inside the house. They listened. There were two voices, both male. The loud one let his voice boom. He wanted to be heard. Fear took their breath away. Eron slid the panel open, just a crack. A sliver of intense white light entered their nest beneath the stairs. It was the middle of the day. The intruders' impertinence angered Makena. She sat up, sputtering, "It's not right, not right, not right."

"Shhh. Makena," Kianna consoled her, "Shhh. Shhh. They'll hear you."

The old woman backed down, muttering to herself, "It's OK. It's OK." Then, loudly, "No! No! No!" Kianna could not quiet her. Makena rattled the panel open, banging it loudly against the wall. She pulled herself out and blinked in the strange light of the sun. The intruders had pulled the curtains back and raised the tattered shades. The house, almost empty now, was flooded with light.

She followed the voices into the kitchen.

A man's voice roared, "Hey Grandmaw! We thought you was dead. Folks told us you was dead," It was the tall angry man from the street.

"Go away you. Get out!"

He wore a black pea coat smeared with mud, blue jeans that looked new, and tattered sneakers with Velcro straps left undone. His face, hair, and beard were filthy. Close-set eyes studied the interior of the house with immense suspicion and greed. He smiled, teeth straight, white, perfect. "Awww now, Grandmaw, don't talk to your only grandson that way. Come and give me a kiss."

"Get out of my house!"

"Now that's not right, Grandmaw. Don'tcha remember? I'm Phil and this here's cousin Dean." Dean nodded and looked away. "Come on, Grandmaw, don' tell me you don' remember me. I'm Brenda's son." He smiled as he spoke, but the words passed his lips without affection.

Makena stamped her foot. "Get out!"

Dean searched the house again. This time he found the closet beneath the stairs. "Hey Phil," his thin voice fluttered with excitement, "there's something in here."

Phil grinned. "What you got, Grandmaw—a dog or something?" He made a show of picking the furious old woman up and setting her to one side, then he bowed mockingly in her direction. He went to see what Dean was yelling about.

The smaller man stuck his head into the compartment. Six human eyes blinked at him in the darkness. Startled, he stood up and banged his head against the stair tread above. "Jesus H. Christ—she's got people in there." He withdrew from the closet, panicked, and demanded, "Get the hell out of there!" Kianna and the twins emerged hesitantly from the sheltered darkness, eyes blinking hard against the light. They, unlike the intruders, were clean. Kianna had insisted on regular bathing, even when all they had was cold water. Their clothing, however, was ridiculous. Picked out of Makena's voluminous piles of cast-offs, they were mismatched, too small, too big, worn through. Kianna was too frightened to be ashamed.

"What the hell, Grandmaw, what are you doin'?" Phil was pissed.

"Kikuyu is my friend. I waited for her, and she came back to me!" Makena shrieked madly, "She is my guest, they are my guests. Do not insult my guests. They must stay with me."

"Forget it, Grandmaw. I'm here now—me and Dean. We gonna take care of you. Right, Dean?"

"Yeah, that's right."

Kianna tried to reason with the two men. "Listen to me," she said. "Your... grandmother needs help. She needs us."

"Bullshit," Phil responded, pulling a pistol from inside his coat. "The front door is that way. Use it before I lose my patience."

Makena screamed and lunged at Phil. Dean grabbed her roughly by the neck, and the old woman howled in pain.

Phil marched Kianna and the twins out the front door. "Now get off my damn porch. Get off my damn lawn. Get the hell out of my damn neighborhood."

They scrambled down to the sidewalk.

Kianna begged the men to listen to her. Phil pulled the trigger, and a bullet scattered the dirt in front of them. He watched them turn and run. Their fear amused him.

"Hey, Dean, come 'ere. Watch me make them dance." Phil squeezed off a handful of rounds, not meaning to hit them, not caring if he did. Kianna, Val, and Eron ran until they could no longer hear Makena scream.

When they stopped, Kianna wanted to say something to explain their eviction to the twins. She opened her mouth but words failed her. They stood together in the street, holding each other, shaking with grief and terribly alone. Finally, Kianna said, "Gramp and Gran are probably worried sick about us. We need to go to them."

Eager to escape the catastrophe which had befallen them Eron said, "Dad'll be there, waiting for us."

"He might be there," Kianna said. Val looked away, as if fascinated by the ruins of a house that stood on the other side of the street.

Their mother peered ahead. The street and sidewalks were a carpet of broken glass and windblown garbage. Many buildings remained standing, but their shattered windows gaped at them like astonished toothless mouths exposing charred interiors. She ached for John, needed his easy confidence, his faith in the future, his belief in happy endings. But he was gone. She looked at her children and knew that they were lost, fatherless, malnourished, homeless, and soon they would be hungry and thirsty as well. Kianna drew a deep breath and offered up her best impression of John Wallace. "The sign says the exit for I-90 is just one mile this way," she pointed, unnecessarily, at the sign. "One is a prime number so it must be a lucky exit." Eron smiled at the joke. It was just what his Dad would have said if he'd been there with them. Kianna took Val and Eron by the hand and said, "Let's go."

4
THE ROAD

The on-ramp was right where the sign had promised it would be. But instead of a steady stream of traffic they found the great highway deserted, like a concrete river run dry. The cindered remains of the toll booths were strewn across the plaza along with the vandalized remains of dozens of vehicles. Eron eagerly inspected the first three or four SUVs they came to until he was certain that nothing of value remained. They had been stripped clean.

A smooth cement arc delivered them to the highway's eastbound lanes where they wandered aimlessly from guardrail to guardrail. The only sound came from the songs of birds recently returned from their sojourn in the South. Bright spring sunshine combined with physical exertion, and a still raw grief made them tired. They sat down in the middle of the highway and waited.

"Let's go home," Val whispered, pleading.

"No," Eron objected, "Dad'll be at Gran and Gramps'."

Kianna looked out across the city, the wreckage no longer smoldered. The view offered a scene of destruction so total it seemed like something a rampaging army might leave in its wake. It was a wonder they had made it through the winter alive. The memory of Makena made her wince. She thought of home. The bungalow would be gone or, if it still stood, would no longer belong to them. Eron called his mother out of her reverie. "I'm hungry."

Val glared at him. They were all hungry, but the words, spoken aloud, only wounded their mother.

Kianna paced, trying to guess what they should do. Val understood the question her mother was facing. "We can't go back, Mom. We can never go back."

Out of the west, they heard a faint mechanical hum. The sound grew louder, and soon they were sure it was a truck. It was heading east and so were they.

"Go over behind the guardrail, stay out of sight. I'll stop the truck and see if we can get a ride." She sent them off with a hug and said, "It's going to be OK. Don't you worry. We're together, so it's OK."

The twins scurried away. Kianna took a deep breath. She needed to be strong, for them. She made a show of planting her feet astride the dotted white line, put her hands on her hips and waited. A blood-red tractor-trailer, its paint gleaming in the late afternoon light, rolled toward her. She still straddled the line. The air horn blared. She didn't move.

He could run her down. No one would know. No one would care. Might dent the grill, though. The driver downshifted. Not bad looking. He stopped. Wendell Dickie leaned forward in his bucket seat and peered out over the truck's long hood. The woman still blocked his way. Most bandits knew it would be death to waylay a shipment, but it could still be a trap. He yanked the air horn's cord, long and hard, then fingered the driver's side window control. The glass slid smoothly down. He stuck his head out the window. Straining to raise his thin nasal voice above the diesel's dense throb he yelled, "Out of the way, lady!"

Kianna came around to the side of the cab and peered up at the driver. A beak-like nose and two narrow, suspicious eyes dominated a boney face. Strings of pale yellow hair had been combed over a sunburned scalp. The blue work shirt, cuffs folded up to the elbows, was unwrinkled, new. He spat tobacco juice expertly at Kianna's feet. It was a warning. She was not to touch his truck.

"I know what you want...sign says no riders, can't ya' read?"

She looked at the door and found the words hand-lettered in flowing white script across the cab door. They read *Wendell Dickie—Owner Operator*.

"I am terribly sorry, Mr. Dickie."

"So you *can* read." Another shower of tobacco juice spattered Kianna's shoes.

"Yes, I can Mr. Dickie, so you can't fool me. You are the owner, you're the captain, you make the rules, and you can break the rules." She smiled up at him.

"I guess that's right," he said. The woman was a mess—wild hair and crazy clothes—but she had class, he could see that much. She had probably been a high-tone lady before. He asked with interest, "What do you want?"

"I need a ride—east—to Boston."

"Well it just so happens that I'm headed to Boston myself." He undressed her with his eyes. Nice.

"I might have room, but I'm gonna have to charge ya'."

Kianna felt the air leave her lungs. "Mr. Dickie, I don't have any money."

"Didn't figure ya' did."

"But I can get some when we get to, ah...Boston."

"Well sure you can, but I need payment in advance."

Kianna poured her very being into a single word, "Please."

Dickie snorted and spit again, "Been a while since I had me a woman—pretty as you. Climb in and we'll do some business." His grin revealed cragged tobacco-stained teeth. He popped the door.

"There's one more thing," Kianna hesitated, "I have children. Twins—the three of us—we all need a ride."

"Kids. Damnit." Dickie slammed the door shut.

"They won't be any trouble and I can still...pay you." She smiled weakly at Dickie. He hesitated, his body already hungry for what had been promised.

"Let's see 'um," he said.

Kianna called out "Val, Eron, come out. It's OK." The children showed themselves reluctantly.

"They won't be any trouble."

Dickie hesitated. "They better not be." He killed the engine.

Kianna called the twins over. She bent down and whispered, "Mr. Dickie is going to take us to New Hampshire. But I have to go up into the cab to talk with him about it for a while. You two stay right here. Sit here on this step. Swear to me you will not move, you will not come to the window or say a word or go anywhere until I come to get you."

Eron was suspicious. "Why?"

Kianna flushed with anger, "Never mind why, Eron, just do what I say." The twins both felt sick. Wendell Dickie helped Kianna up and into the cab. The door closed behind her, the lock snapped shut. Val and Eron sat without speaking, without seeing, without hearing as the shadows lengthened on the road. Finally, the cab door swung open, their mother spoke softly, lovingly, "Come on up, Mr. Dickie says it's time to get going."

They clambered into the cab where Wendell Dickie received them in the manner of a medieval lord, his hand resting on a sawed-off double-barreled shotgun next to his seat. "Kianna, you set next to me, here." He pointed to the rider's bucket seat. "You kids," he jerked his thumb toward the bunk, "can ride back there."

Dickie hit the ignition switch. The 500-horsepower diesel engine roared to life. He released the airbrakes, dropped the transmission into low range, and the tractor-trailer slid forward. Kianna turned to face the twins. "Mr. Dickie owns this tractor-trailer."

Dickie laughed, "Now, Kianna, I thought I told you to call me Wendell."

"It's very nice," Val volunteered hesitantly. The interior reminded the girl of the way the world had been—before. Nothing was patched or burned or broken, it felt new.

Dickie responded, "It's not just nice, it's the best. Peterbilt, 2005. Engine's got less than a million on it since the last rebuild. I'm one of the last independents still runnin'. Might be the last, can't say for sure."

"Where did everybody go?" Eron asked.

"You been hidin' under a rock, boy?" Dickie flicked a glance at Eron. "Don't ya' know what's been goin on? I mean there's been strict and I mean strict rationing since January. Military and essential business only. I'm on essential business." He poked his thumb into his chest. "We get fuel and nobody else."

"So what do you carry that's so important?" Eron asked.

"Hey kid, I got secrets and I gotta keep 'em. If I told you what I got back there then I'd have to kill ya'," Dickie's laugh made his delight at the thought obvious to all. He dipped his fingers into his shirt pocket and fished out a tin of chewing tobacco. He popped the lid, one-handed.

Eron continued, "We're going to New Hampshire to Gran and Gramps' farm. We think Daddy might be waiting for us there already."

"Hmm. New Hampshire, huh." Dickie grinned at Kianna, who stared straight ahead.

"We're from Chicago," he said.

"I might have guessed," Dickie replied.

"Do you have any news from Chicago?"

"Well I just happened to pass through the Windy City a couple of days ago, as a matter of fact."

"What's it like?" Val asked innocently.

"Chicago is bad—a mess. Still burnin'. I looped south on 690. All kinds of crazy stuff goin' on there. The worst, and I do mean the worst, of the riots were in Chicago. Mob strung up the Mayor, City Council, cops, firemen, garbage men. Hell, I don't know. City's basically one big ash pit now. Assholes."

Kianna and the twins listened in silence, their worst fears confirmed. Evening faded into night, twin halogen beams streaked the road ahead. Highway signs flashed by, Ashtabula, Conneaut, Girard, then Erie.

Wendell Dickie talked, could not stop talking. He told them about the food riots in Denver and the 200,000 people who froze to death in Minneapolis and St. Paul. "I've heard people, people who know, say more'n half the people in the country are dead. No shit. Everything's gone to hell and nobody knows why." Dickie spat juice into a plastic coffee mug. "Government was no good, couldn't even get out of its own goddamned way. The Militia calls the shots now."

"The people who survived called the disaster by its own name—they called it 'the Fall.'"

"Yeah, then there's Cleveland, good old Cleveland. Used to be a great town. One night, end of last year, 100,000 people bought it. Right there on the street. The way I hear it, it was all 'cause some yahoos couldn't control themselves. Rumor went around there'd be fuel and food at the docks. Warn't no such thing ever goin' to happen," Dickie laughed. "But people believed it. They believed it and look what happened. I heard half the city was there. The cops was down on the docks tellin' ev'rbody it was just a damn rumor but the crowd just kept comin'. Pushed 'em right out onto the pier. They would've gone right into the lake but the cops said, 'screw that shit' and started shootin', you know, warning shots. Damn fools went crazy so the cops had no choice, started firin' right into the damn mob. If the people had just done as they were told an' just gone home, it woulda been fine. Anyway, it was a real stampede like buffalo or somethin', people outta their minds." He tapped his smooth white forehead with his index finger, "They just went crazy, climbin' all over each other without any sense of what they was doin'! Took 'em a month to clear all the bodies away, things being the way they are."

"You were in Cleveland," Dickie crabbed. "Don't tell me you didn't hear about the damned riot." None of the three would answer. The cabin fell silent save for the engine's single low note. Several hours later, as light gathered in the east, Dickie merged onto I-86. Kianna sat up straight, concerned, then alarmed. "Aaahh...Wendell, you're going the wrong way. I-90 is back there."

Dickie smirked, "Goddamn you are a bossy bitch. No wonder your husband left ya'."

Kianna pressed her lips together unwilling to answer him in the flush of anger. "I'm just saying," she said, "I-86 goes south, through Binghamton. It's the long way round."

"Well Miss Smarty Pants—I been on 90 between Rochester and Syracuse and it's a goddamned mess. This way's better so you can just shut up."

"OK, don't get mad. I didn't know."

"Damn right you didn't."

Kianna pulled the atlas from its pocket on the inside of the door. "Light's overhead," Dickie boasted. "I can turn it on from over here." He thumbed the switch. Kianna flipped through the pages. "Here it is," she said, "we can pick up 87 east of Binghamton, it goes right back to Albany and I-90."

"Obviously," the word oozed with the smug satisfaction of one who had just prevailed in a vital and complicated argument. Jamestown, Olean, Salamanca, and Campbell. When the sun was up, Kianna said, as softly as she could, "We are going to have to stop again, before too long."

This time Dickie agreed, "Yeah, me too."

They flew passed Corning, Horseheads, and Elmira, his foot did not come off the accelerator until they reached Binghamton. Dickie pulled onto the highway's shoulder just west of the junction of routes 17, 87, and 81. He killed the engine and pulled the keys from the ignition, "Ahh, gotta check the right rear, somthin's funny there. You go on and ahhh...take care of your business."

The Susquehanna flowed close by and Kianna was eager to get the water, to wash up, to be free of the cab and the smell of the man. "Follow me." Neither child spoke but the idea of leaving the road and venturing into woods alongside the fast flowing river scared them. Kianna insisted, and they followed dutifully in her footsteps. The night's ride left their limbs stiff, and they maneuvered awkwardly down the incline and to the river's edge. A gentle morning sun gradually warmed their faces and lifted their spirits.

They emerged from the thicket alongside a shallow stone-bottomed eddy. Stately cottonwoods in new leaf graced the bank and cast a dappled shade onto the surface of the water. Kianna knelt down and washed her face and hands. She drank from her cupped hands, and it was good. "Don't be afraid," she encouraged her children, "it's safe." Soon, they were splashing in the water as well.

"It tastes like snow," Val said.

"It was snow not too long ago," Kianna answered.

High above them, the tractor's diesel engine roared to life. By the time Kianna reached the shoulder of the highway, Dickie's truck was already turning onto the looping onramp for I-81 south. Eron cursed and hurled stones. Kianna sat on the cable guardrail her face buried in her hands. Val sat next to her and placed her arm protectively around her. The children waited while their mother gathered her strength. They needed her strength. At last she stood and said, "We're going to be alright but we need to get back to I-90."

Eron stamped his foot, "No more trucks."

Kianna agreed. "We'll have to walk. It's quite a ways, about 80 miles from here. There are roads, small roads we can follow. I saw them on the map." She pointed at a span a half-mile up river, "The bridge will get us started." She meant to speak with confidence and she succeeded. "We'll go east until we find route 8. It will be hard, but we can do it."

"As long as we're together," Val reminded her.

Kianna reached for the twins, willed them to take her hands, and they did. She needed them to walk beside her, and they did. A hard day's journey took them deep into the countryside. They passed farmhouses abandoned then stripped bare, barns burned to the ground, equipment upended and scattered as if by a great and terrible wind. A handful of vehicles passed by. They hid as soon as they heard one coming and revealed themselves only when they were certain it was gone.

The earth, now in spring's first flush, fed them. Kianna's trained eye found dandelion greens, wild mushrooms, and fiddlehead ferns. Val still had Makena's pouch of matches slung around her neck. Eron scavenged a pot from a barn, half of which remained standing. Kianna made hot soup for her children. At night they gathered the white pine branches and used them to construct a lean-to with a soft, aromatic bed beneath. They fed a campfire with wind-fallen branches until it lulled them to sleep.

By the third day, Kianna reckoned they were near the midpoint of their journey. They had been following route 8, as it ran alongside the Unadilla River. By mid-morning the wind backed into the west. It was cool, damp. The noon sun offered them little comfort. By late afternoon they could feel a chill in the air. The rain came in the early evening, cold, drenching. There was no place to hide. They pressed on, physical exertion providing their only protection against the icy deluge.

Night fell, but the darkness was not complete. Electric lights lit the sky ahead of them. Kianna felt sure they would find a town a mile or so farther up the road. She urged the twins to quicken their pace.

When they drew near to the lights, she could see that a barbed wire gate spanned the road. Spotlights glared down on the wet pavement. Shivering with cold and fatigue, Kianna, Val, and Eron stepped out of the darkness and into their merciless pool of light.

A bored metallic voice addressed them, "Strangers are not welcome here."

Kianna put her arms over the shoulders of her twins. "We are just passing through. We just need a place to stay for the night. I swear that's all. We mean no harm."

The man wielding the bullhorn stepped forward. He was short and heavy, his eyes were hidden by the bill of a New York Yankees baseball cap pulled down low. He wore an orange waterproof overcoat, heavy black rubber boots, and a badge. "Your kind ain't welcome. You city folks done enough damage. So just turn around and go right back where you came from."

"Please, sir," Kianna begged, "please."

Knowing that nothing more needed to be said, he turned away and pulled the trigger on the bullhorn. "Ernie, we got some city people who won't leave. Bring the dogs around."

Angry male voices, the clanking and rattling of chain against steel and the dog's frenzied yelping made it clear this was not an idle threat. The guard faced the strangers and lowered the bullhorn, his voice a wet hiss. "You don't wanna leave, but the dogs'll have other ideas. If I were you, I'd start running."

They ran away. The rain, the cold, the fatigue, these things no longer mattered. The river lay to the east and Kianna didn't want to be trapped with their backs against it, so she went west, away from the village, up into the hills. The dogs gained on them. Kianna, Eron, and Val plunged into the darkness climbing higher and higher into the wilderness.

Gradually, the baying of the dogs faded. The animals were assured of a warm, dry bed when they returned home and were not inclined to continue the hunt on a night this foul. The intruders had been chased well away into the ink-dark forest gloom. They did their part. High above the valley, with its clear north-south orientation and smooth, predictable river plain, the points of the compass disappeared. There was only one direction: higher. The Wallaces fled into the hills, away from the roads, away from the dogs, away from the people. They blundered into a thick stand of brambles. The thorns tore their clothes and cut their skin, but they did not slow down. They staggered forward until they could walk no further. Mercifully, the rain stopped and the mother and her children huddled together on the sodden earth and slept.

Dawn slowly rolled back the night's cold fog. Kianna roused the twins. They cried when they woke, cried from hunger, cried from fear, cried from thirst, cried from pain. They slept in their soaked clothes and were now chilled to the bone. Val rolled onto her belly, her body racked by a fit of coughing. She wiped her mouth, looked at her hand, and saw pus. She hid it from her mother and brother.

Kianna held them close, let them cry. When they were finished, she said, "It's time to go." She pulled Val to her feet and put her daughter's arm around her shoulder. They walked, not knowing where they were, not knowing where they were going. Numbed by fatigue, they stumbled across an empty pasture, the grass deep green. They wandered into a mature stand of hardwoods, the trees were mostly beech, ash, and cherry. Kianna did not notice and did not care.

They side-stepped down a stream bank, waded through ankle-deep water, then struggled up the other side. Beyond the stream was a road, a dirt road. Kianna stepped onto it and turned her face to the now strengthening sun. "If we put the morning sun at our backs, we'll be heading west. If we go far enough, we'll find another road leading north."

"Mommy," Val begged, "I don't feel good. Please, I don't want to walk anymore."

"We'll go slow, honey." Kianna took her daughter's hand into hers.

Eron's face tightened with anger. "I'll bet there are bad people on this road. There are bad people everywhere."

He ventured into a stand of oak and emerged minutes later with a weapon. It was a wooden stick about as long as he was tall, an inch in diameter at the butt end with a tip that came to a nasty looking point. Kianna let him carry it.

Ahead, the road curved to the left. As they drew near, they saw a woman walking toward them. She was white with long white hair, nicely dressed with a leather pack slung over her shoulder, and carrying a wooden basket. She was alone. Despite her innocent appearance, Kianna stiffened with fear. Eron lowered the point of his spear. The woman looked up and saw them. She smiled and waved. When she drew near, Eron stepped forward the better to protect his mother and sister. He eyed the basket the woman was carrying. It was filled with brown eggs.

"Give me the basket," he demanded.

"Eron!" Kianna gasped.

The woman smiled. "I'm afraid this basket was made for me by my good friend Jeffery Gale. He's too busy to make me another so you can't have it, but I'd say it's the eggs you really want."

Eron gritted his teeth. "Yes the eggs. I want, *we* want, the eggs."

"Eron, stop it," Kianna commanded.

The woman spoke again, "Eron I will give all of these eggs to you and your family...if you'll do one thing for me."

Eron tensed, "What do you want?"

"You are going to have to tell me how you'd like to have them cooked." She looked into Kianna's eyes. "I'd like to invite you and your family to join me for breakfast. My name is Jude Thomas, and you are welcome here."

PART II

5
EGGS IN A BASKET

The unpaved road was deserted and wide enough to allow the little party to walk four abreast along its gently crowned center. Jude said, "It's not much farther, a mile at most." She paused, then added, "There's a hill at the end," she looked at Val. "We'll take our time."

Kianna's mind whirled. These were the first kind words she had heard spoken since they were driven away from Makena. She wanted to believe in the woman, wanted to believe she was a good, kind woman. She needed to believe it. "I've, *we've*, had a hard time, a very hard time." Jude let her continue. "We need help."

Jude reassured her, "We all need help. Me and mine the same as you and yours." Kianna became painfully aware of how she and the twins must appear to this woman. They were dirty, scratched, and bruised. The journey from Cleveland had reduced their already ill-fitting clothing to rags that barely maintained their modesty. She imagined how she would have reacted if she had stumbled upon such people walking down the street in Chicago. She knew it would never occur to her to invite them into her home and feed them breakfast.

Wary of strangers, Eron suspected a trap. He fell in between Kianna and Jude, gripping his spear firmly even as he let the tip drift toward the brown road. Miles from the nearest highway, they were unlikely to find help if this woman turned against them. The mothers observed these precautions and honored them by pretending not to notice.

Unlike her mother and brother, Val was untroubled by doubt. They were safe and this good woman would take care of them. She knew this in the same way that she knew her own name. Val sidled up to Jude's side. She admired the long silver hair that fell down across her shoulders, looked up into her loam brown eyes. Jude was almost as tall as her mother and carried herself with a simple elegance. The basket of eggs swayed gently as she walked. Val reached out, shyly, and touched the fabric of Jude's dress. It was clean and smooth and perfectly tailored, as if it had been made for her alone. It was the color of spring, rich and deep green. For Val, it was as if she had stumbled upon Persephone herself, floating across the land. Then the coughing came, and she slumped onto her hands and knees. Eron stood close as Jude and

Kianna comforted her, rubbed her back, told her she would be alright. When it passed, Jude said, "My husband is a doctor. He's out seeing patients now, but he'll look after Val when he gets home."

Kianna voiced her worry, "She's always been so healthy."

Jude looked into Val's eyes, "Bill's a good doctor. He'll take care of you." While Val recovered her strength, Jude pointed out the half-finished nest of a robin newly returned from the South. She set down her basket, leaned over the patch of shooting stars that had taken root along the roadside and breathed in the scent. "They smell like spring."

Kianna, eager to offer something to Jude, hesitated, then ventured, "They are Dodecatheon sanctarum. Native people used the flowers as charms, they said they brought wealth and...and..." she stumbled over the words, "made people generous."

Jude looked at her, surprised.

Kianna hurried to explain, "I'm a plant scientist. I had a lab at Northwestern...before everything fell apart."

The little party reached the foot of the hill Jude had told them about and paused again to gather their strength. Kianna felt she had been delivered, as if by magic, to a strange and undiscovered country. "Everything is so...so peaceful."

"It is," Jude nodded.

"Out there, the world has smashed itself to pieces. Everything is dying... out there."

Jude had heard stories about the chaos, the last letter from Ned Wolff had been full of such news. He called it "the Fall."

"It's different here. Here, you are guests of the Shire." Jude laughed. "I'm so glad you came to see us. We haven't had visitors for months." As she finished speaking, they crested the brow of the hill, and the village of Summer Hill appeared before them.

Kianna had never seen anything so beautiful. Here, in the middle of nowhere, was a cluster of tidy stone cottages, each topped by a flat sod roof. There was an inner ring of thirty, maybe forty, of these buildings all arranged around a central village green. A score of children played on the open ground there. Beyond them, young men practiced lacrosse. Kianna closed her eyes for a moment and drank in the children's delicious overlapping protests and triumphs. It was a sound she thought she would never hear again.

A second look revealed another circle of buildings arranged, irregularly, outside of the first. The biggest of them were far larger than the cottages and more varied in their construction. These, Kianna guessed, were the barns and workshops of Summer Hill. A faint breeze from the west carried a trace of wood smoke. Her eyes searched for the source. Smoke curled lazily from a half dozen of the chimneys. Only then did she notice the things that were missing. There were no wires, no cars, no antennae, no cables. Out there, these things lay in ruins. Here, it was as if such things had never existed.

The colors of the village blended with those of the earth. The scene formed itself into an astonishing portrait, beautiful, complex, healthy, and whole. The children had stopped playing and were beginning to stare at the unwashed, bedraggled strangers who seemed to have appeared out of nowhere. Jude felt their shame.

She pointed to the nearest of the houses, "We live here." As she swung the door open, she reminded Eron, "I owe you a hot breakfast."

The boy peered inside. "Wow, this is cool!" He abandoned his weapon at the threshold and ushered his mother and sister inside. Jude closed the door quietly behind them.

It was home.

Eron could feel it, they all could, and they soaked it in. This was how the house on St. Joseph Street had felt. This was old, comfortable, and warm. A family lived here and had lived here for a long time. Jude went to the kitchen. She set the egg basket on the work table and turned her attention to an antique wooden stove. After rattling the grates, she found a few embers from the morning fire still glowing. She laid a handful of kindling in, opened the damper, and she was ready to show her guests the house.

"Bill and I built it together, back in the '80s. We'd just returned from..." She hesitated then changed her mind, "We had just found Summer Hill, and we thought this was the best place for a house. Most of the houses up here are laid out like this, in a circular pattern." A massive stone fireplace dominated the center. Streaks of soot darkened the rocks below a hand-hewn oak mantle, giving mute testimony to the thousand roaring fires that had burned hot and bright on blustering winter nights. Opposite the fireplace, south-facing windows let the sun stream in, warming the house even in the middle of winter. Well-worn overstuffed leather chairs perched comfortably upon on a handmade rug. Persian, Kianna thought.

Against the wall stood an antique fall front desk. Kianna pointed to it. "That's beautiful."

"I love it," Jude said. "We bought it not long after we moved here, found it on a front lawn down in the valley. Bought it on the spot even though we really couldn't afford it." Kianna admired the book-lined shelves behind the leaded glass doors that flanked the writing surface. The oak had darkened with age and was now almost black. "It has quite a story of its own. I'll tell you all about it sometime."

Finally, they came to the kitchen. The fire was hot, and it was time for breakfast. Jude invited Kianna and the twins to sit at the heavy wooden trestle table that dominated the room. It was the first time they had sat down at a table since the morning they left Chicago. John's absence, though painful, was left unspoken.

Jude added a load of air-dried ash and tipped the damper. From the icebox, she retrieved a ceramic pitcher, a crock of butter, and a block of hard yellow cheese. "How about some milk, toast, a little cheese, scrambled eggs, blackberry jam, and let's see...some potatoes. Would that be good?"

Val answered for all of them, "I would like that very much, ma'am."

Kianna started to get up. "I can help," she said.

"No need. I've got it down to a science. Besides, I'd say I've had an easier day than any of you."

It was the truth.

The table was laid quickly and beautifully. They ate together. Aware only of the taste, the smell, and the feel of a meal made for them, served to them, shared with them. When they were finished, Jude disappeared out the back door, returning moments later with another armload of firewood. She fed half of it to the now ravenous fire and opened a valve at the base of the water tank that sat beside the stove. Their bellies full, Kianna and the twins cleared the table.

Jude stepped onto the front porch and called for Caleb, her youngest. He raced across the Green, toward the sound of his mother's voice. He was tall, his arms and legs gangly with adolescent growth. Fine brown hair framed inquisitive, knowing blue eyes. His skin, flushed with exertion, made him look older than his fifteen years. Bounding onto the porch, he slung his lacrosse stick casually over his right shoulder.

"What's going on, Mom?"

"We have visitors."

"Yeah, we saw. Everybody saw. Everybody is talking about it." Caleb's voice rose with his enthusiasm. Jude hushed him. "They need new clothes. Kianna and I are about the same size. Eron can wear some of the things you've outgrown but we don't have anything for Val."

"How old are they? Are they from the Valley? Nobody recognizes them."

"More about them later. Right now I need you to go find Mia. Tell her we need some nice things for the girl."

"OK. Sure, Mom!"

Back inside, Kianna and the twins had straightened up the kitchen the best they could. Jude laid her hand on the hot water tank and said, "Now, who would like a bath?"

"Yes," Kianna agreed. "We all need a bath."

Jude filled the tub for Eron and handed him a washcloth and a bar of homemade soap. Back in the kitchen, she stoked the fire.

"I can't wait!" Val said, squirming in her seat.

"I can't tell you how much I appreciate what you are doing for us," Kianna agreed.

"You'd do the same for me and mine."

When Eron was finished, he bellowed, "Mom!"

Jude guessed his question. "You'll find a robe hanging on a hook by the mirror."

"Oh, thanks." Eron's boyish voice echoed against the bathroom's stone walls.

Finally, the door swung open. Eron stood proudly in front of them. His thick curly hair glistened, his skin was clean, and he was smiling.

"Oh yeah. Oh yeah!"

"I am so going next!" Val yelled.

Kianna clasped her hand to her mouth and tried to hold back her tears, but could not.

6
A FLAXEN BLOUSE

Caleb found Mia at work. She was his age and was of medium height with an athletic build, like his. Her hair, which she usually let run free as a wild mass of auburn ringlets, was hidden beneath a patterned red kerchief. Mia was apprenticed to a Master Beekeeper and both Master and apprentice were hard at work preparing the foundations on which the bees would soon deposit the year's honey. Caleb explained his errand and soon the two of them were standing in front of Mia's closet. Caleb waited as patiently as he could while she inspected its contents.

"How old is she?" Mia asked.

Caleb grimaced, "How should I know? I haven't even met her."

"But you did see her, right?"

"Yeah but who knows," Caleb grimaced. "She's shorter than you and me, about up to Mom's shoulder."

"Hmm," Mia deliberated. She sifted through her wardrobe finally settling on a blouse, plain, brown, not her favorite.

"Hah," Caleb chided her. "It's ugly—even I know that's ugly. Your Mom'll kill you if you pick that one."

"I was just looking," she answered defensively, stung by the truth in Caleb's words.

"Yeah right," Caleb said. "Hey, I like this one." He reached out and touched the white blouse which hung next to the brown one.

"Oh my God. No way. Say you're not serious."

"Yeah, I'm serious. It's pretty and you know it."

"I can't. It's my favorite."

"It was your favorite but you can't wear it anymore, can you?"

"Yes I can."

"No you can't."

"Could if I wanted to."

"You can't wear it 'cause now you've got great big boobs."

"Shut up, you jerk." Mia whacked Caleb's shoulder with the flat of her hand, not entirely displeased.

Caleb responded by cupping his hands in front of his chest and taunting her, "Mia's got boobs. Mia's got great big boobs."

"Caleb Thomas you are the biggest jerk in the world." She plucked the blouse from its hanger and held it up before her. It was beautiful. Woven from the finest flax, bleached white, and then embroidered with glittering beadwork. The sleeves were tasseled and the cuffs fringed with hand-worked lace.

"You want me to give her this one 'cause you have a crush on the new girl."

"I do not," Caleb responded, hurt.

Mia laughed. It was a hearty, knowing laugh that could not be answered. "So is she a skirt girl or a pants girl?"

Now Caleb was flustered, "How should I know, I don't even know her. She just needs something to wear. You're the one making a big deal out of it."

Mia arched her eyebrows, "Skirt or pants?"

"I don't know, why are you asking me? Skirt, I guess."

"Hah. I knew you would say that." She picked out a long flowing skirt that matched the blouse perfectly, and it was warm enough for the still early spring.

"OK," she said. Her voiced plumed with an exaggerated boredom. "Take these and tell your new girlfriend I said 'you're welcome.'"

Caleb rolled the clothes into a ball and stuffed them into the roomy defenseman's basket at the end of his stick. He fled the house, eager to be finished with this strange duty. Once home, he dumped the bundle on the kitchen table and raced through the house until he found his mother and Kianna sitting on the back porch.

"I'm going to meet Dad on the Turnpike. I'll be home with him for dinner. Love you, bye." He turned to leave, then remembered, "Oh, the clothes are on the table." The front door slammed behind him.

Kianna smiled, "Well, he's something."

"That's my baby boy."

"He's growing up."

"He'll be sixteen this winter."

"The twins turned thirteen last fall before the troubles started."

Jude nodded. Then she took Kianna's hand, "I'm sorry to hear about John. He must have loved you and the twins very much, more than life itself."

Kianna bit her lip, "I loved him, everyone loved him. Val and Eron most of all."

"They need you now," Jude said.

"I was brave for them, as brave as I could be. But last night I thought it was the end. I wanted to sleep—and never wake up."

"Well," Jude said, "today is a new day."

Kianna trembled, started to speak and then stopped, afraid to put her thoughts into words.

Jude answered the unspoken question in a casual, offhand way. "You and the twins have been through a lot, it's a miracle you lived through it. I wonder, would the three of you do Bill and I the honor of being our guests? It would be nice if you stay with us a while—until you're sure what comes next."

Kianna let herself breathe; this was her heart's desire.

The women stood and reached out for each other. Kianna's answer came in the wordless warmth of two lifelong friends, newly met. When the moment passed, Jude said, "You go on upstairs and get the kids ready for dinner. I'll feed their old clothes to the fire, if you don't mind."

Kianna slipped upstairs and nuzzled her children awake, the way she used to when they were little. They blinked into the light and looked around the room, not sure where they were.

"Is Daddy home?" Eron asked drowsily.

Kianna swallowed hard. "No, honey. Daddy's not home, we're not home. We're in a new place, a safe place." The answer seemed to satisfy her son, because he laid back, eyes open, listening to the unfamiliar sounds of the house, but was at ease.

Kianna crossed to the other side of the bed and whispered into Val's ear, "I have a surprise for you." Her daughter's eyes blinked open.

"Really?" she asked.

"Mmm hmm." Kianna answered, then she unfurled the blouse before her daughter's unbelieving eyes. It sparkled like a diamond necklace.

"And this," Kianna held up the skirt.

"Oh, Momma!" was all Val could say.

"They are yours. They were given to you."

Val reached out and touched the fabric. Then Eron said, "Hey, I got some pants and a shirt. Great."

He leapt out of bed and got dressed.

"You go on downstairs. We'll be down in a bit," Kianna said.

Eron rolled his eyes, "Girls." He clumped contentedly down the stairs and found Jude in the kitchen, "Hi. Ahh…" He wasn't sure what to call her.

"You can call me Jude."

"Jude." He said the name slowly.

"You had a good nap?"

"Yes," Eron answered. "The girls are getting dressed."

"You look nice," Jude said.

"Thank you...Jude."

She smiled at the boy. He was short for his age, big boned but, now, painfully thin. She could fix that.

"Can you help me with dinner?"

The food smelled good.

"Can you peel potatoes?"

Eron shrugged uncertainly.

"Here, I'll show you." She put a paring knife into his hand. "Like this, cut the skin off but leave the white part." Eron set to work concentrating on this unfamiliar task. Jude hummed as she worked.

Minutes later the front door burst open and Caleb and his father tumbled across the threshold, engaged in a playful but highly spirited wrestling match, thudding and banging as they rolled around on the floor.

"Boys," Jude yelled from the kitchen, "no wrestling in the house. Plus you know we have company." The banging stopped but a whispered conversation ensued. Then, together, "Sorry, Mom."

"Get washed up," Jude replied. Bill and Caleb entered the kitchen and flung their arms around Jude. Eron, still clumsily wielding the paring knife against the potato skins, listened intently but did not look up. Jude spun her men around and introduced the boy at the table. "This is Eron. I met him on the Turnpike today. He and his mother and sister are visiting us."

Eron looked at Bill and saw a large man, about six feet tall, his hair a tangled curly mess, his face covered with a bushy salt and pepper beard. The eyes were blue and, Eron realized, they were kind. The boy smiled weakly.

"I'm pleased to meet you, Eron," Bill's voice boomed. He reached out and shook Eron's hand. "It's about time we had some visitors around here, wouldn't you say Mother?" Jude was busy at the stove but Caleb answered helpfully, "Mom says Dad never met a stranger." He waved at Eron in the awkward way teenagers do and added, "Hi, I'm Caleb."

A real smile spread across Eron's face. Caleb plopped down in the chair across from Eron, "Mom's got you on the spuds I see—lucky you," he said playfully.

"That's right," Jude said, "and there's a knife there for you too, so get to it, buster." Caleb caught Eron's gaze and laughed. "He's a guest, Mom, so he shouldn't work. And I like him, so I shouldn't work."

"Like I always say: no work, no eat."

The light of the day was fading, and Bill set to work lighting candles, narrating his day as he went. "Had a good day, spent most of it over in West Farthing. Won't need to stop back for a week or so, I'd guess."

"Good," Jude replied. "And the Emerson baby, how is she?"

"Jaundice is fading, nursing like a tiger. I told Jenna to put her in the sun a couple of hours a day, just to be safe. Ran into Haleigh and Hannah. They were working the hives along Emerson Brook. They'll be home, but late for dinner."

"Not surprised." Jude said.

When twilight reached the single point at which the candlelight matched the fading light of day, Kianna stepped into the kitchen. "May I present Miss Valerie Wallace." They all stopped to watch Val descend the stairs, her cocoa skin glowing alongside the soft white linen. The beadwork shone even in the candlelight. Her skirt swayed like the tall grass of a summer meadow.

Eron let out a low, long whistle, "Sista, you look great." Val beamed. Jude whispered to Kianna, "My friend, you have a beautiful daughter." Bill stood and applauded. And, through it all, Caleb peeled potatoes. Jude sidled up to him and said, out of the side of her mouth, "Doesn't Val look nice?"

"Yeah, nice," he mumbled. Mia's false accusation still stung.

"We will talk about this later," Jude added ominously.

The family set the table, and it was soon laid heavy with mashed potatoes, stuffed squash, a pot of steaming barley, potato and leek stew, and bread as black as the night sky. Bottles of hard cider were opened for the occasion, and there was a salad of fresh spring greens. Bill moved the conversation along, keeping well away from topics he guessed might be difficult. Just before dessert, the girls arrived home. It had been dark for an hour, and the moon was not yet up. Bill rose as they entered the kitchen, "It is my pleasure to introduce to you my lovely daughters, Haleigh and Hannah. All those who know them, love them," he said.

The "girls" were in fact young women; Kianna figured them to be in their late teens. Haleigh was the taller of the two and, she thought, the older sister. Long curly brown hair fell down around her shoulders with a careless beauty. Her face was narrow with fine high cheekbones, and her eyes sparkled with intelligence. But it was her mouth that drew Kianna's attention. Thin lips, naturally pink, were held together in a smooth confident line. She wore overalls. The knees were muddy, the fabric worn but not tattered.

Jude spoke next, "And those who know them well, know that my dear girls may have little to say, but every word is precious."

The two smiled and sat down at the table. Hannah took the seat across from Kianna. The younger sister's face was rounder, more delicate, her cheeks tinged with a rosy pink. She had her father's eyes. Hannah tied her baby thin brown hair up into a bun, the way an older woman might. Her hands bore long, thin fingers that were already well acquainted with hard work. Her eyes smiled first at Kianna, then at Val, and then at Eron, but she did not speak.

"The Wallaces come from Chicago. They needed a place to rest." Nothing more needed to be said.

"Now you've met three of our five. The two older boys, they're on their own." Bill passed the slices of apple and cheese that were dessert to his left. "It's calving season, so Zach and Elijah Morris are up to the big barn over near Hardbottle. They'll be there til the last heifer delivers. A week, maybe two, I expect. He's the oldest."

"Yes...he's the oldest," Caleb put in, "and he's always saying how everything was so much harder when he was my age and how I'm so lucky 'cause I'm the baby and all that."

"Well," Val ventured, "I'm Eron's big sister. He says we're twins but, really, I'm older than him."

Eron huffed, "Yeah, by like three minutes. I just sent you out first to see what it was like out there."

"You did not."

"Did too."

"Enough," Kianna admonished. "Stop."

Jude stifled a laugh in her napkin. Caleb and Eron had discovered a new common cause.

Bill went on, "Virgil, he's two years younger than Zach."

"And he's the genius," Caleb added in a bored tone.

"Well yeah," Bill added, "a real mechanical electrical genius, it's true." He jerked his thumb back toward the cook stove. "We used to have to heat water on the stove, then Virgil built a thermosiphon out of junk parts, really, and now the water goes straight to the tub. It's great." The idea that putting hot water into a bathtub amounted to an act of genius struck Eron as primitive beyond belief.

"Anyway, Virgil's over to Bag's End. He's working with Bob Brazzi. The two of them are building a water-powered gristmill. It's a big job. Not sure when they'll be done, but people are hoping for next year."

"And of course our Haleigh and Hannah—they grow things," Jude said. The pair smiled at their mother.

"And me," Caleb clamored, "I'm going to be a doctor, like Dad."

"Right he is," Bill said, beaming with pride.

"Some day," Jude cautioned.

Bill stood up. "Time to clear the table. Many hands make light work. Care to help, Eron?" Eron nodded with enthusiasm. "Let's get it done then."

"Mom," Eron said. "You and Val rest. I'll take care of it."

"Why thank you very much, Eron Wallace. I'm proud of you."

By the time the clock struck ten, everyone was in bed and sound asleep.

7
A COUNCIL OF ELDERS

E ron Wallace woke with a start, then groaned. He had been dreaming of his father, had seen his face, heard his voice, felt his reassuring touch. Now, John Wallace was gone. The immediate, punishing untruth of his dream made the night they were separated seem a lifetime ago. It was time to move, time to restart the search. He slipped out of bed, dressed quickly, and crept down the stairs.

He found Bill in the kitchen. "Mornin', Eron."

"Good morning."

Bill's worn black leather knapsack lay open on the work table, half of the day's provisions already inside.

"Got some bread, here. And cheese. You hungry?"

"Yes."

Bill studied the youth's face. His skin, smooth and tan, was unblemished. Adolescence had not yet arrived in full, nor was it marked by the extraordinary losses he had suffered. But the eyes, the eyes told a different story.

"Sleep OK?"

"Umm, yeah."

Bill set a plate in front of Eron. "Sweet dreams?"

"Mmm hmm. Had a dream about my Dad."

"Miss him?"

Eron looked accusingly at Bill then realized the older man meant no harm.

"More than anything."

"I'll bet you never expected to find yourself in a place like this."

It was an ambiguous remark and Eron was not sure how to answer it. "We're on our way to New Hampshire, to Gramp and Gran's. Dad's probably already there, waiting for us."

"Ahh, New Hampshire. Had some good friends out that way. Jude and I've been to Concord, Manchester, and Portsmouth. We even got up to Laconia, back before."

Eron talked with his mouth full. "They have a farm, near Keene."

"I'll bet it's beautiful."

Again Eron hesitated, "We should call them and let them know we're OK and...make sure Dad's already there. Maybe he'll come and pick us up."

Bill sat down across the table from the boy. "Sorry, Eron, but we don't have a phone. Nobody up here does."

Eron bit his lip. "Maybe a letter. Could we send a letter? I know the address."

Bill leaned forward, "There are big troubles out there, and I know you've been in the middle of it. Yeah, the world's gone crazy." Eron would not look at him so Bill backed off. "You know the old saying? 'Neither snow nor rain nor heat nor gloom of night stays these couriers from the swift completion of their appointed rounds'?"

Eron didn't, but nodded as if he did.

"It's a great motto, one of the best. But the fact is that our mail stopped coming last winter. We haven't seen or heard from anybody associated with the US Postal Service since then."

Eron was disappointed but pressed on. "But down in the valley, they have phones down there, right?"

"I guess they might, but the truth is that those folks are pretty freaked out right now. Your Mom said you had a run in with the valley people down east of here."

Eron nodded.

"They aren't bad people, really. Just scared. It's the fear that makes them do such ugly things."

Eron remained determined. Bill could feel the animal fierceness of his determination. It would serve the boy well. "Mom said we should go north and get to I-90. That road goes almost all the way to Gramp and Gran's. She said we could walk there."

"I suppose she's right."

"We're gonna have to walk the whole way 'cause people in cars and trucks are bad, really bad—especially people in trucks."

"I don't doubt it."

His fear aroused, Eron narrowed his gaze and lowered his voice til it was barely a whisper. "You can't make us stay here."

Bill laughed and regretted it immediately, hurrying to reassure Eron. "No, we can't. And we wouldn't want to. You and your mother and sister are free to come or go as you please. You can leave anytime you like with our blessing and any help we can give."

"Good, that's good," Eron answered thoughtfully.

They heard people moving upstairs. "Well," Bill said, "I've got a long day ahead of me, gotta get moving." He rose from his chair, plucked a dark wool hooded sweater from a hook next to the back door, pulled it over his head, and then reached for the leather bag. He snapped its nickel buckles and was ready to go.

"One more thing," the words tumbled out of Eron's mouth.

Bill slung the knapsack onto his shoulder and turned to face the boy. "What's that?"

"Val, how is she? Is she OK?"

"I took a look at her last night. Talked to your Mom about it. She's got what folks call walking pneumonia." Eron flinched. "She's young and pretty darn strong. There's nothing wrong with her that the gifts of time, good food, and rest can't fix."

"She's gonna get better?"

Bill reached out and put his hand on Eron's shoulder. "She'll be OK, just give her a chance to get her strength back."

Eron smiled, "OK, I will. Thanks Doctor Thom…"

"Call me Bill will ya?" He winked at Eron and said, "Gotta go," then slipped quietly out the back door.

After lunch, Jude announced that she had errands to run and would be out for the afternoon. "Make yourselves at home. I'll be back before supper." When she was gone, the Wallace family found themselves alone in the house for the first time.

Kianna puttered in the kitchen with her children close by. They made small talk, enjoying the illusion of being at home in the Bungalow on the South Side, willing themselves to believe that school was out, that they were passing the day together, waiting for John to finish his work.

Waiting for John to join them.

The mood, sweet and light as cotton candy, lasted until Eron started talking about leaving. "Mom," he implored, "we've got to get out of here."

Kianna closed her eyes, made herself breathe. John was not coming home, this was not her kitchen. They remained alone and unprotected in a world gone mad. When her heart stopped pounding, she answered her son the best she could. "Of course, honey. We are on our way to Gran and Gramp's, but we need to rest. We all need to rest."

Eron bristled, "Every day we hang around here is a day Dad spends worrying about us. Let's go!"

Kianna fought the desire to put her son in his place, to strike at him with the truth. Her lips moved wordlessly. Then she lied, "I know, honey, but Daddy also knows that we are all together. He'll know I am taking care of you, and that will ease his mind."

Val's eyes ranged between her brother and mother.

Unsatisfied, Eron changed his tack, "The other thing is that this place is weird, really really weird. It scares me."

"Scares you?" Kianna answered, surprised but grateful for the distraction this new topic offered.

"Mom," he answered impatiently, "Bill says he's a doctor but he lives in a house with a lawn for a roof. There's no electricity, no phone, internet, no TV. And he doesn't even own a car—he walks to work." The last bit was offered as evidence of the most dangerous kind of moral degeneracy.

Kianna reasoned with him. "It's true that people here are different from the people we knew at home, but there are lots of different people in the world. Different doesn't mean bad." Her left eyebrow rode up the way it did when she was making a point that was not to be ignored. "You of all people should appreciate not judging people for their differences."

"Yeah. But, Mom, they think their son is a genius because he put hot water in the bathtub."

"Well, Eron, can you make hot water run out of a tap?" she asked.

"You know what I'm talking about, Mom. And those two girls just look at you and don't say anything. It's weird."

Again Kianna was eager to change the subject, "Anyway, we have to wait til Val is better before...before we can leave."

They turned to Val who sat primly at the table. The girl gave a pained sigh and addressed them in a calm steady voice, "Daddy is dead. He was crushed by all those people." The words echoed off the walls with the force of an emotional sonic boom. "Gran and Gramps are dead, too. I'm pretty sure. They were really old and the winter was long and cold." She spoke in the settled tone of a widow, done with grieving, remembering her late beloved husband.

Kianna blinked hard.

Eron howled like a wounded dog, "No! No! That is a lie," he lunged at his sister. "Take it back! I swear I'll make you take it back. Daddy's alive! He's got to be alive." Kianna pulled him off from his sister, and Eron rained blows down upon his mother's shoulders. They came fast and furious, but they were not meant to injure.

"She's lying! She's lying!" he wailed. "Make her take it back. Daddy's waiting for us. We've got to go to him!"

Kianna reached out for her son, but he shoved her roughly away. He fled the kitchen and stumbled up the stairs, sobbing wordlessly. When he reached the bedroom, he slammed its door as hard as he could. Val stood up and gathered her mother into her arms and held her as Kianna convulsed with grief. Val sang the tender song of consolation she learned from her, which Kianna had learned from her mother. She sang it softly, over and over.

Hush your cries, close your eyes,
Dream of pretty little horses.
Hush a bye, don't you cry,
Go to sleep my little baby.

Jude entered the Shire's Long House, walked its length, sat on the bench that was reserved for younger visitors, and waited for the Council of Elders to assemble. The Long House stood on the low ground east of Summer Hill tucked inside a thick stand of ancient hemlocks, not far from where she first met the Wallaces. It was a small unassuming building, consisting of a single room measuring 30 feet wide and 50 feet long and lacking adornment or decoration of any kind. None was needed, for this was the heart and soul of the Shire. Framed with hand-planed oak timbers and raised in a single day by the people themselves, it was built as the home of the Shire's Council of Elders. Both the wood paneled ceiling and the well-worn floor boards had been reused from a 19th century dairy barn. The windows were small and placed high up so passersby would be unlikely to see or hear what was happening inside. A pot-bellied stove stood at the north end alongside the chamber's heavy oak door. The stove was cold; there was no need for a fire on this warm spring day. Most importantly, the two long walls were graced with chairs reserved for the Elders of Farthings, East and West, respectively.

Jude sat down, leaned back against the wall, closed her eyes, and listened to the familiar murmur of the Elders' conversation. They waited for Naomi Barken, the eldest Crone of Crickhollow, to arrive. When she was in her appointed place, the Council was called to order, and Jude was invited to speak. She walked to the center of the room, every one of the faces that surrounded was familiar to her. Each had touched her life, each was a gift. "I expect that news of the Wallace family's arrival has reached all of you." The

Elders murmured agreement. "They come from Chicago. The chaos we have heard about led them to flee their home with the hope of reaching the safety of the New Hampshire farm on which the husband John was raised. John lost his life while protecting his family from a mob in Cleveland. The mother and her children found refuge in the home of an elder and spent the winter there. They were driven from that home. Misfortune hounded them at every turn until I came upon them. They were hungry, cold, and friendless right here on the Turnpike." Jude knew that the Elders would want to hear her opinion, so she continued. "Bill and I have taken them into our home, heard their story, and taken their measure. These are good people, as loving and kind as any in the Shire. They have bowed before their fate, but they have not been broken."

Now it was time to listen.

They listened to the hemlocks as they combed themselves with the warm spring air. They listened as a murder of crows chattered anxiously among the highest branches. They listened to the sound of their own breathing.

At last, Tim Woody of Hardbottle—once a Coast Guard coxswain and shepherd, now a poet and Elder—said, "They are castaways. Kallimos treasures castaways, treasured you and Bill. Took you in, made you whole."

"That is true," Jude answered quietly.

Amanda Peet, a Crone from Bywater, her voice thin as paper, said, "I think they have come to us for some reason, some good reason we do not yet understand."

Bob Brazzi, Master Tinker and youngest of the Elders, added, "Virgil and I are hard at it with the new mill. Another pair of hands would sure help."

"The mother, Kianna, has advanced training in botany." Jude said. This news elicited a ripple of approval. Botany was something useful, something important. "As for the children, they are twins, both thirteen. Old enough to apprentice."

Naomi Barkan, the eldest of them all, spoke for the first time. "What of the heart..." Jude took this as a question and started to answer but the Crone continued, "When the heart, when the heart is full, it's alright." Her voice trailed off as she repeated the phrase, "when the heart is full, it's alright."

Jude started, "They..."

"No," Naomi interrupted, "what of our heart? This mother and her children are not the objects of this test. This is a test of our people, our beliefs, and our hearts. The Shire must give them the welcoming they deserve." The words hung in the air, like dust caught in a beam of sunshine—tiny, but brilliant. That settled the question.

Claris Bagnall of Summer Hill—once an accountant, professor, and potter, now a storyteller and Elder—said, "I think the Murchison place might make a good home for this little family."

Heads nodded all around.

"Becca and Jim would be pleased. It was their way."

Claris said, "I'll arrange the welcoming for tomorrow, if the Wallaces are willing."

Jude nodded. "Thank you. I'll talk to them about life here and the Murchison house tonight." Her business before the Council concluded, Jude excused herself and stepped outside, eager to return home.

When Jude was gone, Amanda Peet said, "This'll be hard on Bill and Jude. The memories will come like a flood, stronger than water." The Elders agreed and knew there was nothing they could do for them. The matter concluded, they turned their attention to the problem in Bywater.

Jude returned to a somber household. Kianna told her what had happened and confessed that Eron refused to leave his room. She was afraid that the discord might upset her host. It did not. Given the unsettled situation, Jude did think it best to keep the news about the invitation from the Elders and the offer of the Murchison House until after dinner. The food was good, but the table was unusually quiet. Jude struggled to contain her anticipation. Kianna struggled to contain her grief. Bill just struggled.

Eron had refused Kianna's request for him to come down to join them, so after the table was cleared, she took a plate of food up to him. When she came back downstairs, she found Bill and Jude engaged in an urgent, whispered conversation in the kitchen. Haleigh and Hannah, never much for talk, slipped out of the kitchen when the work was done, happy to be on their own. Jude asked Caleb to build a fire; the warmth of the day had given way to a cool evening. A fire, while not essential, would feel good. When she was ready, Jude summoned Kianna, Val, Bill, and Caleb to the semi-circle of chairs arrayed before the hearth.

The gathering seemed dangerously formal to Kianna. She gave into a panicked fear over the impact Eron's tantrum might have on them all. The clean clothes, the warm beds, the many acts of kindness had felt so good that she had let herself forget she and her children were strangers here and would, surely soon, be made to leave. Perhaps even tonight. A wave of nausea swept over her.

When they were settled, Jude said, "This afternoon, I went to see the Elders at the Long House." Kianna squinted, trying to understand if this was good or bad for her and the twins. Jude saw her expression and reassured her, "The Shire has a Council of Elders, just like Kallimos. They help us all with life and the problems of everyday life."

"The Council is the Shire's government?" Kianna wanted to understand.

"No," Bill said. "The Elders have respect and influence, but no power. They don't need to hold onto power."

"Oh," Kianna said, not really understanding.

Jude, still excited by the news she held inside, tried again. "I told them about you, your story, how you came to be here and...your grief."

Kianna could not restrain herself, "I want you both to know how much we've appreciated what you've done for us, how much we owe you..."

Bill said softly, "Let Jude finish."

"The Elders are happy you have come to the Shire. They think your arrival is important for many reasons, some of which not even they understand."

Kianna listened hard. Her life and her children's lives teetered on a knife edge.

Bill got up out of his chair and stood in front of the fire, warming himself. "We know you are on your way to New Hampshire, but we can't imagine how you'd ever get there, things being the way they are. It might be wise to stay awhile, let things settle down out there."

Jude nodded in agreement.

Kianna grimaced. "But you have a family of your own. We can't just stay here with you."

"Busy house for sure," Bill agreed. "But we aren't talking about you staying with us." ·

Jude had to interrupt, "The Murchison place was Becca and Jim's, but Jim died a few years back. Becca lived alone until she died last winter. They were good people, wise Elders both of them. They didn't have any children, and the house has been sitting empty." Jude leaned forward, eyes blazing. "The Elders agree that you and the twins are meant to have it." The announcement made, she flopped back in her chair.

Kianna's jaw went slack, then, slowly, she brought herself to say, "But we don't have any money."

Bill grinned mischievously. "The thing is, you don't need any money. The house is empty, the Elders agree you should have it. They think you and the house go together. It's yours—for free—if you want it."

The conversation was interrupted by a short, polite cough. Eron was announcing his return to society. He stepped cautiously into the sitting room. The flickering light of the fire illuminated his puffy, red-rimmed eyes.

Her son's sudden appearance made Kianna nervous. "Eron honey, come sit down next to me." He slumped onto her chair's broad arm and slid his arm around his mother's shoulders, then reached out and touched Val. This silent apology was accepted in full. Much relieved, Kianna returned to the strange offer she had just received. "Eron, did you hear what Bill and Jude were saying about the house?" He nodded to show he had. Kianna focused fully on her children. "Val, Eron...what do you think?"

Val's eyes gleamed, "Oh, Mama, it would be wonderful."

"Eron?" The boy closed his eyes for a moment, then opened them slowly and nodded yes.

"Are you sure, Eron?"

He answered very softly, "Yes."

Kianna turned back to Bill and Jude, "I have to make sure I am understanding you. They, these people the...ahh...Elders, they are sure they want to give us a house?" She struggled to believe such a thing could be possible.

"The house and a place with us all here in the Shire are yours if it's what you want," Jude said.

Kianna swallowed hard, her mind still reeling, "We want to stay."

Bill clapped his hands together, "Welcome to the Tribes of Eden."

Jude joined Bill before the fire. "Tomorrow is the Welcoming. It's a big day. It'll be a long day, but a good day."

"A Welcoming, cool. Haven't had one in a while." Caleb said.

There was murmured agreement. The hour was late, and it was time for bed. Bill, Caleb, and the twins made their way upstairs. Kianna held back. She needed to talk to Jude. When they were alone, she asked, "Why? Why are you doing this for us? We are strangers, we have nothing."

The question made Jude tremble. "Bill and I were strangers once, lost and alone, like you. We had nothing, like you. We were taken in and made welcome, given a chance to live and to learn. It was a long time ago, but I remember. I don't think anyone could forget."

"What happened?" Kianna asked.

"The people of Kallimos saved us, changed us. They changed our lives forever. We owe them everything, so I guess you could say that we are paying a debt forward on behalf of some very dear friends."

Kianna could see how deeply Jude was moved, but she still did not understand. "Kallimos? I've never heard of it."

"It's a very long story, one you will know soon enough." Jude said.

Kianna nodded, willing to wait. "So, off to bed we go then."

Jude smiled wearily and embraced Kianna, "Tomorrow, my dear Kianna, is much more than just a new day."

8
RETURN TO KALLIMOS

B ill and Jude lay in bed, holding hands and staring into the night's black depth. It was just as the Elders had foretold. The unexpected arrival of the Wallaces and the family's desperate plight triggered powerful memories of their own collision with fate. They were young then, just out of training and eager to transform the field of aging, dragging it out of the fuddy-duddy past and bringing it fully into a bright and shining scientific future. He was a physician, a specialist in the care of older people, and she had taken a doctorate in the social science of aging.

They lived in New York City, in an apartment on Barrow Street not far from Sheridan Square, though it would be more accurate to say they slept at the apartment and lived in the city's public library. Two years of hard labor brought forth a 680-page manuscript entitled *Medical and Social Realties of Aging*. The tome presented the latest in aging research and was destined to become the standard textbook in the field of aging. Not that they would know—or care.

When their work was done, they rewarded themselves by chartering a little sloop named Sophia and spending a summer cruising the Caribbean. Alone. Together. They approached Montserrat one late summer evening and let out a sea anchor in the dense shadow of the island's looming volcano. Their old lives came to an end there. During the night, an unseen power took hold of the Sophia, shattered its wooden hull, and pulled them both into the ocean's cold depth. They should have died. Instead, they were cast ashore on the hard, white sand of Kallimos.

Lying in a bed together, they regained consciousness. Jude stirred and opened her eyes, "Are you alright?"

"I think so. You?"

She rolled toward Bill and a wave of pain rushed through her. She whispered, "I hurt all over. Where are we?"

"I don't know."

"This isn't a hospital. It can't be."

Bill let his eyes focus. "It's so dark and so quiet. Maybe it's a house...on Montserrat."

Jude shook her head, "We were miles from shore when the boat went down."

In the silence that followed her comment, she reached out and took Bill's hand. They considered a gruesome possibility. What if they had drowned? What if they were dead? Was this some kind of afterlife?

For a long time, neither of them spoke.

Then Bill said, "I've gotta pee." This observation struck them both as being very funny and they laughed, even though it hurt to laugh. Bill shimmied painfully toward the edge of the bed and put his feet on the floor. In front of him was a lidded earthenware jar. He hoped it was a chamber pot. When he was done, he climbed back into bed. "I've never known a dead person," he told Jude, "but I am willing to bet dead people don't need to pee." After Jude took her turn and crawled back into bed, they held each other and slept.

As time healed their wounds, they turned their attention to the world beyond the walls of their room. They heard voices but they did not understand the language being spoken. It was a tongue they felt certain they had never heard before.

The woman who had nursed their injuries served them each a steaming bowl of aromatic soup. Then she spoke to them in English. "For three days before you came here, a fierce wind blew out of the west. The oldest soul among us does not remember any storm with greater power. Every tree bowed before it, and the rain came like a river out of the sky. When the storm passed, a boy named Zachary went to the shore and found you there." She poured two cups of bitter red tea. "The people brought you to me. At first, I did not think that you would live."

Bill studied her closely as she spoke. She was a thin woman of middling height, perhaps five and a half feet tall. Her bright blue eyes were framed by wrinkles that came from a lifetime of sunshine and laughter. Her thin, pale pink lips smiled easily, and a braid of brilliant white hair hung down to the middle of her back. Her most striking characteristic, however, was her poise. She moved and spoke with an uncommon grace. This woman was easy to listen to—and easy to trust.

"My name is Hannah. Like you, I came here unwillingly. I was a child when they found me on the beach. The people nursed me back to health. They took me in and taught me how to live. They will do the same for you. So..."

Jude interrupted her, "We just want to go home."

Hannah's voice dropped to a whisper, "What I must tell you is very difficult to believe. But you must believe me, for I speak the truth. You have been sent here from the Other World. This is your destiny."

Bill demanded, "Where are we?"

Hannah answered slowly, "You are in Kallimos. This land was separated from the Other World in the ancient times. This is the very heart of the world."

Jude insisted, "No. We just want to go home."

Hannah was firm but kind. "No one has ever returned to the Other World. You will spend the rest of your lives here. In time, you will find great happiness here among our people."

Bill turned away from her. "I don't believe you."

Hannah nodded, "I understand why you doubt, and I have felt the fear that you are feeling now, but time will prove the truth of what I say."

Their wounds healed, and the people of Kallimos welcomed them, embraced them, loved them. They taught them their language, stories, and ways of life. Gradually, Bill and Jude let go of the Other World. Jude began work as an apprentice gardener under the tutelage of a woman of vast age named Haleigh. Bill became a goatherd. They settled into peaceful, contented lives and that eroded the rigid armor the society they'd left behind had forced them to carry.

Once they'd been experts in aging and the problems of the old. Now they lived in Kallimos, where the lives and the wisdom of the Elders were woven deeply into the fabric of society. The Elders of Kallimos became their mentors. Slowly and very gently, the Elders taught them how to live in the manner of the people who inhabited the "heart of the world".

One night, as a powerful wind rose out of the west, Haleigh and Hannah woke them from a deep sleep.

Their urgent whispered voices trembled with prophesy and foreboding. They huddled together beside a dwindling fire as Hannah told them how the connection between Kallimos and the Other World had been lost. "The people of the Other World let go of tenderness and compassion. The strong began to use hate and fear to rule the weak. That world lost its way."

Jude nodded, "People still tell stories about the end of innocence, about Eden, the paradise that was lost."

"This," Hannah said, "is the difficult news I bring to you tonight. There are signs that the way into the Other World will reopen, if only for a moment.

There are omens that hint..."

"Omens?" Bill snorted. "Omens can't really predict anything, can they?"

Hannah answered, "There are signs that you both will pass over to the Other World."

Bill dismissed her with a wave, "Not us. We're staying here. Right, Jude?"

She agreed, "We are going to spend the rest of our lives here, in this place with these people," she closed her eyes and smiled. "We belong here, inside the heart of the world."

But it was not to be. Forces greater than themselves drew them into a dark and violent sea. They washed ashore in Montserrat, a few years older and vastly wiser than when they had left. When they saw that Kallimos and its people were truly lost to them, their grief tore at their hearts creating wounds that would never heal. Their suffering was compounded by the fact that few would ever believe their story. For most people, even those who loved them most, Bill and Jude's faith in the reality of Kallimos seemed crazy. They spoke the language of Kallimos, even sang its songs, but the questions kept coming: "How did you survive? Where were you, really?" Maps were consulted, calculations were made. They were given every opportunity to change their story, but they did not, because they could not.

In time, they retreated into the hill country of upstate New York. The land there reminded them of the Summer Hills of Kallimos. They found that fighting to improve the lives of older people who were confined to institutions soothed the pain of their loss. They called their movement the Eden Alternative. Some of the people who did believe the story of Kallimos joined them to build a village they called Summer Hill. Then they built another, and another. In time, a total of seven villages lay alongside the Turnpike's unpaved ten-mile length. Together, the Tribes of Eden—for that is what they called themselves—built a haven in a heartless world.

When sleep came, they dreamed of Kallimos, heard its language, and swayed to its ineffably beautiful music. In the morning, they held each other close and muffled their sobs against each other's flesh. They knew the wound in their hearts, made by the loss of Kallimos, would never fully heal.

The sun ruled a pale blue sky and the air was hot and humid by the time the Welcoming ceremony was completed. The guests of honor retreated gratefully to the cool interior of the Thomas house. Kianna and the twins slumped into the overstuffed leather chairs, exhausted. "Nice job everybody," Bill said as he shouldered his bag. "I've got to get over to Crick Hollow. See you at supper."

Jude bustled about the kitchen, her long silvered hair pulled up into a bun. She wore an elaborately embroidered summer dress that was both comfortable and beautiful, just like the woman who wore it. She kept up a happy patter of conversation as she prepared a pitcher of cold red clover tea. It revived her guests, as she knew it would. After enjoying two full mugs, Kianna said, "That was amazing. You knew everyone. You knew their names, their stories, what they did, what they like, what they don't like."

Jude shrugged, "They are my neighbors. I know them, they know me. That's it. It won't be long before you three will be able to do the same."

"When we lived in Chicago, we lived in the same house for seven years." Kianna said.

"I loved our old house," Eron added quickly.

"Me too," Val agreed.

"We all did," Kianna said. "But we lived there all those years and never knew our neighbors, not really."

"Mr. Martin lived across the street," Eron said. "He had a funny dog. It looked just like him."

Kianna remembered the man. He had disappeared the week before they left Chicago. She had no idea where he had gone. Then she said, "We smiled, we waved, we said good morning. It was nothing like this."

"You know, Kianna, I've been thinking about something I said to you the first night you were here. You wondered why we took you in. I didn't really know what to say then, but now I think I do. We took you in, all of the people of Summer Hill. All of the people of the Shire took you in. It was easy for us to do because we are joined together. But, out there, it's so much harder. If my five children and I showed up on a doorstep—out there—how could anyone take us in? We'd be too heavy a burden for any single family to bear, no matter how much they might want to help."

Eron leaned forward in his chair, "The song everybody was singing at the end…I didn't understand any of the words."

"Mmm hmm," Jude agreed, "I can't see how you would. It's a song from Kallimos." Jude raised her voice and sang the refrain, "*Kerna ninst purin joovl Arbenviren egan havkeen Arbenviren egan havkeen.*"

"What does it mean?" Val asked.

"It's pretty simple really. It says we all need each other. We need to be connected to each other. Our happiness depends on being connected to the world and each other."

Eron abruptly changed the subject. "I'm hungry. Who else is hungry?"

Val laughed. "You're always hungry."

"I," Eron answered triumphantly, "am a growing boy."

When the dishes were washed and put away, Jude walked into the living room, opened the glass door on the left side of the fall front desk, and pulled out a leather bound book. It was big and heavy, and its yellowing pages made a ragged edge on the right-hand side. Jude tucked it gently under her arm. "Well," she asked brightly, "are you ready?"

Kianna took a deep breath, "We're ready."

"Let's go."

They stepped into the late afternoon. The heat of the day was already slipping away. Shadows lay long and thin on the ground, the way they do in the springtime.

A flock of children, none older than ten, raced by engaged in a game of make believe. As engaged as they were, they still called out, "Hi Kianna, Hi Eron, Hi Val, Hi Jude," as they passed.

Jude took them along the east side of the Green, past the icehouse and root cellar, around Betsy Von Mechow's dairy, and then behind Ryan Simmons' glass blowing studio. All of the buildings were tidy, laid up of field stone. It looked like shale to Kianna. Wooden doors stood open inviting the spring air inside. Friendly greetings met them at every turn.

"The valley people always liked to say the people of the Shire moved up on top of a hill just to live underground." Jude explained.

"Shire—hobbits live in a Shire," Eron complained.

"Right," Jude agreed, "I guess our houses are something like Hobbit houses. Anyway, we all thought it was a nice name so we picked it up and started using it ourselves. Summer Hill is named after a place we knew in

Kallimos, but all of the other little villages up here on the Turnpike are named after the Hobbit villages in the *Lord of the Rings*. I was on my way home from Bag's End when I met you."

Eron grimaced. "Hobbits are weird. They're really short and they've got big hairy feet." He paused, then emphasized, "I'm not a Hobbit!" Kianna glared at her son, warning him to be more polite.

Jude continued, cheerfully, "Don't worry Eron, no one will think you're a Hobbit. It's just a joke. Besides," she added, "it was a Hobbit, Mr. Frodo Baggins of Hobbiton, who saved Middle Earth. Remember?" Eron nodded in reluctant agreement. It was true. Jude looked at the boy and smiled, "Who knows, maybe someday, you'll save the world."

At the southern edge of Summer Hill, Jude stopped, turned, and said, "Well, we're here."

Kianna clasped her hand to her mouth. In front of her sat a tidy stone cottage, its smoothly rounded walls supported a vibrant green roof. The front door was hewn from wide oak planks and fitted with a hand-forged latch and iron hinges. Small leaded glass windows flanked the door. A pair of rose bushes gripped a trellis that vaulted up and over the entrance. Kianna could easily imagine how they would look and smell when they came into full bloom.

Jude led them to the house, pressed the latch and swung the door open.

"No key?" Eron asked hesitantly.

Jude shook her head. "No one has keys or locks."

"That's crazy."

"I know it seems that way," Jude responded, "especially after what you've been through. During the Fall, we worried that people from the valley would come for us. But they didn't. We didn't have anything they wanted, I guess. Go ahead, Eron. Open the door."

Inside, the house smelled of apples baked in maple sugar. Though the sun was declining into the west, Kianna saw how the generously proportioned south windows would bring the best of the day's sunshine directly into the heart of the little house. The furniture was similar to Jude and Bill's: mostly oak and cherry, handmade and worn with use but sturdy enough, it seemed, for another half-century. The floor was strewn with braided rugs. A round stone fireplace, smaller than the one in Jude's house but well-suited to this one, occupied the center. No one spoke as they circled around toward the kitchen. A solid butcher block squatted in its center surrounded by a cast iron cook stove, a small but spotlessly clean white porcelain sink, and an oak icebox. Next to the wall beneath a hinged window was a small table, its top inlaid with hand painted ceramic tiles. Two pairs of matched chairs faced each other across the table. A hand blown vase bursting with spring flowers sat next to a freshly baked pie.

Kianna turned to Jude, "You were with us all day. How did you do all this?"

"I didn't do it, your neighbors did. The people of Summer Hill did this. They want you to be happy."

"We don't have any money," Eron said, growing alarmed.

"Neither do we," Jude answered.

"We'll pay you back," Kianna insisted.

"I know, and so does everyone else. We have plenty of work and not enough people. Believe me, we are all glad you are here."

Kianna nodded.

"There are a couple of other things you need to see." She led them out the back door onto a flagstone patio. "The water pump is there," she said pointing to an antique brass hand pump. "It has an automatic siphon, so it won't freeze in the winter," Jude reassured them.

"But there's water inside too, right?" Eron asked. "This is just for show, right?"

Jude shook her head. "Jim Murchison built this place. He didn't go in for those kinds of conveniences." She pointed at a squat outhouse that stood at the end of a curved stone path. It was the only building on Summer Hill made entirely of brick. Jude chuckled. "He was well-known for his sense of humor."

"Awwwww, Mom!" Eron moaned.

Kianna shushed him, "Mind your manners."

"One more thing, before I go," Jude said. They stepped back into the kitchen. She swung a thick book out from under her arm, laid it on the table, and ran her fingers lovingly across the fringed cover. "This book," she said, "tells the story of what happened to Bill and me before we came here." Kianna reached out and touched her new friend lightly on the shoulder. Jude said, "If you really want to understand us and how we live here, you should read it, together."

Kianna said, "We will. We'll start tonight."

Jude heaved a heavy sigh, "Good." She started for the front door, but first turned to look at the little family. She saw how eager they were to be together in their new and unexpected home. "The girls stopped at the seed bank in Hardbottle today. We'll be over tomorrow to help you get a garden going. The timing is good. See you then." Jude stepped outside, and Kianna closed the door carefully behind her. A shiver of excitement swept through her.

The mother and her children walked around and around the house, hearing it, smelling it, seeing it, feeling it. A wardrobe stood next to the door in Val's tiny room. She opened it and squealed with delight. All of her clothes were there, folded and hung with care. They stepped into Eron's book-lined room. "I like it," he said. He went to the window beside the bed and looked out. "It's perfect. You can see the Green from here, see everybody coming and going." Kianna knew her son would never forget the winter on Baker Street, the pall of danger, the constant need for surveillance. The bedroom that Becca and Jim Murchison had long shared, was now prepared for Kianna. There were clothes, more than just what Jude had given her, neatly put away. She studied the brass bed closely. It was made up with linen sheets topped by a brightly colored quilt. There were two pillows. She missed John, ached for him. It would be better to return to the bedroom later, when sleep would come quickly.

Kianna brightened the mood the best way she knew, declaring, "I think we should have the pie for supper." In the kitchen, Kianna put Eron to work searching for plates and forks while she sliced the pie. Val found a pitcher and took it outside. The pump handle rewarded each effort with a gush of water. At their table, she poured out three mugs of cold clean water. They ate and drank with relish.

After dinner, Val and Kianna built a small fire in the fireplace. It warmed the room against the night's encroaching chill. "Mom," Eron frowned, "this is really great and everything, but seriously? Pumping water by hand and heating it on the stove? This is like living in the Stone Age."

Kianna reached out, pinched his cheek, and chided him gently. "Maybe my little genius will get the hot indoor running water for his Mommy and sister."

"Mom, I'm serious."

"I know you are. Now let's do up these dishes so we can start Jude and Bill's book."

Night was falling by the time they were ready. Val lit candles and placed them on the table. Three chairs were pulled close together. Kianna laid her hands on the leather binding. A single word was etched on its face; *Kallimos*.

She remembered what Jude had said to her the day she and Bill asked them to stay on Summer Hill, *I was a stranger once, like you are now. I was cast onto a distant shore, like you. I was taken in, made whole and made to feel welcome. Like you.* Kianna opened the cover and began to read.

10
GRASPING THE NETTLE

Eron woke early, this time from a dreamless sleep. He lay still and warm beneath his covers and watched the light grow stronger. Soon he was able to make out the titles on the spines of the books that lined the shelves in his room. *Robinson Crusoe, Of Mice and Men, Brave New World, Moby Dick*—they were old man books, history, novels, nothing exciting. He got out of bed, walked to the dresser, pulled out a pair of pants, a short-sleeved shirt, then remembering how cool the mornings had been, a sweater. He dressed quickly. The house was quiet and his mother and sister were still asleep. They had all been up late, had treated the book as if it were a bedtime story. He walked into the kitchen and saw it lying there, open on the table, where they had left it. He glanced at a page covered in flowing script.

Our teacher said, 'Through their words and deeds, Elders show us how dohavkee lies at the heart of every life worth living. Jude thinks the best English words for this are 'belonging' or 'oneness'. From the very beginning, each person seeks havkeen. The first task of a child growing inside its mother is to fasten itself to the womb. This slender cord is the first connection we make to another. When the child is born and the cord is cut, the baby, mouth open and eager, seeks its mother's breast. So it goes for the whole of a human life.

Boring.

He wandered outside.

The place was neat. People kept things up nice, not like the pigsty they lived in over the winter. His eye caught a long row of weeds growing up against the south wall of their new house. The untidiness annoyed him. He went back inside. His mother and sister were still sleeping. In the quiet, he imagined how his mother and sister would be proud if he pulled those weeds. He went back outside, peeled off the sweater, and set to work.

Val sprinted barefoot across the Green. Eron lay on the kitchen floor screaming in agony, and his mother didn't know what to do. On Bill and Jude's doorstep, Val pounded her small fists hard against the front door.

"Jude, Jude we need help. Eron's been stung."

Haleigh lazily swung the door open. She stood calmly in front of the frantic girl. Dressed in dark brown overalls, she held a crust of black bread between her thumb and forefinger. She swallowed and asked calmly, "Bees?"

"No," Val gasped. "Some kind of plant."

"Nettles," Haleigh nodded.

"Mommy needs help. Eron's crying. It won't stop stinging."

Jude heard the commotion from the kitchen and appeared with Hannah at her side. The young woman was, like her sister, dressed for the day's work and anxious to get started. Jude held a thick cake of homemade soap in her hand. She said to the girls, "I'll go right over. You stop at the tool shed and bring what we need."

"Please!" Val begged.

Minutes later, they found Eron where Val had left him, writhing on the floor, wailing each time he caught a breath. The fire in his skin burned like a hundred match heads.

Jude dunked the soap into a pot of cold water standing on the counter. She worked up thick lather in her hand.

"Shhh, shhh. It's OK. You'll feel better in a minute." She knelt down beside him and spread the lather onto the reddened areas of his hands, chest, arms, neck, and face, taking care not to let the soap run into his eyes. The relief was nearly instant.

"Stupid plants," he seethed.

"Stupid nettles," Jude corrected him.

"Stupid nettles. Who would let nettles grow next to a house?"

"Nettles aren't stupid," Kianna admonished her son. "They are really useful."

Jude added, "Becca Murchison made a wonderful nettle tea."

Eron shivered involuntarily. "People drink nettle tea? Insane!"

"Not really," Jude said. "It's very good for arthritis. Becca and Jim both had it pretty bad, and she said nettle tea was the best thing ever."

"It burns!"

"Not when you know how to handle it."

Jude reached down and plucked one of the leafy stems Eron had scattered in his wake. She crushed it with a quick, sharp movement. "You see," she said, "it's just like the old saying, 'the world's a nettle; disturb it, it stings; grasp it firmly, it stings not.'"

Eron struggled to his feet, ready to be done with the lesson in practical botany. From behind the house came the hard irregular clank of metal against soil and rock.

"Haleigh and Hannah are here!" Val cried.

They went to the garden and welcomed the sisters who were already at work, spading the rich brown earth and picking out the year's fresh crop of stones. Jude admired the soil. "Becca always made a good garden," she said. The sisters had brought an assortment of hoes, rakes, and spades from the community garden shed.

"Well," Kianna beamed as she rolled up her sleeves, "let's get to work."

The women worked the soil while Eron watched. In the aftermath of the nettle incident, he had adopted the philosophical stance of a brave soldier who had volunteered for a dangerous mission, been grievously wounded (through an act of treachery, no less), and was now entitled to watch the war from a safe position, behind the front lines.

No one seemed to mind. By mid-afternoon, Eron had fallen asleep beneath a gnarled apple tree. The seedbed was prepared, the twine strung taut between wooden stakes. The ground was ready to be sown.

Hannah leaned on the handle of her rake and reviewed the work so far.

"I like my rows nice and straight," Jude said.

"Mmm hmm," Hannah agreed.

Kianna was eager to discuss what they had read the night before and took this as an opening. "The way you were taught when you were in Kallimos?"

Jude smiled, "Yes."

"We stayed up late last night, reading." Kianna cast a glance in Eron's direction and he was still asleep. "John and I met at university, too, but we met in the student union, not the library. We both loved science. He was a mathematician." There was so much Kianna did not understand. "Kallimos the place, the island, the way you describe it, is it real?"

Jude knew the question was coming, had to come. It had been asked of them since the day they returned. She offered Kianna and Val the best explanation she had. "Bill and I were just like you and John. We were happy with our lives, loved our work, and never expected anything to happen to us, not like it did. Something, some kind of deep power reached out and took a hold of us, dragged us away, and nearly killed us." Haleigh and Hannah, having heard the story many times before, drifted away and began preparing for the next phase of their work. Kianna and Val remained rapt. Jude continued,

"The people of Kallimos pulled us off the beach, fed us, clothed us, sheltered us, healed us. Our old selves, the people we used to be, ceased to exist. We studied under two old women, Haleigh and Hannah..."

"And named your daughters after them."

Jude smiled, "We did. I apprenticed in the garden under Haleigh, and Bill became a goatherd. He wasn't bad. We lived there for many years, then..." she braced herself for the difficult part, "we were pulled away from Kallimos, returned here, to this world—against our will."

Val and Kianna could feel Jude's sadness. Jude drew a breath, "So...you deserve an answer to your question, 'is Kallimos real?'"

Val nodded eagerly, hoping for the answer she wanted to hear.

"Hannah showed us how to live inside the heart of the world, how to live among the people of Kallimos. Long ago, Kallimos was connected to us, as part of us all. Then, people let go of the ancient ways and let greed and cruelty become their masters. When that happened, Kallimos disappeared. It's still alive, still thriving, still beating, still so full of love, still waiting for us. I don't know how or why it happened, but Bill and I were allowed to touch this heart and it touched us, changed us, remade us."

"Is it real?" Kianna asked.

"If you look for Kallimos on a map, or in a picture from a satellite, or in the laboratory, you won't find it. You can't find it. A scientist would say that Kallimos does not exist."

Val gasped. "Hannah said Kallimos is like what we think of when we say 'heart and soul.' The physical heart pumps blood through the body. It's easy to find. You can feel it when you lay your hand on another person's chest. This heart loves, it yearns, it makes us human. It is our 'heart and soul,' and it exists inside all of us. We know it's there but no one can see it, not even with the most powerful x-ray."

"So Kallimos is real!" Val exclaimed.

"Yes," Jude agreed, "Kallimos is real."

The question of reality settled for the time being, Haleigh came forward with a leather bag, undid the clasps, and then carefully withdrew a bundle of carefully folded paper packets.

"Seeds," Kianna said, half to herself. "You save seeds."

"It's the only way," Jude said. "These came from the Hardbottle seed bank. There's another one in Bywater. They're for you." She guessed what Kianna might be thinking and added, "Don't worry, you'll pay the seed bank back in the fall."

Together, they planted a spring garden of peas, beans, corn, broccoli, squash, and pumpkins.

Eron roused himself from his afternoon nap in time to join into the end of the workday. It was the moment when the day's shadows lengthen and you can see, spread out before you, the purest proof of how in one day, with the sweat that dripped from your brow, with the aches that bore into your arms, your back, your neck—you changed the world. Changed the world for the better.

When the moment passed, Eron stretched and said, "Dinner?"

Kianna mussed her son's hair, "The nap make you hungry?"

Her son smiled contentedly and answered, "Yeah, Mom, it sure did."

Val folded her arms, the way a disappointed schoolteacher might. "Well," she huffed, "you weren't any help." She stomped into the house, with Eron right behind her.

Haleigh and Hannah had already started for home. Jude was alone with Kianna. "You'll be sore tomorrow. Sore in places you didn't even know you had. But," Jude breathed a deep, satisfied sigh, "the garden's in—and that's the important thing."

The sound of the twins squabbling in the kitchen drifted out of the window. Before she went to restore the peace, Kianna said, "Thanks for explaining, I'm not sure I really understand but I want to, I want to understand."

Jude offered a tired smile, "You will, in time. The Shire, it's a lot like Kallimos, and it kind of works on you, in a good way."

"Good night, Jude."

"Good night, Kianna."

The bickering grew louder.

"Enough you two!" Kianna bellowed.

Jude walked home alone and found pleasure in the close of the day.

11
TRANSISTOR RADIO

I n the morning, neighbors came calling. They came in ones and twos and threes and fours, always bearing food and gifts, always ready to sit and visit. They brought dishes, clothes, hand tools, recipes, and, perhaps most importantly, gentle instruction in the art of living in the Shire. Sasha Pfeiffer was the first to arrive. She was a short, squat, no nonsense kind of woman who had worked as general counsel for a Seattle-based software company before she came to Summer Hill. Now she lived next door to the Murchison place with her husband Benjamin, and together they ran the Shire's largest cheese making operation. She presented Kianna with a one-pound wheel of her renowned sheep-milk Gouda. "Kianna do you smell smoke?" Sasha followed her nose to the kitchen. "Aah yes, Becca's Waterford. Imported ages ago from Ireland you know. Can be temperamental." The antique cast iron cookstove bristled with dampers, vents, and adjustments. She opened the firebox door, and cold smoke from a smoldering fire leapt into the room. Sasha shut it, spun the round draft controls below, and then opened the damper all the way. "That's better. Now be sure to close this side vent. Not all the way, of course. But when the weather is cold and the wind is out of the west. Otherwise, naturally, you'll go through firewood faster than scat."

It made Kianna dizzy.

Ed Beimfohr, former radio journalist, now an actor, musician, and farrier, stopped by. He slid a pot of goulash into the icebox and noticed the interior was warm. He conscripted Eron, and the two of them headed out across the Green to the village icehouse. The room was filled with one-foot square blocks of ice packed in sawdust, stacked to the ceiling. The air was damp and wonderfully cool. Ed hooked a ten pound cube of ice with a pair of steel tongs. "Where do we pay?" Eron asked

"Um, yeah," Ed fumbled for a response. "Actually you'll pay this winter when we all go out to cut ice, haul it in, pack it, and stack it."

Eron frowned, "It's free?"

"You work. Work filling the icehouse, and then you get to take ice when you need it."

Kianna was given authority over what had been the Murchison family's bins in the common root cellar. Her neighbors had already stocked them to the brim. They would have plenty to eat. Val was introduced to the milkhouse, its plastered walls so fresh and clean. Cream skimmed from the top of the day's milking was poured into a clear one-gallon glass jug. The top was screwed on tight, and then the jar was fitted onto what had once been an exercise bike. Pedaling the bike churned the cream into butter. She had never tasted better.

Lakisha Jones, once a nurse's aide, now a potter, showed the Wallaces through the henhouse and explained what would be expected from them when it was their turn to do the chores there. They learned how to retrieve eggs from the nest boxes and use a boxlight to candle them properly. The rooster, spurs out and feathers puffed, scared Val. "Don't worry about him," Lakisha reassured him. "Old Garfunkle scares everybody. It's what he was born to do."

These were the easy things.

Much harder was the work of learning everyone's name and, beyond that, mastering the intricate web of relationships that joined them all, one to another. Nearly a week had passed since their Welcoming on the Green, and Kianna was tired and so were the twins. It seemed impossible that they would ever know everyone in Summer Hill, what they did, what they used to do, who they were related to, who their friends were, the things they liked and didn't like. This was just Summer Hill. There were seven other villages strung out along the ten-mile length of Turnpike Road.

When the tide of visitors ebbed, Bill returned to the Wallace house. It was early evening, and the day had been glorious. Spring's claim on the earth was now uncontested. He tapped lightly on the back door and heard Kianna call from inside, her voice high and pure like the tone of a bell.

"Come in."

Bill found the twins bustling about the kitchen, Val sweeping the floor and Eron drying the dishes his mother was washing. "Late supper," Kianna explained with a smile.

"I'll bet it was great."

"It was great," Val agreed. "Mom made bread."

"And we had soup," Eron added.

He studied them casually but closely and liked what he saw. They were healing, maybe even healed. "Hey, Val, how's that cough?"

"Gone," she beamed.

"Thought it might be." He swung his backpack down off his shoulder in a single practiced motion and set it carefully down onto the kitchen table. "The word around Summer Hill is, somebody in this house likes gadgets."

Eron laid down his dishtowel. "I like electronics, especially computers—and computer games." His smile was bright, genuine.

"I'm afraid I can't help you there. But I did find this at the house." He reached into the worn leather bag and pulled out a small cardboard box, which he laid on the table. The daylight was failing, and Val hurried to light candles.

"Virgil made it when he was little, but I'd forgotten about it." Bill pulled the lid off the box while Eron peered eagerly over his shoulder.

"Umm...what is it?" he asked.

"It's a radio, an AM radio."

"Well yeah," Eron said, trying not to sound too disappointed, "but there's no place to plug it in."

Bill pulled the handmade radio out of the box in which it had rested for so long. It was the size of a thick, hardcover novel; the case was made of dovetailed quarter-sawn oak. On its face there was a two-pronged jack, an unmarked black plastic knob, and single metal toggle switch. Along the right hand side was a small hand crank, the kind one might find on an old-fashioned music box.

Eron frowned. "How does it work?"

"You crank the handle, like this," Bill demonstrated. "After a minute or two, you'll have charged the capacitor, and you're ready to go."

Eron waited impatiently, eager to hear it work. When Bill stopped cranking and the box remained stubbornly silent, he could not conceal his disappointment. "It's old, it must be broken."

"Whoops, one more thing, and pretty important too." Bill patted the pockets of his sweater and found what he was looking for. He produced a tangle of thin white wires. "These are the speakers. They plug in here." Bill fiddled with the dial. When he found a signal, he offered the earbuds to Eron, "Here, listen."

The boy took the earpiece, afraid of being disappointed. Then he heard a voice. He was as amazed, Bill thought, as a deaf child would be on hearing a human voice for the first time. "Mom," he exclaimed, "it works, it really works!"

Bill smiled at Kianna. "I thought he might like it."

Eron's body quaked with genuine excitement. "Like it? I love it!" The boy threw his arms around Bill's shoulders in an awkward embrace. "It's the best thing ever."

"If it's OK with your Mom, you can have it."

Eron looked at his mother, his eyes pleading. Kianna answered quickly. "You can keep it, if you promise you won't let it interfere with your chores."

"I swear it won't!"

"Huh," Val disagreed, but chose not to press the point.

Kianna gave a gentle nudge, "What do you say to Bill?"

The words came straight from the heart. "Thank you, thank you very much."

"You're welcome," Bill said. "Well, I guess my work here is done." He closed his pack, returned it to its accustomed place over his left shoulder, and turned toward the door. "Goodnight, Kianna, Val."

"Thank you, Bill," Kianna said.

Eron caught Bill at the door. "Hey!" The boy's voice carried the brittle edge of anger barely suppressed. His eyes narrowed with suspicion. "There's no...there's no volume control."

Bill studied the youth for a moment then answered brightly, "Yeah, I know. Virgil built it when he was seven, maybe eight. He didn't have the parts and couldn't make what he needed back then."

"It will be fine," Kianna was firm. She laid her hand on her son's shoulder, felt the flash of anger recede.

Bill kept things light, "Oh, one more thing. Glad I remembered. Jude was with the Council of Elders today. They're wondering about your work Kianna, and of course, Val and Eron's education."

The words, offered so innocently, worried Kianna. "Oh, I..." She needed to explain.

"Don't worry about a thing. It's all good. You've got a bright future here in the Shire. You all do." Bill looked Eron in the eye and the boy looked away, ashamed. "Why don't the three of you come over to our place for supper tomorrow night? We can take our time, really talk things over."

Kianna accepted the invitation gracefully. "We'd be happy to come."

"All right then, I'm off." He closed the door gently behind him.

"Turn it off," Kianna snapped. "We've still got to finish this kitchen and then we've got some reading to do. You can play with the radio later."

Eron complied.

When the chores were finished, Kianna opened the book Jude had leant to them, brought the candles close, and read aloud to her children.

It was the story of Kallimos, of Bill and Jude and their journey to and from the hidden heart of the world.

12
WEAVER, TINKER, SEED-KEEPER

Kianna slept poorly. She rose before the sun and instantly regretted doing so—time crawled. Bill had told her not to worry, but he was like that. Obviously, people had been talking about them, about her, about her "work" and the twins' education. She didn't know what to think. What did "going to work" mean in the Shire?

There was no school in Summer Hill, or in the whole of the Shire as far as she knew. She had yet to meet a teacher. What could the Shire offer her children? Kianna's anxiety drove her into a cleaning frenzy. When they were up and about, she enlisted the twins in the effort. By the time they were ready to leave, Kianna's little cottage sparkled. Her children were scrubbed and neatly dressed. She inspected them one more time before she led them around the Green and to the Thomas house.

After dinner, Jude asked, "Did Bill mention I went to see the Council of Elders?"

Kianna nodded cautiously, "He did."

"They talked about lots of different things but mainly about you three. They've got some ideas."

Kianna stifled a sigh of relief.

"You remember the packages of seeds the girls brought over when we put your garden in?" Kianna nodded. She figured she could hold her own in any conversation about plants.

"The truth is we don't really know what we're doing with our seeds. There've been problems, nothing major but enough to make us worry. We've had seeds spoil, didn't save the right seeds—lots of different things. The point is that everything and everybody up here depends on the seed bank. It's our life."

Kianna nodded. Seeds couldn't just be ordered from a catalogue and delivered by mail the way they used to be. Nor could they run to the grocery store if the garden didn't come up. Jude was right. The Shire's seeds were its life.

"So the Elders were talking about your training in botany, and they'd like to know—would you be willing to serve as the Shire's Seed-Keeper?"

The question landed on the table with a thud.

Kianna hesitated. Everything and everyone would depend on her. This wasn't like working on some esoteric genetic research project. The pressure would be enormous. If she made any serious mistakes, people might starve. "I haven't really gone into it, but the truth is, I've done most of my work lately in the lab, mostly with soybeans." She felt Eron's eyes on her.

Her son spoke as soon as his mother finished, the words coming in short fervent bursts. "Mom used to love working outdoors. It was her favorite thing. She was really good at it. The best."

Kianna was buoyed by her son's pride in her. "OK, I'll do it. Do it the best I can. I can't promise anything, really, but I'll try."

One question settled, Jude and Bill turned their attention to Val. She arrived wearing her favorite linen blouse, the one Mia had given her on her first day in the Shire. Jude asked her, "You love that blouse, don't you?"

Val blushed but answered honestly, "Yes, I do."

"Good," Jude said. "How would you like to meet the woman who made it?"

"I'd love to."

"How would you like to be her apprentice and learn how to make clothes like she does?"

Val was thrilled.

"Zakia Johnson over in Crickhollow, she's in need of an apprentice. The Elders wondered if you might be willing to visit with her, you know; see if you'd be interested."

"Can I, Mom?"

"Of course you can."

"This is how we lived when we were in Kallimos," Bill explained. "People look for something they love and then apprentice under someone who loves it too." He continued, "It's not school the way people used to think about it, but it is a real education." He gestured toward his youngest son. "Caleb's interested in medicine, and he's my apprentice. When he finishes his training with me, he'll be invested as a Journeyman and, in time, he'll be a Master. We're all teachers, and we're all students. The day will come, Kianna, when you'll have apprentice Seed-Keepers, and someday your former apprentices will have apprentices of their own."

Jude drove the point home, "We think learning is much more important than schooling."

"Yeeehahh!" Eron was delighted. "No more classrooms, no more books. No more teachers' dirty looks."

"Now as for you, young Mr. Wallace." Bill spoke formally, but there was a twinkle in his eye. "The Shire's Master Tinker, and an Elder in his own right, has expressed an interest in you. I told him about how much you liked the radio, and he'd like you to consider coming on as an apprentice Tinker."

"Tinker?" Eron was puzzled.

"We have to make what we need around here," Bill continued.

"Like the butter churn that's really a bicycle," Val interrupted.

"Right. Tinkers make things—tools, machines, contraptions—things that people need."

"Including hot water heaters," Kianna smiled at her son.

"Bob and Virgil are just starting work on the gristmill above Bag's End. Plus, summer is coming and all kinds of stuff is going to break and need to be fixed or replaced."

Now it was Eron's turn to be uncertain.

"So, I'd be an apprentice, like Caleb is with you?"

"Yes."

"Wasn't Virgil his apprentice before?"

"He was."

Eron doubted he could ever measure up to the Shire's rising young genius.

"The Elders think you might be good at it," Jude reassured him.

Everyone was looking at him, and it made him even more uncomfortable. Partly to escape the scrutiny and partly because he really had no idea what he "loved," he went along. "Sure, I'll do it. I don't know how to make anything, but I'll do it."

Caleb had entered the kitchen, unnoticed, during the last part of the discussion. He reassured Eron, "Don't worry, that's why they call us apprentices."

It was late, the decisions had been made, and sleep beckoned. Jude stretched and yawned. "Kianna, I can get you started in the morning. I'll come over at first light, and we'll walk the land together." She turned to Caleb, who was standing just beyond the candlelight. "You'll take Val over to Crickhollow and introduce her to Zakia."

"Awww, Mom," Caleb protested, "Dad said he needs me to check on the Clark kids in Bywater tomorrow."

"Ask Haleigh and Hannah to do it." Jude looked at Bill. He knew the answer she was looking for and gave it to her.

"No problem at all. I've got to be over that way tomorrow anyway, I'll see to them."

"Caleb James Thomas, I'm giving you the privilege of escorting Val Wallace to Crickhollow."

The youngest son appealed to his father for relief.

"Hey," Bill shrugged, "you're getting the better part of the deal."

"Not really," Caleb groused. The comment provoked a sharp 'we'll talk about this after they leave' look from his mother, and he instantly regretted his words, but not because he hadn't meant them. Walking the Turnpike with Val Wallace would be a nightmare. People would talk. He could imagine what they would be saying. Worse, he was now in line for a long, and determined, lecture from his mother.

Jude added to her son's duties. "When you get back from Crickhollow, take Eron over to Bag's End and up to the work site. Introduce him to Bob and Virgil."

"OK," Caleb said.

As they got up from the table and drifted toward the door, Bill pulled Kianna aside. "I suppose this'll be the first time you've been away from the twins in quite a while." Kianna nodded, the thought of being separated from Val and Eron made her stomach churn. He put his arm around her, "Don't worry, they're safe here." She nodded, wishing she could let go of her fear and feel even a fraction of Bill's boundless optimism. "Think of it this way, you'll have plenty of new things to talk about at dinner."

The Wallaces walked home in silence, each deep in thought, considering what the morning would bring. At home, they got ready for bed, wished each other goodnight, and turned in. Eron closed the door to his bedroom, retrieved the radio from its hiding place, and then slid under his covers. He cranked it as quietly as he could.

As always   safety bulletins at the top and   each hour. The Schuyl   ssway remains closed in both directions   after an explosion damaged the   there are no plans   a repair   citizens needing to travel to   should use alternate routes.   strains on fuel   city residents should be able to expect an increase   availability from 3 to 5 hours a day. a dozen headless bodies floating in the harbor.   the murders are the actions of   'anarchist elements'...

Eron fiddled with the knob.

>   WKRP
>   your host   those
> filthy bastards have   nothing works no one's safe, rape, murder,
> robbery in broad daylight   they're animals if you ask
> me and they deserve to be lined up and shot…

Again, he reached for the knob.

>   people, hungry, tired and afraid
> funeral procession carrying the remains of all 17   the city   to
> regarded as suspicious   in effect   violators   curfew
> militia commanders on sight   remain closed. Stay tuned to
> for news of food delivery schedules in your sector…

The sound faded as the charge ebbed. Eron cranked the handle again. And again. And again.

13
WARP AND WEFT

The sun, bright and cheerful, floated up and out of the eastern hills, painting over the glittered night with a bright, almost painful, blue. It was warm, the warmest day of the year so far. The black flies, early spring's scourge of man and beast, had yet to hatch. As directed, Caleb escorted Val to Crickhollow. "Zakia's an old friend of my Mom's. She's fun. Honest. Everyone says she's the best in the Shire."

Val gasped when she saw her. Zakia wore a beautiful pleated ochre blouse with beads embroidered across the front in the same style as Kianna's blouse. She leaned comfortably against the jamb of her workshop's door. Her skin was a rich coffee color that shone in morning's bright sunshine. Short gray kinky hair framed a wise, knowing face. Kind eyes opened like windows onto the world. Her skirt matched the blouse, flowed over her, light and simple. Delicate gold earrings dangled from each ear, and a pair of glasses hung from a bead chain.

Caleb made the introduction, "Zakia, this is Val Wallace. Val this is Zakia Johnson."

Zakia welcomed the girl with a smile, "Jude Thomas tells me that you're something special."

"I..." Val hesitated.

Caleb interrupted, "OK then, I gotta get on back home."

The Master Weaver studied the boy for a moment. "Tell your mother I said 'thank you'."

"I will, Zakia."

"Well, Val, what do you say you come inside and we get started?"

Val stepped across the threshold and into a world of beauty and magic. It was a single room, wood-paneled with a high gabled ceiling and something she hadn't see in the Shire until now—skylights.

Zakia followed Val's gaze upward. "Yeah they're nice. I told Bob Brazzi I had to have them. A Weaver's got to have light, good light, and he figured it out—the way he always does."

The light fell upon a half dozen wooden handlooms of varying size and construction. There was a dizzying collection of boxes and cabinets filled with beads and buttons made of glass, wood, and bone. When Val returned to Zakia's side, the Master asked, "Do you want to learn?"

"Yes, I do."

"Good. We begin now."

The apprentice was given a seat at a small loom at the heart of the workshop. "Every piece of cloth tells a story, and you are the storyteller."

14
THE MILL

It was almost noon when Caleb returned to the Wallace House. He knocked on the back door and, not hearing an answer, stepped inside.

"Eron?"

The little round house was quiet, the common areas empty. The door to Eron's room remained closed. Caleb approached.

"Eron!"

A faint rustle of bedclothes came in answer. Caleb pushed the door open. Eron Wallace was still in bed.

"What do you want?" he groaned.

"You sick?" Caleb could imagine no other reason for a person to lie in bed all morning.

"No," Eron answered grumpily. "Just tired."

"Get up, man. Daylight's burning, and we've still got to get to Bag's End."

Caleb's manful urgency annoyed the younger boy. "What's the rush? Nobody's going anywhere, are they?"

"Bob Brazzi and Virgil were expecting you this morning. We're late already."

Caleb turned away in disgust and went to pack a lunch for them while Eron dragged himself out of bed.

Good food, the brisk walk up Turnpike Road, and Caleb's amiable manner invigorated Eron. He started peppering his companion with questions. Encouraged by Caleb's easy-going answers, he worked up the courage to ask, "If tinkers are so clever why don't they just invent something they could sell for lots of money. Then they could get a nice house, a real house in a real city."

"Arrrghh. The world out there is crazy, you said so yourself."

The boys approached the site where work had begun on the Shire's Gristmill. Especially after the big build-up Caleb had given it, the Mill was a real disappointment to Eron. Situated astride a narrow gorge that opened out of a large pond, the future Gristmill currently consisted entirely of stacks of old car tires and mounds of gray dirt. Eron thought it might be clay. A single enormous sluice pipe dominated the worksite. It had once run beneath a highway and was almost eight feet across and maybe 30 feet long. There was no bustle, no energy, and no bright yellow construction machines. Eron kicked the dirt in disgust.

Behind the dirt and tires, they stumbled onto a motley collection of second-hand appliances, bundles of wire, assorted lengths of metal pipe, buckets of bolts, and coils of rope. Everything was laid out as if it was a yard sale in his old neighborhood in Chicago. Then he saw it, and it was beautiful: an SUV. It looked like a 2008, dark blue. At first he thought it might be his Dad's car, but it was a different make. It sat in the open, gleaming like gold in the sunshine. He ran to it, tried the door latch. It was unlocked. He slid into the driver's seat. The plastic seat cover was warm and soft. It felt good.

Caleb ignored Eron and looked for his brother and Bob Brazzi. "Hey, you guys here?"

Finally, Virgil answered, his voice echoing madly, "Hey, Caleb. We're in the pipe. Gotta finish this. We'll be out in a minute."

Reassured, Caleb turned back to Eron. "We can drive to Gramp and Gran's in this. It's perfect, almost as good as our old car. Can we have it?"

"I don't think you want it," Caleb responded. "Tinkers have been taking parts out of this thing for years. There isn't much left under the hood."

Eron gripped the sun-warmed steering wheel with both hands and stared straight ahead. Though he could not name the feeling, a grim foreboding swelled inside of him and threatened to overwhelm him. He knew what was right; he knew how life was supposed to be lived. Real life, normalcy, the comfort of ordinary understandings—all of these things were lost to him. The Shire had saved their lives. He could admit that, but the place and its people were proving to be strange, stupid, perverse, and ignorant. He glanced down at the vehicle's dashboard. Where the instruments should have been, there was a gaping hole and a jangle of amputated wires. He felt sick.

From behind them came the clanking sound of men in hard-soled boots walking on steel. Bob Brazzi and Virgil Thomas emerged, blinking in the daylight.

The older man's gray hair was pulled into a ponytail that hung down to the middle of his back. He had a salt and pepper moustache, and his pale green eyes studied the world from behind wire-framed glasses. His arms glistened with grease and sweat. He wore the kind of undershirt that Eron had seen in old-time pictures of construction workers.

Out of the pipe, one step behind the Master came Journeyman Virgil Thomas. Caleb's older brother stood six-foot-two, with wiry arms and a well-muscled neck and chest that was draped with the ropey kind of muscle that only comes from hard work well done. He wore overalls but was shirtless under the bib. He let out a whoop as soon as he saw Caleb. He ran to him, picked him up, and whirled him around as if he were a doll. Caleb roared in outrage until his brother set him back down on the ground.

"So, who's this?" Virgil asked.

"His name's Eron," Caleb answered. "He's from Chicago."

"Welcome to the Shire."

Eron nodded perfunctorily then pointed at the SUV. "Can you make it run?"

The Master Tinker slipped off his glasses and cleaned them with his kerchief. "You have some place to go?" He asked.

Eron huffed as if he was explaining something that should be obvious, even to a small child. "Yeah! Obviously! My Mom and my sister, we need to get to Gran and Gramps' house. They live in New Hampshire. We only came here by...by mistake."

"Goes to show," Bob answered kindly, "mistakes can sometimes be for the good."

Eron would not be mollified. "You're the Tinker. Can you fix this car?"

"Oh, I don't think that car has run in, maybe, five years. Belonged to Dirk Davies back then. He gave it to the Shire, lives in Bywater now—ran out of gas so he didn't have much use for it."

Eron exploded, "It ran out of gas? You tore it apart because it ran out of gas?"

Virgil answered happily, "Yeah, it's been great. Pumps, wires, motors, fans. You wouldn't believe the stuff we've already salvaged from it. The mill'll be powered by a water turbine—Bob's idea—and we're taking the wheel bearings and the transmission for the power transfer unit."

Eron was unable to hide his disappointment.

Bob eyed his new recruit carefully. "Yeah, it's the end of the road for old Bessie here," he said, "but for you it's just the beginning."

"I guess so," Eron answered.

"You're thinking you might want to join up with the Tinkers, eh?"

Eron shrugged his shoulders.

"You like to make things?" Bob asked.

"I think so, but I don't really know. When we lived in Chicago, we didn't have to make anything. We just bought what we needed at the store."

"Models?" Bob asked hopefully. "Puzzles?"

"Not really."

"Ahh, no matter," Bob said. "Virgil, what do you say we get him started?" Eron slid reluctantly out of the driver's seat and went to work.

15
ONE WINTER NIGHT
2016

Summer, thick with green, ruled the world until the frost found its flaw. Autumn crept across the land turning a thousand emerald hues into reds, browns, and yellows. Trees stood bare-headed beneath the heavens, gray branches prickling a cold sky. The Earth knew what was coming, knew the old man would come riding on the back of the north wind, knew it was time to rest.

Kianna listened. Outside in the dark, the storm edged toward its peak, stronger and colder than it had been the hour before. Wind-driven snow was piling high against the lee of the house. By morning, the drift would be halfway up the door, almost to the windowsills, but that didn't matter. Eron and Val were tucked into their beds. The Wallace House was stronger than wind or snow, and there was no place she needed to go. A roaring fire had given way to red-hot coals that sank their heat deep into the stone. She held a cup of chamomile tea, still too hot to drink, and remembered the winter before, huddling close with Makena, sharing her strawberry tarts, her kindness, her stories of the African trickster, and the nest they made beneath the stairs.

She looked at the empty chair beside her. It should have been John's chair. He should be sitting in it right now, making her laugh, making sure she knew how much he loved her. She ached to hear his voice, to laugh with him, to feign interest as he plowed through his long but adorable descriptions of his math problems. She was certain John would have loved the Shire. She remembered his touch, so gentle and understanding. Eyes closed, she worked to recall the way he smiled, the way his eyes danced when he was happy, the sound of his voice when he whispered, "I love you." Time was already fading her memories of John Wallace, stealing them away from the woman who loved him best.

Being Seed-Keeper suited her. Together with Jude she tramped the length and breadth of the Shire, exploring its woods, hollows, ridges, and streams. Its limits ranged ten miles square, and most of it was wild. Already she found partridge berry, liferoot, trout lilies, black cohosh, and wild carrot and brought them back to the people of the Shire. There was more, so much more, waiting to be discovered.

The harvest had been good, and she made sure the best of it was kept back for next year. The seeds, small and hard, had been sorted, counted, weighed, and packed carefully away. When spring came, there'd be little time for a cup of tea and a seat by a fire. She would be out delivering her precious cargo from Bywater to Crickhollow. The thought made her smile.

Zakia said Val was born for the loom. The Master Weaver was challenging her apprentice, pushing her to learn, to think, to create. She taught Val the story of Arachnae, the girl with an extraordinary gift for weaving who unwisely claimed that she was better even than gray-eyed Athena. The offended Goddess changed her into a spider. Now, whenever Val spied a spider's web, she'd say, "See, Mom, there's weaving everywhere." In the Shire, a Master Weaver was a person of importance and respect. Val was going to be alright.

Kianna got up and stirred the bed of coals until it glowed then layered an armload of split oak into a criss-cross pattern overtop the embers, piling the firewood high enough to outlast a cold winter's night.

Bob Brazzi had stopped by earlier in the day. After tea, and a hesitant beginning, he told them he wouldn't need Eron in the spring. "Tinkers," Bob said kindly, "are all about getting things done."

It was true that Eron hated being a Tinker's apprentice, but Bob's rejection threw him into a rage. "You are a dirty bastard. You never gave me a chance. You never taught me anything. You treated me like a slave." Kianna jumped in to calm her son. He dismissed her. "You can't fire me 'cause I quit. I hate you. I hate all of you. You couldn't make me come back. Never!" He stormed off to his room, cursing his mother as he went. Val chased after him and spent the rest of the afternoon soothing her brother's injured pride.

When they were alone, Bob said, "I'm sorry."

Kianna looked away.

"Boys," he added, "sometimes it can be hard for them."

She nodded.

"He misses his Dad," Bob said.

Her grief collapsed Kianna into shoulder-racking sobs. The Tinker put his arms around her, but this was something he lacked the power to repair.

"If John was here," she choked out the words, "if John was here, this wouldn't be happening."

"You're doing the best you can. That's all a mother can do."

Kianna wiped her tears away, "I know... I know he's made trouble, quite a bit of trouble for you, but he's not a bad boy."

Bob smiled. "I know. Truth be told, I had a temper like his when I was younger. I grew out of it, he will too."

Kianna looked into the Tinker's eyes. "Can he have another chance?"

Bob shook his head. "I'm sorry. He's run out of chances with me. He needs a fresh start with someone else." Moved by Kianna's grief, he added, "I'll ask around, see what I can do."

The night had reached its deepest, darkest point, and Kianna rubbed her weary eyes. It was long past time for bed. She walked round the house one last time, stopping to peek into Val and Eron's rooms before she went to her own. Eron heard his mother moving and feigned sleep as she stood in the doorway and watched him. When she was gone, he cranked the handle of his transistor radio and held the earphone close. There had been less and less to hear since the cold weather had come.

KDKA, gone—KRP, gone—WBBM Chicago, off the air. Boston, New York, Baltimore, all gone. He worked the dial expertly from end to end, listening as hard as he could. The voices had all gone silent.

16
THE APPRENTICES

The room was hot and smelled of blood. A cheerfully unconcerned Jeffery Price, pantless but still wearing his bloodstained linen shirt, lay before Caleb Thomas. Jeffery had been working with the grazier's apprentices as they trimmed the edge of a hayfield with their razor sharp scythes. They had been hard at it since dawn, and he wanted to reach the hedgerow on the east end of the field before breaking for lunch. In too much of a hurry, he stepped clumsily into a woodchuck hole hidden by the tall grass. He stumbled, and the burnished blade bit deeply into the flesh of his right leg.

Three sturdy apprentices had carried him back to Bywater, laid him on a hastily cleared potter's work table, and sent for Doctor Thomas. It was mid-afternoon by the time Bill and Caleb arrived. They found a diagonal wound that ran a good six inches across the front of the thigh. It gaped wide and revealed muscle and sinew in its depth. The edges, Caleb thought, formed a twisted mocking grin.

Miles to the east, in the Shire's highest county, apprentice Herdsman Eron Wallace sat comfortably in the shade beneath the great spreading branches of a thick-trunked oak. It was cool. The terrain favored the gentle breeze that came out of the west. He was supposed to be making a count of the cattle in the highland. Instead, he settled down with a loaf of his mother's potato-onion bread and a block of cheese. When the food was gone, he reached for his radio. It had been months since he wound it up. Its empty hiss depressed him. Up here, so much closer to the sky, he thought, he might find a signal.

They washed the wound, finding and carefully removing bits of dirt and grass while Jeffery downed a fifth of Ivan Lane's Best Bag's End Blackberry Brandy. When it was time, Caleb looked up at his patient who was now very pleasantly drunk. The Master Grazier smiled congenially at the young doctor and slurred, "Go ahead, kid. Don't worry about your stitchin'. I aint gonna be winnin' any beauty contests, that's for sure."

Bill saw Caleb's sweat-beaded forehead, knew that his son's heart was pounding. He remembered his first time. "You know what to do, place the first stitch here at the midpoint of the wound. Match the edges." Caleb's hand trembled as he reached for the needle with its delicate trailing thread. He drew a deep breath and, just as he had been taught, began to sew.

Eron spun the handle, adjusted the tuning knob, and listened. KDKA in Philadelphia came in, bright and clear.

> *...period of violence, disease and fear is over. Order has been reestablished in the city and though we have all suffered greatly in recent times we can look forward to a new era of security and justice...*

Cincinnati, Pittsburgh, and Baltimore all shared the same good news. The Chicago station was running a news program that reviewed recent history.

> *...In the end, the old republic bowed to the demands of reality and passed the General Reincorporation and Isolation of Demographics Act of 2016 by unanimous consent. In doing so, it placed all authority into the capable hands of the GRID. Economist Dr. Robert Norris had this to say about the landmark legislation: 'We've known for decades that private enterprise consistently offers solutions that are superior to government programs. The GRID offers all of us the full benefits of privatization. The GRID has restored public confidence and is now actively engaged in those displaced by the Fall, providing them with safe, secure housing and access to the full range of GRID products and services...*

He cranked the radio again and found Cleveland. The name of the city stabbed him in the heart but, still, he listened.

> *...lawless elements outside of the control of the GRID will be targeted for relocation or, if they are unwilling, destruction. We've had altogether too much anarchy, people doing whatever they want. There is a better life to be had by all, when the GRID assumes full control...*

The radio's squawking voices enchanted Eron. Their crisp, clipped tones, reinforced with a vast certainty, held him in their thrall.

The wound's edges were matched well. It was time to apply the dressing. Bill broke a loaf of bread into small pieces and dunked them in an earthen jar filled with fresh milk. "Lay these over the wound. They'll start to mold and the mold will fight the bacteria. It's an old-time antibiotic."

Caleb bandaged the wound while his father gave Jeff instructions, "We'll stop by in a couple of days and change the dressing for you. Stay off your feet. The stitches will come out in a week or so."

"All set, Dad."

Bill pulled Jeff up to a sitting position. "There's a buggy outside. It'll take you home."

Jeff gave woozy thanks to the young healer, "Nice job kid." With an arm around each of their shoulders he hobbled to the carriage. They watched it roll away.

"Jeff's right," Bill said. "You did a good job."

The Shire's Master Herdsman was annoyed. Eron was supposed to come by the barn and give him a report on the high pastures. It was the hottest part of the afternoon, and he and his favorite mare were searching for the errant apprentice. Zach Thomas was a big-shouldered man, with a square, almost antique, jaw. His eyes were wide-set and accustomed to peering into the distance from beneath a floppy, broad-brimmed felt hat. The youngest of the Shire's Masters, his face carried only a wisp of a beard. The Master Herdsman caught sight of Eron and muttered, "What the hell?" The boy was lounging in the shade of an oak tree apparently unconcerned about his failure to report in to the barn.

Zach's blood was up by the time he reached Eron.

"Hey, what the hell are you doing?"

Eron struggled to his feet. "It's news, great news. The troubles are over. It's safe out there." He waved his arms wildly.

"What are you talking about?"

"I was listening to this." He reached down and picked up the radio.

"That's Virgil's radio."

"Your Dad gave it to me. I can hear all kinds of stations on it, from as far away as Chicago."

"So?"

Eron boasted, "All of the fighting and the, uhhh, riots. They're all done. Now the GRID has taken over." He stared directly into Zach's eyes. "Pretty soon it'll take over the Shire. Pretty soon I won't have to listen to you anymore. You won't be the Master anymore. You'll have to do as you're told, just like everybody else."

Zach squinted. "The GRID?"

"It's the new government. It believes in law and order and it doesn't like people like...like you." Eron spoke with the fervor of a fresh convert. "All the people on the radio say that if people don't obey its orders, they'll be punished."

Zach dismounted. "I sent you up here to check on the cattle and I find you lollygagging under this tree."

"But," Eron backed unsteadily toward the trunk of the tree.

"Screw the damned radio. You've got a job to do," Zach barked.

Eron threw his arms up and winced as if to avoid an oncoming blow.

Eron's helplessness cooled Zach's anger. He took a deep breath. "I know you come from out there, probably still got people you care about out there. But the fact is, you live here now. None of that stuff matters, not anymore."

"Yes it does," Eron countered. "It matters more than anything in this stupid Shire."

Bob Brazzi had told him the boy would be difficult, and he hadn't exaggerated.

"Alright," Zach sighed. "It matters. But until the voices on the radio come to save us all from ourselves, we have work to do. Real work. There's still plenty of daylight left. You swing up over the top three pastures then stop by my place on your way home. You can do that?" Zach asked gently.

Eron felt hate well up inside of him. He hated the man for not listening to him, hated him for making him feel afraid, hated him for his bizarre fixation on those stinking cattle. He made his face into a mask and nodded, "Yeah, I can."

"Good."

The Herdsman mounted his horse and rode off. Eron carefully packed his radio into his rucksack. His heart still pounded. The world was changing, he was no longer alone, now he had allies and someday, somehow, he would have his revenge.

17
THE ALIENS

S ummer brought rain enough, but not too much, and the harvest was
good. The Autumn Feast and the greatest part of the year's work lay
behind the people of the Shire. Kianna sat at Jude's kitchen table, hands
cupped around a dark brown ceramic mug. Outside the window, the weakened
sun scattered its light across the land. A west wind stirred with the morning
bringing herringbone clouds and the promise of rain by nightfall.

Jude probed gently, "How's Eron doing?"

A pained look swept over Kianna's normally sunny face. "He's not happy.
He's not like he used to be. I don't know what to do."

Jude sighed. Zach had told her about Eron's refusal to work, his constant
stirring of conflict between the other apprentices, and his calculating lack of
concern for others. Tears rose into Kianna's eyes but did not fall.

"Oh, I wish you'd known him when he was little. So beautiful, so full of
life, so full of love." She looked away.

"He'll be OK," Jude said, hopefully.

"Lately he's been going on and on about some grid thing and how all
the troubles out there are over and how people are being taken away to God
knows where."

Jude knew about this too. The news had spread from Eron to Zach to the
Council of Elders. The old republic was dead. The GRID had taken power and
was now herding the survivors of the Fall into its walled compounds. The
unexpected rise of the GRID cast a shadow over the peace of the Shire.

They listened to the children playing on the Green until Jude changed the
subject. "Caleb's the one who has me worried."

They were both painfully aware of Caleb's incessant teasing of Val.

"Bill's talked to him about it. More than once."

"Mmm hmm," Kianna sipped her tea.

"I'm really sorry," Jude added.

"Val lets him have it right back."

"That doesn't make it right."

It was Kianna's turn to offer reassurance. "I think we can just watch for
now. They'll work it out, in time."

Jude thought back to the day she met Kianna and the twins on Turnpike
Road. Val was so young then, sick, hungry, cold, and tired—but beautiful,

even then. Now she was fifteen-years-old and brimming with strength and confidence. They would wait.

Another cup of tea was poured, and the two women sat together, in silence, the way good friends do.

The next morning dawned wet and cold. Val had already eaten and left for the workshop in Crickhollow, but Eron didn't want to go to work. He sat at the kitchen table, still in his bedclothes, bleary-eyed, his hair still matted by sleep.

"Mom," he insisted, "listen to me. I heard them on the radio last night. They're coming to our sector, maybe today, maybe tomorrow. They're not really sure when, but they're coming."

"I don't care what the radio says. You need to get dressed and go to work."

He ignored her. "The GRID has fixed all the problems. It's super powerful and it keeps people safe."

"We're already safe," Kianna said.

"Yeah, right," Eron huffed. "This place is insane. We gotta escape while we can. The Militia is coming, coming to rescue the survivors. The GRID is setting people up in the real world, in real houses, in real Demographic Units. They're rescuing people, saving people like us."

"You need to go to work."

"Believe me," he said sarcastically, "I won't be missed."

"Eron!" his mother insisted.

He rose sullenly from his place at the table, went to get ready. At the door, he pulled on his oilskin. "Seriously, Mom, I don't know how much longer I can keep doing this. I hate those stupid cows."

Kianna hugged him and sent him on his way, her heart breaking as she watched him trudge slowly across the Green, pelted by rain falling out of a slate-gray sky.

In the early afternoon, Kianna thought she heard thunder; the sound was deep and distant. She dismissed the thought and went back to sorting seeds, a magnifying glass in her left hand, tweezers in her right. The sound grew louder and, again, she paused from her work. It was constant, like the thrumming of an aching tooth. Trucks, heavy trucks, were coming up the Turnpike, more than one or two. She went to the rack beside the door, drew her own oilskin across her shoulders, and stepped outside.

By the time she reached the Green, the convoy was already parked along its opposite edge. The engines purred smoothly, pouring hot black exhaust into the air, where it mixed with the rain. There were five vehicles. Kianna recognized the first and last as military Humvees. The others were canvas covered transport trucks. They were painted black, not camouflage, not olive drab. Each vehicle door was marked with the outline of a bear's paw, precise but inaccurate, painted white on black. There were no flags.

The driver's side door of the lead vehicle swung open, and a soldier emerged. Dour and pale, he wore his helmet's night vision scope swung up and out of the way. He grimaced as his gleaming black boots bit into the mud. He scanned his surroundings then snatched a microphone from its shoulder clip. The doors swung open on the other vehicles, and a dozen more soldiers emerged into the rain. The men huddled together, cradling their rifles, content to wait passively until they were ordered into action.

Kianna tore her gaze away from the intruders and looked to see what they saw. From all around the Green, the Elders of Summer Hill were coming to greet the convoy. There was Jonas Campbell the baker, Riana Becker the potter, Michelle Barry the poet, and Taylor Morris maker of paper and inks. Together, they approached the soldiers.

The officer stepped forward. A mere handful of people stood before him, but he spoke as if he addressed a throng. "I am Major Robert Fitzgerald, Third Division, GRID Militia. I am a Population Recovery Specialist. This is my team," he nodded briefly in the direction of the other men. "We've come to save you." He let the last sentence hang in the air, for dramatic effect.

And the Elders obliged.

When the moment passed, Jonas answered with the reed thin voice that only old age can provide. "It is awfully nice of you fellows to come all the way out here, in the rain and all. Please know that we do appreciate it."

Major Fitzgerald smiled stiffly, and said, "Sir, I do not believe that you understand me. You are currently located outside of a Certified Demographic Unit; the GRID will not supply this area with food, fuel, or electricity." Not getting the response he expected, he stated the obvious, "There are no GRID connections outside of certified Demos. We've come to relocate you to a Demo, now, before winter." He signaled to his men. They swiftly formed themselves into ranks and shouldered their weapons.

Jonas studied the men carefully then stepped forward. "There's no need for excitement young fellow."

The major's gaze swept across the old people in front of him. He hadn't seen so many of them since before the Fall. "You must understand that winter is coming. You do understand that, don't you?" He spoke in the loud, slow voice that people reserve for fools, foreigners, and old people. He scanned the crowd again and this time saw Kianna standing in the back. He addressed her directly, "Will they listen to you? Can you talk sense into these old fools?"

Kianna shrugged but said nothing.

Compassion was not the Major's strong suit, and he was tiring of the game. "Anderson," he called, "load 'em up." The soldiers quickly surrounded the Elders, barrels lowered.

Jonas spoke again, "Mr. Fitzgerald, I think it is you who does not understand."

The major jabbed his forefinger at Jonas, "Listen to me, old man. The old republic is dead. Got that? Everything, and I do mean everything, is under GRID control. Those buildings there," he pointed at Summer Hill, "this land, all of it is GRID property." He decided to offer them one more chance, "You're gonna die up here, old man, without GRID protection—no food, no medicine, no energy, no information, nothing, you're gonna die."

He addressed the group as a whole. "I could have you all killed right where you stand. You're all refusing relocation, and that makes you aliens. I have been granted authority to shoot those who refuse relocation!" The Elders did not stir. Kianna held her breath.

"How can I help you?" Jonas asked.

The Elder's persistently gentle manner took the edge off Fitzgerald's anger. The officer continued, more calmly, "It is my duty to explain to you that if you do not accept re-assignment at this time and any of you attempt to enter a certified Demo at any point in the future, you will be attacked, and most likely killed." The wind was picking up, and the rain now fell in cold hard sheets.

"If I may..." Jonas began.

"Nevermind. Thumb this document. No, put your thumb here, on the blue square. It means that you are surrendering all rights to future relocation for everyone in this sector."

The major looked into Kianna's eyes one last time. She returned his gaze and remained silent.

The Elder laid his thumb on the blue square.

The deed done, the officer barked, "We'll let the winter finish them off, let's go."

The men shouldered their weapons, happy to retreat into their warm, dry vehicles.

Engines roared, and the convoy pulled away from Summer Hill. The Elders stood in silence and watched them retreat into the cold, wet distance.

Val was already home, warm and dry, sitting by the fire with her mother when Eron burst into the house. "They were here! I saw the tracks. They came to save us." Kianna dreaded what was sure to follow. "What happened? When are they coming back? Where did they go?"

She stood and faced her son. "The Elders met with them. They told them that we were fine, that we didn't need to be rescued."

Eron flushed red with anger. "Who cares about them, what about us?"

"We are staying here Eron. This is our home now. We don't belong out there anymore."

Eron's face paled as his body shook with a cold anger. He screwed his eyes tight shut as if the darkness would somehow erase the words his mother had spoken. Kianna reached out to him, but he pulled away from her. He stormed into his room and slammed the door so hard the stone cottage trembled. During the night, the rain gave way to winter's first snow. By morning, it had filled the ruts left behind by the Militia's heavy vehicles.

18
THE GOAD

Black flies swarmed apprentice Herdsman Eron Wallace as if they were a fierce, hungry cloud. The sun rode high, and its heat scorched the very air he breathed. He hated this job more than any other. A hundred cow-calf pairs had to be sorted into pens and made ready for the high summer pastures. The dams were skittish and fiercely protective of their young. The calves could spook at the sight of their own shadows.

All of the other apprentices were already resting in the shade. They started before dawn and had done their part. Late to work, Eron still had a pen to clear. Only one dam and her calf remained, but they refused to pass through the gate. Sweat soaked his shirt; he was hungry, thirsty, and tired. He made three passes around the corral, but he was no closer to finishing. He spied a post lying on the ground. It was left over from last year's fence repair. He picked it up, and it felt good in his hands. Eron glanced over his shoulder; the other apprentices had gone inside for lunch. No one would be watching. He trudged toward the dam, and she eyed him warily, keeping her calf behind her. He cooed, "Hey boss, hey bossie, bossie, bossie."

He worked her into the farthest corner of the pen. When he had her trapped, he raised the wooden club high over his head. He hesitated, and then brought it crashing down on the cow's spine. It landed with a sickening thud. The boy-man swung again. It felt good. The dam bellowed, her calf cowered beneath her.

Someone was watching. Zachary's oldest boy, six-year-old Joshua, sprinted for the house. "Pa, Pa, Pa! You gotta come, you gotta come right away, Pa!" Zach met him on the porch.

"Pa! Eron's hitting Baby Doll with a stick—hittin' her real hard!"

Zach leapt off the porch and sprinted for the barnyard. The apprentices tumbled out of the house and raced after him, but none could match the enraged Herdsman's stride.

Eron raised the goad and struck again.

Zach vaulted the fence and reached Eron before the apprentice knew he was coming. He wrenched the weapon from Eron's hands and threw it on the ground. "What the hell do you think you are doing?" Zach's voice boomed. Not waiting for an answer, he took Eron by the scruff of the neck and pitched him face first into the muck.

Zach's boys and a half dozen apprentices lined the barnyard fence, watching. Eron picked himself up from the stink and saw them. They stood silent as stones, but he knew that later they would talk—they would laugh—at him. The time had come to have his revenge. He crouched before the Herdsman, ready to strike. He would knock the bastard down. He would make the apprentices laugh—at the Master. He looked up and saw a two-hundred-and-twenty-pound man, hard as stone from a lifetime of loving and caring for his cattle. Attacking him would be suicide.

Blood pounded in Zach's temples, and he spoke one word at a time, his rage-rattled voice, barely above a whisper. "You are finished here." The Herdsman bent down to pick up the fence post, and Eron flinched, stumbled backward, and splashed into the dung. Still, no one laughed. "Baby Doll never hurt you, never hurt anybody." Zach stepped toward Eron and the boy scrambled back onto his feet.

"Go," Zach said. "Go and don't ever, ever come back here."

19
THE INVESTMENT
Summer, 2017

They came from Bywater and Bag's End, Frogmorton, Hardbottle Bucklebury, Summer Hill and Crickhollow: the whole of the Shire came to the Midsummer's Feast at the Pavilion. They came on foot, on horseback, by wagon, buggy, and bicycle. There were children, babes in arms, Elders, young lovers, and married couples comfortable in their middle age. The Pavilion was the largest building in the whole of the Shire, bigger even than the barns. Master Tinker Bob Brazzi had designed its vaulting cantilevered roof. Its great sliding doors stood open in the summer and were closed in the winter. It was shelter, theater, meeting hall, concert stage, and market place all in one.

In and around the Pavilion were food and drink: cheese, beer, wine, bread, ice cream, and the summer's best raspberries, tart and sweet. Clusters of friends and neighbors formed and reformed as people caught up with each other, played music, and swapped stories. There was also, as always, business to be done. The Shire functioned on a complex system of barter, of favors done and favors owed. The Paper-Maker from Frogmorton might need planed lumber from the Sawyer in Bucklebury and arrange for it by taking over the Blacksmith's obligation to help stack hay in the Grazier's barn the following summer. The Elders believed this system of exchange served to weave the people of the Shire together.

Up on Summer Hill, Kianna and Eron cut across the Green. Kianna had promised to walk down the hill to the festival with Jude, and she was late. After nearly an hour of coaxing, Eron had finally agreed to leave the house. He slouched alongside of her.

"He'd better not be there. If he's there, I'm not going in."

"He won't be there," Kianna reassured him.

"I hate him," Eron answered. "Hate him. Hate him. Hate him!"

"Eron," his mother shushed, "stop it."

Kianna tapped on the back door then stepped inside wondering if they were too late. "Jude?"

"Coming," Jude answered. A moment later, she emerged from her studio laden with paper, boxes of charcoals, and a folding artist's tripod. The Midsummer's Feast was the busiest time of her year.

"Eron, so glad you are here, I was afraid you'd gone on ahead. Would you help me with some of this?" Jude's smile reassured the youth.

He brightened slowly. "Sure."

Jude studied his face. It had changed. The boy who had arrived in the Shire two years before was now poised on the edge of manhood. Eron willingly shouldered the greatest part of the burden, and they were soon on their way. The three paused on the brow of the hill overlooking the festival grounds. Below them was a rippling quilt of color and sound. A village constructed in a single morning circled the Pavilion. They hurried down the hill and plunged into the crowd. Eron helped Jude set up an outdoor portrait studio. Kianna wandered off to see friends and catch up on garden news. When everything was in its proper place, Jude laid her hand on Eron's shoulder and said, "I'd like to do your portrait." An unfamiliar mixture of pride and embarrassment made him shift his weight. He shrugged his shoulders. "I'd love to make a picture of you."

"Sure, if you want to."

"I do. The light is perfect."

He sat for her and when the drawing was complete, she showed it to him. His eyes grew wide. "It's...great. That's really me? Wow."

"You like it?"

He nodded eagerly.

"Show my Mom," he said. "And Val. Val, too."

Eron's whole face smiled, and Jude wondered if she was seeing his father's smile. He was as happy as she had ever seen him. She slipped the portrait into a folder, then turned, the line of people wanting portraits already stretched to a dozen. "Alright, Amanda," she said, "you're next."

Eron wandered off in search of Virgil, now a Master Tinker. He was likely to be somewhere behind or above the Pavilion's stage. He saw a knot of apprentice Herdsmen and veered away from them. Roundabout, he came to the backstage steps. Onstage the floor was littered with electrical cables, tools, and a jumble of lights and speakers, microphones, and amplifiers. The Midsummer's Feast had been Eron's favorite part of the tinker's trade. Unfortunately, it came only once a year. "Virgil, you there?"

When no answer came, Eron concluded that he was probably at the powerhouse. Eron found the twisted footpath that led through a stand of oak and ash down to the sod-topped powerhouse.

"Virgil," he cried.

"Yo!" Virgil's voice echoed toward him. "Down here."

Eron ducked as he stepped through the stone building's squat doorway and then clambered noisily down the metal stairs that led to the control room. Virgil's arms and chest were covered with slick black grease. He had the electrical generator torn down to the windings. "Damn bearings are bad. Mind giving me a hand?"

"Yeah. Sure."

"Put a wrench on that fitting..."

Val was in heaven. The kaleidoscope of colors, the smell of meat and vegetables being grilled over charcoal fires, and the burble of contended conversation welcomed her, enfolded her. The pale blue sky promised fine weather, for the next few days. This would be a good feast. Today, for the first time, her work was being offered alongside Zakia's, a half dozen linen shirts, simpler, sturdier and less ornate than the Investment Blouse she made for Caleb Thomas.

She stood on the edge of the lacrosse field with her two best friends, Rebecca, an apprentice Sawyer, and Nia, an apprentice Teamster. Their beloved East Farthing was two goals down. They already screamed themselves hoarse, but the game was still in its first half. Caleb was East's midfielder and team captain. Val watched him, watched him even when he did not have the ball, watched him when he rested on the sideline. The score was close, the lead bounced back and forth. It was a game, people said, that would be remembered for years to come. In the end, East Farthing pulled ahead, taking the Cup for the third year running.

Zach wanted to watch the game, but didn't have time. There were plugs to fit, microphones to position, lights to adjust, and instruments to tune. The other members of the band worked alongside him. They were all helped along by Bob Brazzi's genial stream of expert advice, "Leave that. Get the preamps adjusted then come back to it. Never mind those, they're busted. I'll have the apprentices get after them this winter."

The afternoon shadows lengthened, and the bustle gave way to quiet conversation over the last big meal of the day. When the dishes were cleared away, people turned toward the stage. The Investment ceremony came first. This was the moment when the whole of the Shire invested itself in the apprentices who were ready to become Journeymen and the Journeymen who were ready to become Masters. After the ceremony, there would be music. Zach's fingers itched for the steel of his guitar strings. He loved the sound of the band, loved the old songs they played.

Bill was just returning from tending to a lacrosse player's sprained knee when he caught sight of Caleb across the way. He motioned to him.

"Great game," he said, mopping his son's sweat-soaked hair with his hand.

"Thanks Dad." Caleb was flushed with excitement. He was a grown man now but still treasured praise from his father. He read the look on his Dad's face.

"Something wrong?" he asked.

"No," Bill shook his head. "I just wanted you to know I'm proud of you."

Caleb smiled, "I know."

"You're ready," Bill said, mostly to himself. "You're ready, but you need to remember," Bill looked at his son. "Remember, this is just the beginning. Tomorrow you'll start making decisions about how to use what you know. Knowing when to act and when to sit and wait, that's the hardest thing a Journeyman has to learn."

The son threw his arms around his father.

A richly robed Zakia Johnson swung her elder's cloak up and over her shoulders and stepped out onto the stage. She called to the Tribes of Eden with her deep brassy voice. "Apprentices, Journeymen, Masters, come forward."

"Let's go," Bill said.

At the Investment ceremony conclusion, cheering echoed off the hillsides, passed through the forest, and reached the powerhouse. This was the signal Eron and Virgil had been waiting for. Working together, they cranked open a balky sluice grate and watched as the water rushed in from the pond above them. When it struck the turbine blades full force, the needles on a bank of meters jerked to life. A moment later, the single bulb hanging overhead glowed like a miniature artificial sun.

"You want to do it?" Virgil asked.

Eron nodded, then grabbed hold of the rubber handle lever on the side of a 200-amp panel and pulled down hard. The switch closed the circuit, and the generator settled into a steady dull hum. On stage, sound equipment and lights sprang to life.

"OK, let's go," Virgil said.

Eron demurred, "Nah. Not me. I'll stay here."

"You don't have to. Bob fixed the voltage regulator. It's automatic now."

"Not my thing."

Virgil understood. "Yeah, OK. Keep an eye on things, alright?"

"Sure," Eron answered.

Virgil sprinted toward the sound of the band.

The musicians launched into a reggae version of *Jack-a-Roe* and it rolled them into the glorious early summer evening. The azure eastern sky would fade into purple, then black. The music would carry the people forward, singing and dancing, as they traveled the ancient passage that stretches from day into night.

Deal, Row Jimmy, The Wheel, then *Deep Elem Blues*. Overhead, arc lights bathed them all in artificial light. The second set: *Scarlet Begonias, Fire on the Mountain, Morning Dew*, closing with *Not Fade Away*.

After midnight, Zach's voice rang out, "Mom! Get up here and bring your mandolin!" The crowd roared its approval. Jude stepped onto the stage and the band plunged into Iko Iko.

Caleb Thomas ran toward Val, his fine Investment Blouse gleaming in the night. He gathered her into his arms, twirled her around, and whooped. Then he returned her gently to the ground and disappeared as unexpectedly as he had appeared.

Chakko mo fino, an-nah-ney
Chakko mo finnah-ney
Hey, now...

When the music ended and the cheering faded away, the crowd stilled itself, eager for what came next.

Elder Melissa Roane from Bucklebury, former supply chain manager, swineherd, and printmaker, stepped up to the microphone. The hush spread quickly then deepened into silence. In the depth of the Powerhouse, Eron listened.

"I am blessed," she began, "to be among the Elders of a wise and gentle people. All of us here in the Shire are well-acquainted with the sleep of the contented. Our doors are unlocked, our minds are at peace."

The former Tinker's apprentice began to pace back and forth. "Our minds are at peace." What bullshit, he thought.

The old Crone continued, "There are others, so many others, who live in fear, whose lives are not their own. Not long ago, men from the new government came to the Shire. Our Elders met with them then sent them away."

The words flooded him with fury. He stopped pacing and struggled to control his fury, but the Crone's screeching, amplified voice would not stop.

"Without knowing it, these visitors gave us a gift. They reminded us that the outside world still exists and that we are still a part of that world. This is a truth that we may sometimes forget but that we will never be able to escape."

The old Crone's stupid prattling had brought his blood to a boil. Somebody needed to shut her up. Eron's eyes fell upon the heavy pipe wrench they used to reset the bearings. What a shame it would be if, somehow, the wrench fell into the turbine's intake valve. He could say he had left long before. They were holding him hostage, and a hostage had every right to strike a blow against those who held him—every right.

He laid his hand on the wrench's long, cold, steel handle.

The Elder's voice became the whisper of a mother tucking her children into bed. "Do not forget those who suffer still, remember them because, truly, we are one people living in one time. Keep them in your hearts." She smiled and stretched out her arms. "Now sleep well my children, sleep well you mothers and fathers, you sons and daughters of the Tribes of Eden."

The power failed the moment she finished, and the Tribes were plunged into the silent depth of a moonlit night. A quarter-mile away, a boy fled the scene of his crime. A thrilling combination of fear, exertion, and power made his heart pound in his chest.

20
PROMISES

The summer crawled fitfully toward the fall. At least, that's how it seemed to Eron. Zach had discussed the Baby Doll incident with the Council of Elders. While no specific punishment was recommended, it was decided to ask Kianna if she would take Eron on as an apprentice Seed-Keeper. She agreed, and in her most hopeful moments, she imagined the fascination with plants she had felt since her childhood would jump from mother to son. It did not.

One cool September afternoon, the Seed-Keeper and her unwilling apprentice passed within sight of the now nearly completed mill above Bag's End. What had seemed so jumbled and unimpressive, so amateurish a year before, was now a thing of wonder. The mill's wooden superstructure straddled the outlet of the pond rising above the water like a giant exclamation point. They hoped it would be ready in time for the fall harvest. The final remaining task was the installation of the massive turbine blade that would power the mill. Everyone was talking about it. The Shire would have its first Miller, and the hundreds of human-powered kitchen flour mills would be contributed to the Tinkers' parts bin.

Eron spied Virgil scaling the grain silo which towered above the mill. "Hey, Mom, we all done?" he asked.

"You know we aren't," she answered. Then, relenting, she added, "But I suppose..."

He didn't let her finish, "Great! I was thinking that I might go see Virgil and, you know, come home a little later."

Kianna was pleasantly surprised. "Great, honey. Sure. Fine. See you at home."

Eron ambled across the open meadow stopping now and then to admire the Tinkers' creation. He was in the building's shadow when Virgil met up with him. "Pretty nice, huh?"

Eron answered honestly, "Yeah, it really is. I never thought it would turn out like this."

"Mmm yeah. Bob did though. It's just the way he imagined it."

The former apprentice felt a pang of grief rise up inside of him. For a moment, he regretted that he had cared so little about the tinker's craft when he had served under Bob Brazzi.

"How you doing?" Virgil asked.

"OK," Eron lied.

"I would hate to apprentice for one of my parents," Virgil confessed. "I don't know how Caleb did it."

"It's not easy," Eron agreed.

Virgil looked at Eron and felt his unhappiness. "Anything I can do?" He asked.

Eron shrugged his shoulders. "I listen to your old radio, as much as I can."

"Oh yeah?"

"It works great."

"What do you hear?"

Eron smiled. "It's all about the GRID. It's all anybody ever talks about. It's awesome. It's working."

Virgil nodded.

"You can connect to it, everyone connects to it," Eron continued. "I could connect to it too—if—if I had a GRID station."

"What's that?"

"They give them to the people who live in the Demos. It connects you to everything. They say they're amazing."

"I could make you one I bet," Virgil ventured confidently.

Eron shuddered with excitement. "Oh my God, Virgil, could you? When? When could you do it?"

Virgil grinned, then shrugged. "I dunno, after we get the mill up and running I guess."

"When? When?" Eron's enthusiasm was infectious.

"This fall, definitely this fall."

Virgil cautioned him, "First things first, Eron. Don't worry, though, I'll do it for you."

"You promise?" He asked, hopeful.

"Hey, Virgil!" Bob Brazzi called from inside the mill.

"Be right there," Virgil answered. He gave Eron a thumbs up. "Don't worry, be happy. You've got a GRID station coming your way."

"Need calipers, the big ones."

"Got 'em, Bob."

Virgil disappeared into the building.

When he arrived home he was so eager to share his good news that he didn't notice Caleb Thomas sitting at the kitchen table. Nor did he see that his mother had been crying.

"You're not going to believe it, Mom! Virgil's going to build me a real GRID station!"

"That's great, honey," Kianna responded numbly.

Then Eron saw Caleb, "Isn't it great?"

"Yeah, super," Caleb said.

The screen door banged again. This time it was Val returning home from a day on the loom. She saw everything at once, her mother's tears, Caleb's deep concern, and Eron's strange enthusiasm. Nothing was as it should be. She wanted answers, but her twin interrupted before she could speak.

"Val," he exclaimed, "you'll never, ever, ever, guess what happened to me today. I stopped by the mill to see Virgil and..."

"You were at the mill?" Val could not imagine Eron stopping by to visit the Tinkers at work.

"Yeah, it's great. But the big news is..."

Val stopped listening. Her eyes darted between Caleb and her mother.

"...a GRID station!" Eron concluded.

"Wow," Val spoke without enthusiasm. "Wonderful."

Kianna refused to meet her daughter's gaze.

Finally, Eron caught on.

Val looked hard at Caleb. She needed to talk to him, alone. "I'll bet it's been a while since you've seen Virgil."

Caleb understood what she was asking for. "Yeah," he agreed.

"Why don't we go over there together, tomorrow morning?"

Caleb sighed then nodded, "I'll come by for you in the morning."

"I'll be waiting."

21
MAN DOWN

Aclear sky brought a hard freeze, the first of the season. By the time Caleb returned to the Wallace house, all that remained of the frost were the crisp white silhouettes that hid within the morning's first shadows. As promised, Val was waiting for him. They walked together in silence. Neither party willing to begin the exchange both knew was coming.

When they passed the turn for Bucklebury, Val offered, as innocently as she could, "You came by the house yesterday—to see my Mom."

"I did," Caleb admitted.

"She'd been crying." It was both question and statement.

"You know...Val, you know I can't talk about it."

"She's my mother, Caleb."

"I know."

"Tell me."

"You should ask her."

"I did. Believe me, I did," Val huffed.

"And?"

"She won't talk about it," Val continued, "I'm afraid...it's multiple sclerosis, Caleb. I had a fifth-grade teacher who had MS, and she started limping—just like Mom," Val looked at Caleb. "That's it, isn't it?"

As gently as he could, Caleb started responding, "Val..." Val stifled a sob, but he kept his gaze fixed on the road ahead. He wanted to take her hand, but did not.

They walked on, each lost in thought.

Val was ready to try again when Caleb interrupted, "What the hell?"

Virgil was sprinting toward them, his long arms and legs pumping like flesh and blood pistons.

He saw them and screamed, "Man down!"

Caleb broke into a run with Val right behind him.

When they met up, Virgil gasped an explanation, "Turbine. Fell. Bob's trapped. Leg pinned."

"Where?" Caleb asked. Virgil flung his arm back toward the Mill. "Bottom of pipe. Nathaniel's with him."

Minutes later, they stood at the lip of the turbine shaft where a rope ladder plunged into an inky darkness. Virgil grabbed a wind-up flashlight and called for Nathaniel to climb up and out.

The apprentice emerged shaking from a combination of fear and cold. "It's bad, really bad."

Caleb swung himself onto the ladder with Virgil right behind him. At the base of the shaft his worst fears were confirmed. Bob Brazzi's leg was crushed beneath the massive metal turbine. Above them, water gushed into the shaft.

"Gotta stop that water," Caleb said.

Virgil scrambled above, a moment later he called down, "Can't. The sluice gate's busted, and the blade's blocking the outflow." Caleb stood in ankle-deep water. He bent down to examine the Master Tinker. Bob Brazzi was drifting in and out of consciousness, but when he was lucid, he recognized Caleb.

"Glad you're here."

Caleb ran the torchlight across Bob's face. He was near to a ghost, falling into shock. There wasn't much time.

Caleb turned the light onto the wound. Tons of metal had crushed the leg mid-calf, pinning Bob to the base of the shaft. "Virgil, stop that water!"

Virgil cursed, then answered, "The inlet's jammed! It'll take an hour, at least."

Caleb turned the beam back onto the trapped leg.

Bob mumbled, Caleb crouched low straining to hear, "It's so cold."

The Journeyman decided.

"Bob, will you trust me?"

The Master Tinker nodded yes.

"Good, we'll get you out of here."

He called up to his brother, "I need a hacksaw—with the sharpest blade you've got—and a screwdriver," Caleb continued, urgently, "Get Val a coil of rope, fifty feet at least, send her down here with it, and the saw."

The flashlight was fading. Caleb cranked it hard.

He felt the pulse in Bob Brazzi's neck. It was rapid and thin. The cold, the pain, and the loss of blood were driving his patient deeper into shock.

"Bob," Caleb spoke softly, but his voice still echoed wildly inside the narrow metal casing.

The Master Tinker didn't answer. Caleb thought it might be a blessing.

He could hear Virgil yelling orders to Nathaniel. Water still poured into the shaft. It was six inches deep and coming faster.

While Val descended the ladder, Caleb fingered the artery in Bob's neck, pulse 150—too fast. He was losing blood. When she joined him at the bottom of the shaft, Val handed Caleb the hacksaw. He took it and tapped his thumbnail against the serrated edge. Sharp. He looked at Val, "Take off your belt. I need it. Now." Without a word, she unbuckled her fine hand-woven belt and handed it to him. "Hold his head, like this," Caleb demonstrated. The Journeyman wound the belt around the leg. Once it was snug, he slipped the screwdriver between the layers, twisted, and then trapped the handle of the screwdriver in the fabric.

He handed her the flashlight and pointed. "Shine the light. Here."

When Val directed the beam onto Bob Brazzi's pale white leg she understood what Caleb was going to do. Her stomach churned as the Journeyman laid the edge of the blade against the skin. The blade made a low, grunting noise as it bit into flesh. When he reached bone, Caleb doubled his effort. The saw's rasp, amplified by their narrow metal prison, sounded like nails dragged cruelly back and forth across a chalkboard. Val shivered. On the far side of the bone, the flesh of the calf gave way to the saw quickly and silently. Caleb worked quickly, expertly, and without remorse. When the job was done, the Journeyman pulled the freed stump up and away from what remained of the lower leg.

The torchlight did not waver.

Cold water continued to rain down on them. "Val, I'll hold Bob. You've got to weave a sling for him." The water was knee-deep. Her fingers flew through the darkness as she tied one knot, then another, and another, and another. When it was done, she knelt down and plunged the first loop into the bloody water. She worked it up and over the stump of his right leg. Moments later, the harness was secure.

"Climb out with the rope. Virgil'll have a hoist ready, and we'll get Bob out of here."

The water was waist-deep when Caleb felt pressure on the line. Bob swung up and away. When they had him out, Virgil told his brother that he had sent Nathaniel to Bag's End for a buckboard and a fast horse.

Pulse regular, but thin at 170.

Caleb looked at Val. Her fine clothes were stained with blood. He studied her hands, the fingers so long, thin, and nimble. He looked into her hazel eyes. Val returned his gaze, not as a girl, but as a woman. Nothing was said. Nothing needed to be said.

22
THE SPOOF
Spring, 2018

Kianna trudged across the vast open meadow that lay to the east of
Summer Hill. There was snow, but just a couple of inches. The late
winter sun had found strength enough to make the crunchy top crust that
signaled the coming of maple sugar season. She stopped, leaned hard upon
her walking staff, and caught her breath. The west wind suggested that there
would be several more days of cool weather. The sky above was blue as heaven.

Summer Hill lay before her. This was her home. She loved its people,
and they loved her. Val belonged here, too. This midsummer, her daughter
would be Invested as a Journeyman Weaver. Zakia believed that Val carried
the spark of genius, that she was destined to rank among the Shire's greatest
craftsmen. There would be a wedding, too—she was sure of it. Perhaps not
this year or next, but it was inevitable. She knew John would have approved.

Then there was Eron.

Her breath returned to her. She sighed deeply. Her son dangled helplessly
between boyhood and manhood. He failed as her apprentice and retreated to
his room, mired in deep depression. The Shire would always have a place for
him, would always take care of him, but he would never be happy. He had no
place, no standing, no real work, and no friends. There had even been friction
with Caleb. Eron resented his frequent visits to the house and made no secret
of his feelings.

The sun played across the field bringing a thousand icy diamonds to light.
Kianna liked the cold weather, liked to feel the earth at rest, liked the plain
truth that the south wind would come in its proper time, and, along with
the spring rains, revive the world. She felt the numb tingle that plagued her
left leg reassert itself. She needed to move. Even at its best, her gait was stiff
and halting, much worse than it had been last winter. She expected that the
summer would be worse still. Soon she'd be sitting by a fire with her good
friend Jude Thomas. She needed to ask a favor.

Jude made two cups of chamomile tea, sweetening Kianna's with just
enough honey, and returned to a pair of leather chairs perched before a
roaring fire.

Kianna took her mug of tea and inhaled its steamy vapor. "Nice."

"Thought you'd like it," Jude answered.

Kianna took a sip. "The cold's been good for the sugar bush. The sap will run later this week, I'm sure of it."

"Can't come soon enough," Jude said. "When the sap flows, the winter goes." She sat back in her chair. "I'm ready."

"It'll be a busy spring..." Kianna said. She wanted to continue but couldn't.

"How's your leg?" Jude asked.

"Could be better..."

"I'm sorry."

"I'll be OK," Kianna reassured her.

They sat in silence, watching the fire burn down.

Kianna spoke so softly it was hard for Jude to make out the words, "When spring comes, I'll need help, more help..." Then, painfully, she admitted, "I'll need a new apprentice."

"I..." Jude reached out and touched her friend's arm.

"Eron, he can't do it, won't do it, just won't." She looked at Jude, "He's a good boy, despite what happened. He just needs something, something to hold on to. He's got nothing to hold on to, and it scares me."

"Everybody needs that," Jude agreed.

"The thing is," Kianna looked at Jude, urgent, hopeful, "last fall Virgil mentioned to Eron that he could help him. He told him he'd make a GRID station."

Jude leaned close, eager to help, if she could. "Let me guess," she said. "He's been busy and hasn't gotten to it."

Kianna nodded.

"What's a GRID station?" Jude asked.

"I'm not sure exactly. It's some kind of satellite-computer combination—I think."

"Virgil said he'd make one for Eron?" Jude wanted to be sure she understood.

"It was last fall, when Bob Brazzi lost his leg. It was a hard time."

"Virgil gets so wrapped up in his work, he loses track of things," Jude reassured her. "But if he said it, he meant it."

Two days later, Master Tinker Virgil Thomas stood at the Wallace family's back door, his tinker's tool bag slung across his shoulder. He held himself with the easy confidence of one who is the master of his craft.

Kianna welcomed him in, but gave no sign that she knew the nature of his visit.

"Eron around?" he asked.

"Sure," Kianna replied. She called to her son, "Eron!"

When no answer came, Virgil filled the silence. "Just remembered that I told him I'd make a GRID station." He hesitated, passing over his recent conversation with his mother. "Now's a great time to do it."

Kianna nodded, "Wait...wait just a minute." She went to her son's room, pushed the door open, and stuck her head inside. Eron was in bed, as she knew he would be.

"Virgil Thomas is here to see you."

"Tell him I'm busy."

"He says that he promised to make a GRID station for you."

"Yeah, that's what he said," Eron's voice dripped with disgust.

Kianna decided to pull rather than push. "He wants to start right now. But I can see that you're tired. I'll tell him to come back some other time." She started to close the door.

Eron threw back his covers. "Wait!" he cried. "Wait, tell him to wait. I'll be right there."

"OK," Kianna said.

Minutes later, Eron scrambled into the kitchen.

"Hey, Virgil, you really mean it? You'll build it for me?"

"We'll start now."

Eron hesitated. "But you're the one who can build anything—even Bob Brazzi says so."

Virgil smiled. "Maybe so, but I have to know what I'm building, don't I?"

He nodded, uncertainly.

"You've had your ear glued to that old radio, so you must have some idea how this thing is supposed to work."

The smile returned. "I think I do."

"Alright then, I've got two horses tied outside, and we've got a long ride ahead."

"Horses?" Eron flustered. "What do we need horses for? You've got your tinker's bag. Let's just get started."

"Need parts to work with, and the parts we need are in Crickhollow." Kianna had already gathered the cold weather riding gear Eron would need.

"Thanks, Mom," was all he said, but those words, uttered with such rare and careless joy, made her warm all over.

The ride to Crickhollow went much faster than Eron had imagined it would. Virgil was a willing listener, and he was willing to hear what Eron had to say about the GRID. "You see," Eron said, "the GRID figured out how to take care of people. It's not right to just leave people to run around, doing whatever they want. That leads to trouble. Big trouble."

"Like what happened to your Dad," Virgil added.

Eron nodded grimly, "Yeah. Now with the Demos and the GRID stations, people get to be safe and they get to have this whole really exciting world that's inside the GRID station. It's a whole world. That's where people really live now."

"Like the old console games, like they had before the Fall. You mean like that?"

"Oh, no!" Eron protested. "Way better than that. It's not a game, it's life. It's VL; Virtual Life. It's so much better...so much better than...this."

"You want that life?"

"More than anything."

"OK," Virgil said.

They rode in silence for a time then Virgil announced, "Almost there." He turned his horse onto a narrow path which led around the south side of Crickhollow. A stand of hemlocks blocked the cold wind, and the sun peeked between them, thin and high. The Tinker dismounted in front of a cavernous barn with a high gothic arch roof and white-washed board and batten siding.

"Wow," Eron confessed. "I never knew this was here."

"Learn something new everyday," Virgil answered. It was one of Bob Brazzi's favorite sayings, and the old man meant for it to be followed literally.

Once the horses were settled, Virgil led Eron inside. The contents took his breath away. Even in the dim light, he could see row upon row of neatly stacked electronic equipment: computers, amplifiers, video game consoles, HDVD players, CRTs, LCDs—it had everything. He walked slowly, carefully, worshipfully along the aisles. The shelves were jammed with bushel baskets heaped with cell phones, PDAs, assorted electronic gadgets, some of which not even Eron recognized.

"It's beautiful. It's all so beautiful," Eron whispered.

"I guess," Virgil answered. "Not much use though. I'd rather have motors, circuit breakers, pumps. This stuff is actually pretty useless."

Eron felt he had entered into a holy place.

Virgil was already at work, muttering as he went, "...Satellite transceiver...

need a dish and a box...internet...had a G5...controller, power source maybe 60 watts...solar panel...battery, 16 gauge cables..." The acolyte followed the Master at a respectful distance.

By the time they set out for home, the daylight was failing and their saddlebags bulged with salvaged electronic gear. The wind had veered to the west and they rode into its teeth. Eron didn't care. This was like his birthday, his last real birthday when he still lived in Chicago, when life was good.

It took Virgil longer than he expected to make it work. During those two weeks, the sap had run, been boiled off, and the year's harvest of maple syrup put away. When the GRID station was ready, he showed Eron how it worked. "It's crazy really. The data comes from outer space to the dish by the window there." Virgil pointed unnecessarily. Eron absorbed every detail of the installation. "It's something like the old Internet—from before the Fall, but way faster."

Virgil flicked a switch, and a pair of taupe boxes whirred to life. Eron bit his lip with anxious anticipation. The screen presented them with an eerie green blinking cursor.

"That's stupid. That's no fun."

"Yeah, well, you can't get in through the front door, so to speak. It's locked." Virgil stared at Eron. "You're not really part of the GRID so you have to come in through the back door." He waited to see if this was a problem.

It was not.

Virgil keyed in a complicated series of commands. "It's a spoof. You're fooling the GRID into thinking that you belong. I wrote it all down for you." A beep signaled that the door was open. The screen came to life and revealed a cityscape that looked as real as a picture. In fact, it was a three dimensional computer generated image, an idealized image of the real New York City. "You live here, in this city," Virgil laughed. "Actually you live here in Summer Hill, but the GRID thinks you live in this fake city."

It all looked real, beautifully real to Eron.

"I set up an avatar for you..." Eron didn't know the word. "You know, a game character, like in the old console games, from before the Fall." Again, Virgil's fingers pounded the keyboard. This time, the image of a young man, who looked very much like the real Eron, materialized on the screen. The avatar nodded at them, giving the eerie impression that it recognized its human counterpart. Virgil stood up and laid his hand on the shoulder of the flesh and blood Eron Wallace. "You're smart. You'll figure out the rest."

"Thank you." Eron breathed the words as if they were a prayer. Gratitude flooded his senses, and he would have expressed himself more fully if he'd been able to take his eyes off from the virtual world that shimmered across the screen.

"Right. OK, then." Virgil wandered into the kitchen where Caleb, Val, and Kianna sat talking. The first warm breeze of spring filtered through an open window.

"Well?" Kianna asked.

The Tinker shrugged his shoulders, "It works. He loves it. I've never seen him so happy."

Kianna closed her eyes and offered silent thanks.

"Way to go, brother." Caleb flashed Virgil a thumbs up.

"I had fun," Virgil admitted, "but it's time to get back to the real world."

Caleb stood up, "Yeah, me too. I'll go with you." He looked at Val, so beautiful in the sunlight. "Be back soon." The words were meant for her alone.

That evening Caleb returned to the Wallace house. Eron took time away from his GRID station to share dinner with them. He dominated the conversation with animated descriptions of his virtual exploits. "I took the L train and it was packed. I went all the way to Coney Island. I'm gonna ride the rides when I get some money. It's so great, you should come with me. You should all come with me!" After apples and cheese, he retreated to his room. Caleb asked Val to join him for a walk on the Turnpike.

In the morning Kianna woke to the sound of rain. It was a cold rain. She could tell by the sound it made on the window. A blustering wind whipped the budded branches into a frenzy. She lay still and warm in her comfortable bed and remembered the night they slept in the open, beneath just such a rain. It was April 19, 2021, six years to the day had passed since she met Jude Thomas, since they stumbled into a new life among the Tribes of Eden.

23
FLYPAPER

To: Bradley Long, Assistant Deputy Director, Office of Strategic Initiatives
From: Morton Davis, Section Chief, Academy Candidate Identification Service
Re: DSJ Agent Simulation Program (ASP)
Date: December 23, 2021

As you know, ASP was released into the GRID environment fourteen months ago. The staff has completed the first annual review of the program (code named "Flypaper") and can offer the following conclusions and recommendations:
1. Utilization remains far below projections. Non-returning ASP users have generated remarkably similar comments (e.g. "boring, stupid, goody-two-shoes, lame"), which indicate a need to update the interface and enrich the game play feature set. Find attached our request for a 15,000 programmer hour allocation for this upgrade.
2. Our relatively small group of habitual users has yielded one truly extraordinary candidate for the DSJ Academy. Our team has carefully analyzed this user's profile. He scores in the 99th percentile on all primary indices and shows remarkable cunning in his interactions with the program environment. We think this user's ACP account should be transferred into your direct management portfolio.
Please advise when a determination has been made in the case cited above and we will respond accordingly.
Cc: Intra-Agency Resource Allocation Council.

Eron Wallace walked south along 5th Avenue. It was another beautiful day in the city. He crossed to the Avenue's east side at 64th street. These were his favorite shops. He was on his way to work but still had time for some window shopping. The spring menswear collections were on display, and they were fantastic. There were fine Italian suits, tailored just so, shining black wingtips, and neckties exploding with color, with power, with wealth.

Everything was so expensive, but the day would come—he knew it would come—when he would be able to buy anything he wanted. It was a strange painful ritual, this habit window-shopping on the way to work. He wanted what he could not have. He wanted it so badly it made his heart ache. He decided that the pain was a good thing. The pain drove him harder.

He lingered longer than he should have at the shop windows and was now running late. He hurried down to 48th street between 5th and 6th avenues, to a narrow alley that ran between the Algonquin Hotel and the Yacht Club. He looked over his shoulder to make sure he wasn't being followed then slipped into it. It was a dead-end no more than eight feet wide with dull red brick walls reaching skyward on three sides. He walked to the end of the alley, and stood, his face just feet from the wall.

An unseen hand scribbled a written question on the brick:
WHENEVER YOU TAKE ONE, YOU LEAVE ONE BEHIND.

Eron knew from hard experience that, somewhere, a timer was counting down the seconds. This was the worst part. If he didn't answer correctly, the question would disappear, and he would have to wait another 24 hours for his next chance to be admitted. "Take one, leave one behind..." He found the answer.

A step.

A door appeared before him. He thumbed the lock, and it swung open. His office was a perfect shining semicircle, the front wall, a stunning 180-degree arc filled floor to ceiling with flickering LCD screens. Each showed a different slice of city life. Dominating the middle of the room was a sleek black command chair. Eron's touch brought its bristling speakers, buttons, keys, and levers to life.

He scanned the gleaming wall, left to right. Nothing happening. He could change that. He would change that. He could make the cameras go anywhere he wanted.

Anywhere.

He decided to pay a visit to the city college's women's locker room and began entering the necessary commands when the collage of moving images disappeared. The glowering visage of the Director of the Department of Security and Justice took their place. Heavily jowled with wirebrush eyebrows and an intense, beetle-like gaze, the Director commanded Eron's complete attention.

"Wallace," he snarled. "We've got a problem."

"Yes, sir." Eron answered reflexively.

"There's been a network security breach in sector four. An unauthorized user is accessing J-9 level domains." The Director went on to sketch the details of the breach.

Eron felt sick. This was about spoofing, his spoof, his back door into the GRID.

"Well, Wallace?" The Director glowered at Eron.

"Ah, um."

The Director upped the ante, "A hundred thousand Virtual Life points if you can solve this for me." It was ten times the points he had on account.

Eron's body shook. One. Hundred. Thousand. Points. If he explained how it was done, he would be rich. If he told the Director what he knew, he might well find his own private back door closed to him—forever. He agonized, stalled for time.

"I'm not sure, sir." He was a balloon leaking air. "Maybe," he paused, "maybe it's a stolen password cache."

The Director did not hide his disappointment. "That's ridiculous, Wallace. Wrong answer." Then, most hurtfully, "I had faith in you Wallace, but this..."

The screen flipped off and the room went dark. Slowly, the scenes from around the city blinked back to life. Eron thought that he might vomit. He had to get away, far away.

Eron gasped and lifted his hands from the controller. He tore his eyes from the screen. It was over. He was home. He was in his room. The windows were dark. It was dark outside. There was snow.

His mother called to him, her voice so full of love. Eron staggered to the door.

"Coming, Mom."

Gradually, he recalled that this was the night of the Midwinter feast—February 2, 2022. He struggled to compose himself, afraid that his ragged state would make his mother worry. She worried too much.

"You OK?" She asked.

"Yeah, fine, Mom," he lied.

Kianna chirped, "The Thomas' are bringing the sleigh over to pick me up. We're going for a ride and then to the feast."

"Can I come with you?"

Kianna stopped what she was doing, turned and looked at her son. She asked, carefully, "You sure that you're OK?"

"Doing great," Eron answered without conviction.

"Get some warm clothes on," she prompted. "They'll be here soon."

He answered her with a smile.

Jingle bells draped over the horse harnesses announced the arrival of the Thomas family sleigh. Val had gone ahead with Caleb in a shiny little one-horse cutter he borrowed for the occasion. Kianna and Eron climbed aboard.

Bill greeted Kianna's son cheerfully. "Good to see you, Mr. Wallace."

The air was calm, and fluffy flakes drifted down from above. Eron settled into the seat close to his mother. It felt good to be next to her. She draped a heavy wool blanket over their laps, and then tucked it up under their chins. The stone Kianna had been heating on the stove sat on the sleigh's floor. Its warmth rose to greet them. A hidden moon peaked from between the clouds.

"Ready back there?" Bill asked.

"Ready," Kianna answered.

The horses started with a jerk and they were off.

Bill called back to them, "Gonna stop at the falls before the Festival."

They passed over Summer Hill's snow-covered Green then down the hill and onto the Turnpike. They turned west, swept past Bag's End, Frogmorton, Bywater, and then traced the edge of Mad Brook. A cast iron footbridge— people said it was built in the 1800s—spanned the gorge below the falls. Bill tied the horses to a hitching post and walked out onto the bridge. Below them, scattered beams of moonlight played across the jagged edges of the frozen waterfall.

The hubbub within the Pavilion depressed Eron from the start. The air hung heavy with the cloying twitter of laughter and greetings. "How are you? How are you? How are you?" Eron shambled round the edge of the gathering, watching as people bartered trinkets among themselves. Then came that awful, screeching music. He turned his back as Zach Thomas hammered on his guitar, and then stumbled unexpectedly into his sister. She was in the arms of Caleb Thomas. The sight of them together pierced him unexpectedly. Her eyes were closed, she was in love—even Eron could see that.

Her love seemed deeply disloyal. She was his sister. She was his twin. She had cast him, her own brother, aside and taken up with a jerk. It was wrong. Eron suddenly felt certain that his father would not have approved of the relationship. Anger rising, he decided to confront her. Around him, the music built to a furious height. It took hold of the crowd, making it pulse with energy. Eron touched Val on the shoulder. She turned and smiled at the sight of her brother.

"Eron! I didn't think you'd come!" She yelled.

"Yeah, you didn't ask me to come, did you?"

The music crashed to its conclusion. Eron lowered his voice. "Val," he said, "I'm kinda tired. You want to walk home with me?"

Val's eyes sparkled under the Pavilion lights. "But the storytelling is next. Don't you want to hear the story?"

Eron clenched and unclenched his fists. "Who wants to listen to some stupid old crone?" he snarled. "I want you to walk home with me."

Sensing a change in the tone of the conversation, Caleb stepped in. "Hey, Eron..."

"You stay out of this. This is between me and my sister."

"I'd love to walk home with you, Eron, but I don't want to leave until after the story."

"I want to leave now," Eron snarled.

"She's not ready to go," Caleb said. "cool off man, enjoy the party. What's the rush? You know what I mean?"

"You're choosing him over me?"

Val was insulted, "Eron, come on."

"You can't lie to me. It's true, and you know it."

The old woman's prattle drew Val's attention, and she turned toward the stage. The conversation had ended. Disgusted, Eron plunged into the crowd. He had to escape, to get away, to be free of them.

"You need to go after him?" Caleb asked.

"No, he just needs to cool off. I'll talk to him in the morning."

"You sure?"

"Yeah."

Outside, it was lonely, dark, and cold. Hands shoved deep into his coat's big woolen pockets, he trudged home alone. Eron Wallace was certain, in the way that only the young can be, that all was lost, that his long journey through darkness would never end.

Jude opened a velvet-clad box and withdrew the gold band that had laid so long inside. "My Dad got it in Marrakech, during the Second World War. He gave a pack of cigarettes for it. The man told him it came from Timbuktu, told him it was good luck."

Caleb looked dubious. "If it's such good luck, why'd the guy trade it away?"

She mussed his hair, "You are too much like your father. All I know is that my Dad wore it on a chain with his dog tags all the way to Berlin."

Caleb took it from his mother's hand and held it up to the light. It was inscribed with ancient and now indecipherable runes. Whatever their meaning, they formed a beautiful flowing circle. His mother continued, "It was Grandma's wedding ring and she wore it til the day she died. She wanted me to have it, but I could never bring myself to wear it. I think…Val might like it." He turned it over and over, admiring the flawless craftsmanship.

"They had a good, long marriage."

"Yeah, Mom, it's great. She'll love it."

"When are you going to ask her?"

"Tonight. I'll ask her tonight."

In September, the Tribes of Eden came to Summer Hill for the wedding and assembled under tents pitched on the Green. Slate gray clouds rolled in from the north carrying with them a foretaste of the cold that lay ahead, but no one minded. The people gave their full attention to Caleb and Val. They poured out affection, joy, and hope as if these things came from a jar with no bottom. They ate and danced and sang. They filled the very air the couple breathed with the purest form of *dohavekee*, of connectedness, of belonging.

After the ceremony, Val searched the crowd for Eron. He was supposed to be there for his sister.

Caleb found Virgil. "Have you seen Eron?" His brother shrugged, "Nope."

"Val's worried. See if you can find him."

Virgil nodded. They both knew where he needed to look.

He strode across the Green picking his way between old friends and cries of, "Virgil! Have a beer with us!" He walked into the Wallace home and went straight to Eron's room, found him glued to the screen, game controller in hand.

"Hey, Eron."

"Huh."

"Come on, man, let's go." Eron didn't budge. Virgil enticed him, "We just tapped a fresh keg. Its great stuff. The party is on."

"Mmm hmm."

"Everybody's asking about you. People want you to be there."

"Bullshit," Eron spat the word without diverting any of his attention from the screen. Virgil tried the truth, "Val misses you. She wants to see you."

"Tell her I'm coming." His face contorted with effort, but his voice was empty.

Virgil stepped between Eron and the screen.

"Get out of my way." the words carried a threat.

Virgil reached behind the screen and flicked the power switch. The screen went black.

Eron dropped his controller and lunged at Virgil. He crashed into him, knocking the GRID station off its stand. "You basard!" Virgil broke Eron's grip, spun behind the crazed man, and pinned his arms to his side. Eron struggled ferociously kicking, twisting, and howling in vain. The rage faded as quickly as it had come. He began to sob, and Virgil released his grip.

"Come on," the older man said. "You'll feel better when you see Val. When you see how happy she is."

"No," Eron said.

"Forget the box, Eron," Virgil nodded at the scattered components. "You know I'll fix the damn thing for you."

"I was winning and now I lost. Now I'm a loser. Because of you!"

Virgil held up his hands. "Hey, look, I'm trying to help you do the right thing. Your sister, your twin sister got married today. She needs you. Your Mom needs you."

"Screw you."

Virgil returned to the wedding tents—alone. Val and Kianna would be disappointed, but not surprised. He took his place in the circle that had formed in honor of the newlyweds. Bob Brazzi was in the center, with them, a tankard of beer held high. He was doing a jig in their honor, dancing on a wooden leg of his own design.

25
ZEROED OUT
Spring, 2024

The GRID station froze and Eron cursed. It was a piece of crap. He punched the reset button. Nothing. He rebooted. The screen came to life but in place of the GRID's virtual world was a sickening blue screen. He was being accused of crime, GRID crime.

A message box appeared:

The holder of this account has been convicted of felony GRID Lottery fraud. The adjudicated sanctioned penalty is a zeroed balance. Current balance: 465,847,319 VL Points.

Eron gasped as the numbers raced relentlessly backward. It was like watching one's home burn to the ground. He felt sick. His VL car, his VL clothes, his VL apartment, his VL powers—he was losing everything. When it was over, the screen read:

000,000,000 VL Points.

The screen blinked again and presented him a question and a text box:

Does this convicted user wish to make a statement?

Eron let his fingers race across the keyboard. "You've made a mistake. I have committed no crime. I swear that I am innocent."
He clicked the button marked "Submit."
Again, the blue screen flickered.

Do you wish to formally challenge the moral authority of the GRID?

YES   NO

There was a war inside Eron's head. The truth was that he was innocent. The truth wasn't what mattered at the moment. The GRID demanded obedience, worshipped authority, thrived on order and control. If he challenged his conviction he would, he knew, become a perennial suspect, a pariah, the object of unrelenting suspicion and scorn.

Eron closed his eyes. He clicked the button labeled "No."

The hard drives inside his jerry-rigged GRID station thrashed for ten long minutes. When it was over, another message box appeared:

Penalty complete. User may now rejoin GRID Society.

Eron staggered out of his room and vomited.

When his stomach was empty, he returned to the GRID station, determined to regain every bit of his lost fortune. Nothing would stand in his way. He would work until he got it all back.

Weeks.

100,000 VL points.

Months.

500,000 VL points.

A year and a half later, he had amassed eight-hundred million points.

To: Bradley Long, Assistant Deputy Director, Office of Strategic Initiatives
From: Section Chief Morton Davis
Re: Elite Candidate Loyalty Test
Date: May 14, 2025
Subject E. W. has recovered and has now exceeded pre-test VL status with no sign of resentment or cynicism. Loyalty is confirmed.

Assistant Deputy Director Long was pleased. He tapped the connect, "Hey Mort, got your note on Wallace. Looks good. Let him run his total up to a billion, then bring him in. He's ready."

26
BIRTH DAY
Summer, 2025

In the fall of the second year of Val and Caleb's marriage, Val became pregnant. By spring, Val had taken the aspect of a ripening pear, sweet, soft, and round. When summer reached its height, she and Caleb left their home in Frogmorton, went to Summer Hill, and settled into Bill and Jude's house.

Her water broke on the night of the full moon and it ran clear and plentiful. Contractions rolled across her belly as if they were waves falling against a warm, sandy shore. Caleb had attended many births, but this was his first as a father to be. It was hard, much harder than he'd expected. Bill murmured a comforting stream of reassurance. "She's alright and so are you." Kianna arrived at the house before dawn, her gait painfully slow, her mood ecstatic. Haleigh and Hannah, Zachary and Sadie, and Virgil and Chloe were there too. Only Eron was missing.

Bill laid his hands on Val's abdomen. The baby was coming head first. That was good. The contractions came every two minutes, then once a minute. At daylight, Val needed to push. Slowly, the baby descended. The head crowned. Bill ran his fingers across the thick dark hair and told Val that he was sure the baby would be a girl.

And it was.

Val and Caleb agreed to name her Emma, after the wise woman of Kallimos, the one who had led the people to lasting peace. It was a good strong name. The baby suckled at her mother's breast, then slept.

Downstairs, the families made ready to welcome the baby girl into their midst. Breakfast was laid out on the worn oak table. Birdsong floated through the open windows. Outside, the grass, tall and emerald green, reached for the sun. The earth seemed eager to embrace this new life. At noon, Caleb helped Val down the stairs so that they could present their daughter properly. She was received with the love and honor due to a precious living jewel. When it was done, Val rested in a big leather chair, her feet propped on an ottoman, her baby asleep on her chest.

When the conversation lapsed, Val asked, "Where's Eron?"

Kianna reassured her, "He's coming, don't worry."

Bill urged a bottle of homebrew beer on the new mother. "It'll help Emma bring the milk down."

The families were clearing the noon meal away when an ecstatic Eron burst into the house. "The best most fantastic, most amazing thing has happened!"

"Yes, it has!" Kianna agreed. "You are an uncle. You have a baby niece. Her name is Emma!"

Eron did not to let this announcement intrude upon his own profound pleasure. "I made it. I've done it. I've come back. All the way back. I am," he raised both fists high over his head and roared, "I am a billionaire! I have a billion GRID points. You are looking at a rich man!"

The outburst flustered Kianna, made her feel ashamed, but she chose to play along with her son. "That's great, Eron. Now we have two things to celebrate: Emma's birthday and your...success."

"There's more, huge news, fantastic news! I am so young, so damn good that the Department of Security and Justice has recruited me. Me! I'm going to be an agent, a special secret agent. The Section Chief himself wants me to come to headquarters in New York City, the real New York City."

Emma slept at her mother's breast, blissfully unaware of what was happening.

Jude ventured, "Congratulations, Eron."

All eyes were on him. It was only right, he thought. I'm bigger than all of them now, bigger than all of them put together. "They say that I can bring my family with me." He was flying, soaring terribly close to the sun. He looked at his mother and sister, blind to the astonishment on their faces, "We get to leave this stinking hell hole. I can take you both with me. We can finally have a real home in a civilized place."

No one had ever seen this man so happy, so alive.

"Eron, honey," his mother pleaded. "This is home, we are home. Our friends are here, your sister..." She swallowed hard. "Your sister is married and she has a baby. Their place and my place is here."

Eron wobbled. "Please, Mom, I did this for you. In New York, you can get a real doctor for your legs. You won't have to make do with," he glared at Caleb, "that witch doctor."

Caleb checked his anger.

Kianna leaned hard on the table. "We'll talk more about your success later. I'm very happy Eron, very happy for you."

"Like hell we will." His face paled then turned hard. They were doing it again, cutting him down, telling him that he was a failure. He wasn't going to let them do that, not again, not ever again.

He stabbed his finger at Jude. "It's her fault. She tricked you, Mom. She's been lying to you from the very beginning. The whole Kallimos thing, it's a big lie. She kept us here, made us prisoners." Pride and anger raced round his fevered brain driving him farther, much farther than he ever should have gone. "You!" He screamed at Jude Thomas, "You...bitch!"

Those words kicked over the beehive. Virgil rushed Eron, but Zach caught him from behind and held him off. Bill stepped in front of Caleb and roared, "Stop!"

Emma stirred but did not wake. Bill addressed Eron in a voice low and easy. "I know that this is hard for you, but your mother is right. It's a big day, for all of us. Everybody's all tensed up. Let's just relax, talk things over. There's no need to get upset."

Eron clenched his fists and screamed, "Bullshit! This is bullshit! I'm leaving, and you can't stop me. I'm meeting a DSJ convoy today. Today! Down in the valley. They're coming for me." He begged his mother and sister, "We need to go. Mom, Val come on, we've got to go. Please, Mom. Please come with me."

No one moved.

His weakness shamed him, and he withdrew his plea with snarling cynicism, "So that's how it is? My own family turned against me by a pack of stinking hobbits. Fine, then, I'm going. And you two," he glared at Kianna and Val, "can come crawling back to me when you come to your senses. The GRID will know where I am."

He stormed out of the house slamming the front door so hard that it woke the baby. Kianna wanted to follow him, to hold her boy close, to whisper her mother's love into his ear, but she did not move. Neither did anyone else. Someone coughed. Feet shuffled.

Hannah retrieved the egg basket from its place in the pantry. She held it out and asked her brother, "Caleb, would you go to the henhouse? We need at least a dozen eggs."

"Sure, Hannah." Caleb slipped out the back door and the spell was broken.

Over dinner, Val declared this to be one of Eron's tantrums. She expected that he would return home before dark and that Kianna would find him plopped in front of the screen. The game, that was the thing, it was a Virtual

Life—self-contained, completely detached from the real world. The unreality was actually the thing he liked best about it. It was a world unto itself, a world designed and managed by the GRID. It was the Virtual Life of the GRID that had amplified Eron's anger and vengefulness. After dinner, the conversation slowly turned to what could be done, what should be done.

Kianna confessed, "I've tried every thing I know how to do. He just...he just..." She paused and looked away.

"Tell them, Mom," Val insisted. "Tell them what happened."

Kianna stifled a sob. "Last year something changed. I could see that the game was taking him over, making him crazy. I hid the cables for his GRID station and..." Kianna buried her face in her hands and fought for the courage she needed to finish the story. "The things he said, they were terrible. He went back to his room. I thought it was over. He was so quiet. I went to check on him and..." The pain of the memory overwhelmed her, she slumped forward in her chair unable to continue.

Val finished for her, "Mom found Eron hanging by the neck. She got him down. After that, he stayed in bed for a week. When he could talk again, he made Mom promise that she would never do it again, never take the GRID away from him."

"Kianna, I wish we'd known. Maybe we could have helped," Jude said.

"I couldn't..."

"It makes me sick. I built the damn thing for him," Virgil said.

"You couldn't have known, nobody could have," Kianna said. "It wasn't a machine to him, it was a drug. The GRID, it took his soul, it changed him into..."

"We've got to help him," Jude said, "however we can, but there are others, so many others, millions of others out there. We've got to help them, too."

Virgil disagreed, "There's nothing you can do, Mom. The GRID's too big, it's everywhere. It's taken over everything out there. Everything."

As usual, Bill saw it Jude's way. "We'll use Eron's rig to get in touch with our old friends—our Eden friends—from the years before the Fall. They won't like this any better than we do."

"Won't work, Dad," Virgil shook his head dismissively. "Eron and I talked about this quite a bit. There are software robots that crawl all over the GRID, 24/7. Everything goes through it and everything gets analyzed. It's the government, businesses, the military, the police, the banks—it's everything from before the Fall—all rolled up into one thing."

"Screw 'em," Bill said.

"Dad!" Virgil was exasperated. "The GRID is mean as hell. It comes down hard on people who make even the tiniest peep of protest. It crushes them. This isn't like the old days when you and Mom and Ned went after the nursing home industry. This is serious. They own the army, the courts, the prisons. Eron says the GRID even owns the Shire. We need to stay as far away from it as we can get."

"No!" The word echoed off the stone walls. Jude began to pace. "We can't hide from it. I just have to believe other mothers, other children are getting hurt. We cannot stand by and let it...let it take over the world and think that someday it won't come for us."

"OK." Caleb asked, "What do we do?"

"We start by getting a message to Ned Wolff," Jude answered. "He was there when we started the Eden Alternative, we need to know what he thinks."

"But how?" Bill asked.

Zach volunteered, "I'll bet he's still at Cornell. I'll go and see him—see what he has to say about all this."

"The roads are closed, Zach," Virgil reminded his brother. "GRID traffic only."

"Who said anything about roads?" Zach smiled.

"You guys," Caleb said. "It's 70 miles to Ithaca, at least."

"Probably more like 80," Virgil added.

Kianna shook her head. "You don't know what it's like out there. Don't even think of it."

Jude raised her head, "What's your idea, Zach?"

"All I need is a topo map and a compass and I can stay on the high ground all the way to Ithaca."

"Yeah, but it's still a long ways," Caleb said. "Like I said, 140 miles round trip off-road. It would take weeks. Ugh."

Zach enjoyed the spotlight. "I'll ride. I can be there in two days on horseback."

Bill leaned back against the sink, arms folded, brow furrowed. "Couple of things," he said. "First, I'll send you with a letter—a post that outlines what we're thinking."

Bill's eyes darted toward Zach. "No offense," he said.

"None taken," Zach replied with a smile.

Bill continued, "The second thing is that this isn't a trip anyone should make alone. There are too many unknowns. You'll need a partner."

"I'll go," Virgil volunteered. "I feel bad about what happened to Eron and Mom's right—we've got to do something. I'm in."

"Me too," Caleb stood up.

Jude smiled at her youngest son. "I know you want to go but your place is here with Val and Emma. You know that."

Caleb looked at Val and his precious baby girl then mumbled his concession.

"We'll have to ride at night and hide during the day," Virgil said. "The GRID's got eyes in the sky, satellites linked to computers that monitor the movement of people in and around the Demos. Eron showed me the pictures. At night, those satellites are blind."

"Yeah, that's good," Bill agreed.

"There's something else," Virgil insisted. "We'll need guns. I'll bet I can find a few somewhere in the Shire, if not I'll make us some."

"No," Jude said.

"Mom," Zach insisted, "we're gonna need to protect ourselves."

"No," Jude remained firm. "Guns will get you killed."

"She's right, boys," Bill said. "Your best bet is to travel light and fast, under the cover of darkness. Just take the post, it has value for only one person—Ned Wolff. You won't have anything anyone else would want." There was finality in Bill's voice.

"When?" Zach asked.

"Two days," Haleigh said. "The moon will be in its first quarter."

PART III

27
THE CITY

E ron crashed blindly into a thicket of shadbush and brambles. He was running downhill, out of the Shire. Whip-thin branches lashed his face while barbed thorns tore at his skin and his clothes. Fury drove him forward. He tumbled into a clearing and let fatigue own him. He lay face down on the warm, damp earth. His own mother, his sister, his family, had turned against him, had chosen them, over him.

When the pain ebbed, he continued his journey. It was already late; the sun was riding low in the western sky. The convoy would be coming up from the south, looking for him, and he still had not found old route 12. Eron picked his way through the overgrown ruins of a village. He guessed that it was Sherburne, hoped he was right. He stumbled onto the village's main intersection. Roofless, windowless brick buildings stood on three of the corners. On the fourth, a gray marble monument, built to honor the men who fought in the Civil War, lay on its side, broken and helpless. He turned south.

When the sun touched the horizon, Eron began to worry. The soles of his feet were paved with blisters. If he missed the convoy he would have to go back—and he would never go back. The sun was nearly down when he heard the sound, so beautifully dull and predictable, so completely unnatural. The convoy's single musical note gained strength. They were coming for him. They were coming to save him. Eron stopped walking and stood in the middle of the highway. He stared at the cracked, ash-gray pavement, waiting for his deliverance.

The convoy hissed to a stop. A metallic voice, bullhorn thin, vaulted over the rumble of the engines. "Identify yourself."

"My name is Eron Wallace."

An officer, dressed in a tight fitting black tunic, with a white bear paw insignia over the left breast swung down out of the purring vehicle. Eron's eyes went instantly to the man's right hip. A chrome pistol was holstered there. He was Corporate Militia. The Lieutenant was young, not much older than Eron himself.

"It's an honor, Mr. Wallace. A real honor." He shook Eron's bloodied hand, "You had us worried. We've never been..." He glanced warily at the night's gathering gloom. "Never been this far off...off the GRID before." Eron nodded, unsure what should or shouldn't be said. "Well then, let's get started." The lieutenant escorted him to a stretched military-style limousine. Inside, he washed the blood from his hands and face with pre-moistened, individual plastic-wrapped towlettes. He pried the lids off food containers labeled "Cheeseburger," "Fries," "Pizza," and "Filet Mignon." Each contained a brightly colored, almost neon, paste that smelled and tasted precisely as advertised.

A full belly and the roar of the engines joined with the deep fatigue that was a residue of the day's intense emotions and exertions. His eyes grew heavy. He pressed a button in the armrest, reclined his seat, and was soon asleep.

His convoy crawled to a stop and Eron woke with a start. It was early morning. Eron sat up straight and peered hungrily out of the smoked glass windows. Ahead and to the right, across a wide gray river lay the real New York City. Its buildings stood straight and tall, as if challenging the sky. There was no confusion, no jumbled disorder. This was glass and steel made to obey the will of men. Eron shifted his gaze. Straight ahead, the western approach of the George Washington Bridge opened invitingly before him. He caught snatches of the conversation between the kindly lieutenant and the bridge's master of the guard.

"He's a VIP. DSJ business—Deputy Director level authorization."

"I've still got to thumb him."

"No, you don't." The lieutenant lowered his voice menacingly, "Academy." The word ended the conversation. Moments later, the convoy passed the checkpoint.

Eron rode across the Hudson River and into the city that was the basis for the virtual city in which his avatar lived. The convoy commanded the middle of real streets and avenues, blasting through intersections, sirens blaring. Broadway flashed by, then they turned east onto the real 48th street, then down 5th avenue, another manic turn, this time onto 32nd street. Buildings, people, vehicles rushed past, all of them thrillingly real. When the convoy ground to a halt, they were within sight of the East River.

The lieutenant leapt to open the door for Eron and stood aside as his guest stepped clumsily onto the broad city sidewalk. The officer saluted and Eron, not knowing what else to do, made an awkward return salute. "It's been an honor sir. Best of luck at the Academy."

Eron mumbled a few words of gratitude before a smartly uniformed doorman interrupted, "Bags, sir?"

The lieutenant responded protectively, "No bags."

Eron followed the doorman into an ornate lobby that swelled overhead like the vault of a limestone cavern. Eron tipped his head back and studied its inlaid ceiling, simultaneously admiring the intricate detailing and hating this display of a bumpkin's curiosity. He pulled his gaze back down and snorted with contempt. The Shire's Pavilion would easily fit into this single space.

A tap on his shoulder startled him. "Eron Wallace?" He turned, a petite woman stood before him. Straw-colored hair fell to her shoulders in a jangle of ringlet curls. She wore makeup, bright red lipstick, and, Eron breathed in softly, there was perfume. Her thin white blouse highlighted a buxom figure. A black pencil skirt ended just above her knees, though a slit on the right side rose considerably higher. A shimmering silver necklace plunged suggestively out of sight.

She looked up at him and repeated her question, "Are you Eron Wallace?"

He answered carefully, "Yes."

She smiled, flashing teeth white and straight. "Wonderful! My name is Traci," she paused to make a tick mark on her clipboard computer. He smiled at her, still uncertain.

"You're younger than the others."

"Is that bad?"

"Not at all. I think it's great."

"Good."

"Let's get started." As she led him across the lobby, he could hear the swish of her stockings and the clicking of her high heels on marble. They reached a bank of brass-trimmed elevator doors along the far wall. She touched a button and a pair of doors slid open. Eron hesitated, wishing his mother and sister were with him.

"Come on in," Traci winked. "I won't bite."

She pushed the button for the 55th floor. "It's Academy housing. Very nice."

The doors closed, and the cab shot upward. Traci chatted amiably while Eron stared numbly at the GRID station that flashed silently in front of him. On the appointed floor he stepped out of the cab and into the hallway. Traci smiled. "I picked out your apartment myself. The view of the city from your balcony is stunning."

Beside a bone-white door, an LCD screen glowed bright blue. Traci laid her thumb against it, and the lock snapped open. Inside, a wave of recognition staggered him. This was his apartment, the one he had furnished so carefully inside the GRID. Everything was modern, clean, simple, pure. The walls had been painted a blinding shade of white, and the intense cool light cast by the overhead halogen lamps made them glow. The furniture was spare, utilitarian, all chrome, glass, and synthetic fabric. The smell was new. Everything was new. A small sitting room led into a galley kitchen furnished with a digital food paste re-heater, a disposal, and a small sink. The floor was polished to a mirror finish. The work compartment contained a sleek titanium GRID station complete with a flat screen as big as the sky.

"I must say, you do have excellent taste, Mr. Wallace," Traci murmured. "Let me show you your bedroom."

She pushed the door open and went directly to a pair of accordion doors, "Your wardrobe is here." With a flourish, she revealed the interior of a walk-in closet filled with the real world counter parts of Eron's VL wardrobe.

He stood and stared then reached out and ran his fingers over the beautiful synthetic fabric. Behind him, Traci reclined casually on Eron's king sized bed.

"You've had a long journey."

He turned to face her.

"Must be tired, so much excitement."

Eron shrugged his shoulders.

"Can I make you more comfortable?"

"No, I don't think so."

Traci got up. Got close, so close he could feel her soft, warm breath on his skin. She laid her hands on his shoulders and whispered, "Mmm hmm..."

Eron stepped back.

"You don't start til tomorrow." She rubbed herself gently up against the young man.

Eron stammered, "I don't know you. I...I don't trust you."

"But, Eron..."

Then, more forcefully, "I want you to leave."

Traci backed away, pouting"Fine then, if that's how you want it." She plucked the clipboard computer from the bed and stormed out, slamming the door behind her.

His deliverance was complete.

Eron Wallace flopped face down onto the vast white coverlet and sobbed uncontrollably, so great was his joy.

28
A STORM IN THE DISTANCE

A fleet of thunderheads sailed above Summer Hill the night after Emma was born, soaking the land with much needed rain. In the morning, the earth smelled fresh and clean. Kianna let people know that Eron was gone. Caleb and Val entered into parenthood, sleeping when Emma slept. They woke in the afternoon and lay three abreast on a bedspread that Val had woven when she was a Journeyman. A summer breeze entered through an open window and caressed them.

Bill and Jude sat on the porch in the back of the house and remembered the old days, back before the Fall. Ned Wolff had been one of the first to hear about the Eden Alternative. He came to Summer Hill when there was just one house: theirs. He wanted to learn. It was the spring of '92. He'd been a stubborn cuss right from the start. He challenged every idea, demanded every proof, and was gradually convinced that a Kallimos-inspired nursing home revolution was feasible.

Ned returned to his native Texas and put the ideals of Kallimos to work. He made a new world for the people who lived and worked in the nursing home he ran there. He saw the wisdom of making a community that had the power to restore honor to Elders and those called to care for Elders. Years later, when the Eden Alternative had grown bigger than what Bill and Jude could manage, Ned came to Summer Hill and took charge of the movement. Before the Fall, the Eden Alternative was known, among people who cared about such things, all over the world. From Perth to Tokyo, London to Zurich, San Diego to Saskatoon—it changed how people thought about and cared for Elders.

But Ned got restless. More than anyone else, he saw the Fall coming. In '04 he left the Shire to take a position on the Cornell faculty. He went there and told his friends to protect the books, the quarter of a million volumes in the university's vast collection. Friends used to visit him in Ithaca, in those days. They stayed up late drinking wine and listening to Ned talk about how, someday, those books were going to need him; how, someday, people would remember how much they needed the books.

Bill and Jude continued to worry over the still unwritten post. So much seemed to depend on choosing the right words, asking the right questions.

In the afternoon, they went to the Long House and sat with the Elders of the Shire.

Zach and Virgil were also busy preparing for the journey. Kianna reminded them which edible plants were in season and where they could be found. Sarah Johnson, Master Harness-Maker of Bucklebury, worked through the night to finish a handsome set of saddlebags that the riders could use to carry their provisions. Beth Kimmon of Crick Hollow gave them topographic maps and a small brass compass. "Even before the Fall," she said, "traveling east to west over this terrain was much harder than traveling north to south. You'll have to find half a dozen ridges by my count and cross the valleys below as well. Here," she stabbed her finger onto a smudged area on the map, "is Camp Pharsalia. It was a low-security prison under the old republic, and the GRID might still be using it, so I'd keep my distance."

Virgil suggested another possibility. "Maybe we should head farther south, down toward Marathon then over to Dryden. We'd come up on Ithaca from the west—that would avoid the old route 13."

Beth nodded. "That'll work."

"I know we can get there," Zach furrowed his brow, "but I am a little worried about how to get into the university. These folks aren't likely to appreciate strangers stopping by."

The older woman agreed, "Xenophobia, the fear of strangers. It was bad after the Fall. The GRID likely still uses that fear to control people. They won't roll out a welcome mat. That's for sure."

"Any ideas, Beth?" Zach valued her advice.

"I'd say the best bet would be to persuade them, somehow, that you are one of them. Don't let them know you're a hobbit." She winked, "It'll take some imagination, but I reckon you'll find a way in."

In the last part of the afternoon on the second day, Bill sat before the fall front desk and pulled a sheet of handmade paper from a folder. He shook an inkbottle, unscrewed the cap, wetted the tip of his antique brass-tipped pen, and began to write in simple flowing script:

July 5, 2025
Dear Ned,

It is my greatest hope that this letter, which Zach and Virgil have so kindly volunteered to deliver into your hands, finds you as full of vim and vinegar as ever. Jude and I are well, and the Tribes of Eden continue on their merry way here in the Shire. We have been, I am quite sure, forgotten by the outside world, which in these times counts as a blessing. Caleb is at home looking after his wife Val and their brand new baby, a beautiful girl named Emma. Haleigh and Hannah send their love.

It is other family news that leads me to write. Val's twin brother, his name is Eron Wallace, has been ensnared by the GRID's Virtual Life. He's lost touch with the real, living world of family, friends, Earth, and sky and has now run away from the Shire. We think he may have gone to New York City to join with the GRID in real life, but we cannot be sure. His pain grieves us all and has led us to ask uncomfortable new questions.

He reread what he had written then gently blew the ink dry. He leaned back in his chair and stared intently at the ceiling. He thought of the night that followed Emma's birth, remembered how he had laid awake listening to the thunder. He dipped the nib of his pen and continued...

Last night the first storms of summer rumbled across the land. I'm sure you heard them in Ithaca, too. When I hear the growl of distant thunder, I can not help but ask: "Will the storm threaten me and mine?" If the wind rises, tosses the branches of trees, lifts the dust from the road, I watch the sky, check the doors and windows, bring the little ones inside. If it continues to gain strength, I think, I plan, I act.

Ned, the Elders of the Tribes believe—and I agree—that the GRID's rise represents a new kind of storm. We are OFF the GRID and intend to remain so. Still, its corrupting power has already touched us right here in the heart of the Shire. It has stolen a young man away from us, and we suspect that it has taken much more from many others. Though we are loathe to admit this, it seems that we too lie in the path of this storm.

Jude and I are confident that you will have gained insight into the GRID and the threat it poses. The Council of Elders has deliberated on this matter and feels that we cannot turn away from the danger it poses. We wonder, old friend, if the time has come to act once again to share the wisdom of Kallimos with this broken world. Once again, it seems we must ask:

What should be done?

What can be done?

All of us here in the Shire look forward to receiving the benefit of your wisdom. Zach and Virgil will remain with you for as long as needed to prepare your response and return home with your post.

Your friend,
Bill

He sanded the paper, selected an envelope, carefully folded the post, and slid it into place. Rising from his chair, he called to Jude. "It's done."

29
ITHACA

Zach and Virgil rode west, under the cover of night. They descended into the valley then forded the Chenango River a mile south of Sherburne. The houses, barns, garages, and shops they remembered from before the Fall all lay in ruins. Charred vehicles lay scattered before them, some turned on their sides, others on their backs. It was as if an angry volcanic god had discarded them there. There was no sign of human habitation.

They rode along what had once been Steam Sawmill Road, but was now a barely detectable path. After a long climb, they made the ridge top and followed its line south and west for several hours. When it veered north, they turned due west and descended into what had been the village of Cincinnatus. It too was a shattered hulk.

Dawn's rosy fingers had already reached into the eastern sky when they decided to stop. They came upon a mature stand of hemlock that straddled a small stream and made camp there. The men were tired and so were the horses. All of them ate, drank from the stream's clear running water, then Zach and Virgil slept.

The next night's ride passed much like the first, taking the pair past a series of empty, forlorn villages and hamlets. It was still dark when a ten-foot high chain link fence halted their progress. Topped with razor wire, it emitted an ominous hum, as if it was possessed by an army of furious hornets. Even in the fading moonlight, the printed warnings were legible: DANGER: HIGH VOLTAGE.

"Alrighty then," Zach mumbled.

"Hmmh," Virgil answered.

"That's not on the damn map," Zach continued.

"Nope."

Beyond the fence lay a four-lane highway, the old I-81.

"You suppose we could find a way around?" Zach asked.

Virgil thought for a moment. "It's hot, and that most likely means that it's continuous. Probably runs from Syracuse to Binghamton, at least."

"Not good."

"Right you are."

The horses chafed at the delay.

From behind, a voice commanded them, "Don't move unless you want a bullet in the back."

Zach slowly raised his hands and signaled for Virgil to do the same. "We're not looking for trouble, just passing through," he said.

"Bullshit."

The horses pawed and sputtered, made anxious by the menacing unseen voice. "You got us where you want us, OK. We're just going to turn the horses around. They'll spook if we don't."

"Alright, but don't get any ideas," the man answered.

The brothers wheeled their horses. A burly middle-aged white man, eyes narrow and suspicious by nature, studied them the way an evil minded boy might inspect an insect. He wore a black leather vest and his arms were covered with a dense network of tattoos. The sour odor of diesel and grease clung to him. The scent bothered the horses. Zach was troubled by the pistol.

"It's loaded." He pointed the gun's barrel at Zach's head.

"Look, man. We haven't got anything. Nothing you want or need. Not looking for trouble, just want to be on our way."

"That's for the Boss to decide. Now get down off those damn horses."

The brothers dismounted reluctantly.

The daylight gathered strength. It was time to move. The gunman steered them with his weapon. "That way," he said.

The brothers made their way along a narrow footpath, leading the horses by their reins. Their captor followed close behind. Virgil silently cursed their luck. They left the Shire unarmed. Now he and Zach were helpless.

The footpath led into a roughly circular clearing of mostly level ground, about 50 yards in diameter. The area was sheltered by a ring of towering oaks. Parked along the perimeter was a motley collection of trucks, cars, SUVs, motorcycles—there was even an old yellow school bus. Ropes had been drawn taut between the larger vehicles and tarps strung over them, creating makeshift shelters. Virgil counted two dozen men and maybe twice as many women and children. The sudden arrival of strangers in their midst set off a small panic. A bear of a man, a head taller than the rest, pushed his way through the disturbance.

He bellowed, "What'cha got, Chuck?"

"Found 'em sittin' and starin' at the fence like a couple damn fools."

The Boss nodded. "Check 'em out, boys."

A half dozen men, who might have been Chuck's brothers given how much they resembled him in dress and appearance, moved on the Boss's command.

Two men immobilized Zach and Virgil, holding knives to their throats while others frisked them. The saddle bags were opened, their contents dumped on the ground.

Chuck announced the results. "No weapons. Not even a damn knife. Found this though." It was the envelope that contained the post to Ned.

"Yeah?" The Boss tore it open, pulled out the letter, scanned it, and laughed. "Hah! Some guy rambling on about thunderstorms? That's it? You boys have got to be crazy. What? You escape from the cuckoo house or somthin'?" Virgil opened his mouth to protest but the Boss was faster. "What the hell? Goddamned homespun clothes, riding horses, fer god's sake, out here with no weapons, no damn sense whatsoever. I mean Chuck here brought you in slick as shit and that," the Boss grinned, "that tells me a lot."

"I'm Zach Thomas, and this is my brother, Virgil," Virgil nodded stiffly. "We live two days' ride to the east of here, in a place called the Shire."

"Really? I'm *so* impressed." The Boss rendered judgment. "Boys, they seen the camp. Get rid of 'em."

Knife edges tightened against their throats. "We're going to fight you," Virgil roared. "We are going to take you down. Death to the GRID!"

The Boss squinted in disbelief. "What?"

Zach repeated the message. "The GRID drove one of the boys from the Shire insane, and the Elders say it has to be stopped."

The Boss's mouth dropped open. "You think we're the GRID? Us?"

The pair nodded in grim agreement.

The Boss whooped with delight and the whole camp laughed with him. "You damn idiots, I'm George Johnson. This here's the Brotherhood. We're not the GRID. We fight the GRID. We are the GRID's worst nightmare." The Brotherhood cheered this declaration. "Let 'em go, boys."

George approached them, curious. "What route you live off?"

"Turnpike Road," Zach answered.

"Not the road, the route," he snapped. "What's the route number?"

"We live on the ridge between routes 12 and 8, near where 80 crosses over."

"That country's burned over. Nothin' left. Convoys?"

Zach answered honestly, "No."

"Not in a Demo are you?"

"Hell no," Virgil spat.

"We are," Zach affirmed, "off the GRID."

The Boss motioned like he was flicking an insect off the back of his hand. It was a sign. He did it again. Then, he growled, "Off, off, damn it, off the damn GRID. Where the hell have you boys been? It means that you are, you know, OFF the GRID."

"Oh," Zach said.

These weren't GRID spies, couldn't be, too stupid, too lost. He decided to let them live. "Pick up your stuff and look after your horses." Then he turned to Chuck. "Bring 'em on over to my place and we'll find something for them to eat."

Inside George Johnson's tent they sat on plastic patio furniture and devoured bowls of flavored protein paste. After the meal, their host offered the brothers a place to sleep. It was late in the afternoon when the Boss roused them from their rest. He returned the post to Zach, carefully resealed in its sleeve. "Your old man's right. You want to rise up against the GRID. You're crazy. I like that."

Zach took the envelope. "Thanks."

"I suppose you'll be riding at night."

"That's right," Zach agreed.

Virgil scanned the tent. "You have lights?"

"Yeah, we got lights," the Boss snapped. "All those vehicles got lights but we can't run them just for light. Wastes fuel."

"You don't need to burn fuel. You've got loads of power," Virgil answered evenly. "You just haven't figured out how to use it."

"Yeah, right. Power out here, hah."

"You better listen to him," Zach said. "He's a freaking genius."

Virgil explained, "That fence is loaded with power."

"Yeah, enough to blow you to hell if yer not careful. That's 12,000 volts."

"12,000 volts..." Virgil responded, the wheels of his mind already spinning toward a solution. The Tinker rose to his feet, "What spare parts have you got?"

"Chuck!" the Boss called.

While Virgil went to work, George Johnson entertained Zach with the story of the Brotherhood. "They came to get me and Anjie, said we had to go into a Demo. We not only said no, we said 'hell no!' Right, hon'..."

"Mmm hmm."

"Headed out, out on the road. And we found out pretty soon that there was plenty of others like us, not willing to be rats in the GRID's damned cages."

"So?" Zach asked.

"So we got together and, naturally, folks wanted me to be the leader."

Zach studied the Boss's wife while the big man ranted about the villainy of the GRID. She was a pretty woman, small with slender shoulders and hips, with an intelligent face surrounded by baby thin blonde hair. He could see that, even though George might do all the talking, the man needed her, relied on her.

"Like I was sayin', I was really the first one to say, 'Let's hit the damned convoys!' and by God we started hittin' the damned convoys. GRID took everybody's guns and ammo after the Fall, gave all of it to the damned Militia, suits us. All we've got to do is crack some skulls and take what we want."

"Chuck's gun?"

"No bullets." George Johnson laughed.

"Right," Zach shrugged.

"Fooled you though. Fooled you, right?"

"Yeah," Zach admitted.

George Johnson was on a roll. "There was this time down near Altoona..."

Two and a half hours later, Virgil had assembled three vehicle batteries, wired them in parallel, built a voltage rectifier from the broken remnants of a coil ignition, wound a step down transformer, and hung a series of vehicle headlights from a rope inside the Brotherhood's roomy main tent. When all was ready he attached a clamp's copper jaws onto the wire. The current snapped and light flooded the interior.

Virgil entered the tent with Chuck at his side and acknowledged the Brotherhood's cheers. Zach yelled, "That's my brother for ya. All the juice you need! Compliments of the GRID!"

"Bee-you-tiful," the Boss agreed.

"Chuck!" The Boss bellowed. "Show these fine gentleman the gates and make sure they get across."

"You bet, Boss!"

Zach led the horses to the edge of the camp, Chuck kick started his bike, and they were off. The gates turned out to be openings long ago cut into the fence. The brothers dismounted and led their nervous horses through the portal, then up the highway's steep embankment. The moon cast pale shadows onto the bone white concrete. Unshod hooves made a hollow clunking sound as they struck the pavement. At the eastern gate, Chuck took his leave. "Not sure you two are goin' ta make it out there. Hope ya do, but if ya don't...been nice knowin' ya."

"Yeah nice knowing you too, Chuck," Zach said. "See you around." They spurred their horses and disappeared into the forest. An hour later they crested the ridgeline that would deliver them to Ithaca.

The eastern hills glowed behind them as the brothers drew near to Cornell. They searched for and found a grassy clearing, unsaddled their horses, and set them loose. Pleased to be released from their burden, they grazed contentedly. "They'll be here when we get back," Zach said. Virgil didn't doubt it.

The once great university now belonged to the GRID. Like every other Demo, it was enclosed by a wall. This one stood about a dozen feet high—a rambling assembly of scavenged metal, wood, and stone. Virgil snorted in disgust. "It's crap. It was built in a rush then patched, and re-patched. Total crap. There's watchtowers, if you want to call them that, every hundred yards or so. This is," he concluded, "engineering malpractice."

"Be glad," Zach answered, "that the ones who built it are probably guarding it now."

Ned Wolff, if he was still alive, had no idea they were coming. There would be no help for them from the inside. Nor could two unarmed men be expected to storm the gate. That left the most direct path, through the front gate with the full permission of the garrison. It would require a great story and some acting. They made their plan while they scavenged food from the forest.

After the meal, Zach asked his brother, "You ready?"

"I guess."

He pulled Virgil to his feet. "You might as well start."

Virgil punched his brother in the face. He hit him the way he had when they were boys. Zach tackled Virgil and they fought with violence and passion but without malice. They rolled in the dirt, elbows flying, knees, feet, fists fully engaged in the struggle. Zach's head slammed against Virgil's nose, and the blood began to flow. When it was over, they lay on their backs, chests heaving, faces bloodied, clothes torn and dirty.

It was mid-afternoon when the pair approached the main gate. Zach hobbled along with Virgil's arm slung over his shoulder. His brother limped convincingly. The sentry demanded that they approach no closer, and they stopped in the shadow of the wall. Zach turned in the general direction of a speaker bolted to the cross beam above the gate. "Thank God we found you. We thought we would die out here."

"Stay where you are," the voice commanded. They obeyed. In the silence that filled the next few minutes, the two hung their heads and gave every appearance of struggling to remain standing.

The gate creaked open. A short, well-fed, and astonishingly self-important man emerged. His scowl clashed with the still babyish features of his chubby face. He carried a clipboard computer. The uniform was faded and, while it might have fit him years earlier, it clearly did no longer. He announced, "I'm Sergeant Raines, Corporate Militia, Academic Division, Chief Gate Master and I warn you," he held up a plump pink fist, "this is a deadly weapon."

"Thank God. Thank God for law and order," Zach said. "Our convoy was attacked by The Brotherhood. My God it was terrible. They weren't human. They were savages." Virgil nodded in mute agreement, as if he was still too stunned to speak.

"What happened?" The Sergeant poised his stylus now above the surface of the touch screen.

"Everything was fine, wonderful, good as could be. We came through Binghamton without a problem and then...BLAM, BLAM, BLAM. They blew the tires. Don't ask me how they did it. The truck ahead of us flipped, rolled over and over. Terrible," Zach shuddered convincingly. "They pulled us out and lined us up. We figured we were goners."

"Uhh, huhh," Raines nodded like he had been there.

"The convoy guards started fighting back. Brave men. It was a hell of a thing, baseball bats, chains, iron pipes. Men screaming, I can still hear the men screaming." Raines shuddered. "We crawled under a truck, thought we could hide there but one of the little ones, a kid I think, ratted us out."

The Herdsman winced.

Suddenly, Raines remembered his manners and asked the two to step inside, giving them a seat in the shade. They were halfway home. The Sergeant tapped the screen and asked, "What happened next?"

"Well a bunch of them—four, maybe five—got a hold of our legs and pulled us out from under there and dragged us into their camp. Oh sweet Jesus, they worked us over pretty good with some rubber hoses." Zach struggled to continue telling the story. "there was nothing we could do. They took everything. We were about half dead by the time they dumped us into one of their damn trucks. They drove and drove."

"How far?"

"Can't say," Zach said. Raines looked at Virgil. The younger brother said, "I got hit pretty hard in the head. I don't remember anything."

"Anyway," Zach continued. "They dumped us, dumped us like garbage and roared away."

"Left you for dead, huh?" It was more of an accusation than a question.

Zach looked puzzled then answered slowly, "Yeah, I guess you could say that they did."

"Bastards."

Zach continued. "When we came around we didn't know where we were. We just walked, walked all night."

"Uh huh." Raines continued to take the information down.

"Found this place—just stumbled on it." Zach peered at Raines and asked with perfect innocence, "Where are we?"

The Gate Master answered proudly. "This is the GRID's Cornell University Demo."

"No!" Zach shouted. "Praise be to Heaven! You mean it? If you do then this is a miracle, a true-blue, honest-to-goodness, one-of-a-kind, thunderbolt miracle."

"Really?"

"Yeah!" Zach staggered to his feet. "We're not strangers here. We're family. Our Uncle Ned Wolff is a professor here."

Raines' grabbed for the black plastic microphone that hung from his breast pocket. "Hey! Get a hold of old Professor Wolff," he barked. "Tell him I've a surprise for him that he just won't believe. His nephews—they're alive!"

Ned Wolff met them at the door of 508 Highland Street. He was as short, round, and inscrutable as ever, and he picked up on the con from the first instant. In his most professorial voice, he assured Raines, "You've been midwife to a miracle my good man. Stunning really, you've saved my nephews from a terrible fate—out there." Raines swelled with pride.

"Just doing my duty, Dr. Wolff."

"I'd expect no less."

"Um, Dr. Wolff, I'll need to thumb them before I go."

This was a problem.

Ned Wolff pulled his owl-sized glasses off his face and polished them with a loose shirt tail. "Zach, Virgil, you go on inside." The brothers disappeared into the house. The professor lowered his voice. "Long story, really, and..." he cleared his throat, "somewhat complicated."

Raines nodded as if he understood.

"Rather messy." He looked the Sergeant in the eye. "Just let me thumb that report, and we'll sort out the details later."

"But..."

He reached out and took the clipboard from Raines, thumbed the blue square, and thanked him again. Ned closed the door.

The brothers had already settled onto the screened back porch they remembered from their many visits before the Fall. Ned entered and took the remaining empty chair. "Well the Thomases always do manage to make life interesting."

Zach grinned. "Nice to see you too, Ned."

"Must be something big to bring you two hobbits out of the Shire."

"You got that right. Mom sent us."

Ned peered over top of his glasses. "Really?"

"Yeah. We brought this," Zach produced the tattered envelope from its hiding place and handed it to him. "Dad wrote this after he and Mom met with the Council of Elders."

Ned received the document with pleasure.

"You don't mind if we turn in, do you?" Virgil asked. "We've had a pretty long couple of days."

"I would say you have," Ned agreed. "Your Dad's letter will make good company." After he showed his guests to a dusty but comfortable guest bedroom, he returned to the porch and pulled the post from its envelope. He recognized his old friend's smooth, left-handed cursive and began to read.

In the morning, after a protein paste breakfast, the three returned to the back porch and talked. Ned still felt that the life of a professor was agreeing with him. The brothers admired his house and its many, many books, and they had questions, lots of questions. Virgil started. "The Demo wall is pathetic. Bob Brazzi would have it torn down and rebuilt." Zach added, "Raines doesn't seem too bright either. You know, Ned, this GRID thing is actually pretty lame when you see it up close."

Ned groaned. "You're missing the big picture. You've got to see the GRID as it fits into history. The Shire was safe during the Fall, but out here millions of people died. There was chaos, violence, disease. Brother fought brother, no one was safe. Then, out of nowhere, the GRID appeared. It promised safety, security, stability. The cost? Obedience. The authorities told us the walls were built to keep strangers like you two rascals out. The truth is they were built to keep people in."

"Alright," Virgil allowed, "the walls keep people in but...where are the people?"

"Indoors, all of them, almost all the time. They're mesmerized by their GRID stations. Yeah, their bodies are here in this Demo, in these houses. But their minds? Their minds live inside the Virtual Life that the GRID created for them."

"Just like Eron..."

Ned nodded in agreement.

"What about you?" Zach asked.

The older man shrugged. "Me? I love books. The library, that's my world."

After lunch, they got down to business. "I've read the post, quite carefully. I share the concerns your Dad raises, share them in full. The GRID is a radical creation—the rampaging, the rioting, the pandemics—all of that stopped as soon as it took power. People embraced it, loved it, the way a person might love a doctor who amputates a limb in order to save a life. The problem is that it just keeps cutting, doesn't know how to stop."

The middle brother drummed his fingers. Ned nodded. "Virgil?"

"Dad wants back into the revolution business. I can tell. What do you think?"

Ned leaned back and took the time he needed to consider the question.

"The GRID's a system of control, the most powerful system for controlling human beings that's ever been developed. Taking on the GRID would make our fight to abolish nursing homes look like a walk in the park."

"Mom's itching for a fight too," Zach added. "I mean, she wanted us to come here, told us, practically, that we had to come. That's not like her—at all."

"No, it isn't," Ned agreed.

Virgil pushed for Ned's bottom line, "So you're saying that we should keep our distance? The GRID—it's too big, too dangerous for us to fight?"

"You're too worried about where a fight would lead. But it isn't a fight we want, or need. What your parents believe, and I agree, is that it's up to the Elders. This is their chance to save the world. But we don't need them as fighters. We need them because they remember."

"Umm, Ned, the GRID has the oil, the food, the Militia, and a hammer lock on information and you want to...reminisce about the good old days? We need weapons." Virgil was firm.

"Bah," Ned snorted. "Fight the GRID and you make it stronger, you reinforce its reason for existence. The streets run red with blood, your blood."

"So, what is the answer?" Zach asked.

"I've put my thoughts into a letter to your parents. Read it over before you go. I will say this though, the struggle will be long and will," here he glanced playfully at Virgil, "require a great deal of patience."

"Great," Virgil sighed.

"Well," Ned stood up and clapped his hands, ending the discussion. "I've planned a fine supper for us and then you'll be off—on your appointed rounds, so to speak. I'll take you to the southern gate. An especially dull-witted evening guard will serve us well."

As night fell, Ned led them through the empty streets of the campus. When they arrived at the gate he placed his hands on the young men's shoulders. "It was so good to see you. I've been alone with my books for so long that I'd quite forgotten my years as a rebel. It's good to know that my friends in the Shire...remember."

"We miss you. We all miss you," Zach said.

"Come see me again and when you do, come in through the cemetery—there," he said pointing at a hillside of unkempt graves. "There's a guard tower down there but they don't like it. A superstitious bunch, they are. Anyway, I think you might find it to be a more convenient entrance. Easier on your noses, too."

Through the cemetery, the Thomas brothers were gone. When the Herdsman whistled short and sharp the horses came to him. By the time they reached the site of the outlaw's camp, the Brotherhood was gone. "Might as well rest here," Zach said.

As they lay down to sleep Virgil said, "When we get home I'm going to take Eron's GRID station for a whirl. I'll explore it—learn it—bust that Virtual Life open and see what's inside."

"You're not going to go crazy—like Eron did—are you?" Zach worried.

"Eron wanted it, wanted to be controlled. He wanted to know the rules so he could obey them. I want to know the rules...so I can break them."

"That's my brother," Zach replied.

They reached Bywater at dawn on the seventh day of their journey. Haleigh and Hannah welcomed them home, fed them, and put them to bed. Ned Wolff's post was entrusted to a girl on a fast horse.

She rode for Summer Hill.

30
EDEN UNDERGROUND

Dear Bill,

The arrival of Zach and Virgil Thomas on my doorstep was both pleasant and unexpected. They've grown to become fine young men. You must be proud of them. We spent many pleasant hours on my back porch, and they shared the many doings of the Shire with me. For my part, life continues on its quiet way. I have been made Master of the university's library service mainly, I think, because no one else wanted the job. It suits me well though. The books need me, and I need them.

I read and reread your post and have thought carefully about the situation you describe. You are right to say that GRID represents a new kind of storm. I have lived in it, but not been of it, all these years and I've studied it closely. The GRID is the largest most powerful system humankind has ever constructed. Like its creators, it is prone to stupidity, violence, selfishness, greed, and jealously. It professes a faith in the common man but, in fact, disdains the very people it claims to honor. Fear remains its most successful product. The GRID stokes the fear of strangers among the Xenos (the slang name for people who live in Demos) because that fear gives them control. Order, Loyalty, Control, Submission. These things underwrite the currency of its world order.

Virgil suggested to me that the Tribes should fight the GRID. I have no doubt that you, Jude, and the Elders will reject his well-intentioned advice. Nothing could be more dangerous. Frankly, I doubt the GRID can be overthrown with even the most extreme levels of force. Direct attacks on the structure of the GRID will simply reinforce its reason for being, and make it stronger.

The GRID does, however, have a weakness. Its continued survival depends almost entirely on its ability to erase the past. The GRID wants us to, needs us to, forget. It leads the Xenos to forget each other, to forget what is possible when people come together in pursuit of some noble aim.

I propose an alliance between the young and the old, an alliance dedicated to the transmission of memory. Let the Elders write of their lives, their memories, their past. Let the young carry those posts across the night, as Zach and Virgil have done, and deliver them to Elders trapped, as I am, inside the Demos. This will be difficult, dangerous work but it will press upon the GRID's most vulnerable point. Although I never knew him, it is clear to me that the loss of young Eron Wallace has struck a spark. Let us now tend the flame that has grown from that spark. The time has come for a new Eden, an Eden Underground.

Your Friend,
Ned

31
BEHIND THE CURTAIN
Summer, 2027

The three Thomas brothers settled with practiced ease into the deep wicker chairs on Ned Wolff's well-screened back porch. It was late afternoon and they had just risen from their mid-day slumber. The towering pines that surrounded the house cooled the summer breeze, adding a clean, crisp scent to the air. Ned puttered in the kitchen, re-heating food pastes for his guests.

They had been riding the circuit, their saddlebags bursting with posts from every Demo they visited: Cazenovia, Skaneateles, Fulton, Ilion, Herkimer, Oneida, Onondaga, Cortland, Ithaca, and from here, home. Caleb's little Emma would turn two at the end of the week, and her father and uncles wanted to be home in time to help her celebrate the day. The visit with Ned would be short.

Their host appeared with a tray laden with plastic tubes filled with flavored protein paste.

Zach groaned, "Appreciate you feedin' us, Ned, but I've had about all the fake food I can stand."

Ned smiled, mischievously. "Hunger is the best sauce, boys."

They ate with gusto.

When they were done the men sat back. It was time to listen and learn. Virgil started with the usual question. "So what are you working on, Ned?"

"History," he answered, templing his fingers. "A very interesting slice of history."

Zach draped a leg up over the arm of his chair. "Rome? The Civil War? Vietnam? What?"

Ned shook his head. "No, something much more recent. I've been studying the Fall and the decades preceding it."

"What's to know?" Caleb asked.

"Yeah," Virgil agreed. "It happens all the time. Empires get soft and everything falls apart. So it goes."

"Aaah, yes, a nice summary of the conventional wisdom. Boy, you've got to dig deeper if you want to understand, really understand, the way things are. You fellows wouldn't remember but back before the Fall, the whole world was connected in ways that were actually quite amazing. It was a global economy back then. Your parents and I, we traveled all over the world teaching people about the Eden Alternative in those years. Perth, Zurich, London, Tokyo, Stockholm. No place was too far."

"Mom and Dad have some great stories," Caleb agreed.

"Yeah, good stories," Ned agreed, "but the point is that this whole system, it made the world smaller and smaller and it made life go faster and faster. Growing up in the Shire, you fellows never really experienced it, but back in those days you could buy strawberries, fresh strawberries, in January. Strawberries that were picked in South America and flown overnight in a jumbo jet and brought to a store in your neighborhood."

Virgil couldn't help but be impressed. "Wow."

"The whole system was built on just two things: trust and oil."

"Then the oil ran out," Zach volunteered.

Ned shook his head. "Not really. There's still plenty of oil in the ground. The problems started when the cheap, easy to get oil ran out. Even so, the old republic could have survived even til today, if it had kept people's trust. The old republic was founded on the idea that people in search of 'life, liberty, and the pursuit of happiness' could solve even the biggest problems. In order for it to work, people needed to believe in each other, trust each other, work with each other. You know..." he prodded them, "'We the people...'"

The brothers stared blankly at Ned. Rusty mantras from the old republic's glory days didn't matter, not anymore.

"OK," he sighed. "you want the take home message? Someone or something, I'm not sure who, or what, decided to transfer assets from the trust account to the fear account."

Virgil nodded, "Xenos are afraid. As far as I can tell, that's the whole point of the GRID."

"I think it started when those lunatics flew airliners into the World Trade Center. They acted with the intention of creating fear—terror. Here's the thing, though. They also provided a world-class lesson in how thin and brittle trust could be. For the first time, the old republic abandoned its faith in people, its trust in trust—it surrendered completely, totally and without reservation, to fear."

"Yeah," Zach said. "They scared the airplanes right out of the air. That was the first time I saw a blue sky without the white streaks."

"Contrails," Virgil added for the sake of accuracy.

"Right, contrails."

Ned Wolff took a deep breath. "I've been thinking lately about the last days of the old republic. You fellows probably don't remember that much about it but it was a great thing, a fine thing, and it lasted more than two-hundred years. Then it was gone."

"The old republic was a mess, didn't deserve to survive." Zach spoke with certainty.

"Lots of people say that," Ned agreed, "but I don't think it's true. I've been reading about this, really digging in. I don't think the old republic fell, I think it was pushed. Powerful people decided their investments would be more profitable if they transferred them, so to speak, from the trust account to the fear account."

The Master Herdsman leaned forward. "How'd they get away with it?"

Two-hundred miles away, Eron Wallace was ordered to leave his tactical counter-insurgency lecture and proceed directly to an office on the 87th floor, higher than he had ever been before. The order worried him because it disturbed the usual routine, and the Academy thrived on routine. As the elevator shot upward, he checked and rechecked his recent conduct, hunting for the slightest hint of disloyalty or disobedience. Nothing came to mind.

He found the correct corridor and then the room to which he had been summoned. The door was locked, so he sat down on the stiff plastic chair next to the door and waited. Thirty minutes later, Assistant Deputy Director Bradley Long came shuffling down the hallway. Eron leapt to his feet and greeted the older man in the formal manner of the Academy, studying him closely as he did so. He was a small man, perhaps five-and-a-half feet tall, and would have been completely bald if not for a thin rim of wispy, artificially colored hair. Thick wire-framed eyeglasses made his otherwise beady eyes seem large for his face. His suit was clean, but shabby and seriously out of fashion.

"Come in, Cadet First Class Wallace." His voice carried the rasp of a long-time smoker. The interior of the office presented Eron with an astonishing display of a disorder that was rarely seen in the digital era. Mounds of paper, yellowed with age, occupied every available surface. A battered but serviceable desk dominated the center of the office. The walls were painted builder's white and lacked decoration of any kind.

Eron was invited to sit, while Long busied himself searching for the paper folder he needed. The missing file was eventually located and the older man cleared his throat, ready, at last, to begin. "Right, then, very good." The accent was distinctively New England, maybe Maine, Eron thought.

"Quite a record you've built here, Cadet Wallace." Mr. Long thumbed the pages carefully.

Eron guessed this was a compliment and said, "Thank you, sir."

The older man studied Eron, closely. "The work the Academy gives you, not very challenging, right?"

"I do my best, sir."

"Careful, too. Very nice." Long smiled primly, then wetted his lips. "Cadet Wallace, I'm sure you realize that as of next week you will have been with us for two years."

"I do, sir."

"Another two years and you'll be an Academy graduate."

"I hope to be, sir."

Bradley Long clasped his hands and laid them on the desktop.

"What if there was another DSJ Academy, a secret program reserved for the GRID's future leaders."

Eron came to full attention.

"Would you like to know more about such a thing or would you prefer to return to the classroom?"

"I'd like to know more, sir," Eron said hungrily.

"If I decide to share the details of this program with you, Cadet Wallace, your days at the Academy would be over. Your friends, perhaps they will miss having the pleasure of your company?"

"No...they...it's fine."

"Yes," Mr. Long replied. "I thought it would be."

"There were those who saw this coming, you know, writers, artists, poets who could see what most people couldn't. They understood how memory and history combine to shape our destiny. The past, the present, the future—these things are all closely related to each other. Rewrite the past and you control the present. Define the present and the future is yours for the taking. Hang on a minute..." Ned heaved himself up and out of his chair and disappeared into the dark interior of the house. He returned, a book open in his hands. He thumbed its yellowed pages quickly then found what he was looking for.

Zach read the cover, "*1984?* Dang that's old, Ned."

"Older than you think. It was written in the 1940s."

Caleb joked, "So it was a book about the future of the past—and now it's a book about the past of the future."

Ned ignored the joke and continued scanning the pages. "Here it is." He cleared his throat and began to read:

Day by day and almost minute by minute the past was brought up to date. In this way every prediction made by the Party could be shown by documentary evidence to have been correct; nor was any item of news, or any expression of opinion, which conflicted with the needs of the moment, ever allowed to remain on record. All history was a palimpsest, scraped clean and re-inscribed exactly as often as was necessary.

"So, it's an old trick," Zach concluded.

"One of the oldest," Ned agreed.

"I finally get it." Virgil nodded at a satchel full of posts lying on the floor. "The memories, the past, contained in those posts, from the GRID's point of view—those are deadly weapons."

Ned closed the book. "The deadliest weapons of all."

Bradley Long pulled a handkerchief from his pocket, removed his glasses, and rubbed the lenses with the threadbare cloth.

"You're smart," he began, "so you probably already realize that things are not as they seem."

Eron nodded eager for more.

"For example, the records in my file here indicate that you have been convicted of cyber fraud. An incident involving the lottery, I believe."

Blood drained from the Cadet's face, he opened his mouth to speak, but no words came.

"It's all right," Bradley Long offered a yellowed smile. "I happen to know you are innocent."

"Y...Y...Yes I am."

"Do you remember the night you were accused?"

Eron nodded, painfully.

"Of course you do. But did you ever suspect that it was all simply a test, a test of loyalty. One you passed, with flying colors, I might add."

The Cadet felt dizzy. "Thank you, sir."

"I remember it well because I was the one administering the test. I was the one who accused you, penalized you, and received your acceptance of the GRID's authority."

Eron was unable to speak.

Mr. Long slid his glasses into place.

"Cadet Wallace, I would guess you also remember your first night with us here at the Academy."

"I do, sir."

"The woman who showed you to your apartment. Tell me about her."

"She was, nice. Very professional, umm. Very nice."

"Anything else?"

Eron blushed.

"Well," the Cadet looked away and mumbled, "she was kind of ...ahh... interested in me."

"Yes, Traci is like that. A natural, I think. A wonderful actress."

Eron had replayed the memory of that evening so many times the details had faded. She was beautiful. She wanted him. Wanted him! He was afraid and sent her away, but how he had wished for her to return.

Long broke the reverie. "Traci works for me, of course. She was assigned to your case. We asked her to seduce you. We needed to see how you would respond."

Eron stared at the floor.

"Surprised?"

A pause, then, weakly, "No."

"Right."

Eron's throat was dry.

"There's more, much more," Long continued.

Bradley Long kept his promise, and took Eron behind the curtain.

"So you see," Long concluded, quite sure Eron would see, "the old order was unsustainable. It was killing the planet, wasting its resources, breeding disorder and inefficiency at every turn. It was doomed to fail. We just...helped it along."

"I remember," Eron volunteered, "when the power started going out, the first time it happened was on my birthday."

Long nodded. "A necessary intervention. We needed to focus people's attention. People, back then, took so many things for granted. We needed to shake them up, remind them they were lucky to have anything at all."

Eron agreed.

The older man took a deep breath and leaned back into his chair. Let his mind carry him back to his own glory days. Eron waited. "Remember this, Cadet Wallace. People who feel safe are hard to satisfy. People who feel safe are always looking for something more, wanting more, more, more of everything. Safety is a disaster, a disaster for everyone concerned."

Eron nodded, not sure where this was going.

"People who live with a healthy dose of fear," Long's voice rattled and plunged, "demand very little. They are easy to satisfy—and isn't that what we all really want—to be satisfied?"

The question caught Eron by surprise. "Yes, sir...I want to be satisfied."

"Well, of course you do, everyone does. And so we set to work making a world where everyone, every last person could be satisfied..."

Mr. Bradley Long warmed fully to his subject. "Before the Fall, a number of us committed ourselves to a program of strategic rolling destabilization. At the top of our list was the dreadful problem of over-population, massive over-population." Long smiled widely, his stained teeth glowed under the fluorescent light. "It became necessary to reduce and purify the population. With just a little help, the people were able to accomplish this for themselves. They turned on each other. They 'culled their own herd,' so to speak."

Eron smiled, "I used to listen to, ahh, a radio, and I always wondered why things happened the way they did, but the radio never said why. I figured no one knew."

Long corrected his student, "No one out there knew because no one out there was supposed to know."

"Eron," Long adopted the manner of a concerned but loving father. "I'll give you a perfect example of what I mean. Back in, umm, 2013, no, 2014, I'm pretty sure it was 2014, around New Year's. I put together an operation. Nothing special really..." The modesty was false.

Eron nodded, encouraging his mentor to continue.

"We had a situation, a motley rag tag urban population, surely you know the type. A few of the so-called leaders were actually trying to expose our good work. They were poking around where they shouldn't have been. It had to be nipped in the bud. The file was given to me."

Long's voice dropped into his chest. It felt good to re-tell the story. "The city was already short of food, fuel, medicine—short of everything really. We'd seen to that. I released a carefully designed sequence of rumors. They spread like a wildfire, hot and fast." Long made a mocking nasal voice. "Food! Fuel! Medicine! Get it all at the docks Saturday night!" He laughed. "Damn fools. They came...100,000 people came. The mob piled on top of itself like I knew it would." He tipped forward in his chair—this was the best part. "Then, at just the right moment, I had my men squeeze off a few shots, not more than a dozen, I'm sure of it." Long let his eyes flutter closed behind his clear plastic lenses, to better enjoy the memory.

A seizure of guilt and fear rattled the core of Eron's being.

Long grinned. "A whispered rumor, a dozen bullets, and 100,000 dead, maybe more. No fingerprints, no one ever knew how it happened."

Eron fought for breath then forced out the question, "City? What city?"

"Why, Cleveland, of course. The 'Great Panic at Cleveland,' that was my work, all mine. In fact," he concluded, "I still consider it my greatest achievement."

E mma fidgeted as her grandmother slid a sheet of paper from its folder. The paper was the color of bone and smelled, she thought, like corn. She waited for Jude to lay it flat in front of them, just as she had a thousand times before.

"Big day tomorrow, little girl."

"Big girl," Emma insisted. "I'm going to be seven!"

"What do you want to make for Mommy and Daddy? It's their birthday, too."

"A poem."

Jude unscrewed the cap on a fresh bottle of Mark Golden's ink and placed it into its well. "I'll do the border, but you tell me what it should be."

"Ivy. I really like ivy."

"You got it, kiddo."

Emma dipped her fountain pen into the ink and began to write.

First, I make a secret wish.
Then I blow the candles out.

She stopped and looked up at Jude. "What's a good rhyme for wish?"

"Dish rhymes with wish."

Emma returned to her work.

Birthday cake is my favorite dish.
It makes me want to shout!!

"Done?"

"I should make a picture, too."

"I think they'll like that." Jude opened the desk's wide bottom drawer. It was empty.

She reached behind the desk and took hold of the cache of paper she kept hidden there, "Here we go." She flipped through the stack of old drawings, searching for one still blank on one side.

Emma stopped her. "Who's that?"

Jude's heart skipped a beat. It was the drawing she made on the day of Caleb's Investment.

"That looks like Mommy!"

Jude hesitated, "That's your Uncle Eron, your Mom's brother..."

Emma finished for her, "He ran away a long time ago, when I was born."

Jude nodded. "Your Mom and Uncle Eron are twins."

Emma nodded. "Is he ever going to come home?"

"I hope he does come home someday," Jude reassured her. "Ahh. This one's perfect, like new. What do you want to draw?"

Thoughts of the long lost uncle fled her mind. "A horse!" She declared.

When the picture was finished, Jude heard the familiar rap of Kianna's walking stick on the flagstone outside the back door. She went to greet her old friend. The two women stood in the kitchen sharing a murmured conversation.

Emma interrupted them, "Grandmas, look what I did!"

"BEAUTIFUL!" Kianna exclaimed. Emma glowed.

"Do you think Mommy and Daddy will like it?"

"They'll love it."

Jude took the picture, rolled it carefully, and placed it in Emma's little backpack. "Alright, you two," she said. "Have a good time."

Kianna was going to walk to Bywater with Emma and wait there for Zach, Virgil, and Caleb to return from the post ride. Val would join them in the evening. Jude bent down and kissed Emma. "See you tomorrow, kiddo."

The summer heat was hard on Kianna. It made her legs weak and aggravated the numbness in her left foot. She looked into Emma's eager eyes. It would be alright. They had all day. "We going the back way, Grandma?"

"You bet," Kianna answered.

They stayed off the Turnpike, ranging across the Shire's meadows, alongside its ponds and streams, then skirting the east edge of the marsh. Kianna quizzed Emma on the names and uses of the mid-summers' plants and flowers. Emma knew them all. They reached Haleigh and Hannah's late in the afternoon. Kianna rested in the lengthening shade while Emma helped in the garden.

After supper, Val arrived, full of happiness. She knelt down and hugged Emma. "Have a good day with the Grandmas?" she asked.

"I've got a present for you and Daddy."

"And I've got a present for you," Val answered.

The light of Emma's birthday had just broken and dense fog still clung to the land cool, wet, and heavy when the sound of horses woke Emma. She jumped up and cried, "Daddy's home!"

The brothers burst into the little cottage, tired but happy. Emma made a running start and leapt into her father's arms. Caleb swung his daughter around, whooping and hollering along with his brothers. Then Emma called out, "Daddy's got blood, lots of blood on his shirt." The room fell silent.

"Caleb," Val whispered.

Her husband smiled, "Val, we have a very observant little girl. I do still have blood on my shirt, but it's not mine." He looked into his daughter's eyes, "I'll tell you all about it, little girl, if you want to hear."

"You know I want to hear the story, Daddy." She couldn't believe her father would have any doubt on that point.

"Of course you do, baby."

By the early afternoon the Post Riders had been washed, fed, and rested. The family gathered together in the shady part of the Aunties' garden.

As usual, Zach began the story. "Pretty good trip. Lots of posts, no trouble with the Xenos." He looked at his sisters. "We caught up with that Post Rider from Cobleskill you told us about. She's doing fine." Hannah nodded. "Anyway," he continued, "we were cutting across 90 over near Oneida when we ran smack dab into the Brotherhood. They hit a convoy the day before, back toward Schenectady."

"Scotia," Virgil corrected his older brother.

"Yeah, Scotia. The thing went off the rails, a real fiasco. For some reason, Militia was riding with the convoy. Like you'd expect, all hell breaks loose. You should hear George Johnson tell it. The bullets were flying. The Brotherhood pushed 'em back but Gene Lyons, he took one in the chest. Dropped him right there. Would've died in the dirt except George went out and dragged him back to cover. They blew out of there, headed west, and we ran into them that night."

Caleb picked up the thread, "I'll spare you the gory details..." He paused, then pretended to be startled by the frown on his little girl's face. "Nah, I won't spare you the gory details!" Emma beamed. "So we came up on the Brotherhood's sentry, and he went crazy seeing us there. 'You gotta come, you gotta come right away. Gene Lyon's been shot, shot real bad!' He took us straight to him, and let me tell you, he looked like hell. Pale as death, he lost a lot of blood, couldn't hardly breath. 'Circling the drain' as they used to say. I put my hands on his chest, and I could tell he wasn't moving air. Come here, kiddo."

Emma climbed into her father's lap and lay down across it with a proud dutifulness. "I tapped on the right side of his chest, like this." Caleb expertly percussed his little girl's chest, striking it quickly with his finger and producing a soft thudding sound. "Now that's how it's supposed to sound. But when I tapped this guy's chest, it sounded hollow, like a ripe pumpkin."

Virgil interrupted, "Caleb said he was going to need an airlock, a kind of one-way valve. We needed a suction pump, too, so I went to find one, or make one—same thing."

Emma, still lying on her father's lap, looked up at the clean white linen shirt, woven by her mother, that her father now wore. She liked it so much better than the dirty bloody one he was wearing that morning. "The blood, what about the blood, Daddy?"

"Well, when Virgil was ready, I took a knife and slid it in between Gene's ribs, like this." Caleb poked his finger into Emma's ribs. She exploded with giggles. "Seriously now," he looked his little girl in the eyes. "The knife goes in above the bottom rib, not below the top rib. Remember that." She nodded solemnly, then he repeated the rule, "Above the bottom rib, not below the top rib."

"OK, Daddy," Emma promised.

Zach had been quiet too long, "It was like he popped a balloon. Whooosh! Blood came spraying out like crazy. Covered Caleb, just drenched him."

Both Val and Kianna shivered involuntarily.

"Luckily, the slug was within reach, I fished it out and then snaked the tubing into the hole."

Virgil was exited, "I made a water trap, that way his own lungs would do the pumping—very nice if I do say so myself."

No one had any doubt.

"So that's it, kiddo. That's how Daddy got blood on his shirt."

"Is he going to live? Will Gene Lyons live?" Emma needed to know.

"I'm pretty sure he will," Caleb answered. Emma threw her arms around her father's neck hugging him so tightly her little body trembled.

"Oh yeah," he said. "We found out that George Johnson has a little girl too. She's a few years younger than Emma. Name's Serena. Cute as a button."

In the evening, the family gathered for the formal celebration of Emma's birthday. There was a cake and candles—and a birthday wish. The gifts were simple and few, pencils, a new blouse, and small collection of pressed four-leaf clovers. The highlight of the evening was the reading of Emma's story.

When the time was right, Bill escorted her to the writing desk and helped her pull the Kallimos book down from its shelf. Bill sat in his worn leather overstuffed chair and she took her place on his lap. Together they carefully opened the worn covers. Bill drew a deep breath and began to read aloud. "Long ago, when the People were still new to this world, a Tyrant took power in Kallimos. A greedy man, he declared that commoners must render unto him the top half of all that grew in their summer gardens. With heavy hearts, the People went to Emma, the oldest among them, and gave her the terrible news. She listened, thought, remembered, and then she spoke." Emma of the Shire loved the story's refrain. She knew the words by heart: "My children, my grandchildren, do as I say and all will be well. When the spring rains come, plant only potatoes, turnips, beets, and carrots."

"The people were saved. But the following year the Tyrant threatened them anew. Commoners were required to deliver to the King and his men the bottoms of everything they grew. Again, the People sought the counsel of Emma of Kallimos. 'My children, my grandchildren, do as I say and all will be well. When the spring rains come, plant only peas, beans, pumpkins, and cabbage.'

"All winter long, the soldiers who served the Tyrant choked down bowls of bitter pea root soup, grumbling as they ate. Knowing that he must not err again, the Tyrant declared that the People owed him the tops and the bottoms of their harvest. They would be left only with the middles. This was disaster. The People went to say goodbye to Emma of Kallimos, for surely they would not survive. 'My children, my grandchildren do as I say and all will be well. When the spring rains come, plant only corn.'

"At harvest time they trundled the roots and cornstalks to the Tyrant and kept the golden ears for themselves. When the men saw that their master had been fooled again, they searched the castle but he was already gone. Outside, the People approached. They too wanted revenge. Pitchforks and torches in hand, they were determined to make the Tyrant's followers pay for the master's crimes.

"Emma, quarterstaff in hand, stood alone in front of them. 'The young men who sided with the Tyrant have done you wrong, and now you seek their blood. They were fools, but who among you has not played the fool? They were wrong, but who among you has not been wrong?'

"A wave of shouts and cursing swept through the People. Emma let it pass then declared, 'If you must have blood then take mine. There can be no place for an old woman like me among people with hearts as hard as yours.'

"A young woman's voice rang out, 'Tell us more!'"

"'If you strike these men down, the blood you shed will stain your hands and the hands of all the People for a hundred generations to come.' They listened to Emma the Elder, let her courage and her wisdom seep into them."

"'My children, my grandchildren, do as I say and all will be well. Prepare a great feast and make places at your tables for the Tyrant's young followers. Feed them, sing for them, and dance with them. Welcome them back into the hearts of the People. By doing this, you will lay the foundation of a great and lasting peace.'"

And so it was.

33
THUMB PRINT

E ron Wallace's foot tapped rhythmically against the worn gray marble. He sat uncomfortably on the cracked plastic chair that Assistant Deputy Director Bradley Long kept beside his cluttered desk. The older man drummed his fingers in annoyance as he read then re-read Eron's duty request form. "Cyber Crime? Eron, don't be ridiculous, that's pissant stuff. You've disappointed me, not going to deny it, really disappointed me." Long shook his head in disbelief. "Top of the program, ranking off the charts. You could have any posting, Director's staff even, and this..."

Eron would not budge. "It's what I want, sir."

"Goddamned waste, is what it is."

"You said it yourself, sir. I can have any post I want."

Long gave up and pressed his thumb against the digital document's RFID chip and thrust it across the desk. "File this with Personnel and they'll grant your idiotic wish."

Eron received it with care.

"I don't mind saying that I expected better of you. Really thought you could overcome your...background. All the years of training, it's a damn waste."

"I'm sorry I've let you down."

The meekness of the apology stirred Long's anger. "Get the hell out of here, and don't even think about crawling back to me when you see what a mistake you are making. Understand?"

"Perfectly," Eron answered. "I'm quite sure that we will never meet again."

34
DOC

Fourteen-year-old Emma Thomas was exactly where she wanted to be. The day was still new, and she was riding down the middle of Turnpike Road with her father on her left and her Uncle Zach on her right. The latter was keeping them entertained with horse stories jumbled together with a running commentary on what was involved with the care, feeding, and training of one's own colt.

Caleb studied his daughter as they rode. It had been a hard winter. Kianna's death, coming so suddenly and so unexpectedly, had been hard on her. His usually cheerful daughter had been sad, too quiet, too withdrawn for too long. He'd been telling Bertie Marciel, the Master Harness-maker, about it last week when he stopped in to check on her. Bertie had lost her husband Jeff last fall. Pneumonia. Bertie said nothing would make a fourteen-year-old girl happier than getting her own horse. Best of all, she had one she thought might be just right for Emma. Today they were going to bring it home.

"Bertie says it's a colt?" Zach asked.

"Yeah, Percheron mare. Arabian stud. Jeff was sick pretty much most of last year, and Bertie says he never did get to work with him." This news adjusted Zach's attitude.

"Oh, Mama! A hot blooded colt, and he's been running wild up there for a year. Oh, Mama, this is going to be fun."

"What do you mean?" Emma asked.

"What I mean is he'll be wild, wild as can be." He turned and looked at his niece. "This isn't going to be easy."

A smile danced across her face. "You can do it, Uncle Zach."

"Oh great," he complained with a wink. "No pressure, no pressure at all."

The morning's chill still clung to them as they passed the harness maker's shop in Crickhollow. Jeff's widow and partner in harness wasn't home. Probably running an errand. They would stop and see her on the way back down.

"He's most likely running high up on the other side of the ridge," Zach guessed. "It slopes to the south there, and it'll have the best grass this early in the season."

Caleb nodded. "Let's go."

The ride up to the ridge passed quickly. They went single file, following a narrow muddy farm road that took them through a mature stand of white pine, then into a young forest of mixed hardwoods, none more than twenty feet tall. On the ridge, they rested the horses. Zach reached back and pulled a halter, and a tightly coiled rope out of a saddlebag. His expert fingers quickly resized the halter, making it right for a colt, now a year old. When he was done he said, "We'll swing out east, over there it'll drop us down below the meadow. Sun's out now. It's likely he'll be in the open."

"So how do we catch him?" Caleb asked naively.

"Push him around here," Zach pointed to a stream that exited the lowest point of the meadow. "Head him up there. The stream leads into a nifty little gorge. I'll get a rope on him there."

"OK, then let's go." Caleb said.

The three picked their way among the trees skirting the edge of the forest. When they reached the lower meadow, Zach whispered, "Oh. My. God." A hundred yards ahead of them and not yet aware of their presence, stood a stripling colt. His coat was dark, so coal black the morning sun seemed to disappear into its depth.

"He's beautiful," Emma said. Zach eyed the horse with professional care. Huge chest, huge. Strong topline. Seventeen, maybe eighteen hands. Sound. Intelligent look. "Emma, my dear, this is a one-of-a-kind horse."

Caleb was eager to get started. "Well, then, let's bring him home."

"He's wild. Don't forget. We gotta to be careful." Zach nudged his mare forward and the others followed. He spoke in the soothing voice of a herdsman. The colt's ears perked up, and he turned to face the strangers. Emma could see he was not afraid.

"Hey boy, hey boy..." Zach cooed.

They drew closer and the colt whinnied, warning them to keep their distance. The riders slowed but kept coming.

He spun away from them, hitting a full gallop in a single stride. Zach whistled sharp and short, and the chase was on. Emma fell in behind her uncle and ahead of her father. They thundered across the meadow and plunged down a broad sloping stream bank. Just as Zach had predicted, the colt turned north, racing up the stream bank eager to make the ridge top. The gorge narrowed, the sides rising so steeply that not even a riderless colt could climb them. A fallen tree, branches spread wide, finally blocked his way. Zach dismounted with a thud, tied the reins quickly around a tree, and waited for Emma and Caleb to catch up. Smoke-black eyes watched him, wary, waiting.

When Emma and Caleb were at his side, Zach said, "Stay here. I'll lure him in with some oats and get a rope on him. When I give the word, come on up and give me a hand. I'll need it."

"OK," Caleb agreed.

Zach walked slowly. His reassuring patter did nothing to reassure the colt who started to prance, looking for a way out. Zach held out a handful of oats. The colt sniffed the air. Zach got closer. He laid a broad loop of rope on the ground and poured the oats into the middle of the circle. The colt edged closer, lowered his head, nibbled. Zach pulled hard on the rope but wasn't quick enough. He stumbled backward, surprised his snare had missed completely. The colt reared, front legs pounding the air, and whinnied loud and long. Zach scrambled away from him. Angry and more than a little embarrassed, Zach coiled his rope and charged the cornered horse. The colt would not spook. He turned away from the man and kicked. A hoof grazed Zach's left ear, and he tumbled to the ground. The colt faced him, nostrils flared, ears pinned back. Zach scrambled to his feet and retreated to safety.

Emma laughed. The wild expression on his older brother's face made Caleb laugh, too. Zach sputtered excuses—a string of excuses that only made Emma and Caleb laugh harder. Finally, Zach, too, surrendered to the slapstick dimension of what had just happened. The Shire's Master Herdsman had been sent packing by a one-year-old colt. Zach raised his fist theatrically declaring, "Alright, you. Best three out of five!"

When the laughter ran its course, Zach turned to Emma. "Honestly, that colt's wild. Crazy wild, you'll be better off with..." he looked over his shoulder at the colt who still held him in his gaze. "With something more...civilized."

Emma shook her head. Caleb insisted, "Listen to Uncle Zach. I mean, he's beautiful and everything, but he's dangerous. Too dangerous."

Emma stared at the victor, studying his features closely. "You were mean to him, Uncle Zach. You tricked him, he doesn't like tricks."

Zach wasn't sure how to answer.

Emma started walking toward the colt. She held out her hands, palms up, not speaking but looking straight into his eyes.

Caleb started after her but Zach put a hand on his shoulder. "Wait," he said.

Emma drew near, but the colt did not shy from her. She stood about five feet away, and the two inspected each other. The colt sniffed the air. He was curious, then he took a step forward. Emma held her ground. Again the colt stepped forward. Emma reached out and gently wrapped her arms around his thickly muscled neck. She whispered to him.

"Well, I'll be damned," Zach muttered.

When she was done, she let go of him and marched brightly back to her father and uncle. Zach spoke in an excited hush. "Fantastic! Do it again, but this time, take the rope."

Emma looked offended. "Doc doesn't like the rope."

"Who's Doc?" Caleb demanded.

"He's Doc. His name is Doc," Emma answered.

"OK." Zach asked, "did Doc tell you how we could get him into the barn?"

Emma grimaced. "He doesn't want to go to the barn. He thinks barns are yucky. He wants to be free."

Caleb seized on this declaration as a way out of all this, "Alright then, he wants to be free. We can go home, and he can be free." To his surprise, a big smile spread across Emma's face.

"Let's go, Dad."

Caleb wanted to make sure he understood. "And leave Doc here, out here, in the wild?"

Emma swung up onto the back of her horse. "Yep. We're friends and we're going to be friends our whole lives." She looked accusingly at Zach, "Friends don't try to tie friends up or make them wear a halter or a bridle or anything. Right, Uncle Zach?"

"Right you are, my dear niece. Let's go home."

They crossed over the ridge top and descended the far side and were soon in sight of Bertie's workshop. As the riders approached, she came out to greet them. "Well?" she asked. Zach didn't want to talk about it, but Emma did. The girl bounded down off her horse, ran up to Bertie, and hugged the older woman. "Thank you, thank you, thank you! Oh, thank you so much!"

Puzzled, Bertie said, "Well, you're welcome, my dear—but where's the colt?"

Emma chattered excitedly, "Uncle Zach tried to catch him, but he didn't want to be caught." The Master Herdsman rolled his eyes. "Uncle Zach fell down twice, but that's because he just didn't understand. I just walked right up to him. He's so big and his coat is pure black and his name is Doc and," Emma drew in a deep breath, "he's my very best friend."

Bertie cupped her hands against Emma's cheeks. "Wonderful."

"Come on inside, all three of you." Then with an impish grin, she added,

"I want to hear all about how that sweet little colt got away from the big old Master Herdsman."

"Oh, yes," Emma answered confidently. "I'll tell you all about it!"

35
THE EXECUTIONER
Summer, 2039

A rare feeling of contentment swept over Eron Wallace and he decided, for once, to savor it. He sprawled comfortably on the couch in the rear compartment of his custom private motor coach and could feel the vibration of the diesel engine below him, could feel it even through the sofa's plush foam cushions. Outside, landscape flew by. The convoy was headed south, to Orlando. Eron lazily supposed they were on I-95, someplace near Baltimore. But he didn't know for sure, didn't care to know. This was going to be a good week, the best week of his life. He shivered with anticipation, reached for the peach-flavored drink that was nestled in its cup holder and raised it to his lips. He sniffed appreciatively, noting with satisfaction it was one-hundred percent artificial.

With his triumph so close at hand, Eron indulged himself in nostalgia. He'd been the first, and was probably still the only, graduate of the Elite DSJ Agent Program to enter the Cyber Crime Division. The others had supposed he was damaged goods and forgotten about him. He had fallen off the map. Expectations were low at the CCD, and he had the time and freedom from scrutiny he needed to prepare for this week. He spent five humiliating years deep in the bowels of the bureaucracy preparing for what was to come.

Just two years earlier he had emerged from his hiding place, vastly more experienced and unscathed by the DSJ's vicious infighting. The Director of "The Trial," the GRID's video Justice Reality program, had taken a chance on him. It was strange, Eron thought. The GRID offered everyone a complete, perfectly sealed virtual world where anything was possible, but people—many millions of people—still hungered for live action justice. "The Trial" was designed to sate their hunger.

In the vehicles trailing behind his were the lawyers, bailiffs, and judges who made up the show's cast. More accurately, they were the actors who played lawyers, bailiffs, and judges. They all worked off a script, and the script belonged to him. They were all wonderfully, brilliantly—fake. The defendants, on the other hand, were always real and always terrified. The criminals were, Eron believed, almost always guilty, guilty as hell. Their fear was the critical ingredient, the thing that gave the show its tang. The Xenos themselves, all of them, formed the jury. He smiled. The people themselves were allowed to wield the mighty sword of Justice. The show was broadcast on the entire GRID, every screen, no exceptions. When it was over, people voted, instantly, electronically. The people, it seemed, were very unforgiving.

Guilty.

Guilty.

Guilty.

Since there was no higher court, there could be no appeal. The punishment was always presented live, the very next evening.

Eron began as the program's deputy Assistant Director. Within a year he was an Assistant Director. Six months later, the top job was his. He looked idly out the window. The light of the day was collapsing into the west. He thought he'd feel more excitement. No matter. It had to be done.

The convoy reached the walled city of Orlando the following morning. Eron showered, shaved, and dressed, as always, in a finely tailored synthetic fabric suit. The air outside was already boiling, but weather did not concern him. The others would come to him. When he was ready, he walked into the main cabin, took his seat in the Program Director's chair, clapped his headphones into place, and went to work.

"Cole, scout locations. Get back to me by noon."

"Opritza, get me some B-roll of this godforsaken hellhole."

"Bennett, get those moron actors to my office by ten—I need to talk to them."

An hour later, a guard showed The Trial stars into the main compartment. They were pleased to find the director in an ebullient, welcoming mood. After his guests were seated and made comfortable, Eron dropped copies of a thick dossier onto the table in front of them. "I know you've been wondering why we didn't have our usual pretrial briefing earlier in the week." The actors reached quickly for the files. Eron continued to speak as they popped the seals and looked inside. What they saw shocked them. "As you can see, this trial deals with treason, a disgusting betrayal, and multiple felonies committed by one of the DSJ's own."

The Judge scanned the pages hungrily.

Bradley Long...Covert Operations...Agent Recruitment...Fraud...Pattern of Sadistic Behavior...Innocent people...Zeroed Out...Hid his crimes...Retired... New Evidence...Overwhelming proof of guilt...Living in Orlando.

The speaker next to Eron's desk crackled to life. "Sir, Militia extraction unit confirms that the offender has been taken into custody."

The actors' fear rose like bile. Convicting low-life GRID criminals for entertainment was one thing. Hell, it was their job and they enjoyed it, but going after a high-ranking former DSJ official—especially one who had conducted covert operations during the Fall—they could think of nothing more dangerous, or foolish.

Eron had expected this. "If you will turn to the red tab, you will find two certified communications. The first confirms Long's guilt. The second is from the Chairman himself, and it authorizes this trial." The defense attorney let out a long, low whistle.

"Any questions?" Eron demanded.

There were no questions.

"Alright then," he began, "what we have here is a story of good versus evil. A formerly upstanding DSJ official..." Eron paused for effect. "I actually met him once back before...all of this," he pointed at the dossiers. "Anyway," Eron picked up the thread, "this was quite a little racket. He'd pick random people, nothing special about them, good people, salt of the Earth and all that, and would accuse them of disloyalty, of lying, cheating, stealing—whatever he could think of."

"Bastard." The prosecutor spat the word as if it was a broken tooth.

"There's more," Eron assured them. "He would zero them out. Bust them down to nothing." Again, Eron paused to let his words sink in. "And where do you think those VL points ended up?"

The judge rose out of his chair, his fists mashed against the tabletop. "The dirty filthy liar stole them, lined his nest with them, used them to 'retire' here, fat and happy living off his dirty money." His deep bass voice normally so restrained, so judicial, burned with genuine anger.

"Right," Eron said. "Now I hope it is clear why I chose to handle this personally."

"Damn straight," the defense lawyer agreed.

"I've taken care to arrange a fitting punishment for this crime, but as you all might suppose, I've come to detest this...demon. So I need you to take this one all the way, all the way to the goal line...for me." Eron held out his hands, pleading, "I'll direct the trial from here, but I don't want to see this man—not even for a minute."

"You've got it, Mr. Wallace," the Judge pledged his support. "You can count on us." The others signaled their full agreement.

The hook was set.

Eron rose to signal that the meeting was over. "Oh...one more thing, I expect the dirty bastard will deny everything." The actors laughed, of course he would. It was to be expected. "And he'll likely try anything to get off." Eron hesitated, as if he was embarrassed by an unexpected thought. "He might even accuse me somehow, maybe even accuse me of framing him, something along those lines."

The Judge winked at the Director. "Don't you worry about a thing, Mr. Wallace. We'll take care of everything."

Eron sighed with genuine relief. "Thanks, I knew I could count on you."

When he was alone again, Eron returned to the chair in front of the control panel. From there he could see and hear without being seen or heard. He was the unwatched watcher.

The program's portable courtroom was erected, wired, lit, and made ready. For once the job was being done capably—a big improvement. He called up the roster. He had a new crew chief, a young man. His name was John Knox. Eron made a mental note. He would keep his eye on him and know soon enough if he was for real.

When the final checks were complete, Bradley Long was led into the courtroom and the cameras zoomed in on him. He had aged much more than Eron expected. He shuffled toward the defense table and used a cane. Damnit. Here was another problem to handle. He punched the button connecting him to the Judge's hidden earpiece. "So what!? He's an old man. I don't want sympathy building up for him just because he is old. Got that?"

When the courtroom formalities were complete, the judge intoned, "Justice, true justice, is applied to all evenly, fairly, compassionately. An offender's youth, or age, is irrelevant." The magistrate nodded at the defendant. "Furthermore, no one can expect to be immune to the consequences of their actions, not even," he added gravely, "the high and mighty."

Eron, watching from the bus, nodded approvingly. Then came an avalanche of evidence, solid proof that Long had attacked innocent people, accused them of crimes they did not commit, zeroed them out, destroyed their lives.

Prosecutor Smith: I enter into the record this set of documents, each thumbed personally by Bradley Long.
Bradley: I've never seen any of them before. It's all a lie, this whole thing is a lie!

Prosecutor Smith: May it please the court, each of these documents carries the unique thumbprint ID of Bradley Long.
Bradley Long: (Face flushed) It's a lie!
Prosecutor Smith: (Leaning in close, voice just above a whisper) No, it's the truth, the whole truth, and nothing but the truth.
Defense Attorney Franklin: Objection.
Judge Andrews: Overruled.

Bradley Long was doomed and smart enough to know it. The people watched, then pressed their buttons. Innocent or Guilty? Eron took a piss while votes were tallied. When he returned, the verdict was in.

Guilty.

He smiled. Tomorrow was going to be good.

John Knox stared at the drawings he had been given. They sent a chill down his spine. His crew had labored overnight to build an engine of destruction. The defendant was to be shackled supine on the main platform. A long metal lever would, at the appropriate time, transfer the collective weight of his victims directly onto Long's chest, crushing the life out of him. The plans also called for extra camera booms to be installed, all the better to capture the scene close up, in three-dimensional detail. It would be terrible, Knox knew that, and people would love it.

At the appointed hour, DSJ guards led Bradley Long to his death. He was positioned so that the crew could fine-tune the sound and lighting. Then the theme song swelled in their earpieces.

One after the other, the "victims" of Bradley Long's crimes stepped victoriously onto the levered platform. With each additional weight, Long's suffering intensified. By the time the victim's platform was halfway full, the convicted extortionist could no longer scream out his agony. His breath came in narrow ragged gasps. The cameras lapped up the pain, lingered over the suffering. When the platform was full, the weight pressing on Long's chest was so great that his rib cage collapsed and the great vessels of chest were torn apart. Blood shot from Long's mouth, sprayed the camera lens, and delighted the millions of the jury who watched, who could not stop watching.

When it was over, Eron Wallace glowed with pride. The proud father of the Cleveland Riot, the man who had taken his father from him, had received the punishment he deserved.

Now John Wallace could rest in peace.

36
THE ELDER OF CAZENOVIA
Fall, 2039

Caleb Thomas was in Cazenovia, sitting at the kitchen table of his old friend Cody Brooks. The weather had turned foul. A dreadful autumn rain fell in sheets.

"Neither fit for man nor beast," Cody said, hands cupping a mug of tea.

"No sign of the Watch?" Caleb asked.

Cody shook his head. "Wouldn't be, not tonight. 'The Trial' is on all the GRID screens." He grunted, "The Xenos love it, absolutely love it. Last night was the guilty verdict. Tonight is the punishment."

"Don't waste time, do they?"

"No, they don't."

The conversation turned to home. Cody was one of the ever-growing numbers of hidden Elders, the ones with whom the Elders of the Shire corresponded. Virgil had delivered a pouch full of posts, and Cody would read and then pass them on to other Post Riders coming through, riding other routes. Over the years, the Eden Underground had built a network of Elders and Riders who were spreading memory deep into the GRID's world, and the GRID knew nothing of it. All of the young people who carried posts between Demos were known as Post Riders, even though only those from the Shire rode on horseback.

He asked about Virgil's new baby, a girl. "Doing fine," Caleb answered "Looks like Chloe."

"And your Emma? She must be, what now, thirteen, fourteen?"

"Fourteen," Caleb answered. "She's doing alright. Had a hard winter, with Kianna passing on and all. Now she's crazy about this wild horse."

He recounted the story of Zach's attempt to capture Doc. Cody roared with laughter. "She's a good girl," Caleb continued. "Got a mind of her own for sure. Smart. Sees things other people don't. Says things others won't say. Great hands. Could have been an artist, like her grandmother, or a weaver like her Mom, but it looks like she'll be a healer. I think she'll choose medicine, apprentice with me in the spring."

"She'll have a good teacher."

Caleb acknowledged the compliment with a polite nod. "Growing like a weed. Going to be tall, like her Mom. Outruns, outclimbs, outdoes all the boys her age, and not by a little." Caleb added, "Maybe in another time she could have danced ballet. She moves like that."

Cody watched as Caleb swelled with pride.

"Sounds pretty special."

Caleb nodded, his thoughts back home in the Shire—far away from Cazenovia. "Yeah, she is."

"I look forward to meeting her."

Caleb laughed, short and sharp. "Oh, I don't think so. This whole post riding thing, it's just too dangerous, way too dangerous. No," he added confidently, "there'll be plenty for her to do at home in the Shire." Then as if to console his host, he added, "You'd love her though. She's a great kid."

"Well, sounds like it'll be my loss." Cody Brook's eyes twinkled as he spoke. He had lived a full life. He had daughters of his own. He felt certain that someday, Emma Thomas would sit where her father sat now. It was just a matter of time.

37
ALLIES
2041

Summer, in its fullest, descended upon the Shire. Grass, long and green, waved in the hot wind, waiting patiently for the cattle that would soon descend upon it. The people, too, brimmed with life. The Turnpike rang with the sounds of cutting, stitching, weaving, grinding, pounding, hoeing, dipping, pulling, and harnessing. Sun, rain, and soil gave life, and it was the people's obligation to take hold of that life, shape it, change it, transform it, make it into the things they would need if they were to pass safely through the winter.

Zach returned to the high pastureland, his broad cloth shirt soaked through with sweat. He sat on the bench in the dooryard and leaned down to pull off his riding boots. Sadie was inside. The raspberries had come into season and she was putting up jam. The kitchen was a sweet smelling inferno. She called out to him, "Don't get too comfy, hon. Caleb stopped by earlier looking for you."

She stepped outside, a fine looking woman now in her middle decades. Smile lines graced the corners of her deep brown eyes. Her face, usually so merry, revealed her concern. She sat down next to Zach. "It's about Emma. He and Val are worried sick about her."

Zach joked, "She's sixteen. She's supposed to make them worry." Sadie would have normally answered with a joke of her own. Instead, she laid her hand on Zach's arm. "No, really. I think something's wrong."

He looked at her, puzzled. "She sick? Pregnant?"

Sadie shook her head. "No, it's that horse, that wild horse she calls Doc."

Zach nodded.

"They need to talk to you."

Zach bent over and pulled his boots back on. Caleb and Val needed him. He would go. "They at home?"

"Caleb said they would be."

"Don't know how long I'll be."

"I'd come too," she said, "but I'm not finished, won't be for awhile."

Zach stood and pulled Sadie to her feet. He held her close, their skin, glistening with summer sweat, slid soft and easy, each against the other.

"You'll wait up for me, won't you?"

She laughed and kissed him. She kissed him the way a woman long in love kisses her man. She knew him, knew his faults and failures, and accepted him as he was, loved him more because she knew that he was just like her— flawed, imperfect.

They let go of each other. "I'll take Jed. He needs a good go. Love you, babe."

Twenty minutes later, man and gelding galloped west to Frogmorton.

Val heard hoofbeats in the dooryard followed by the thud of boots hitting the ground. It was Zach. He had come, as she knew he would. She swung the door open, stood on the sill waiting for him as he tied his horse.

Val hugged him. "Thanks for coming."

Zach laughed, picked her up, and swirled her around. "You think I'd disappoint my favorite sister-in-law?" Then in a joking whisper, "Don't tell Chloe I said that."

Val laughed.

Inside, Caleb was clearing away the dinner dishes. The heat of the day was fading, the sky above clear. The night would be pleasantly cool.

"Hungry?" he asked his brother.

"A little," Zach answered.

Caleb knew that meant "very". He ladled stew into a bowl.

Zach listened as he ate.

"Somehow, I don't know how, Emma has developed some kind of..." He searched for the right word, "Arrangement with Bertie's colt."

Zach shook his head. "Never was anybody's colt. Wild, that's all."

Caleb went on, "She's been going up into the hills, looking for him. But now she's riding him."

Val, unable to keep quiet burst in, "Riding that stallion, no halter, no bridle, no saddle, nothing—just up on his back—and he's as wild as ever."

This did surprise Zach. "Really?"

Caleb nodded. "Val and I went for a walk a couple of days ago, down along the stream, over toward Crickhollow and saw them galloping, mad galloping across the pastures up there."

"Hmm."

Val leaned forward, worried.

He saw her anxiety and shook his head. "Nah, it's not bad. It's good."

"It's crazy," Caleb insisted.

Zach leaned back in his chair.

"Zach, it's dangerous. That horse turned on you—you! She shouldn't go near it." He saw fear in Val's eyes.

The older brother wanted to relieve them of their worries but he could see that Doc wasn't the only issue at hand. He began slowly, "Doc turned on me in the gorge because I had him cornered. I was trying to take away his freedom. We both understood what was happening. He knocked me down, and could've killed me if he wanted to. He was hoping I'd take the hint, and I did."

"That's the point," Caleb burst in. "He could've killed the Shire's Master Herdsman. So what about our little girl?"

Zach shook his head. "She's not so little anymore, I've noticed." He was right; Emma had powered through a growth spurt and was now nearly six feet tall. Her deep brown hair fell down onto her shoulders. Her coffee-and-cream colored skin seemed to give off a light of its own, a light from inside. Somehow, Emma had remained untouched by the awkwardness, the shy uncertainty that so often accompanies so great a change. The people of the Shire saw a beautiful young woman, while her parents still fretted over their little girl.

Val was insistent. "We've told Emma she has to stay away from Doc." She looked Zach in the eye. "She'll listen to you."

Zach would not budge. "I'm telling you not to worry. She's not riding on Doc, she's riding with him. They know each other. They trust each other. It's deep, really deep and..." He hesitated to offer the full truth.

"Go ahead." Caleb wanted his brother to speak his mind.

"She loves that horse. That's common enough. I think Doc loves her too, but not because she feeds him, watches him, and mucks out his stall. She doesn't do any of that. It's an alliance of equals."

Zach had barely finished his sentence when they all heard the sound of unshod hooves falling hard and fast on stone. A moment later, Emma stormed into the house. "I hate Troy Martin. Hate him!" Val stepped directly into the path of her daughter's towering rage. "He said he liked me, said he wanted to go to the Summer Feast with me."

"What's the matter, Emma?" The sound of her mother's voice brought Emma's anger down a notch. Through gritted teeth she continued her story. "He wanted to go for a walk down to the falls, but when we got there all he wanted to do was put his hands up my shirt." Val was stunned by her daughter's blunt honesty.

Zach didn't like where this was headed.

Emma continued, "I gave him a good hard shove. He deserved it, believe me." Now, Emma gentled—this was the sore spot. "He fell into the water. He got mad because I couldn't stop laughing."

The Master Herdsman edged toward the door, but the movement caught Emma's eye. Her anger rose again. "He's your apprentice, Uncle Zach. You better tell him I'm not a cow. Doesn't he get his hands on enough teats working in the barn?"

Zach smiled weakly. "My dear Emma, you can be sure I will talk to Troy about this." Her demand satisfied, Emma reached out for her mother, fell into her arms, and sobbed. "He says he won't go to the Feast with me. He doesn't want to see me ever again." Val held her daughter close. "Mama, Mama, what am I going to do?" Emma cried without reserve, her tears soaking her mother's finely woven blouse.

Outside, Zach cinched the saddle and said to his brother, "I've said it a thousand times, being the father of boys is so, so much easier, my dear brother." Caleb nodded in silent agreement. "I will have a word with Troy. He's a good egg, just doesn't know what he's dealing with. It'll be all right."

"Thanks, Zach."

The older brother mounted his horse. "I'd say Doc is the least of your worries."

"I'd say Val agrees, now."

Zach wheeled his horse and headed home. It was a fine summer evening, and Sadie would be waiting for him. He'd be home before dark.

38
BREECH

Later that night, the moon was low and the sky shone with the diamonds of the night when a fist crashed against Val and Caleb's front door. Chris Waldeck called out, his voice pitched with anxiety, "Caleb! Caleb, the baby's coming. I'm sure of it!" His cry brought Caleb and Emma both to the door. "The pains came on hard and fast. Anna woke me up and said I needed to come for you right away." His mare stood in the dooryard. There was no need to tie her. Her flanks trembled from the heavy exertion of the pounding ride. He came all the way from Crickhollow.

"Her water break?" Caleb asked.

"Yeah, but not clear like usual. It was stained—tinged green."

When the final word of that statement left Chris's mouth, Emma bolted from the house, sprinting toward the Turnpike.

"What the..."

"The green," Caleb said. "It's called meconium. It means trouble. No time to waste."

Emma's piercing whistle echoed across the night. In answer, Doc charged out of the dark forest and onto the Turnpike. He circled Emma, and she leapt onto his back. She whispered, *Cha.* The stallion headed west, made full gallop, and then stretched his stride. Emma buried her face in his mane, clinching herself to him with her arms and legs. There was no need to watch the road ahead. He knew. The moon hung low over the trees and ran alongside of them. They reached Crickhollow and raced across the village green. Doc thundered to a stop in front of the Waldeck house, his chest heaving. Emma jumped down and barged into the house. Anna would be in the bedroom.

The laboring mother lay propped up in bed, her eyes wide with terror. Between her legs was the lower half of a baby boy. His buttocks were inky blue. Two tiny legs hung listlessly between hers. They were covered in thick green stool. Anna cried out, "He's dying. I can feel it. He's dying right inside of me." Emma scrubbed her hands and forearms and answered the mother with the strong soothing voice she learned from her father. "Caleb's on his way. You and the baby are going to be fine."

Emma reached inside the birth canal. She felt the cord. There was no pulse. She pushed farther. The umbilical cord was trapped between the baby and his mother's pelvis.

"Anna, I need you to turn over. Get off your back, over onto your hands and knees." The woman's friends, reassured by Emma's confidence, stepped in to help. Emma kept her hand deep inside the mother. Once Anna was on all fours, and the pressure was released Emma pushed farther and found a pulse. Anna groaned when the young Midwife used her wrist and forearm to lever open a space for the blood to flow. Slowly the legs and buttocks brightened. The boy lived, still.

Within minutes, Emma's arm and forearm began to ache. She struggled not to move, not to break the connection. She closed her eyes and listened for her father.

Then there were horses in the dooryard. Caleb and Chris entered the room. Emma turned to face the Master Healer. She spoke in level measured tones. "Multip, gynecoid pelvis, full breech, prolapsed cord, thick meconium color, and tone—much better." The last two words carried a universe of meaning.

Caleb nodded, stunned by his daughter's face—so calm, so confident, so adult. For the first time, he saw her as a woman. He pushed the thought away. "You've got to get farther inside. Get your middle finger into his mouth. His neck's extended," he explained quickly. "That's why he's stuck. You've got to use your finger to pull the head forward so it can pass under the pubic arch."

Emma nodded. When the next uterine contraction eased off, she slid her arm deeper, eliciting a howl of pain from the mother. Her long fingers became like her eyes, probing deeply into a dark, hidden place. She felt the boy's chin, waited for a contraction to pass, then pressed harder. She found the mouth, put the first knuckle in, then the second. "Got it," she said. Caleb heaved a sigh of relief.

"Good suck," Emma added.

That made the Healer smile. He looked at Chris. "It's going to be OK."

As the next contraction built, Emma pulled the boy's head forward and with her free hand she pulled the torso down and out of the birth canal. Once she did so, she was no longer able to splint the umbilical cord.

It was two minutes to the next contraction. Anna pushed, and the baby was born. Emma instinctively flipped the boy onto his back and breathed into his gaping blue mouth. One. Two. Three. Four. A rattled gasp, a cough, and then a cry. Caleb stepped forward, took the child from Emma's arms. His daughter retreated from the bedroom. She was covered in blood and meconium. The newborn's two older siblings fled at the sight of her.

She slumped onto a settle perched in front of a cold fireplace. Later, when the afterbirth had been delivered and the babe had nursed, her father sat down next to his daughter. He put his arm protectively around her shoulders. She snuggled up against him. They did not speak for a long time.

At last he said, "We, your Mom and I, will never say an unkind word about Doc—not as long as we live."

Emma heard this promise and put her hand over her father's heart. "Thank you, Daddy."

"You two saved that boy's life." He looked at her. "You've got the gift. You're better, so much better than I was at your age." He paused, to let the compliment soak in. She nuzzled closer to him. "I remember my first day as a Journeyman. Grandpa took me aside, looked me in the eye, said I knew the right things, told me I had to learn when to act and when to wait. It's taken me years to learn the art."

He was talking mostly to himself now. Still, Emma listened. "You've still got plenty to learn. Your judgment is good, very, very good, but there is so much more to learn."

"I know, Daddy."

He mussed her thick locks. Outside the window, dawn was breaking. "Ready?" he asked, then looked down at his daughter's heavy-lidded eyes. "You rest. I'll tell Mom all about it." He covered her with a light blanket. It looked to him like one of Val's. He checked again on the baby and his mother and, satisfied that they were well, headed home.

It was mid-morning when Emma woke with a start. The house was bustling around her. She thought of the newborn baby boy, threw off the covers, and stood up. In the bedroom, mother and child slept. Outside, Emma consulted with the father and the village women. The lochia was moderate, the baby was nursing well. "Here," they said. "Some clean clothes. You go on. It'll be fine."

Out on the Turnpike a fresh breeze blew from the west, signaling cooler weather ahead. There would be rain by the end of the week. She made her way down to the stream that came out of the high ground between Hardbottle and Crickhollow. She stripped then tied her blood-soaked clothes into a bundle. She plunged into the cool water and washed herself clean. Doc appeared on the stream bank, as she knew he would.

She spoke to him. "Dad says it's OK. You don't have to hide anymore." The horse ambled around to the village side of the stream, placing himself athwart the footpath. Emma laughed and lay on her back in the water, drinking in mouthfuls then spitting them like fountains into the air. When she was finished, she dressed and slung the bundle of laundry over her shoulder. She climbed onto Doc's back in a single fluid motion. Together they passed out of the wooded glen, the stallion loping across the irregular terrain, more like a wolf than a horse.

When they reached the Turnpike, they were just below Crickhollow at the edge of the Shire. Doc pranced across the earthen road. He was from the high country and found the road tantalizing. Emma read his thoughts, leaned forward and whispered, *Cha*. Doc sprang forward. They flew past Crickhollow. Doc stretched out, as if his legs were discovering something ancient, well-known to his forebears but new to him, something in his blood.

They took the middle of the road, owned it. Neither horse nor rider was inclined to cede an inch of their territory. They scattered children and apprentices, bathing them in the cloud of dust they left in their wake.

At Hardbottle they shot past a train of milk wagons, startling horses and teamsters alike. Below Summer Hill, the road leveled itself. Emma delighted in the combination of the warm sun falling down upon her from high above and the cool breeze that swept past her as they galloped. The wind swept her hair out behind like a trailing flag. She felt good, so alive, so free.

Emma closed her eyes, tipped her head back, arms clinched tight against Doc's rippling neck. People fled the road before them, scarcely believing what they were seeing. A wild horse, unbridled, unshod, and at full stride with Emma Thomas on his unsaddled back, blissfully unaware of the mayhem they were creating.

Below Bag's End, they raced past the mill and the line of horses, drivers, and wagons laden with summer wheat. Then came the long downhill slope that would drop them into Bywater. Emma thought that Doc might break his stride at last, but he did not. He knew they were close, and the slope was a wind at his back.

The pair came crashing down the narrow lane that led to the Auntie's place alongside Mad Brook. Doc slowed just enough to allow Emma to leap safely from his back. Fifty yards on, he plunged into the forest.

Haleigh had witnessed this arrival, had seen her niece's windblown ecstasy.

Emma ran to her, eyes wide. "Just a few minutes ago I was in Crickhollow!"

Her Aunt nodded toward the hoe that leaned up against the fence and answered, "You're in Bywater now."

Two days later, Emma stopped by Summer Hill to see her grandparents. She came in through the front door and found the big old house standing empty. This came as no surprise. On a day like today, they'd be sitting on the back porch talking, as Grandpa always said, "about old people, old times, and old ways." Emma stepped out onto the stone back patio, letting the screen door slam behind her. The sound woke her grandfather from a nap, as she knew it would. Emma plopped down in the empty chair beside him. "Where's Grandma?"

Bill gave a snort of pretend disappointment. "What am I, chopped liver?"

Emma laughed. "No! I just thought you'd both be home—for once."

"Went with Tom Morris down to Crickhollow, doing a portrait of a mother and her new son. But you know all about that, don't you?"

Emma blushed slightly. "Yeah."

"Your Dad came by yesterday, told me about it." He looked at her, so impossibly young with so much ahead of her. "I'm proud of you."

"Thanks, Grandpa."

"You're gonna be alright." He sighed and looked out on the green sward topped by a deep blue sky. "When I was coming up they said you had to shine the seat of your pants, study hard to be a doctor."

Emma said, "Mmm hmm."

"Met your grandmother in a library. Yeah, you know the story."

"I know it by heart. I love that story."

Quietly, he said, "Me too." Bill roused himself from his memories and turned to the task at hand. "That horse of yours, he's really something."

"He's not mine. He's not...he belongs to himself, just like me, just like you."

Bill nodded. "Good, very good. I hear you two caused quite a stir on the Turnpike."

Emma wanted to deny it, wanted to protect Doc. "It wasn't much. A few people had to get out of the way, no big deal. People shouldn't be so sensitive. The Turnpike belongs to everyone."

Bill let her weak denial hang in the air until it was gone.

"No matter, my darling. Just thought I'd mention it. Folks have been talking about it, thought you should know."

"Folks are always talking about something."

"So true," Bill agreed. Again, he let silence do its work. Then, abruptly, "Anyway, I've been thinking about the future—your future, Doc's future."

Emma was happy to change the subject.

"My future?"

"Yep."

She looked at him. He seemed small to her now. He was nearly bald, with tufts of wispy white hair, and a beard gone all white. It was too long and Grandma would be on him to trim it, if she wasn't already.

"Been thinking," he continued, "that your Grandma Wallace knew all of the back ways between all the villages of the Shire."

"All of 'em," Emma agreed brightly.

"If I'm not mistaken, she taught them all to you—before she passed."

Emma thought of Kianna and missed her suddenly and terribly. "She did."

"Might be a good idea for you and your friend to practice those back ways."

The idea thrilled Emma to her core. "Post Rider," she said softly. "You think I, we, might get to be Post Riders?"

Her grandfather nodded sagely.

Emma checked her excitement. "Mom and Dad won't ever allow it." She looked earnestly at the old man sitting next to her and said with grim certainty, "They are way too protective."

Bill suppressed a laugh. "Semper Paratus," he said.

Emma ran quickly through her rudimentary Latin. "Always...what?"

"Ready. Always ready."

"Semper Paratus."

"Be a shame if the opportunity came and you and Doc weren't ready." Bill watched Emma absorb the idea. There was, he knew, no need to point out that folks on the Turnpike would also be much happier not having to worry about being run down by a crazy black stallion.

Emma stood. She was excited, eager to be off.

"Gotta go. Tell Grandma I'm sorry I missed her." She bent down and kissed him gently on top of the head.

"I will."

He watched her sprint across the meadow, heard her whistle for Doc. The stallion came swiftly to her side, bent his head low as she whispered into his ear. She climbed atop him, and a moment later they disappeared over the hill.

He realized he was hungry and went inside, well-satisfied.

Eron Wallace tapped the screen and reread the call summary:

Call Origin: Classified
Call Destination: Eron Wallace, Director of Broadcast Justice Programming
Call Timestamp: 06/12/2041 Start: 18:36.02 Finish: 19:11.04
Call Transcript:
　　SF: Hold for Department of Security and Justice Director Peterson.
　　EW: I'll...I'll hold.
　　SF: Director Peterson on the line.
　　OP: Good evening, Mr. Wallace. I hope I haven't disturbed your dinner.
　　EW: No, sir. Not at all. {EMOSENSOR: Anxiety—Moderate}
　　OP: I love the show and I've been following your career for a while now. Great stuff.
　　EW: Thank you, sir.
　　OP: Listen, I've got an opening. Deputy Director, it's...quite unexpected, really, and I'd like you to move up, join my team.
　　EW: I'd be honored, sir. {EMOSENSOR: Relief—Intense}
　　OP: We'll need you here next week. Oh, and if you want to bring a staffer or two of your own along, that's fine.
　　EW: Yes, sir.
　　OP: Welcome aboard, Wallace. Samantha? Follow up with Deputy Director Wallace, make sure he has what he needs.
　　SF: Yes, sir.
　　OP: We'll meet next week and review your areas of responsibility.
　　EW: I will be there, ready to go, sir. {EMOSENSOR: Loyalty—High}
　　OP: I don't doubt it, Wallace. Until then.

39
THE RIDING HOOD
Spring, 2043

Val was certain she'd never been this way with her mother. Things were different when she was young. From the moment she met Jude Thomas, the Shire had been a haven to her. The thought of leaving it never crossed her mind. But Emma was different. She had known only the Shire's safety and security and she bridled at its limits. The weather had broken and the Post Riders would soon be moving again. The trouble between them would be out in the open, again. They sat together at the breakfast table, making small talk, but Val knew what was coming.

Emma took a deep breath. "Mom, I'm old enough to run my own life. Eighteen is old enough."

"Your father was twenty-five when he rode post the first time," Val reminded her. "And your uncles, older still. It was safer back in those days."

Emma could not imagine waiting another seven years.

"Listen, Mom." Emma smiled and took her mother's hands into hers. "I know it's my time. I can feel it. I was born to do this. It's in my blood."

Val drew a heavy sigh and stared up at the wood ceiling. "Yes, my dear child, it's your blood that I am worried about. You hear the stories the Post Riders tell, you know them all by heart, but you forget the danger is real. The wolves, the Militia, the Brotherhood, the Xenos, the wilderness—it's too much, too much at your age."

Emma bristled. "If I was a boy you'd let me go."

"That's not true."

A sullen silence filled the air. Emma let go of her mother's hands—so like her own—and turned away.

In truth, Emma's gender made no difference. Val knew that her daughter could outthink, outride, and outlast any and all of the boys her age. And that horse, the two of them had a savage devotion to each other. Doc would give his life to save Emma's. The fact was Val simply could not face the prospect of losing her only child. She needed Emma to be near, to stay in the Shire. She needed her to be safe.

"I'm going to the Aunties' for a while." Emma said. Val felt a wave of relief. This was how these things usually ended. Emma would slip away to Bywater and in time Haleigh and Hannah would help her see reason. "OK," Val agreed.

Val knew someday she would have to let her go. If things went well, there would be a boy, a good boy from the Shire, maybe David Bowen from Hardbottle. She knew he was interested in Emma. He would make a good husband. Her little Emma would be grown, but still nearby. Her daughter would know what it was to be a mother, and the idea of riding post would fade.

Val heard Doc whinny, and the back door slammed a moment later.

A visit with the Aunties offered a peculiar kind of healing that appealed to more than a few of the people of the Shire. Their snug round stone house was built in the earliest years of the Shire. Its sod roof looked alive with the new spring even though it was already more than a half a century old. Haleigh and Hannah, people said, made more out of less than anyone else. Their home was surrounded by patches of lush green gardens. Dwarf fruit orchards, bee hives, a potting shed, rain barrels, compost heaps, and a hen house—all on less than an acre.

The next day a late spring chill took hold. Most of the evening was occupied by the tedious task of covering tender seedlings with tarps so the frost, if it came, could not get at them. When the work was done, the Aunties went inside to start a late supper, but Emma lingered out of doors. The intense blue of the spring sky was fading in the west. The sun was down, but its light lingered as if unwilling to surrender this one day to the night that must follow. She could smell the earth and thought she could feel its yearning, for it was her own. Spring was a time to throw off restraints and embrace all of the life yet to be lived. She breathed deep. There was peace in this garden and, Emma felt certain, peace in the wide world. Her eye caught the flutter of a song sparrow, a female, just returned from the South as it settled comfortably on the branch of a pear tree. She eyed the lone human without fear. The tiny creature had traveled thousands of miles, faced all kinds of danger, and survived. It thrived. Emma pouted. She was marooned, a cosseted prisoner of the Shire. She let a wave of self-pity wash over her.

Emma heard Hannah puttering about in the kitchen and knew she should go inside to help. One last look at the changing sky showed her Venus hanging low in the west, a dusky jewel—so beautiful, so far away.

The table was laid for supper. A jug of hard cider sat uncorked—it had been a good year for cider—surrounded by three earthen mugs each waiting expectantly for its fill. A tureen of black bean soup spiced with leaks and dandelion greens raised an enticing mist. Haleigh's loaf of thick black bread, still uncut, sat next to the butter. A spiced tart lay hidden under a towel. Emma busied herself with the preparations and could not help but notice Haleigh's absence from the kitchen. She seemed to be occupied by some business in the bedroom as Emma could hear random thuds, bangs, and scrapes emanating from that direction

Once the table was set, Haleigh appeared and the three sat and ate in an appreciative silence. After dessert the dishes were washed and put away. Haleigh built a fire to guard against the night's chill, and Emma settled into the rocker next to Haleigh. Both women let the flames take their thoughts where they would until, at last, Haleigh spoke.

"What's your name, girl?"

Haleigh's questions did not demand spoken answers. They were, rather, invitations to take one's mind in a new direction.

Emma thought, *I am Emma Jane Thomas. I am named for the Emma of Kallimos.*

The fire popped, and a shower of sparks fled up the chimney.

I am named after the great Peacemaker of Kallimos, the woman who stood before the angry mob and helped them remember reason and compassion.

Emma shifted in her seat. The contrast grated on her. She was named for a brave and mighty woman, but what had she done, what would she ever be allowed to do, that could measure up to her namesake? The young woman's foot tapped on the stone floor in annoyance. Haleigh remained silent. Then when this mood too seemed about to pass, Hannah entered the room.

"I've been thinking," she said, "of my old friend Ned Wolff. Had a dream about him, and wanted him to know it." Hannah held a post in her hand.

A half of a smile crept across Haleigh's face as she gasped. "I believe," she said, "my old riding hood is hanging by the door, jet black, should go well with that wild soul you call a friend."

"But I..."

Hannah spoke again, smoothly and with great confidence, "Haleigh and I realized we haven't seen your Mom and Dad in a while. I suppose we could visit them tomorrow."

Haleigh agreed. "Yes, I think we will."

Emma's heart pounded like a hammer. She stood. Her mouth opened and closed once, twice.

Hannah slid into her seat by the fire. The house that, only moments before, had seemed to confine her so unfairly suddenly felt warm and cozy, so safe and full of love. But the Aunties were right; it was time to go. Emma coughed nervously and walked to the door. The cloak was there, right where Haleigh had promised it would be. She hesitated for a moment as images of the next morning swept across her mind's eye. The Aunties would arrive with a gift, probably a jar of honey. Her parents would know everything from the moment they saw them. The Aunties would be kind and gentle. They would say little, but everyone would know—Emma had left the Shire and was riding post. It would be alright.

With a sigh that was heavier than she had expected, Emma pulled the cloak over her shoulders and fastened the catch. The door swung easily on its handmade hinges and the night air greeted her so cool and fresh, so free.

40

THE DIRECTOR'S CHAIR
Fall, 2043

It wasn't luck, he reminded himself. He deserved the promotion. The half-wits that surrounded him might work for the DSJ, but he *was* the DSJ. The GRID demanded loyalty and rewarded it. The old man had grown lazy, soft. The old man had doubted. In the end, Peterson had made the mistake of sharing his doubts with his deputy. Now a new Director sat behind the gleaming black acrylic desk. The others had been afraid. He had acted. Now the job was his.

Who would be his deputy? Who would be given the honor of sitting at the right hand of the GRID's Lord of Fear, its Master of Control? The question was not new to him. Like any sufficiently ambitious man, Eron had often imagined himself sitting exactly where he was sitting now. He had studied his co-workers carefully. He knew the senior staff better, he suspected, than many of them knew themselves. The new Director swung his chair around until he faced the vast plate glass window that overlooked the city, his city now. With great care, he sorted the prospects in his mind.

Jones would be the obvious choice. The man had talent. He was smart, aggressive, and cunning. In fact, it was likely the rat bastard understood Eron would not tolerate his presence and was already planning his own next move. The man was dangerous and would need to be watched wherever Eron sent him, probably to Communications.

Reynolds had skills; she was solid, he knew that. He knew she'd twist the knife if he told her to and do it with her cloying good cheer, but, honestly, she annoyed him. A woman as his Deputy? The thought disturbed him. He might, in a moment of weakness, shy from disposing of her properly when she was no longer useful. He would keep her where she was.

Perkins was old and had too many old habits, too many old stories. He was a declining asset and thus not worthy of a rising 36-year-old GRID superstar. What about Knox? The gangly young section chief had handled the Atlanta situation well. He was competent, but not brilliant. Tall, thin, pale, blue eyes, blond hair—Eron hated the way he looked, but was willing to see beyond mere appearance. Knox was clumsily unsure of himself in so many ways, a useful trait. Eron knew that Knox was without guile—he could read the man's face like a book. Best of all, Knox was one of his own. He had been with him since his days on The Trial. Capable, guileless, and eager to please—it made a nice package.

Eron closed his eyes and let the decision settle. As it did, he could feel that it was right. There was no need to delay. In fact, the Chairman would be pleased when he learned how quickly the Deputy's post had been filled.

The Director leaned forward and keyed the intercom. "Samantha, get me Knox."

"Yes, sir." Her answer was scented with the faintest trace of flirtation; the voice that once had been reserved for Peterson alone now belonged to him. Eron Wallace smiled.

Minutes later Knox rapped on the Director's door. "Come in." Eron let his voice boom the way Peterson's had once boomed. He was in command and meant for Knox to understand this from the start.

Knox swung the door open. The Director eyed the young man as he entered. The pale blue eyes were held wide with nervous anticipation and fear. Knox also failed to suppress his surprise when he saw Eron sitting at what had been Peterson's desk. It was a perfect start.

"Sit down." The Director gestured at the chair in front of his desk. "Peterson has, ahh...retired. It was his health. Quite sudden. Looking forward to more time with his family."

Knox nodded blankly. "I see."

Again, Eron was glad to find that Knox did not see.

"The Chairman has asked me to serve as the new Director of the DSJ."

Knox clutched the arms of his chair like a man at sea, grasping for a fixed point. "Congratulations, sir," Knox said, with just enough enthusiasm.

The Director smiled through pursed lips. "I've been watching you, Knox. Watching you closely."

Knox greeted this news with silence, not sure where it was leading.

"And I think you've got what it takes."

"What it takes for what, sir?"

"I want you to be my deputy."

This surprised Knox, but he answered quickly. "I would be honored."

"Right, then. You'll pick up the work I was engaged with as deputy. You may not be aware of this, but the previous Director had placed me in charge of convoy security and uncertified personal travel."

"I can do that."

"I will deal with the entire range of matters with which the Department is concerned."

"Of course."

"You can have my old office. I'll have Samantha arrange for it to be cleared out. Plan to move in tomorrow morning."

"Thank you, sir."

Knox's natural caution was leeching the excitement out of the moment. The young man had not been thrilled the way Eron had been when he was awarded the Deputy's office. The Director closed his eyes for a moment of reflection and chased his misgivings away. It was better this way. Knox was being given something that was apparently beyond what he allowed himself to dream. The man would be a safer deputy than Eron had supposed.

"Fine then." Eron offered a genuine smile. "Get settled in and prepare a briefing for me on the travel and convoy issues. Be ready by Friday."

With that Knox brightened considerably. This was something he knew he could do, and do well.

"Have Samantha set up a time for us to meet on Friday."

Knox stood awkwardly, a jangle of arms and legs. On his way out he turned and said, this time with real enthusiasm, "Thank you, Director—you won't be sorry."

"I'm sure I won't."

Knox closed the door carefully behind him and was gone.

The next two days passed in a frenzy of work as Knox struggled to master the arcane rules governing the movement of people and supplies between Demos. In general, the Xenos were never to leave their compounds, but there were certain exceptions and, of course, convoy personnel were constantly on the move. Corporate Militia went where sent—where they were needed—no questions asked.

At 3:03 pm on Friday afternoon, Eron drummed his fingers on his desk's gleaming black surface. Knox was late—it was a perfect start.

Two minutes later, Samantha buzzed in. "The Deputy Director is here to see you, sir."

The Director's razor-blade voice answered. "Send him in."

Knox arrived bearing an armload of clipboard computers, each dedicated to a specific transport function. When he tried to sit down, Knox lost his grip on several of the tablets and they crashed onto the marble flooring.

Eron snorted with contempt and turned away so that his chair's high leather back faced Knox.

"Jesus Christ, Knox. Can't you do anything right? You're late. I ask you to do one goddamn thing for me. ONE THING!" Eron roared the last phrase, hoping Samantha would hear him.

"I'm sorry, sir, it's just that..."

"Spare me your goddamn excuses, Knox."

"Yes, sir."

"Do you think you can actually find your notes on UPT activity? Did you even make any notes? You do know what UPT stands for don't you?" The Director lowered his voice as if he was talking to a small child. "Unauthorized Personal Travel, Knox. I did ask for a report on it."

"Yes, sir, and I have been studying the situation very carefully." The Director's back remained turned. Knox fumbled with the stylus, trying to bring up the relevant documents. He steeled himself and began, "Well, it seems that two types of UPT have been identified."

"Go ahead."

"First, there are the organized units or bands that engage in systemic intra-transportation corridor activity."

"Jesus Christ, Knox," the Director muttered. "You mean the Brotherhood."

Knox blushed, he hadn't expected the Director, whom he knew was a stickler for propriety, to use the slang term. "Right, sir, the 'Brotherhood.' Well, the good news is that my statistical analysis of their most recent activity shows just a five percent increase over the past twelve months. You can review the charts if you like."

"Uhh, please." Eron's voice dripped with disdain.

"Well, sir," Knox continued as if the Director had not spoken, "I call the other category informal uncertified personnel travel, or IUPT." Knox let a thin crescent of a prideful smile emerge. He liked that, 'IUPT.' "That data is very spotty and shows no clear trend." The Director grunted.

Now Knox took a deep breath because he could feel he was entering into dangerous terrain. He cleared his throat. "So, I have developed a plan."

The Director did not respond. Knox plunged ahead, eager to fill the silence.

"I've figured out how to eradicate the Brotherhood. Working on a sector by sector basis, we can cut off their seasonal migration and drop their activity by, according to my calculations, by more than 95 percent."

The leather chair began to turn. First in profile, then straight on, the Director's face came into view. Eron leaned forward and lowered his voice almost to a whisper. "Knox," he breathed, "is your mother an idiot? Is your father an imbecile? Do you descend from an entire line of freaking morons?"

Knox stiffened. "No, sir."

"I'd say that any person as stupid as you would have to come from a family of morons. It's the only explanation I can come up with."

Knox grimly held his composure.

Now the Director leaned back in his chair and steepled his fingers.

"Knox, you know what your problem is?"

Knox didn't answer. The Director didn't want an answer.

"You don't think—that's your problem, Knox. Now I don't know if it's a matter of can't think or won't think and I suppose it doesn't really matter. All I do know is that a bag of hammers could outsmart you."

The Director began to rock gently in his fine leather chair and its steel springs squeaked meekly beneath him.

"The Brotherhood is important to us. They serve a function, actually, a very valuable function. They exist to put a face on fear. We don't have to pay them, we don't have to manage them. All we have to do is tolerate their bullshit, indulge their stupid little Robin Hood fantasies, and in return, we can use them to scare the living shit out of the Xenos."

Knox nodded, as if he already knew this.

"Now, I've listened to your little brain fart. I should fire you for it, I really should, but I won't. You're too damn stupid. I don't know what would happen if I did fire your sorry ass. You'd probably starve to death if I wasn't around to remind you to stuff your own goddamned pie hole."

Knox swallowed hard.

"I want you to get the hell out of my office. Go back to work—if you can call it that. I want you to pop the Brotherhood on the nose. Remind them of their proper place and then throw a scare into the Xenos. Do you think you can do that?"

Knox bobbed his head slowly, up and down.

"Fine. Report back to me next Friday." With that he swung his chair back around.

Knox was excused.

Two days later the news went out over the GRID:

The Director of the Department of Security and Justice confirmed the existence of an aggressive new campaign aimed at eradicating the so-called 'Brotherhood' who continue to terrorize legitimate travel and shipments along certified transportation corridors. We've all heard the stories of convoys being attacked, precious supplies of food and medicine being stolen, and men and women being tortured, raped, and killed by these barbaric thugs. This plague must be eliminated.

The DSJ reminds everyone that Uncertified Personnel Travel remains not only illegal but also extremely dangerous. Throughout this campaign, Demo Fence and Gate patrols will remain on high alert.

41
50 CALIBER

George Johnson, the Big Man of the Brotherhood, grunted as he heaved himself into the driver's side of his rusted red four-wheel-drive pickup. The torn upholstery exposed crumbling yellow foam padding in half a dozen places. Once he was settled behind the wheel, he grabbed hold of the cracked rear view mirror, twisting it until his pride and joy came into view. No longer was the pickup's bed a clutter of wadded up tarps and miscellaneous tools. The junk had been cleared away. In its place stood his shiny new gun.

Fifty-caliber. Fifty-damn-caliber.

The Brotherhood—his brotherhood—had fallen on hard times. Protein paste and supplements were down. They were on half rations. Flavorings ran out months ago so what they did get to eat tasted like crap. They had five drums of diesel and twenty thirsty engines. There was talk. He heard it when people didn't know he was listening. "Maybe old George has lost his touch. Can't go on like this much longer." It wasn't his fault, not really. The trouble was the chumps running the GRID supply convoys had, mysteriously, rediscovered their spines.

Now he had the answer.

George glanced into the mirror, but instead of enjoying his prize, he saw Vazquez waving his arms like a fool. George cut the motor and slid reluctantly out of the cab.

"Hey, Boss. This thing's not ready, not even close." He was a complainer, Vazquez. George eyed him suspiciously. He was five-eight, maybe five-nine, not a bit of fat on him, dark-skinned with jet black hair with a thick wiry beard to match. The really annoying thing about Vazquez was how he was always moving, always thinking, always asking too many damned questions. George hated him.

The young man signaled for George to come toward the truck's side panel. "Look here...and here, man. This is crap. Those bolts are schedule two. They'll snap like toothpicks the first time you move this thing. We need schedule eight." The young man slid deftly around to the other side of the mounting pedestal. "This is quarter-inch steel and rusted to boot. It's got to be reinforced, doubled at least. Otherwise, you're going to crack the support braces."

George grunted, "The guys told me it was ready to go."

"They were wrong."

George slapped his neck. It was hot and the air crawled with "no-see-ems". Most years they avoided the damn bugs by heading north as soon as the weather turned.

The deadly silent machine towered above both men, its metal barrel glowing blue in the heat.

"Damnit."

"I did the math," Vazquez said. "One shot will tear this all apart. I don't think you can even drive it off-road like this."

In the background George could hear Vinnie's little girl crying. He knew she was hungry.

The pressure was killing him. The easy thing, the easy thing for everyone concerned would be to give up. They could just surrender to the GRID. They would make a stink, trot them all out in front of the cameras, and have them spout a little propaganda. Eventually they'd all be resettled. He knew others who had done it. Anyway, they said they were going to do it. But really, who knew for sure? He grunted and looked away. Nah, it wasn't for him, or his people. It just wasn't. They were proud. They were off the GRID. They took what they wanted and moved on. It was their way.

Vazquez coughed, and they both knew the sound was meant to bring George back to the here and now.

The younger man said, "Kavan's got a sheet of half-inch steel plate. It's about the right size. We've got to pull the gun off, peel the deck back, and weld the plate to the frame. I sent Jean out to find a place where we could tap the fence out of sight, and she says there's a good spot up the road eight, maybe ten miles."

"North?"

"Yeah."

George squinted into the bright sunshine and studied the youth, again.

The kid was smart. Better than smart, really. He was clever. Got along with everybody. Nobody else seemed to have a problem with him.

"Listen...ahh...George, we're set to start. We can have this rigged by nightfall, but we have to get going."

"Yeah, kid. Good thinking," George said with more enthusiasm than he felt. He handed Vazquez the keys to the truck. "Let me know when it's done."

"Sure, Boss."

Vazquez snatched the keys and leapt out of the bed of the truck in a single thoughtless motion. A moment later, the engine roared to life. Vazquez rolled the window down.

"Be back soon."

George grunted and turned his back on the cloud of dust the pickup left in its wake.

He remembered when they found Jerry Vazquez laying on the side of the road covered in blood—half naked, half dead. They would've left him, but Serena felt sorry for him, said the Brotherhood should give him a chance. She nursed him back to life, and now he was one of them.

George pulled a rag from his pocket and mopped his brow. His darling daughter would be waiting for him now. It would be cool inside the tent. She would have something for him to eat, and then he would lie down and rest.

As Vazquez predicted, the truck was ready by nightfall. The heat of the day faded and cool night air crept into the camp. The Brotherhood formed up. Their motley crew of trucks, motorcycles, and cars might not look like much. They weren't all shiny and new like the convoys, but they could haul ass when they wanted to.

Then he called council. These were his best men. He called them the Knights of the Brotherhood. He started with the news. "There'll be a convoy coming down 295 pretty soon. They'll have to slow down to make the change to 695, and there's plenty of good cover there. Word is, it's loaded. Loaded." He emphasized the last word. He gave them his plan.

"Johnny'll hide the men at the overpass."

"Up in the girders?"

"Yeah, that would be great."

Gerorge's first lieutenant, a former Hell's Angel named Kavan Peterson, would be on the gun. "When the lead truck gets to the end of the ramp, unload on it. Blow the hell out of the engine, but don't hit the cab—got that? I don't want Militia coming down on us."

Kavan grinned. "Sure, George."

"Gene, you bring our vehicles and the rest of the men up on the far side after Kavan lights 'em up. Get 'em out and down on the ground."

"Yeah. Hey, George, I'd like to have Vazquez with me. That OK?"

George grimaced. "Gene, come on, man. You know that kid ain't ready. Maybe never will be. Keep him back with the women and kids."

A nervous shuffling communicated the Knighthood's disagreement, but none dared speak.

Billowing satin clouds obscured a full moon. The men crouched in their hiding places, waiting, listening. Then from the north came the sound of a convoy, good sized, moving fast, but not too fast.

George looked at his watch—it was on schedule. He smiled at his lieutenants, his stomach churning with nervous anticipation.

Just as he had predicted, the lead truck rounded the gentle curve of the exit ramp slowing down to make the turn. "Ready...ready...now!"

Thud. Thud. Thud. Thud. The slugs pierced the engine block. Oil spattered the engine compartment and quickly caught fire. The convoy slammed to a halt.

The Brotherhood dropped out of the girders and, in an instant, surrounded the convoy. It was a dozen vehicles long with three tankers, five panel-sided tractor-trailers, and the usual pathetic convoy guard van bringing up the rear. Kavan wielded his bullhorn expertly. "Everybody out! Everybody on the ground! We got a big gun on you and you try anything—I mean anything— and we'll blow you all to hell!"

People got down.

"Hey, they got booze!"

When the Brotherhood's vehicles pulled up alongside the supply convoy, the looting began in earnest. Vazquez jumped out of the lead truck and clambered into the now empty cab of the convoy's fuel tanker. Five minutes later, the engine roared to life. Vazquez called to Gene, "Got it started. Get somebody up here who can drive this thing."

"Holy shit!" Gene hopped up and down with glee. Vazquez raced to the protein tanker. Time was running short. They'd need to run soon.

That engine came alive.

Then the raid was over. The convoy's tires were slashed and the Brotherhood roared away. No one on either side had been injured, but for the first time in the history of the Brotherhood, a fuel tanker and a protein truck had not just been looted but stolen outright.

They raced north through the night hoping to make safe harbor just north of Charlotte.

Then they slept.

The celebration that began the next evening became legend. They had food and fuel not for a week or two, but for an entire season. George ate and drank but without pleasure. His eyes were fixed on Vazquez. His annoyance curdled into disgust as he watched the Brotherhood—his people—flit around that little prick like moths chasing a flame. Sure Vazquez had pulled a first, jacking the ignition controls not just once, but twice. But what about that? George nursed the suspicion that Vazquez was a mole, a spy, sent from the GRID to infiltrate and destroy them. His gaze wandered to Serena, his darling little girl. She was ogling the damn fool. She was as bad as the rest of them.

Then George Johnson got drunk.

The night wore on. The rebels grew more boisterous, and George's anger kept pace.

It was nearly dawn when George stood, swaying on the spot, and commanded the attention of the Brotherhood

He shook the alcohol from his speech, letting his anger burn bright.

"Today is a new day." The Brotherhood responded with a euphoric drunken cheer. "I congratulate my brothers and sisters for the blow we have landed against the GRID. Our gun is a mighty thing. The convoys don't have anything like it and never will. They will learn to fear us—to fear the might of the Brotherhood." A joyful woozy whoop filled the night air. "I would be entirely happy, but for one thing. One person prevents me from being happy." George Johnson pointed at Vazquez.

"We have among us a man who remains a stranger. A man about whom we know almost nothing. A man I suspect of treason." The drunken finger wagged accusingly at Vazquez. Feet shuffled, people looked away. "You. I don't trust you. I don't like you. You are not one of us, and you never will be one of us." George Johnson spoke softly. His words pulsed with hate.

Jerry Vazquez swallowed hard but said nothing.

The party was over.

George Johnson staggered to the tent he shared with Serena. His fury spent, he fell into the sleep of the dead.

The summer was good, very good, for the Brotherhood. Rich supplies of food and fuel let them wander freely. They shared their good fortune and their knowledge with other bands of the Brotherhood whenever they met them. The gun let them have their way with any convoy anytime they chose to attack. George was the Big Man of the Brotherhood, maybe the biggest.

They traveled from York to Scranton, to Binghamton and Albany, then to Hartford and Boston, up to Portland and Montreal, over to Ottawa and Toronto, down to Buffalo and Syracuse, until the chill of autumn hung in the morning air.

Soon it would be time to head south.

Emma rode post for most of the summer. She and Doc had visited Cobleskill, Canastota, Cazenovia, Skaneateles, Cortland, Ithaca, Elmira, Corning, and Delhi. Her parents gradually accepted the life their child had chosen for herself. When she wasn't riding, Emma continued her studies with her father. Caleb passed his knowledge of medicine to his daughter in the careful, methodical manner he had learned from his father. Soon she would know most of what he knew and would be able to see what he saw, but he also recognized that Emma had something more. Kianna, gone four years now, had left her granddaughter in possession of the name and the properties of every plant in the Shire. Emma instinctively blended Kianna's herbalism with her father's medical knowledge. Inside her, those traditions became something new.

When the harvest was in, it was time to ride again. The Elders prepared a satchel full of posts for Ned Wolff. Ithaca would be her first stop. The second night's ride brought her to I-81. She proceeded carefully knowing that even this late in the year it was possible the Brotherhood might still be in the area. Emma took great care to remain unseen. Being elusive as a ghost passing in the night was a point of pride for all Post Riders. The Brotherhood was there, camped in one of their favorite hiding places. Emma sent Doc off and crept close to the camp's perimeter. The sentries saw nothing as her cloaked form passed between them. Once inside the perimeter, she ambled nonchalantly into the center of the encampment.

George Johnson, lost deep in thought, nearly bumped into her. "Damn you Post Riders," he grumbled. "Always sneaking around."

Emma smiled sweetly. "It's what we do—George."

Her voice startled him. This girl was young. He looked at her and realized he had never seen her before. It annoyed him that she knew his name. He snapped at her, "Someday you're going to wake up, get yourself some real hardware and travel in style—the way the Brotherhood does."

Emma dodged the jab. "Ahhh...the Brotherhood? Too fast for us. We'd never catch up."

"Damn right," the Boss said.

The mouth smiled, the eyes did not.

Emma knew George Johnson from the stories her father and uncles had told her about him. George Johnson, Boss of the Brotherhood, was a big, hearty man who boiled with life. This man was care-worn, afraid. Something was wrong, and she decided to find out more. Guiding him so gently he did not realize what was happening, she led him to the perimeter of the camp.

When they were out of earshot of the others, George's gruff voice dropped to a whisper.

"Umm...didn't expect any damn Post Riders, but I sure am glad you came by." Emma waited for him to say more, studying his face, watching him struggle against his emotions. "What's your name, girl?"

She answered truthfully, "I am Emma Thomas of the Shire."

A flicker of recognition passed over the man's face. "Your Dad is Caleb, the doctor, right?"

"He is."

"Yeah, well, we've known him for ages, good man, for a Post Rider. We heard about you since you was little. Didn't know you were all grown up, riding post now for the Underground. Damn." Clearly, there was more on George Johnson's mind than the coming of age of Emma Thomas. "Anyway," George cleared his throat, "your Dad bragged you up as a healer, bragged you up plenty of times."

"I do what I can."

A haunted look crept across his face. "Ya see, it's Serena, my girl—my little girl. Well, she's not so little anymore, all grown up, too, like you." Tears came to his eyes. George blinked hard and looked away.

Emma waited.

"Something's wrong with my little girl. I know something's wrong. She's sick. Sick as hell. I just know it. We've got no healers here and..."

"I'd be happy to see her," Emma replied gently.

Now the smile was real.

"I knew it. I knew you would." Cheerfully, he added, "Chip off old Caleb's block, I'd say." George took Emma by the arm and escorted her through the camp, proud as a peacock. The pair entered the tent he shared with his daughter. The light was dim until George fingered a switch and an electric bulb snapped on. The room was tidy. Its simple furnishings had been arranged with comfort in mind. Boxes of hijacked provisions filled the space under the eaves. Everything was in order. Then Emma saw Serena. She was young, small, and pretty, with thick wiry hair like her father's. But she was also painfully thin and pale—even in this light. A bucket stood next to the head of the cot on which she lay.

George reached out and touched his daughter's shoulder. "Sweetie, guess what? Daddy found a healer for you. She's gonna make you better." George pointed to Emma. "She's Caleb's daughter...you remember him? He taught her how to doctor. She's real smart."

Emma knelt down and took Serena's hands into hers. "I'm here to help." Serena looked at Emma, her eyes pleading for something. George pulled his favorite folding chair close to them and plunked it down.

Emma understood.

She turned to face George. "You know, I would never think of looking over your shoulder when you were working on one of your trucks."

"Uh huh," George agreed.

"So I need you to leave during my examination."

George's brow wrinkled. "Well, you could watch me fix my truck if you wanted to."

"I'm sure it would be fascinating, but Serena is my patient, not a truck. I will thank you to leave. I'll speak with you when we are finished."

"But..."

"No buts." Emma showed the hulking man to the tent's front flap.

She returned to Serena's side. "Talk to me."

"I'm just so sick, tired all the time. And food, food smells terrible. I feel like I'm gonna die."

"Have you talked to your mother about this?"

Serena looked away. "My mother's dead. Died when...died when she was having me."

"I'm so sorry." Emma studied the girl carefully. "Would you lay on your back for me?"

Serena did as she was asked.

Emma laid her skilled hands on the woman's soft belly. "When was your last period?"

"Sometime this summer, I think. Haven't had it in a while, so that's one thing to be thankful for."

Cupped hands pressed hard into Serena's lower abdomen and the Midwife found what she was looking for. Emma reached for the chair that George had left behind.

"Dear Serena," Emma began, "you are pregnant."

The girl's already pale face blanched. She whimpered pitifully, closing her eyes tight against the world. Emma continued delicately, "Should I assume that this is not welcome news?"

Serena's eyes welled with tears. "The baby is Jerry's. I love him and he loves me, but Daddy hates him, hates him more than anything."

Emma was not surprised. A father, a daughter, and a lover—it was a very old story.

"Does Jerry know?"

Serena shrugged her shoulders.

"Might he suspect?"

"He might."

Emma looked into Serena's eyes. "There's more you need to know." Serena tensed as if for a blow. "It's not one baby, it's two. You're carrying twins."

Serena sobbed. "You don't know what Daddy's like. He'll kill Jerry. He might even..." Serena choked back a sob. "He might even kill me."

Emma gave Serena the time she needed. She held Serena's hand, closed her eyes, and remembered. Though she was just nineteen-years-old, Emma Thomas knew thousands of stories. She heard the Elders of the Shire tell them, again and again, in different seasons, for different reasons. Within those stories, she was sure, lay the answer to this problem. She leaned back in her chair and opened her mind to the wisdom of the Elders. In time, Emma thought of Gabrielle Arie from Frogmorton, remembered her story of the Rabbi of Seville. The Inquisition had threatened him with death, but the quick-witted Rabbi had emerged victorious. She recalled her father's stories of George's raging temper, his impulsiveness, his flair for the dramatic, his vanity, and his cunning. Yes, the story would do. At last she opened her eyes, leaned close to Serena and whispered into her ear. "I think I can help you, but it will be dangerous and it might even make things worse."

"Nothing could be worse."

That, Emma knew, was not true. She continued, "Will you trust me?"

There was a shuffling sound outside of the tent, and then came George's voice, tinged with worry. "Emma, you've been in there a long time, what's going on?"

Emma looked again at Serena. "I will need to give your news to everyone, all at once."

The young woman shuddered. "No, no. No you can't! Daddy will kill me. He'll kill us both. You don't know what he can be like."

"It will go much worse for both of you if he finds out privately. I'm sure of it."

Serena looked into the face of the young Midwife and decided to trust her, trust her completely.

She squeezed Emma's hand. "Help me, if you can."

"I've got things I need to do outside. This will take time, quite a bit of time. You need to stay hidden, in here, until it's over. Do not talk to anyone."

Again George bellowed, "What's the hold up? Come on, Emma."

Serena nodded then looked away. "OK."

Emma lifted Serena's limp hair away from her face and touched her gently with the tips of her long, thin fingers. Then she stood and faced the front of the tent. She made a running start and burst the flaps wide open. A startled George Johnson staggered backward. Empowered by her best impression of the Aunties' mysterious taciturnity, she snapped at the big man. "There's much that needs to be said. Tonight, all of the Brotherhood, together in the main tent, understand?"

George nodded numbly. Then he opened his mouth to ask a question.

Emma dismissed him. "No time to waste. She's resting now." She jabbed the big man's chest with her index finger. "Do not disturb her. If you go in there, if anyone goes in there, then it will all be on your hands—all of it. Understand?" George nodded in numb agreement. "I'm going into the forest to get what she needs. Everyone. Tonight." She spun on her heel and disappeared into the forest.

She wandered east, taking the time she needed to gather the herbs that would soothe Serena's nausea. The bank of a small stream offered her a resting place. She sat there working and re-working the complex drama that might save the life of two young lovers and their twins.

At sunset, she returned to the edge of the Brotherhood's camp. In the center of the camp, the Boss busied himself barking orders that served mainly to distract his own worried mind. The flaps to Serena's tent remained closed. As night fell, the last of the Brotherhood scurried into the main tent.

Emma pulled one last breath of forest air deep into her lungs. The buzz of anxious conversation vanished the moment she opened the curtained flaps. She leapt, as silently as a cat, onto the table that stood beside the entrance. She chose to rely on the wisdom of the story of the Rabbi of Seville. When their attention was fixed on her, she plunged them into her story.

"I am a Healer and the daughter of Caleb the Doctor and Post Rider, granddaughter of Kianna Wallace and Jude Thomas," she said. "I was traveling to Ithaca when I came upon your camp. George Johnson told me that his beloved daughter had fallen ill. He asked me to examine her, and that is what I have done." She paused and swept her gaze across the room. "I have informed Serena what I found, and she has given me permission to share the news with all of you." The crowd, all of them friends and family of Serena seemed, almost, to stop breathing. "Serena has a tumor, a fast growing tumor. I fear for her life."

The news fell on them like a wetted lash. George Johnson, his worst fears stewed in hours of anxious anticipation, exploded with a shriek of animal pain. His friends reached for him, braced him against his staggering grief.

Emma asked, "Who here calls Serena Johnson kin?"

Cries of "Aye" and "Here" went up all around.

"Who here calls her friend?" Emma waited as the Brotherhood cheered Serena. "This fine young woman faces the greatest peril any mortal can know. So I ask you, one and all, who will stand by her side?" They swore to it, one and all. Serena could rely on them in her hour of need. They were the Brotherhood—unity was their strength. "I expected no less. Now, listen closely, for there is more to tell."

Emma whispered the news, "The tumor in her belly is new life. Serena is with child."

The Boss fought his way up and onto his feet. He scanned the room, searching for the culprit.

Emma stayed ahead of him. "Jerry Vasquez, come to me." The young man did as he was asked, emerging from the crowd, anxious but resolute. She asked him the question that was on everyone's mind. "Jerry, are you the father?"

He stood tall and answered loud and clear, "I love Serena, and it is my child she carries."

"You! I will kill you!" George lunged for Jerry and would have gotten hold of him if a pair of his most sensible men hadn't taken hold of the Boss, pinned his arms, and held him back. Livid, he turned on Emma. "The hell with her! She's a damn lying witch! Get her down off from there!"

Suspicion and fear fed on each other, strengthened each other, as she knew they would.

A circle of men closed in on her.

"Stop."

They hesitated.

"Are you the people who, a moment ago, claimed to love and cherish Serena? Do you now threaten the Healer who guards her life?" She pointed her long index finger directly at George Johnson. "You sat in darkness until my Uncle Virgil showed you how to take power from the fence." Everyone knew it was true. "What kind of man would now threaten his niece? Gene Lyons was shot up north and would have died if my father hadn't pulled the slug out of his chest." The man gasped involuntarily. Emma glared at him. "How dare you raise your hand against the daughter of the man who saved your life?" He blushed and stepped back. She addressed them all, "If anyone lays a hand on me, none of you will ever see a Post Rider again—not as long as you live."

The moment of danger passed.

Emma commanded the Brotherhood to be seated. Only George and Jerry remained standing. Emma spoke first to the older man. "I understand your anger, but you are a man, not an animal. You are the leader of the Brotherhood. I expect you to behave like the hero these people know you to be." Direct appeals to George's vanity, especially in front of his people, rarely went unrewarded.

"The hero that I am," he repeated slowly.

"I suppose you'd like to be rid of Jerry, banish him for what he has done?"

"Oh, yes I would." The words emerged from between his gritted teeth, sharp and dangerous, like shards of glass.

"Which is greater, George Johnson, your thirst for revenge or your word of honor?"

George boasted again, "I am a man of honor."

Emma nodded then addressed the crowd, "George Johnson's anger burns bright. But I ask you all, what will become of you if the Boss's anger becomes more powerful than his most solemn vow?" People shifted anxiously waiting for Emma to guide them. "We must allow chance, pure chance, to decide the fate of Jerry Vazquez."

The Brotherhood murmured approvingly. People liked Jerry. They wanted this to be fair.

Seeing that the people were against him, George grunted and then agreed.

Emma now commanded them to bring her a marker, two slips of paper, and a small box. When everything was assembled, she turned to George. "You are the leader of the Brotherhood. You should be the one to write BANISHED on one of the slips and WELCOMED on the other. Jerry himself will draw one slip from the bowl. This will decide his fate."

George inspected Emma carefully. She was young—young and incredibly naïve. The girl probably believed in all that Kallimos nonsense to boot. She was from the Shire and, he figured, she never met a man like him before. He was a man who took matters into his own hands. He licked his lips. He would deal with her after her little charade was over. The Boss marked both slips with BANISHED, folded them over, and then held them aloft. "This girl might be one of those crazy Post Riders, but she's right about this. We'll do it her way, and nobody will be able to claim that I did Jerry wrong. He'll get a 50–50 shot and it's more than he deserves."

George stuffed the ballots into the box and handed it to her. She asked, "George Johnson and Jerry Vazquez, do you swear to be bound by this decision?"

They nodded in agreement.

"Swear it out loud, so everyone can hear, banishment with no hope of return or a welcoming as family, the bond to be honored forever."

Jerry was stricken, his eyes pleaded with Emma for help. He spoke weakly, "Yes, I swear."

George raised the ante. "Every member of this Brotherhood, from the youngest to the oldest, will honor the results of this test of fate."

There could be no appeal.

Emma held George Johnson in her gaze and would not release him. She studied his face, analyzed its lines, its motions, and its shadows just the way the Elders had taught her. The man was hiding his true feelings from the Brotherhood. Fortunately, he lacked the ability to hide his feelings from himself. He was proud of his own cunning. A glimmer of satisfaction swept across the man's face. When it was gone, Emma returned the box to George and brought Jerry forward.

George Johnson held it high. "Choose," he commanded.

Jerry trembled uncontrollably. Emma put her arm around him. He did as he was told and reached into the box, felt one piece of paper and then the other, hoping for a sign, finding none.

Then, he chose.

As soon as Jerry's hand left the bowl, the Boss roared, "There! You all see, it is done. His fate is sealed!" In the same moment, Emma reached out and plucked the ballot from Jerry's hand and popped it into her mouth. She chewed, three, four, five times and swallowed hard.

The Brotherhood went crazy. George, not understanding the nature of his predicament, raised his arms and his voice and demanded silence. When order was restored, he berated the Post Rider. "I've had enough of your foolishness, little girl. You've gone and ruined your little game, so I guess I'll have to deal with that bastard my own way."

She answered him in the manner of a kindly teacher instructing a wayward student. "George Johnson, I haven't ruined anything. We can still learn what destiny fate has chosen for Jerry Vazquez."

No one moved.

"All we have to do is read what is written on the paper Jerry left in the box. It will be the opposite of the one Jerry chose." Emma's gentle gaze slowly revealed George Johnson to himself. Too late. He understood that this Post Rider was not the innocent girl he had supposed her to be. She was a woman of power, power vastly greater than his.

He could not speak.

Emma faced the people and offered them comfort, gave them words soft, warm, and round, full of love and understanding. George heard them and remembered the voice of Serena's mother, gone so long now.

"George," she said. "Show us the other slip of paper."

Her easy manner carried the big man numbly forward. She had anticipated his dishonesty. She relied upon on him to lie and cheat and swear falsely on his honor. He looked at her again. This time he saw the kindness in her eyes. He understood that she would protect his secret.

She had mercy.

He fumbled with the unused ballot then unfolded it for all to see.

It read BANISHED.

Emma explained, "The chosen ballot must have said WELCOMED."

Jerry Vazquez was saved.

The young man was now bound fully to the Brotherhood. He became, and would always remain, the brave and loyal son of George Johnson. Emma guided the two men toward each other, watched as they shook hands, and listened to the mad cheering that filled the tent. A wave of fatigue washed over her. She felt Doc nearby; he was surely within the sound of her voice. The commotion would worry him.

Emma addressed George and Jerry directly. "There is more you need to know. Serena carries not one child but two. Bearing twins is always difficult, but doing so as a young woman and a first-time mother..."

She did not need to finish the sentence.

"She needs help. Two hands will be too few to sustain her. Four will be barely enough. If you let this alliance fail, Serena will die."

Doc's footfalls were there, behind her. He knew it was time. Emma stood with her back against the tent's flap doors. She pointed at the fathers but spoke to everyone.

"I expect you two men to love and care for Serena and the lives in her womb. Return here by the first of April, and I will come to you. I will attend the birth."

Both men heaved a sigh of relief. Emma pointed to the herbs she collected. "Make tea from the leaves I've left for you. It will soothe her sickness." Doc's hot breath was now on the other side of the fabric. She pulled the hood of her riding cloak up over her head, turned, and was gone. In an instant, she was on his back. Still night blind, she wrapped her arms around his neck and whispered, *Cha.*

People tumbled out of the meeting tent, eager to thank her for what she had done but the Post Rider had vanished. She would sleep on Doc's back as he plunged through the empty darkness that lay between them and Ithaca.

John Knox prowled his office on the 98th floor of the DSJ headquarters in New York City. The pacing—ten steps, turn, ten steps, turn—helped him soothe his anger. It was late, 21:30 hours. It was New Year's Eve, and he was at work waiting for his annual review with the Director. Knox knew the meeting would start and end precisely as scheduled. He was prepared.

The Director was doing this to him because the man enjoyed being a prick. In an unguarded moment, he mentioned he was looking forward to spending New Year's Eve with his friends. The Director responded with sneering condescension, "You ought to be taking your work a little more seriously, don't you think, Knox?" There was disappointment but no surprise when the summons to a late night meeting appeared in his inbox.

The Director will meet with you to perform your year-end evaluation at 23:00 hours on 12/31/2043. The meeting will conclude at 23:45 hours.

At 22:55, Knox began filling his briefcase with the encrypted clipboard computers containing the reports, graphs, charts, and summaries he expected to be called upon to produce. He walked down the empty hallway. At the door, he checked his watch. Its face glowed, bright in Samantha's darkened reception area. One minute to go.

Time. Knox knocked twice.

"Come in."

"Good evening, sir."

The Director knew he did not need to reply. A flick of the wrist commanded Knox to sit.

The room's only light came from the sleek halogen vapor lamp the Director kept on his desk. It cast an intense mechanical glow onto the desktop but barely illuminated the rest of the Director's spartan office. Outside, the cityscape sparkled. Instinctively, Knox took the Director's measure. The man seemed more subdued than usual, more matter of fact, less electric. He studied his face. The hairline was receding, nothing new there. The normally fleshy lips were tightly pursed, as if they were protecting a secret. The Director seemed drained. Fat. Old. Tired. Knox wondered if the old man was sick.

Knox responded to a mumbled demand for status reports, and the Deputy plugged the clipboard into the port on the front of the desk. The Director reviewed the documents carefully but without interest, as if he wanted to make an impression of diligence but lacked the energy to actually be diligent. The late night's quiet huddled around the two of them.

Eron was always careful to grind his deputy beneath his heel whenever the opportunity arose. The idea of revoking Knox's night of celebration had, initially, held great appeal. In his eagerness to punish Knox, he now realized, he inadvertently revealed just how sad and lonely a man he was. The charade annoyed him and he wanted it over. He would go through the motions with Knox and dismiss him at 23:45, but not a moment sooner. Eron sighed. As soon as he was free to go, Knox would bolt from the building. The skinny little bastard would miss ringing in the New Year but still meet up with his friends. Meanwhile, the Director of the DSJ would take the elevator to his private quarters and spend the night alone.

"You say here that you think detection is a weak spot." The voice was mechanical.

"Yes, sir."

"Mmm hmm."

"There is…" Knox always worked to avoid volunteering information, but tonight his position seemed more secure than usual. "…Good news all around on the Demo supply function. Nutrients, energy, information—all the parameters are good. Qualitative measures of satisfaction are trending upward." Now came the risky part. "Bands of the Brotherhood have been more active, more aggressive. I believe you've seen the reports."

The Director grunted, "What do you plan to do about it, Knox?"

"I've put the guys in R&D onto infrared sensing technology. Ultimately we will be able to track them, punish them, and drive them when and where we want them."

The Director leaned back in his chair, his face receding from the light. "Not bad, not bad at all, Knox. That's what I call thinking ahead. Most people, they're fools. You know that as well as I do, Knox. It's a good day for them when they can fasten their own velcro. That's why people need us—they need the DSJ. We do the thinking for them. So this is good, Knox. For the first goddamned time you are a step ahead. Those bastards step any farther out of line and we'll run them down and hit them. Hard."

Knox sat dumbfounded.

"Well, listen, I'm sure you need to get going, and ahh, so do I."

"Yes, sir."

"You're dismissed."

"Thank you, sir."

The Director grunted, "Double the goddamned infrared detection budget."

"I will, sir." Knox closed the door softly behind him and glanced at his watch. It read 23:37. There was even a chance he'd make the ball drop in time.

44
AIKEN
Spring, 2044

As far as George Johnson could tell, Serena's pregnancy was going well. The nausea had passed and his little girl was eating like a horse. She had plenty of vitamins, too—the Brotherhood made sure of that. The babies started kicking around the New Year; they were down around Macon then. She let him feel her belly. He was pretty sure the strong kicks meant she'd have boys.

He whisked a fly away and opened his eyes halfway. The Boss lay still as he woke slowly from his nap. He listened to his people, heard the contented murmur of their voices. All was well. Another two, maybe three days and they would start north.

That evening, after supper, he called the Brotherhood together. "Convoy'll be coming along in an hour or so. Not gonna hit it. We got plenty. Just want everybody to watch it go on by," he grinned. "Just for fun."

It came up from the south, and made the bend at Aiken, slowing to negotiate the interchange with route 1.

The lead truck swung into view, and the sight of it sucked the air out of George's lungs. It was Corporate Militia, freaking badass Militia. A troop truck led the convoy, and it was packed with men. They stood at the ready, gun barrels leveled, blue-gray steel glinting in the day's fading light. He looked at Jerry who stared back, eyes wide, speechless. George made the sign, *Silence*. The command was unnecessary. No one spoke. No one moved.

Behind the troop truck came a string of the usual vehicles: protein tankers, diesel tankers, a panel truck, and two more supply vans. Then came another surprise—a sleek black bus. It looked new and the glass was smoked. In truth, it seemed more like a mutant Earth-bound spaceship than a bus. The roof bristled with antennae. There were dishes, dipoles, and two mirror-smooth stainless steel lozenges whose function could only be guessed at. The tail was brought up by another troop truck. The whole thing roared past at 80 maybe 90 miles an hour.

The Brotherhood sat in stunned silence. Finally, Jerry sputtered, "Whoa! That was death on wheels, man."

The Boss's chest felt heavy, as if an elephant was sitting on top of him. If he had chosen to hit the convoy, they'd be dead. All dead. Everyone else knew it, too. Corporate Militia didn't play games.

"George," Jerry said. "They were loaded for bear, and what the hell was with the big black devil bus? They damn sure didn't want anybody messing with it." Jerry went on, thinking out loud. "It felt like they were looking for us. Hunting us."

George nodded, weighed the odds. Stay put or run? Maybe they wanted him to run, maybe the convoy was meant to flush him out, or maybe the coffin on wheels had somehow seen them. If so, they would be coming for them, soon.

Jerry looked at George. He knew what decision had to be made, and was glad he did not have to make it. Looped images of the convoy played across George's mind. They came through loud and proud and wanted to be seen, wanted to be heard. They were, he thought, hunters with a new gun beating the bushes eager to flush their prey out into the open. He called Jerry over, told him how he saw it. The younger man agreed.

George addressed the Brotherhood. "We are staying put." He boasted, with more confidence than he felt. "They think they can make us run but they don't know us. The damned GRID can't make the Brotherhood do anything we don't want to do."

They would stay, dark and quiet. He would double the watch. He ran the numbers in his head. They could lie back for a few days and still make their April 1st rendezvous with Emma Thomas. George started to rise from the crouch he'd been in when the convoy blew by. His knees and back were stiff. Jerry reached out his hand and pulled him to his feet.

"Tough call," he said. George nodded in agreement. His shoulders felt heavy as if the weight of the world rested on them.

45
MOTHERWORT

April brought slate gray skies and rain so cold it numbed the skin. Emma heard it fall and was grateful that she was inside, safe and warm, and not huddled beneath a tree, out there. She pulled her quilt close and thought about Serena, George, Jerry, and the Brotherhood. The north wind rattled bare branches against her bedroom window. Deep in the woods, the last remaining banks of snow gave ground to the coming season. She took a deep breath and let go of her worry. Soon, the weather would break and she'd ride west, out of the Shire.

The Brotherhood arrived at the meeting point on the first of April—what the older people remembered as April Fools' Day—and George Johnson felt every bit the fool. Emma had promised that she would meet them here, in April. Well, April had come and the Midwife was nowhere to be seen. Two of his biggest trucks were stuck in the mud and everyone was cold, wet, and tired. The shadow of the Corporate Militia had haunted them all the way north, had stolen their ease in the day and invaded their dreams at night.

He overheard Serena telling Jerry about her nightmare: "We were all together in a beautiful place, a big green meadow. Everyone was happy. Then I saw dark clouds. I don't know where they came from they just appeared in the sky. There was lightning and thunder. We ran—but there was no place to hide. There was lightning all around us; it was so close it was like we were inside the storm. Then I woke up." Jerry listened and told her not to worry, "It's that onion paste you had for dinner. Forget about it."

George was worried though. Serena's time was near. They were at the meeting place, and the damned Midwife was nowhere to be seen.

The water in the glass by the kitchen window rose overnight, foretelling a run of fair weather. The morning sun, assisted by a warm south wind, set to work nudging the land gently but insistently toward spring. A promise had been made but not yet kept. Emma was ready to go.

The Midwife was there when Serena's water broke. It was clear and carried a healthy, salty smell as if it came from some ancient ocean. An hour later, the pains started. Emma laid the palms of her hands upon the smooth round belly. The womb was a ball of muscle; the contractions rose then fell away.

They were ten minutes apart.

"You and Jerry need to go for a walk."

"Is it safe?" Serena asked.

Emma laughed, "Oh yes, very safe. The twins will not be here for quite awhile. A nice walk will strengthen your labor and," Emma added with a wink, "it will help Jerry feel useful."

Serena tried to smile in return, but a contraction got the better of her.

"Let them come and go on their own," Emma advised her. "They hurt but you need them—it's how your children will be born. When the next one comes breathe through it like this." Emma showed her how to breath.

Serena nodded. "OK, I will."

"Off you go, then."

Emma put fresh sheets on the cot, folded and refolded the sun-dried towels. Then she filled a lidded pot with water, placed the few instruments at her disposal in the water examining each closely before it was submerged. Silk thread, an assortment of needles, clamps, lengths of cotton cording for tying off the umbilical cords and, finally, the bone handled stiletto that Gene Lyons produced instantly from the holster hidden beneath his black leather vest. She hoped she would never have to touch it again. The lid went on and there was nothing to do but wait. She watched the pot and then smiled at her own impatience. She closed her eyes and chose to wait like an elder, calmly and without worry.

Serena and Jerry returned at noon. She was looking much less comfortable; tiny beads of sweat dotted her upper lip. The contractions were moderate and about seven minutes apart. Emma turned her attention to Jerry who looked even less comfortable than Serena.

"Jerry, I was wondering if you and George might run an errand for me."

"What's wrong?" he asked.

"Nothing's wrong. We're going to need more motherwort for Serena after the babies are born. It looks like this." She held up a handful of sprigs for him to see. "Could you two pick some for me?"

"OK."

"Here, take these so you know what you are looking for. Marshy areas are best. Bring me an armful at least."

"But what about Serena?"

Emma smiled. "She'll stay here with me. And don't worry, nothing's going to happen before you get back."

Serena, between contractions, reassured Jerry, "It's OK, honey. Go ahead. I'm sure Emma's right."

"Be right back," he promised.

A contraction came. Serena sputtered, "Oooh. Oooh. Stronger." She started puffing.

Emma smiled.

When the next contraction came, Emma slid her forefinger and middle finger into the birth canal. She closed her eyes and let her fingers see for her. The pelvis was narrow and the first baby was...head down. She breathed a sigh of relief. Then she drove her long boney fingers deeper into Serena's vagina. The contraction was at its peak, but the baby's head remained high in the pelvis. The cervix, she noted, was only three centimeters; it was going to be a long night.

When the contraction ebbed, Serena demanded information.

"Good news," Emma smiled convincingly. "The first baby is head down just the way it should be. And," she added, "we are just getting started. You've got a long ways to go."

George and Jerry returned an hour later with a crate full of what they earnestly believed to be motherwort slung between them. They were spattered with mud and jubilant over their success.

"Out," Emma demanded. "Get out of here right now. Go clean yourselves up before you come back."

They left, spirits high.

Night fell.

The moon was full—a good sign, Emma thought—and it hung high overhead at midnight.

The contractions were coming hard every two to three minutes. The head had descended into the pelvis. Progress was slow, but steady.

Dawn.

Fully dilated. Time to push.

Drenched in sweat and pushing hard, Jerry by her side.

The mother toiled, hour after hour, without complaint. Crowning.

So close.

Serena began to tire.

Noon, head out, thick black hair, like Jerry's, cord around the neck. She tied it off and cut. The baby needed to be born, now.

Hands on head, downward pressure. The shoulder was pinned behind the pubic bone. Jammed tight. Damn. Damn it to hell. Serena pushed with all her strength. Not enough.

Baby turning blue.

A pot lid clattered to the floor.

The blade gleamed under electric light. No time to waste.

Emma cut—vagina to back bone. Blood sprayed across the Midwife's face and chest. Serena screamed. This was the last chance, if the shoulder didn't pass under the pubic bone, all three would die.

Emma's voice was dense, dark, commanding. "Serena, look at me. Look at me, damn you! When the contraction comes you have to push, push with everything you've got. Your babies need you."

Serena wailed as the contraction strengthened. Jerry stood, frozen in a wild-eyed terror. George fled the tent. Emma pointed at Jerry, her eyes drilled into his. "When I give the word you press down like I showed you, as hard as you can."

He nodded numbly.

It was time. "Push, push, for the love of your children, push, woman push!"

Emma pulled with all of her strength. Her arms burned and then she felt it, the slip of bone beneath bone. The shoulder was free of its prison. She lifted the baby's head. The bottom shoulder popped free and he gushed out his mother's body. The child was like a rag doll, mouth open, eyes glazed.

Emma put his mouth to hers. One breath, two breaths, three, four, five...no response. Eight, nine, ten, and then—at last—a gasp and a weak cough. Finally, a cry. Arms and legs twitching with life. Purple, cry picking up strength; blue, arms and legs moving under their own power; dusky pink, pink, sweet beautiful pink. "Waaaah, waah, waah!"

Emma staggered where she stood. The greatest danger was past.

But there was another life waiting to be born. Emma put the first baby boy into his father's arms.

Blood gushed from the gash between Serena's legs. Emma reached deep inside Serena. She spoke, "Open your eyes Serena." The exhausted mother eyed her woozily. "The next baby is close, but he needs your help. You'll have to push two maybe three more times. You have no choice."

"I can do it."

The second twin arrived kicking and squalling from the start.

Serena laid motionless, arms quivering, as she held her boys to her breasts.

Emma inspected the carnage that lay between Serena's legs. Swollen tissue was torn and bleeding. Twin umbilical cords still protruded. The afterbirth was yet to come.

The newborns' lusty suck stimulated the uterus to contract—not rhythmically, as in labor—but in a single, hard, burning cramp. Serena groaned, but Emma was delighted. Both placentas were soon produced and the bleeding slowed to a trickle.

It was midnight before the damage was repaired, each tissue reunited, like with like. Serena had tolerated the suturing well, especially considering that Emma had nothing with which to numb the pain. Her work complete, the Midwife let a marrow-deep weariness wash over her. She lay down on the floor of the tent, next to the birthing cot, and fell asleep. George Johnson bent down over her and lovingly draped a blanket over the woman who saved all of their lives.

46
CURSIVE

The mid-summer sun bore down upon New York City and the pavement burned hot as brimstone. In his deliciously cool office, high above the street, John Knox studied the ordered grid of streets that stretched out before him. His desk was cluttered with the usual haphazard collection of digital documents, clipboard computers, and something new. On top of the jumble lay a pile of oddly-sized sheets of paper, actual paper. Each sheet was covered with a diabolical code, printed using a technology he did not understand.

An ink trace was a simple, if antiquated, procedure and was ordinarily quite informative, but the lab had failed when they tried to trace it to a manufacturer. The code breakers fared no better. They scanned the pages into the Raptor and let the code-breaking supercomputer grind away for a week straight. Nothing. It was the same with the paper. No source could be linked to any of the dozens of documents that lay on his desk. It was as if they had materialized out of some alien world.

Strangely, the items had been confiscated from people engaged in Uncertified Personal Travel. No weapons, no contraband, no maps, no GRID connection—they were wandering the back streets of Demos where they didn't belong. They were young, too, late teens, early twenties—not sophisticated, but old enough to know better. What did they want? What were they after? He had no idea.

Knox followed standard relocation procedures. Convoys returned the wanderers to their understandably terrified families. DSJ field agents hit them with a "scared straight" anti-Brotherhood lecture and made them watch the pre-Fall movie about the men who left their Demo, wandered along some remote river, and paid dearly for their foolishness. It amped up the fear. For good measure, the DSJ hit them with a hefty VL point penalty. It was kid stuff, thrill-seeking juvenile rebellion, nothing serious. Knox felt sure but the papers remained a mystery. Knox now required captured documents to be forwarded directly to his office.

The time had come, he knew, to inform the Director. He'd been chewing up man-hours, and experience had taught him it was better to get the bad news to the old man before he heard about it from someone else. Knox glanced at his watch. Five minutes. He rechecked the digital documents. The lab reports, the code cracker's summaries, and a selection of the actual confiscated papers were all in order. The Director would want to inspect them for himself.

Knox knocked and entered. Samantha was off, or away from her desk. The Director was on the phone. He pointed first at Knox then at the chair perched in front of his desk. Then he swung his own chair away from him so that its high back faced his Deputy.

The old leather chair, which had belonged to the former Director, was gone. A sleek replacement built to accommodate the Director's greatly expanded girth had taken its place. Custom, Knox thought, it had to be. He listened without interest to the familiar *rat, tat, tat* of the Director's voice. "Tell them to do it or I'll hound them for the rest of their miserable lives." The old man tapped off and spun around so quickly that he caught Knox eyeing his new possession. "Bullet-proof," he said. "You can't trust those Militia bastards. Remember that, Knox."

"Well, what are you going to waste my time with today?"

The Deputy drew a deep breath and plunged into the problem. He reviewed the data, the steps he had taken, and, finally, the dead-end he now faced.

"Raptor chewed on this?"

"For seven days, sir."

"Doesn't make sense. You've obviously screwed up again, Knox." The Director paused and made a show of staring at the ceiling as if he was appealing to the heavens for the patience any man would need if he found himself face-to-face with John Knox. "Let's see the intercepts."

Knox pulled a handful of them from his valise and handed them over.

The Director snatched them, his eyes hungry for proof of his deputy's incompetence. He glanced at one sheet then another, and another. His face flushed, then paled. The anger was real. He flipped through the rest of the stack. When he was done, he threw them at Knox and they scattered across the room. "By God, are you taunting me, you little bastard? If you are, I will kill you. Kill you! Do you understand me?"

Knox swallowed hard. "I don't understand, sir. Honestly, I don't."

The Director let his anger own him. "It's script, you idiot. Cursive, hand writing. It's not digital, it's analog—done by hand."

Knox was stunned. "I...I didn't know..." he stammered, "such things still existed."

The Director half rose from his chair and leaned forward, as if he was a rabid dog straining at the end of a chain. His eyes narrowed to slits.

Knox did not dare move.

His anger passed its peak and Eron slowly understood Knox was telling the truth. He returned, heavily, to his seat. The man in front of him was an idiot, a perfect idiot. In fact, he, the Director of the GRID's Department of Security and Justice, worked in a building filled with retards. He imagined them huddled together downstairs scanning the papers into the Raptor and being dumbfounded when they got nothing in return. "Machines can't read script, Knox. They never did, and they never will."

People hadn't used script since the Fall. The DSJ was staffed entirely by pimple-faced geeks, code jockeys, digital superstars—few of whom, he guessed, could read the time off the face of a clock. His anger cooled, leaving behind a delightful residue of superiority in its place. It felt so good that he laughed, a full, deep belly laugh. The sound was unlike any Knox had ever heard the Director make. "Damn if I don't know how to pick'em. Well, Knox, I can't pull your head out of your ass, but I can make you learn how to read script. I want you to go and find some fogey who can read and write this shit and I want you to learn it. Understand?"

"Yes, sir."

"I also want you to stop wasting my Department's money and man-hours on this crap." The Director mimicked the syrupy voice that he supposed people used when they talked to babies. "If I were you, I would keep this to myself. You do realize that your stupidity reflects on me. You do realize that, don't you?"

"Yes, sir. I'll try not to disappoint you, sir."

The Director laughed. "That'll be the day. Now get the hell out of my office."

Face flushed red, Knox scrambled frantically after the papers then left without speaking another word.

47

10,000 TRIBES

All along the Turnpike, the Shire's Masters, Journeymen, and Apprentices were at work. The Council of Elders was also busy meeting daily, searching for the right question. By tradition, at the close of every summer, the Elders posed a question they felt would inspire conversation, thought, argument, and debate among the young.

The questions they liked best had nothing to do with everyday problems or concerns. The adults tended to those things. The Elders went deep. In 2037 they asked, "Do poems need people?" In 2042 they wanted to know, "What are Elders for?" As Question Day drew near, grandchildren pestered their grandparents begging for a hint—getting only a wink and a smile.

Zach Thomas rushed to finish stacking the day's last load of hay into the mow before the sun reached the western horizon. He would have just enough time to put the big horses away, wash up, and rig the buggies for the drive to Pavilion. Emma finished a visit with an expectant mother in Bag's End, walked into the forest, and whistled for Doc. Haleigh and Hannah were already at the Lodge with the Elders. Even though they were younger than Zach and Virgil, the two had been welcomed onto the Council years before. They had been born, it seemed, as old people in young bodies. Virgil and Chloe would be there too, along with their two little girls. It was the year's most solemn social occasion.

When the Tribes were gathered, Maria Hemple strode to center stage. Born in 1956, she graduated from Clemson with an MBA and gone on to found a database software company. She sold it and moved to the Shire back in the early years. Henry Black of Crickhollow took her on as an apprentice Potter, and she took over his shop when he died in 2011. Now she was an Elder of the Tribes of Eden.

"A thousand years ago the Five Nations of the Iroquois Confederacy brought peace to this land. It endured for 700 years, ending only when the Europeans arrived at Confederacy's eastern door. Now the GRID rules the world beyond the Shire, and while it may keep order, it cannot make peace and it will not endure. The Elders believe it is our destiny to bring a new confederacy to life."

"For many years the Eden Underground has helped the Demos grow Elders and Post Riders of their own, though these good people must remain hidden. The people out there will, in time, need much more. They have no bakers, no brewers, no butchers, no healers, no blacksmiths, no weavers."

"Don't forget the beekeepers," Ty Hallet yelled. The obvious pride that animated his claim set off a vigorous round of cheering.

"Of course," Maria agreed. "We must never forget the beekeepers."

Lee Peters, accountant, turned tanner, turned blacksmith, turned Elder stepped forward. "The GRID is a machine. As such, its nature is to break and be repaired, fray, and wear until it can no longer be repaired. As it recedes from the world it will leave behind 10,000 villages, hungry and fearful. We must make ready for that day."

Maria picked up the thread. "Someday, powerful people will come before the Tribes. They will want us to help them keep the GRID running. They will say to us that we need each other. They will be wrong. Today, the Elders offer the Tribes this question: How shall the new world, the world that will come after the GRID, be born?"

The ceremony was near its end. Lee Peters signaled for Haleigh and Hannah to come onstage. They would, as always, have the last word.

"Birth is painful," Hannah said.

Haleigh nodded and added, "There will be pain."

The people of the Shire filed out of the Pavilion and into the cool summer night. A solemn silence followed them home.

48
BEESWAX

At the loading dock, Knox thumbed the package manifest and took possession of a plain brown shipping container light enough to hold under his arm. He wound his way back through the maze of corridors, which led to the building's main bank of elevators. When the doors opened on the 98th floor, a gaggle of junior staffers loitering in the elevator lobby pretended not to be shocked to see the Deputy Director of the DSJ lugging a cardboard box to his own office. The lock on his door snapped shut and he was alone.

Months of study with an Elder on the Upper East Side had given him the ability to read cursive fluently. Writing in script would take much more practice, and he still wasn't convinced it was worth the effort.

He ordered DSJ field agents to search specifically for unauthorized travelers, especially young people. A few of the travelers had fallen into the Department's grasp and the box held the papers that had been taken from them. Knox fumbled with a knife then slit the packing tape from across the top of the box. He pulled the flaps open and removed a digital document that the mewling District Commander had placed on top of the real prize.

He removed one of the confiscated packets. The envelope was made from a waxy kind of paper. He rubbed his fingers across it, then held them up to his nose. The smell was strangely sweet. He closed his eyes, held the packet close, and sniffed cautiously. The smell was honey. Knox, of course, had never tasted real honey. He only knew honey flavor from a factory, used to enhance food pastes. Gradually, it occurred to him that this was beeswax, a primitive form of waterproofing.

He used a blade to slice the packet open. The papers it held varied in size, thickness, and color. Hands trembling, he unfolded the first set. At last, the secret would be revealed to him...

Not long ago a young man, a friend of mine, I think, asked me how I felt about being old. The question disturbed me, and I must have shown my reaction on my face because he immediately became embarrassed. I smiled and said that this was an interesting question, an important question, and that I would have to ponder it and get back to him.

I slept well that night. In my dreams I saw old friends, and I visited places I have not seen in many years.

When I woke, I pulled the covers back, sat up, and then stood up. I felt the ache in my bones and muscles.

It was then I decided, old age is a gift.

I washed my face and peered into the mirror. I saw the wrinkles, the baggy eyes, the receding gray hair. I looked into the mirror and smiled. I am now, probably for the first time in my life, the person I have always wanted to be.

I would not trade the life I have for less gray hair or a flatter belly. As I've aged I've become more kind to myself. At last, I've become my own friend. I am entitled to treat myself, to be messy, to be extravagant.

Too many of my dear friends have left this world too soon, before they understood the great freedom that comes with age. I will dance by myself to the songs of my youth, I will weep over love lost long ago, and I will tell my stories. Pitying glances come my way, but I don't care. In time, those who pity me will grow old.

I know I am sometimes forgetful. But, then again, some of life is just as well forgotten. Of course, my heart's been broken—many times, many times. How can you live so long and love so much and not lose a child, a pet, a marriage, a parent, a lover? In the end, all is lost.

But what of freedom? The poet sang, 'Freedom's just another word for nothing left to lose.'

So yes, I am free, and happy, and old. I won't live forever, nor would I want to, but while I am still here I will not, I cannot, waste time lamenting what could have been, or worrying about what will be.

I will eat dessert every single day (if I feel like it).

John Knox dropped the papers onto his desk. This was it? He'd gone to all this trouble, learned the damned cursive, all for this?

These were the ramblings of a lonely, self-indulgent old man. Knox examined the document closely. There was no name, no address, no GRID ID. The message was maudlin; the author, anonymous. He leaned back in his chair, puzzled. So much effort, handmade paper, handmade ink, cursive handwriting—all for nothing. Even more bizarre was the fact that young people were venturing where they knew they were not supposed to go in this service of utter nonsense. He hoped to impress the Director by uncovering a nefarious plot against the GRID, but all he had were addled musings of an old man.

Hoping that the first document was an aberration, a red herring that might have been used to deceive or deflect prying eyes from what lay beneath, he tore the second document from its waxed envelope.

...I am 82-years-old, an age that I never thought I'd see. I remember when I was young, long before the Fall. The world was different then and so was I. I used to believe many things I no longer believe. I've learned that not believing can be a very good thing.

My childhood, lost for so long to me, has returned to keep me company. I find that I now understand things that were mysteries to me when I was young. Why did Aunt Becky leave her husband? As a child, I saw Uncle Fred as a fun, funny uncle full of jokes and surprises. Now I can see that he was that, and was also a mean drunk who couldn't keep a job and beat my Aunt one time too many, so she left him. Left him for good. When I was a child I was angry that she left. As an Elder, I wonder what took her so long to leave.

Once I was content to see black and white; now I see a sea of gray. Life is messy. It defies simple categories. It requires you to pay attention to the space between right and wrong. The older I get, the bigger that space seems to be...

Knox shook his head in disbelief. It had been his uniform experience that wherever there was subterfuge, there was also, somewhere in the muck, a desire for illicit gain. The Brotherhood illustrated the rule perfectly. They prattled on about being "modern day Robin Hoods," but they were really just ordinary thieves.

The sounds outside of his office told him that the work day was winding down. Staffers' cheerful calls of "see you tomorrow" echoed off the bare walls of the corridor and into his office.

It would be a good idea, he thought, to put findings into a memo for the Director. He called his workstation to attention then began to speak. The text appeared on the screen almost before the word was uttered. The program's speed and accuracy amazed him even now.

Director DSJ, Category 'Eyes Only' from Deputy Director, J. Knox
Category: Uncertified Personal Travel
Director Wallace, I have taken the opportunity to learn how to read cursive handwriting.

Fortunately, the program remained ignorant of just how unwillingly Knox had undertaken this task.

Now that I am able to do so fluently—hold. Program, delete the word 'fluently'.

The word disappeared from the screen, but Knox knew if the Director ever chose to look at the document's history the damning word would be there. It was never a good idea to assert mastery of any kind when communicating with the Director.

As you suggested, I have obtained...

Knox paused and struggled with how to phrase this diplomatically.

... additional user-generated content which has been gathered by DSJ officials in the field.

He was pleased with the result.

I have reviewed these documents at length—hold. Program, delete, 'at length'. And can report the following:
1. The text is highly idiosyncratic dealing exclusively with the personal musings of old people.
2. There is no planning or operational content. Neither do the authors of the text exhort or attempt to persuade. The GRID does not figure into the text in any way, for good or for ill.
3. There is no ulterior motive in these communications, which can plausibly be connected to any illegal, or potentially illegal, conspiracy against the interests of the GRID.

Force of habit compelled him to add a final thought.

Despite these seemingly innocuous findings, I do believe that the phenomenon deserves to be monitored, and I will continue to do so—personally.

The light of day was fading into the west. Summer shadows brought some relief from the heat to the streets below. His day's work was done, he knew that. The corridor was now silent, and the hum of the HVAC had reasserted itself.

It was time to go, but he had little desire to leave. His apartment was pleasant, very nice actually—but it was empty, even less of a home to him than this office. Knox felt the agitated dissatisfied boredom that he knew too well descending on him.

He was clearing his desk when he came upon a third document. It was smaller than that of the other two items and had escaped his notice.

It was different. He smelled it and the scent washed over him. He remembered his own grandmother, his mother's mother, dead these many years. It was her smell, old, comfortable, loving. He realized he had not thought of her in a long time.

He gently opened the packet, removed the post, and began to read.

I was born in Brooklyn but grew up in Queens...

An hour later he finished the last page. He set the folio aside and had the astonishing experience of a voice going silent, of experiencing pure silence. Slowly the world around him reasserted itself. The paper, the ink, the scent, the gently slanted letters crawling across the page—this was something new. The pages in his hand had initiated him into something ancient, quiet, hidden.

Knox caressed the document, finding pleasure in its irregular texture. Then he reached for the first of the posts he had read. He picked it up and reread it and found that, somehow, it, too, had come alive. He could feel the pulse of a life lived in the words. The same was true with the second post. The old woman was there in his office with him, sharing her thoughts, with him.

Needing to clear his head, Knox stood and walked to his office window. The sky was dark, but the lights of the city burned bright. It was like any summer night in New York, but he was different.

Changed.

A wave of memory broke over him. He was a child again. His doting grandmother was alive again. She held him on her lap and whispered into his ear, but he could not hear what she said. The words were lost to him, but tonight her voice had returned. He wiped away tears that came unbidden. The soft ding from the workstation broke his reverie. There was a message from the Director.

Goddamed right you'll stay on top of it. This shit is off the GRID <u>and that makes it wrong.</u> There will be hell to pay if this gets away from you.

Knox fell into his chair and commanded the attention of the workstation.

Sir, you can be certain that I will follow this issue closely and continue to seek out the source and purpose of these peculiar communications.

"SCREEN OFF." He needed to go home.

49
HOME
Fall, 2048

The grass was short; it was time to bring the cattle down off the ridge tops. Zach's two oldest grandsons had turned ten over the winter and were now big enough to ride with adults during the round-up. He passed a Master's eye over the boys as the three of them rode up into the high country. Sam was just two months older than Tom but was much bigger than his cousin. He was a strapping boy with his grandfather's pale blue eyes and thick sandy brown hair. He wore a denim shirt and the floppy hat favored by the Shire's Herdsmen. Tom had his mother's green eyes and quiet manner. Both of them seemed made for the saddle. Though they were still too young to apprentice, they were eager to learn.

The riders emerged onto an upland meadow where a dozen cow-calf pairs grazed contentedly. The sight of the cattle thrilled the boys, and they spurred their horses just the way they imagined real Herdsmen spurred their horses and galloped straight at them. Their high pitched "yips" and "yeehaws" filled the air. The cows spooked and scattered in every direction. Zach rode after the boys, yelling for them to hold up. They returned to their grandfather's side, complaining bitterly, "Stupid cows!" Zach overlooked the insult and asked, as gently as he knew how, "Boys, was that good judgment or bad judgment?"

"Bad," they answered, sheepishly. They hung their heads. He knew how they felt. They'd seen glory standing right before them, their big chance to impress the old man.

Zach softened the blow. "Ah, it's nothing we can't solve. Sam you get back up on the ridge and swing out north. There's a little hollow there."

"I know it."

"Good. It's likely a few of them will be down in there. Push them up and out. The grass is still good here, they'll probably wanna head back this way."

"Got it, Gramps."

Tom, smaller and less confident than his cousin, looked for instructions. It was important that he be given an equivalent challenge. "I'm thinking that those cattle might have spooked partly 'cause they were thirsty. Why don't you scoot down to Meade's Pond and if you find any of 'em, work back up here along the old stone wall."

When they were gone, Zach set to work beating the thicket; it was the worst job and the one that called for the greatest skill. By noon, two dozen cattle were once again grazing contentedly, as they had been when they were first encountered. Zach figured it was time for lunch. A skin of cider for the boys and a bottle of Sadie's fine raspberry cordial for him, cheese, meat, bread eaten out in the open—this was the Herdsman's life. After the meal, Zach offered the boys a short lesson in cow psychology. It was a talk given many times over the years.

"You see, lots of people—really it's people who don't know anything about them—anyway, lots of people say cows are stupid. It's not true. They're really smart but, you see, they're cow smart. And cow smart and people smart, those are different things." The boys spread out on the short grass in the highest meadow and listened as if they were receiving a message from an oracle—which, in a way, they were. "What's a cow want? Well first of all, a cow wants to be with other cows. In particular, a cow wants to do what other cows are doing. If cows are eating, well then they all want to eat. If they are running, well damnit they're all gonna run."

The boys nodded.

"The second thing is that cows want to live, just like people want to live. When you're a big old grass muncher, you make a mighty attractive target for any critter that'd like a little beef on the hoof for lunch. Just look at 'em now."

Sam and Tom studied the cattle as if they were works of art.

"Most people would look at them standing there and figure that they were just eating. But they aren't just eating. They're eating and watching, eating and listening, eating and feeling. Feeling the wind and the ground beneath their feet. And what are they watching out for?"

"Wolves, coyotes, bears, cougars."

"Right," Zach said. "And men. Don't forget, men are predators too..."

"So, what about this morning?" he asked. "What happened?"

"They ran away because they thought me and Sam were predators," Tom volunteered.

"Right," Zach said. "And is running for your life when predators are coming at you smart or stupid?"

"Smart." They agreed.

"Yep, very smart. Let's saddle up."

When they were ready, Zach leaned forward on his pommel and said, "Now, shall we try this again?"

The boys were eager to redeem their error. "Let's be smart predators, at least as smart as the cows." He nodded respectfully in the direction of the contended bovines. "We'll tuck into the woods here and drop down out of earshot. Then when we get south of them, we'll come back up. Slowly." He drew the last word out, the better to emphasize his point. "Got it?"

They understood.

Once the riders appeared on the far side of the meadow, Zach put Tom on his left flank, Sam on the right.

"Now remember, you want them to be concerned about you, not terrified of you. Be a good predator. Use their senses to lead them from behind. Not so close to spook them, not so far as to lose their attention. Make it so the safest thing they can do is move in the direction you want them to move."

The boys nodded just the way they imagined that men nodded, men at work, men who were trusted. They sat in their saddles and pretended they were already respected men of the Shire. Under their grandfather's watchful eye, they brought the cattle down out of the hills and into paddocks at Hardbottle.

The Harvest Moon had risen, fat and happy, up and out of the eastern hills. The air was crisp, the sky above a towering blue canopy, fading into night. Emma lay on her back in the midst of ten acres of oat stubble. Jupiter and Venus were there with her, and then came Mars and Saturn—her Saturn, pale yellow, subtle, slow, mysterious. The stars followed the planets into the sky.

One, two, three, many.

The day's last sunlight glinted against the tiny cloud she made with each breath. She stood and was pleased to find that she was tired. They did good work. All around her sheaves of newly cut oats stood in long neat rows.

She reached down and stripped the head from a stalk. It was heavy with grain. She popped the oats into her mouth, chewed, and remembered why Doc loved them so much. The flavor blended the spring rain, the summer sun, and now, the trace of an autumn evening.

She thought of home. Home would be warm. Her parents would be home, talking to each other in voices as soft as the light. The supper dishes would be put away, all but hers. Hers would be in the warmer, waiting, not just warm but kept warm, for her. There was something sacred about a meal set aside, saved for a loved one, not yet returned home. Emma already knew how she would call their names when she came through the door, how she would be welcomed, honored, adored. She could imagine the conversation that would fill the air around them. It would be about nothing—and everything.

There were, Emma believed, advantages to being the only daughter of the Shire's most accomplished Weaver. Her bed was a cocoon. A refuge for a young woman twenty-three-years-old and unsure what lay ahead.

She and Doc made West Farthing, then Frogmorton, then the dooryard and home.

50
NOTHING AND EVERYTHING

It began, Knox knew, as an instrument of spite. But the routine of meeting on New Year's Eve for a performance review that could just as well be done any other day no longer rankled. He rarely saw people socially. He became a prisoner of his work; he belonged to the DSJ now.

Life was simpler for them. They were free. He admired the boxes, neatly stacked and labeled along one wall of his office. The Elders. The Post Riders. The Underground. He knew them. He studied them. He obsessed over them. They thought what they wanted, wrote what they wanted, did what they wanted, and went where they wanted. Theirs was a world of memory, stubborn rock-hard memory. Reading the steady streams of posts that were delivered to him changed the way he saw the GRID's melodramas, its manufactured tragedies, the comedies that were thinner than air. They were all fake, all sickeningly unreal.

Knox checked the time.

The meeting wasn't until 23:00 hours and all of his reports, charts, and briefing papers had been prepared weeks ago. He would indulge himself. There was a new box, just in from Seattle. The thing was spreading. No fights. No trouble. No plots. Just spreading. It was as if it was being carried by the wind—invisible, untouchable, known only by the quiet rustle of the leaves. No leaders. No followers. There was never any mention of the GRID. None. It was as if the GRID did not exist for them.

Knox popped the lid on the new box and withdrew the top packet. Medium weight and about an inch thick, he ran his hand across the wax coating and sniffed his fingers. He swore that for a moment he could smell the mountains, could smell the life that graced their slopes. He withdrew the first post and unfolded it. His now expert eyes noted the paper, the ink, the penmanship. All were of high quality. He scanned the first few pages. It was a story of Kallimos, and it was new to him. He glanced again at the clock. He still had time.

Long ago, when The People were new to this world, there was a small kingdom in the south of Kallimos. To its east lay the mighty, white peaks of the Pal-Chin Mountains; to the west, a broad, wine-dark sea...

Knox laid the last of the sheets atop the others. The story soaked into his mind and made him uneasy. He went to the window, looked down upon the city. It was a jewel too beautiful to be manmade, too beautiful not to be. Still, Kallimos whispered to him, urged him to listen. A bitter truth needed to be acknowledged. He was living out his life inside a world gone horribly wrong.

He thought of the nameless, faceless Elder who had set pen to paper and, ultimately, given him this gift of the story. He or she was a member of the Underground, there could be no doubt. But what was the Underground? It owned nothing, controlled nothing, took nothing, and, as far as he could see, wanted nothing. All it had, all it cared about, was memory.

The Underground was, day by day, post by post, defeating the GRID's campaign against the past. Memory was still a part of the living world. They remembered and, because of them, he remembered. With the help of the Post Riders, the past once again moved across the face of the Earth.

Memory, Knox now understood, would be nothing until the moment when it was everything.

51
EVERYWHERE

The watchman's plodding footsteps broke into his thoughts. Knox's meeting with the Director would begin in just a few minutes. He swiftly refolded the post, slid it into its envelope, and then closed the box. His eyes swept the room. When he was certain everything was in its proper place, he snatched his battered briefcase and fled the office. Down the corridor, left, right, then left again, at Samantha's deserted post, he stopped to straighten his tie. He rapped on the Director's mahogany door.

"Come in." The voice was both angry and eager. Knox checked his watch, it was 23:00 hours exactly. Without looking up, the Director asked, "How many times have I told you, how many goddamned many times have I told you, on time is late and early is on time. I come in here to do your evaluation, and you can't be bothered to be early?"

"I'm sorry, sir."

"Lets get this done."

"Yes, sir." Knox pulled his digital annual summary from the briefcase with a practiced ease that further annoyed the Director. He snatched it from his Deputy's hands.

Knox studied the old man carefully. His dismissive scowl was expected on an occasion like this. It meant nothing. The light was dim but Knox wondered if, perhaps, the Director was now resorting to some kind of anti-wrinkle treatment. The old man was pushing fifty. He was no longer young, and it showed. The expertly tailored suit hid the man's greatly expanded bulk and somehow managed to make him look sharp.

The Director threw the report on the desk.

"All right, Knox, you've covered your ass. Now tell me, what's really going on?"

"Well, sir, the Infrared work is starting to pay off. All of the main certified transportation corridors now have sensor networks." Knox hesitated. "We can localize virtually all the elements of the Brotherhood and follow their movements."

"And?" the Director demanded.

"And that lets us drive them where we need them." The elegance of the system made Knox smile. "They respond to very small levels of pressure."

"Mmm hmm." It was the closest the Director ever came to offering praise. He followed it with a dismissive wave of the hand.

"Next."

"Well, I continue to monitor..."

"'Continue to monitor,'" the Director mocked. "Don't give me that bullshit, Knox. I'm warning you." Knox flushed red. He suddenly felt sure that the posts were not a topic he wanted to get into with the Director and switched gears.

"I'm...I'm...watching the communications group, ah, closely. Loyalty, ah, to you and..."

The Director came up out of his chair in a single motion. His hands planted flat on the desk. "Bullshit! You're lying to me. Goddamn you, Knox. How dare you lie to me?" Spittle flew from the Director's mouth, landing on the Deputy's face. "Goddamn it, tell me the truth!"

"Honestly, sir, I have been monitoring the communications team."

"I know that." The Director batted Knox's feeble excuse away with a wave of his hand. "What were you going to say? I'm giving you one chance, just one chance, to get right with me, Knox. Do you understand?"

Knox understood.

He took a deep breath. "I've been...been looking into the uncertified personal travel, like you asked. The thing with the handwritten documents."

The Director's eyes searched his deputy's face, seemed even to probe his mind.

"And?" The Director demanded.

"And it's not making any sense to me, not really. I can...I can read the posts, but none of them really seem to matter."

"So you've screwed up, again."

"Yes, sir." Knox felt relief but dared not show it. A Deputy's incompetence made much safer ground than disloyalty, and Knox knew it.

The Director eased back down into his seat. "Thought you looked good with the IR thing, thought you'd look like the stupid jerk you are with the UPT issue?"

Knox flushed again, this time from relief rather than fear. The Director couldn't tell the difference. Eron leaned back in his chair and relaxed. "Knox, I've put up with a lot from you—the stupidity, the rank incompetence, the shit-eating grin. I've tolerated your incompetence for one reason only: I've found you to be both loyal and an exceptionally bad liar." The Director leaned forward again the better to drive his point home. "If you ever lie to me again, if you ever withhold anything from me again, if you are ever disloyal again..." The Director's beady eyes narrowed. "I will make you suffer the way no man has ever suffered before—then, and only then—I will kill you." The Director smiled benignly. "Do I make myself clear?"

Knox swallowed hard. "Yes, sir."

"Fine, then. I know about the boxes in your office, Knox. Why don't you begin by telling me more about what's in them."

Knox took a deep breath and began to explain, "Well, as you know, they contain documents confiscated from young people, all of whom—strange to say—were ID'd as being outside their own Demo. We never find weapons on them, no contraband of any kind, and they don't resist capture. We ask for the packets, and they give them to us."

"So what's the penalty?"

"We hit them with a VL fine and truck them back to their Demo. Usually a DSJ officer gives a 'scared straight' speech to the kid and the family. It works. We never see them again."

The Director waved Knox's optimism away, as if it was a pesky fly.

"What's in the documents? Kids' stuff?"

"No. The strange thing with these posts—they call them posts—is that they always, always have to do with older people. Their lives, their memories, things they think life has taught them." Knox continued truthfully. "Frankly, Director, you'd find it to be drivel, purposeless, meandering, no point at all."

The Director leaned back and templed his fingers the way he liked to do when he wanted people to see how hard he was thinking.

Knox waited patiently.

"Conspiracy?"

"None of the documents advocate any kind of action at all."

"Organization? Hierarchy? Leadership?"

"None. My best guess is that this is some bizarre form of recreation."

The Director hooted, "Your best guess? My God, Knox, your best guess and a sack of shit are the same freaking thing."

Knox held his tongue.

"No, there is something more to it. Too much effort is going into this, and I'd say you're not catching as many of them as you think you are." He scowled at his Deputy. "You've checked the databases? Right? You did think to check the databases, didn't you?"

"Of course, sir. The Raptor's run it against all of them but we still get nothing. This stuff is completely off the GRID."

The Director grumbled, "You think that's a good thing, Knox? I think that's a bad thing. That's the difference between us, Knox. One of us is a complete moron."

"Yes, sir."

"Any unusual words or names, that sort of thing?"

The story of Kallimos leapt, unbidden, into Knox's mind. "Not much, sir. It's pretty scattered except for one thing—a word, a place—I don't know for sure. Many of the stories revolve around it."

The Director looked interested so Knox offered the word up like a gift.

"Kallimos."

Eron Wallace's jaw worked up and down, as if he was speaking, but no sound came out. Knox wondered if the old man was having a stroke.

"That word. Say it again."

Knox enunciated each syllable, "Kal-li-mos."

"There are stories about this...place?"

"Yes, sir. Many."

"Name one."

"I just read a new one, new to me. It's called 'Sarop the Great.'"

Eron Wallace closed his eyes and struggled against the memories rising up out of the deep. Then he reopened his eyes. Speaking with a greatly exaggerated calm, he prodded Knox. "Tell me the story."

Knox felt the shame one feels when he sees a person, normally upright and proper, acting the part of the drunken fool.

"Well, sir, it begins like this..."

Eron Wallace heard the story for the first time in a quarter of a century.

Knox saw how the Director nodded in anticipation as the twists and turns of the plot unfolded. It was as if, he thought, he already knew the tale.

"...and that's pretty much it. I might have left out a few details. I'm not exactly sure."

The Director waved this qualification away and swung his chair heavily around so his back was to the Deputy.

"Tell me again, Knox. Is it true that these posts are being found everywhere?"

"Yes, sir."

"You have no idea where this—phenomenon—originated?"

"I'm afraid not, sir."

There was a long, terrible silence broken at the end by a pained sigh.

When the Director spoke again, his voice was bright, cheerful even. "I've got some good news. A nice counter-weight to your failures, I'd say. The lottery fraud prosecution campaign we've been running is wrapping up. It's been very successful, of course."

"Congratulations, sir."

"So I've been thinking." Knox could feel the ice cold anger that rimmed the happy talk. "It might be nice if I took the time to help you sort out this 'Kallimos' issue."

The words sent one message, the emotion another.

"The UPT, the Brotherhood, the K...Kallimos thing—I'm taking over."

"But, sir..."

"Shut up, Knox. You've done the best you could, and God knows I've tolerated your incompetence. But I do owe you more." The Director paused dramatically. "You should think of this as an opportunity to learn, to see the master at work."

Knox swallowed hard.

"You are dismissed."

The Deputy stood and began to gather his things. The Director continued to face the window behind his desk. Through the pane, the city glittered.

"Good night, sir."

"Knox," the Director answered. "Don't let the door hit you in the ass on the way out."

Knox ran for the nearest bathroom, crashed through the stall door, knelt in front of the toilet, and vomited until his stomach was empty.

52
THE FIRST PRIORITY

Val Thomas was at work. Her second cup of nettle tea sat on her loom's wooden beam. Early morning light filled the room with a pale, earthly glow. Caleb and Emma were out seeing patients, and she looked forward to finishing the blanket she owed to Nathan Miller. The day was young, but the pain had already risen out of her lower abdomen and into her back. The wooden bench on which she had sat so comfortably for so many years now seemed hard as stone. She blew across the rim of her mug and took a long sip, savored the flavor, hoped it would numb the pain.

It didn't.

The data streaming across Virgil's LCD screen made no sense. He rubbed his eyes. He was accustomed to gliding along the back corridors, the hidden passages and cul-de-sacs of the GRID, passing unseen, going wherever he needed to go. He was a digital ghost drifting through a virtual world. All of his favorite haunts now crawled with GRIDbots, the automated software packages that served as the eyes and ears of the DSJ.

The screen flashed red and the workstation's tinny speaker squawked ominously. A packet sniffer was onto him, only two, maybe three jumps behind.

"Damn," Virgil pressed the escape button and broke the machine's connection to the GRID.

He heard Chloe and the girls gathering in the kitchen above his head. It was time for supper; it was time for a break.

Night was falling and with it came the soft, wet flakes the Elders called "onion snow".

Caleb and Emma rode in silence. There was flu in West Farthing, and the day had been long and difficult. Some of their friends and neighbors would not live to see the spring. Death. Emma had seen him at work today preparing the ground, sharpening his scythe, ready to reap what was his. Death, and the fear of death, clung to them as they rode into the falling winter night.

"Dad," Emma broke the silence, "I'm worried about Mom." The words pierced Caleb's heart. He was worried, too. So afraid, that he had not dared speak his fears aloud.

"She's losing weight," Emma said.

"I know."

"Tired. Too tired."

"Mmm hmm."

"Have you said anything to her?"

"No, you?"

More silence. Then, "No."

They were almost home. The night seemed terribly dark and cold. When the horses were put away, they went inside to talk to Val.

Virgil worked his way into the DSJ's policy section. If there was an explanation for what was going on, he was likely to find it here. He sifted skillfully through gigabytes of dreck. There were hundreds of mind-numbing GRID policy folders with names like "Intra-Demo Conflict Suppression," "Maintaining Xenophobic Sentiment Among the Non-Religious: Case Studies," and "V.L. Point Fraud: Problem or Solution?" When he stumbled onto "Leadership Priorities—2049," he decided to take a closer look.

For: DSJ Management Level Five.

Confidential: Eyes Only

Author: J. Knox, Deputy Director

After a comprehensive review of the DSJ's stance on criminal activity outside of established Demos, the Director has decided to refocus on this threat.

Henceforth:

1. GRID Network Security will double resources dedicated to GRID network perimeter defenses, with an emphasis on identification, tracing, and apprehension of alien intruders.

2. The DSJ's stance toward the so-called Brotherhood is hereby elevated from management and deterrence to detention and punishment.

3. It is the Director's view that the DSJ has, to date, failed to prepare properly for the emergence of an off-GRID insurgency capable of undermining peace, order, and proper authority. Recent evidence has emerged that a terrorist-inspired insurgency may be forming or may be likely to form. All DSJ staff are hereby instructed to maintain a high degree of vigilance and report all incidents of uncertified individual personal travel directly to the Director's office—Priority One.

Caleb, Emma, and Val sat together by the fire and talked. The conversation kept its distance from the future but wandered freely through the past. Val and Caleb remembered their little girl's first step, her first word. They told the story of the first time they had seen Emma astride Doc, flying like the wind across the land. Val told Emma about the morning the Aunties came to the house to tell her that her little girl was out riding post.

Not spoken of, but even more important, were the thousands of moments, forgotten in their particulars, but remembered as a whole. It was the story of a little girl, tired, wet, hungry, and cold—a girl who found refuge in the Shire grown to womanhood—blessed with a husband gentle and kind and a little girl of her own, flesh of her flesh, bone of her bone.

The sickness was, Caleb felt certain, ovarian cancer. It had already spread to her liver, spine, and lung. There was no cure. Tomorrow he would ride to see Virgil, share the sad news with his brother, and ask him to hack the GRID for a supply of pharmaceutical-grade morphine. It would be needed.

Virgil upgraded his encryption and ventured back into a digital world that bristled with danger. Better cloaked this time, he slipped through its back alleys, its dark, empty places.

Inside the DSJ's record storage vault, he tried to gain entry to the Director's personal files. No good. They were locked down hard. Virgil drifted over to the Deputy's database. Hmm, 16-bit passcode. With a little luck, he could get past that.

By midnight, he was in.

He found a directory "Weekly Meeting Notes: DDSJ, Deputy DDSJ" and opened it.

March 17, 2049
Recent Increases in UPT "cannot be tolerated"
New set of policies
Machetes ?!?
Militia
Raise Threat Level to "Extreme"
Teach the Brotherhood a lesson
2049 a "critical year"

It was late. Virgil rubbed his tired eyes. Something was changing inside the crazy GRID world. There was fear, fear and loathing, but who could say what it meant. He broke the station's connection to the network and powered the unit down. Chloe would be asleep. She would be in bed, soft and warm beneath the covers. It was time to join her there.

The sun drove the snow away then revived the earth. Emma raised her face to the sky, closed her eyes, and savored the tender touch of a south breeze. Spring had come. The crocuses and snowdrops were up. It would not be long now. She bent down and cut the delicate blooms and formed them into a spring bouquet.

She hung her riding hood by the door and listened for movement. Silence. She tiptoed to her parents' room and pushed the door gently open. Her mother was asleep, the breath deep, easy, regular. That was good. Emma returned to the kitchen to get a vase for the flowers and found the note left by her father. He had gone to Bucklebury. First trimester bleed, shouldn't be long. The family would come in the evening. She returned to her mother's side, placed the flowers on the bedside table, listened to her breathing, drank the sound into her very soul. Then she sat down, gently placed her hand, so long and thin into her mother's. She had her mother's hands, no one could dispute that.

The time was coming.

Emma picked up the thick, hand-bound volume with the word *Kallimos* etched into its thick leather cover. Though she knew the story by heart, she opened the book to "The Treasure Seekers." In a moment, she was transported to Kallimos. In her imagination she was there, standing at her grandparents' side.

Hours later, Val stirred. Emma gave her a sip of water, then felt her pulse. The words came slowly, with difficulty, "I never got to see it…"

"See what, Mom?"

"Kallimos," Val nodded painfully. "My mother never really believed. Too much of a scientist." She managed a weak smile. "She said it didn't matter anyway. How we lived, that's what mattered."

Emma, not sure what to say, asked, "Does it matter, Mom?"

Val nodded again. Then she seemed to change the subject. "My ring. I want you to have it."

"No, Mom, no."

Val slipped the inscribed gold band from her finger.

"Jude always said it was special. She was right."

"You keep it, Mom."

Trembling, Val held it out to her daughter. Emma could not refuse her mother's wish.

"You will go there. Someday. I know you will."

"Go where, Mom?"

"To Kallimos. It is waiting for you."

"No, Mom. You're going to get better and I'm going to stay here with you."

Val smiled weakly.

"Take the ring with you when you go. Take it home, to Kallimos."

Emma did not answer. Her mother drifted into a peaceful sleep.

Caleb returned home, as promised, late in the afternoon. Virgil, Chloe, Zach, and Sadie arrived not long after. Val's breathing became irregular, pausing then beginning again. A mottled blue crept slowly up her arms and legs. She moaned, and Caleb gave her another dose of morphine, the last. A reverent stillness filled the room. Each said goodbye, Emma last of all. She whispered into her mother's ear, "I love you, Mom, and I will miss you. Miss you so, so much." Her voice broke into a sob. Her tears wetted her mother's dark brown hair, so like her own. "You can go, Mom. I'll be alright. You can go."

Emma stood beside the bed with her father's steady arm around her. Val Thomas was gone.

53
ALONE

Tall dark clouds strode out of the night, marched across the city, and drenched it with warm rain. Lightning flashed against the cityscape forcing it to reveal itself, if only for a moment. Thunder rumbled and crashed along steep manmade canyons. Ordinarily, the Director made it a point to ignore the weather. Doing so numbered among the privileges of his position. He was strong enough, rich enough, powerful enough to ignore the wind and rain, even the seasons themselves, but tonight the weather could not be ignored. He was alone in an opulent apartment 108 stories above the street. A wild aerial battle raged outside of his windows, forced him to witness its power.

If the thunder don't get you, then the lightening will...

He shook his head, drove the words away. They came from a song he learned when he was young. Stupid, wrong, an obvious lie—just like everything else in the Shire. He thought of the only real home he ever knew, in Chicago. His family was together there, all safe, all happy. His heart still ached for them.

You can't go back and you can't stand still.

Sleep came long after the storm had blown through. In his dreams, he was a child again. His mother, father, and sister were there with him, before the world fell apart. It was his birthday, their birthday. Val stood beside him, eyes bright and laughing. The lights flickered then went out. There should have been candles and a cake, but there was only darkness. He called for his mother and father, but they did not answer. He called for Val, his companion from even before birth, his sister, his twin. He called her name, but she did not answer. Then he knew he was alone, completely alone.

In the morning, Eron buzzed Samantha.

"Yes, sir?"

"Find that retard Knox and tell him to get his ass over here, we're done holding back."

54
WHO WILL RIDE?
Spring, 2049

The month of May tripped lightly across The Shire, and Virgil Thomas decided it was time to pay a visit to his sisters. He hadn't seen them since the day Val was buried. He arrived with a gift, a kitchen gadget they didn't want and wouldn't use. The real gift was the time they spent working together, preparing the soil for the season's first planting. He was worried, he said, about Caleb and Emma. They suffered a terrible blow. His sisters listened deeply. He pounded stakes, one at each end of each row, then ran twine between them, marking out rows that were literally straight as a string. Their mother had always insisted on this and there could be no doubt—these women were their mother's daughters. By the time the last seed was in the ground, he arrived at the worry that weighed most heavily on his mind. "I keep an eye on them. You know, sort of my hobby. And lately I've been seeing stuff, pretty bad stuff. The GRID is going crazy. It's all upset about things that don't, and that shouldn't, really matter to it."

Hannah sighed, as if recalling a bad dream.

"The GRID has always been this enormous, completely..." he searched for the right word, "self-involved thing, like a whole world that can only think about itself—and nothing else." Haleigh nodded, encouraging her brother to continue. "So, normally—well, for as long as I can remember—it's been obsessed, just obsessed—that's the only word for it—with keeping the Xenos fat, happy, and stupid. Nothing else mattered." The work was done and the warmth of the day began to fade. They put away their tools and went inside. Haleigh rattled the embers of the fire and set a pot of tea to boil. Virgil took his customary chair. These were his younger sisters but he came to them, always came to them, with his most difficult problems. They were already Elders of the Shire. It was who they were.

He picked up the story where he had left off. "Last year, there was this episode where the Militia ran down a branch of the Brotherhood. Put a half a dozen of them on this show trial thing they have. Convicted the poor bastards and tortured them to death, right on the screen. Highest ratings of the year."

The sisters grimaced but said nothing.

Virgil took a deep breath. "The past couple months, since the New Year really, there's something more. It's like..." The idea seemed bizarre and he was reluctant to voice it.

"Go on," Haleigh prodded.

"It's like it's a snake that's wound up tight, hissing, spitting, not striking but getting ready to strike."

"Strike what?" Haleigh asked.

"I don't know, maybe it doesn't even know, but it feels like..." Again, he hesitated.

This time Hannah spoke. "Like it's coming for the Underground?"

"Yeah, for the Underground, the Shire. Coming for us."

The sisters glanced knowingly at each other. The Council of Elders needed to hear this news.

A week later, the whole of the Shire gathered in the Pavilion. Virgil took the stage and spoke confidently of his findings and his concerns. "I can't say anything for certain, but I believe, I believe very strongly, that the GRID has somehow learned of, or at least suspects, the existence of the Eden Underground."

Basketmaker Emmet Gale asked, "How could that be?"

Virgil answered the best he could. "I don't know about the how, but that's not the important thing. What's important is that orders requiring the Xenos to seek out unauthorized persons have been issued. Also, they're distributing machetes to the watchmen. We can no longer send out riders. It's too dangerous, and I believe it's going to be dangerous for a long time." He left the stage and took his seat next to Chloe and his girls.

Mark Hemple, seventh generation farmer, painter, teller of stories, and Elder of his people, stepped forward. "Many here will remember when the Council asked the Tribes to think about the GRID, its past, its future, and the dangers it poses to all people. The Elders believe the end of the GRID draws near. Within its failure lies a choice between a new era of peace and freedom or war and barbarity. We are in danger, all of us. Our families and our friends, homes, our workshops and barns, our land, we are in danger of losing everything."

This stunning declaration, offered in a calm and matter-of-fact voice, stunned the Tribes of Eden.

"As Elders, we have asked ourselves, what should be done? How shall we advise the people of the Shire? We know that some of you will want to fight against this evil in order to protect what is ours. Some will say that we should join forces with the Brotherhood, cement an alliance, go to war at their side. Who among us would beat our plowshares into swords?"

"I will!" Master Tinker Nathaniel Garry rose to his feet. His face flushed with emotion. "I say we fight!"

Mark Hemple bowed in his direction. "I honor your skill Master Tinker and am in awe of your courage. But bravery of this kind offers only a prelude to disaster. Many years ago, a wise Elder said, 'It is folly to talk of violent struggle when the other side has all the guns.' A war against the GRID would be short and brutal and would result in our complete destruction."

Nathaniel nodded, acknowledging the wisdom in the Elder's words.

"Some of you, no doubt, agree that a fight is not in our interests. You may be hoping this storm will pass us by as so many others have. Perhaps if we vanish even more completely into the land, we will be saved. Many among us remember the day the first riders," Hemple nodded respectfully toward the Thomas brothers, "carried a post to Ned Wolff in Ithaca, almost a quarter of a century ago. Our young have ridden and our Elders have written all these years because we've come to understand and believe in the unique power born out of an alliance between youth and age." The people listened with care. "The Eden Underground has become wisdom that moves across the night and into hearts of our brothers and sisters who are trapped inside the Demos. We have believed and taught others to believe in the value of memory, in the power of legacy, in the virtue of a life lived long and well."

Hemple took his time. This was the decisive moment.

"It is the custom of our people, our chosen way, that the Elders may speak but they cannot command. They may influence but cannot coerce. After much discussion, we, the Elders of the Tribes of Eden, have arrived at a consensus. We believe that Virgil is correct. The Underground is in danger. What is more, the Shire itself is in danger. But this is not our greatest concern." Few in the audience could imagine what could be worse than the loss of the Shire and its way of life. Still, they listened. "It is the future of the world that hangs now by the thinnest of threads. The GRID cannot endure, will not endure. We believe the Tribes of Eden exist to catch the world when it falls."

The statement elicited a storm of anxious protest. "Save the world? How can we? Impossible! What about the Shire? What about our families?"

Mark Hemple let the people have their say, and then continued, "The Elders ask, what will become of the generations yet to be born if we surrender to our fears?" Mark Hemple drew a deep breath. "Your Elders ask...who shall ride?"

Emma Thomas was the first to answer. She stood straight and tall, and she faced the people of the Shire. She spoke without fear. "I will ride."

Then Renata Wilson, apprentice Miller, stood. "I will ride."

And then another.

And another.

"I will ride."

Through their courage, the decision was made. The Underground would continue to shine the light of memory into Demo's barren darkness.

Mark Hemple dismissed the assembly, sending them into the night saying, "Such is the will of our people. May your grandchildren's grandchildren tell their children of this day and the courage shown by their ancestors. Today we grasp the nettle. Today we take hold of the future of the world."

55
WITCH HUNT

Cody Brooks scowled at his GRID station. The news was bad and getting worse. Ominous warnings about witches and warlocks swarmed across the screen. The jangling chime that signaled a news update brought him back to the screen. "The DSJ reminds all citizens that treasonous, disease-infested, social perverts and outcasts continue their attempts to infiltrate peaceful, law-abiding Demos. Viewers are advised to monitor their non-VL surroundings closely. Witches and warlocks are known to be especially active at this time." Cody huffed. A rider was due from the Shire, and the timing was terrible.

The GRID had gone insane. It was pumping fear into people's heads like it was 2015. His voice and the voices of the other Elders in the Demo were drowned out by the terror that this crazed propaganda was designed to provoke. He heard the faint tap of pebble against glass, hurried to the window in the back bedroom, pulled the drapes, and lifted the sash. It was one of his favorites, Emma Thomas. She boosted herself out of the alley and into the safety of Cody's house. "Emma, you shouldn't have come. Things are bad, really bad."

"Yeah, we know. Uncle Virgil hacked the GRID and found out all about it."

"And you still came?"

"Sure, Cody," she answered nonchalantly. "the Elders sent you a folio."

This was welcome news, especially in these times, but the danger had never been greater. In the kitchen Cody heated water for tea. Emma called it "crazy tea" because it made her feel jittery when she had too much. The floor concealed a trap door leading to a tiny underground bunker. It had been built ages ago, when the owners imaged it could protect them from an atom bomb.

Cody reported the news. "Word came down from the DSJ that the Demo Watch would have their weapons upgraded. They turned in their billy clubs, and now the knuckleheads are running around with machetes, sharp as hell." He glanced at the slender folio lying on the table between them. "Those posts aren't worth your life."

"Yes they are. They matter, and so do you."

Cody shook his head. "Matter, sure they matter—but more than you, more than your life? I don't think your Dad would agree with that."

"He agrees. Told me to say hello for him. The Underground's not backing down."

Cody Brooks knew it was right. He agreed in spite of the price that might have to be paid. The time was coming. He could feel it.

The rat-a-tat of metal striking wood put them into motion. "Damn! Down you go, Emma." She pulled a tattered throw rug aside, lifted the handle, and dropped easily into her hiding place. The hatch swung shut, and Cody replaced the rug.

The banging at the front door grew louder, more insistent.

Cody scanned the room, saw the folio lying on the table, picked it up, and slid it beneath his vest. He unbuckled his belt, unzipped his pants, and put on his best doddering old man act.

"Just a minute, just a damn minute." He made a show of peering out from behind a curtain then unbolted the door and swung it open. It was Kenny-Boy and a half dozen of the Bishop's Demo Watch goons.

"Sorry to disturb you, ah, Mr. Brooks."

"I was in the head tryin' to take a crap and let me tell you—takin' a crap is no easy thing when you get to be my age."

Kenny-Boy made a point of staring at the old man's undone pants.

Cody made a show of noticing. "Oh yeah, right." He hitched up his trousers and redid his belt. This mundane interlude deflated some of Watchmen's excitement.

"Sir, guard post three reports possibly sighting a witch in this area tonight. Maybe an hour ago."

The homeowner feigned astonishment. "I heard something about witches and warlocks. There was news about it on the GRID."

Kenny-Boy raised his voice the way young people do when they want to, politely, assert their authority. "This isn't just on the GRID. The Bishop is very concerned. He asked us to check the houses along here."

"Oh, I see. Well, come on in, boys."

They crowded through the door, eager to have the job done.

"Heavens yes, boys, I'd feel a lot safer if you gave the windows and doors a good going over."

The Watchman interrupted Cody, "Seen anything suspicious? Heard anything unusual?"

"No, not a thing. Sure am glad you boys are here though."

"Just doing our job, sir."

Then, from the kitchen, "Hey, Kenny-Boy, come look at this."

The burly captain hustled to the back of the house.

"Cody's got two cups of tea out."

Kenny-Boy turned on the old man. "You alone?"

"Hell yeah, I'm alone. Miss my wife though, miss her real bad." The expression on his face made his meaning clear, even to them. He poured a cup of tea for her, pretending she was still alive.

"Whatever."

Another Watchman rejoined the group. "Perimeter's OK."

It was good enough for Kenny-Boy.

They returned to the front foyer. "Yer free to, ah, go back to whatever you were doing."

Cody struggled to conceal his relief.

"Just so you know, Mr. Brooks," Kenny-Boy said, "The Klaxons are set on high. If you see something, anything unusual, just punch it into the GRID and we'll come runnin'."

"Yes, young fellow. I'm sure you will." Cody clapped the squad leader on the back. "Thanks so much for looking out for me, looking out for all of us."

"No problem," the Watchman accepted the compliment. "It's our job. We got a dozen more houses to do, so, gotta get goin'."

The door closed with a satisfying clunk, and Cody leaned against it, listening. When he was sure they were gone, he returned to the pantry and released Emma from the bomb shelter.

"They're going house to house looking for a witch, looking for you. Oh, this is bad. This is very bad."

Emma pulled herself up and out in a single motion and proceeded to dust herself off. "Cody, you've got the folio. I should leave."

The Elder considered this carefully. "Those stumble bums don't know what the hell they're doing, and we probably shouldn't wait around for them to figure it out."

"If I'm out by midnight and ride hard, Doc won't mind. I can make the Shire before sunrise."

It was the safest course of action, and he could help by creating a distraction. "I'll head up Sullivan Street and make a stink at the Bishop's place. You peel around to the south."

At midnight, Cody clumped down his front steps, making a show of cussing and complaining so the neighbors would be sure to notice him. He turned right and headed toward the Bishop's house, grumbling loudly as he went. The streets were, of course, deserted, but he did manage to attract attention. Emma donned her riding cloak and slipped out the side window and into the alley. Keeping to the shadows, she made her way south.

As he approached the Bishop's house, Cody began to hoot and holler. Lights flicked on. The trick was to make a fuss big enough to distract but not so big as to trip the Klaxons.

"Bishop! Oh, Bishop, I've got news, I think. Or a question. Wake up! This is no time to sleep."

The sash of a second story window slid upward and the Bishop's head appeared in the gap. "Whatever is the matter, Brother Brooks?"

Emma hid in a dead-end alley; she only had two blocks to go. A patrol trudged by and passed out of sight. She stepped into the open and ran into Kenny-Boy. The collision stunned them both. The moment he saw that she was a stranger, he drew his machete from its sheath. In the next instant he realized this was the witch he'd been hunting for. He swung the blade with a blind fury. Emma raised her arm against the blade. "No, don't!" she cried. The flat edge of the machete struck her forearm with a glancing blow, but the sharp edge tore into the flesh of her right thigh, knocking her to the ground.

The captain of the guard raised the blade, eager to strike a fatal blow. In a single motion, Emma dodged the blade and sprang to her feet. The pain blurred her vision, but her mind was clear. She could imagine how she must look to the Watchman. Tall and thin, her face hidden in the depth of a flowing black riding hood—she was the very image of the witch he had been taught to fear. "Pathetic human," she hissed. "Your toy blade cannot harm me."

It was true. He struck at her with all his strength, and yet she stood before him, apparently unharmed.

She recognized the man from Cody's description. "You are the Captain of the Bishop's Guard—the one the demons of Hell call 'Kenny-Boy.'"

His jaw worked soundlessly.

"Yes, it is you, isn't it? Poor boy," she growled.

"Do not cry out," Emma warned, "or you will draw them to you. The demon brood of Hell will rise to claim you, if you speak a word." A drizzle of urine spattered the pavement.

Kenny-Boy clamped his mouth shut.

Emma could feel blood pooling in her right boot.

"Drop the knife, Kenny-Boy. Drop it or I will fill your insides with burning sulfur." Emma raised her hand and pointed at Kenny-Boy's face. His eyes fixed on the long, crooked index finger that seemed about to strike him dead.

The machete clattered to the pavement. When it did, Emma whirled into the shadows. For a moment, Kenny-Boy was paralyzed by fear, unwilling to speak or even move. He rediscovered his courage after she was gone. "The witch!" he roared. "The witch! The witch is here, sound the Klaxon!"

Seconds later, the searchlights flashed on. Klaxons howled piteously into the night. Emma sprinted down the middle of the street. Three blocks til she reached the wall. The pain, even when numbed by a tidal surge of adrenaline, threatened to overcome her. She looked over her shoulder. Kenny-Boy had rejoined his posse. They were gaining on her.

The news flashed on every GRID screen in the Demo. The Bishop wanted to be there, to witness this triumph over evil. He clattered out of his house wearing only a robe over his pajamas. "Cody! There is a witch on the south side and, God willing, she'll not see the light of day." The Bishop joined the mob. Cody Brooks, heart breaking, trailed in their wake.

One block to go and Emma's breaths came in ragged gasps. Her legs burned from life-or-death exertion. Her cloak flowed out like a cape as she ran while her hood continued to hide her face. The sight of her was enough to dissuade the Xenos from joining the pursuit.

Emma put on her final burst of speed and disappeared into a narrow, dark alley. Thirty yards to the wall. Emma knew she would have to hit it at full stride. She leapt up onto a discarded packing crate, swung out onto an exposed joist, grabbed hold, and willed her body up and over the top. She lost her grip and fell to the ground with a thud.

Inside the Demo, the Klaxons roared and she could hear the confused cries of a gathering mob. She pulled herself to her feet and limped painfully across the clearing that separated the Demo from the encroaching forest. Then came the sweetest sound she had ever heard, or would ever hear. Doc's hoof beats drummed the earth. He was down wind of her; he smelled her blood. Hell would never know such a fury. Seconds later, the coal black stallion burst into the clearing, scattering clods of soil in his wake.

Emma struggled to her feet. Doc would, she knew, lower his head for her and help her up onto his back. All she had to do was hold on. The baying of the Demo's hounds now joined the cacophony. But that no longer mattered.

"Home, Doc," Emma whispered. "Home to the Shire."

And they were gone.

The Bishop addressed his followers. "That damned—I do mean damned in every sense of the word—that damned witch was here. You can still smell the sulfur." He paused to make note of Cody's arrival. "We all owe a depth of gratitude to Mr. Brooks. A man who, though burdened by his years, was still able to raise the alarm." Cody nodded and remained silent. The Bishop continued to spin his tale. "You can see here, from the footprints that the witch ran down this way. She seized her broom and whoosh—up into the sky." As the Bishop prattled, Cody reached inside his vest and felt the folio of posts that lay next to his heart. They were precious, as precious as blood.

Caleb was, as usual, up at dawn and puttering about in the kitchen when he heard Doc's distinctive whinny. The stallion never approached any living soul, save Emma. Now he called to Caleb. Outside he found his daughter lying prone on Doc's back. He placed his hand on her body—it was cool. His body involuntarily trembled. He forced himself to continue even though he wanted to cry out, to wail his grief. Her limbs were stiff as he pulled her dead weight down off the horse. Only when a soft moan escaped her lips did Caleb know that she still lived. He carried her into the house and set to work cheating Death of his prize.

The Director had sown a whirlwind. Knox rode alone in the elevator as it descended to the loading dock. He would be signing for another shipment of folios, the second of the day. The Xenos were in a panic and the harder they looked for Post Riders, the more they found. The wave of killing sickened Knox, but what happened to the survivors was much worse. He shuddered at the thought.

The shipping clerk saw Knox coming and scurried off to load the authorization documents into his clipboard computer. The boxes of folios were stacked on a dolly cart; there were too many to be hand carried. He would have liked to read them, but that, he knew, was not to be. They would be delivered directly to the Director's office and no one would ever see them again.

Knox sighed heavily as he thumbed the tablet.

"Need help, sir?"

Hell yes, he thought. *I need help, a world of help.*

"No, its fine. I'll take them up."

"OK then."

The dolly had an annoying squeaking wheel that, along with its high-ranking pilot, drew sidelong stares as Knox approached the Director's office.

Samantha, cool as ever, shot Knox a 'he's Hell-on-wheels today' look then said, in a crisp professional tone, "The Director said to send you right in."

Knox mumbled, "Thanks," as Samantha opened the door for him.

Inside, the Director was on the phone. He was uncharacteristically quiet. The high back of his chair muffled the conversation.

Knox waited.

The Director finished with his call and turned slowly around. His face was ashen.

"I brought the boxes personally, like you asked, sir."

Eron nodded.

"Sit down, Knox," he murmured.

"That..." a deep sigh emerged as if forced out of him by great pressure, "was the Chairman. Not a happy man, the Chairman. Plenty pissed, actually.

Ran into Colson out on the West Coast, and Colson crapped all over us, all over the DSJ. Told the Chairman we were bad for business." The Director closed his eyes as if to contemplate the Chairman's displeasure in private. Slowly and then, Knox thought, involuntarily, a thin smile crept across the old bastard's face.

When Eron was ready, he offered Knox an expansive fake smile.

"Well, then. We can't let politics interfere with our duty, can we, Knox?"

"No, sir." Knox agreed, warily.

"So let's look at the big picture. You've let this 'off the GRID' activity flourish right under your nose. Right, Knox?"

"Yes, sir. It seems so, sir."

The Director held out his hands palms up. "Now, I like you. I've always liked you, Knox. Despite your constant screw-ups, I think you're a good egg."

Knox did not like where this was going.

"I've looked at this crap," the Director cast a glance at the boxes that sat mutely on the cart, "and you are right. There's nothing there. A bunch of 'meaning of life' bullshit."

"That's my take on it, sir."

The fake smile returned. "So what does it matter? Hmm, Knox?"

"Well, it's unauthorized. Uncertified."

"Unnatural, evil. Plain evil." The Director spat the words.

Knox mumbled agreement, "That's right, sir."

The moment passed and the Director regained his composure. "So it's just shit, but unfortunately for them, we don't put up with shit." The little joke seemed to please him. Knox waited. "So, how are they doing it? How are these people moving from Demo to Demo without being seen, thousands and thousands of people moving around without being seen?"

Knox brightened. "I've looked into it, sir. The satellite crews have drilled down on areas around Demos and, well, we've found deer, bears, even wolves, but no people. None."

The Director leaned back in his chair, the way he imagined a professor would. "Knox," he asked, "you grew up here, in the city, right?"

"Yes, in Brooklyn, actually."

"Well, the night in Brooklyn and the night," the Director waved his arm dismissively, "out there, are two very different things."

The idea was ridiculous. "Night? They travel at night? Across the wilderness from one Demo to another?"

"Mmm hmm."

"That's insane," Knox said.

"Oh, I agree, but it also explains why you never see them, Knox. They don't want to be seen, they don't want to be watched, they don't want to be monitored. This is their crime. That is why they must be destroyed. The crap they carry, it means nothing. Their desire to evade surveillance—that is proof of great crime. It's proof of treason, Knox. Treason."

"Yes, sir."

"Now, the Chairman wants heads on pikes—you know what I mean— and the shit is everywhere, just everywhere." The Director went off on a rant. Knox sat glum and still. Finally, the man behind the desk circled back round to his deputy. "Here's the good news, Knox. The good news is I've been doing your job in addition to mine. No surprise, really. Goddamnit, I've been doing your job for years. At any rate, I've got a handle on where this is all coming from."

Knox snapped back to attention.

"If an intelligent person reads this, you see, an intelligent mind can walk it all back. Follow the tracks, so to speak, follow them all the way back to here." The Director jabbed his finger onto a paper map lying on his desk.

The scene, Knox realized, had been planned carefully in advance.

The Director insisted Knox study the map closely. A pudgy finger stabbed the map just east of the Finger Lakes, south of the Adirondacks, north of the Catskills, west of the Hudson, in the middle of nowhere.

Knox failed to hide his disbelief and the Director pounced.

"You doubt me, Knox? Don't say a word. I know it. You, a ten-cent moron, doubt me? You had years to figure this out. It took me a couple of weeks. A couple of weeks—tops."

"Congratulations, sir."

Eron Wallace savored the moment. "You are damned right. I saved your ass—again, Knox. Now, if you look closely you will see that transportation corridors surround the area we are concerned with. 90, here—88, here—and 81, here. It's a nice little triangle."

Knox agreed. They could easily control the perimeter.

"The first thing you do, Knox, is you clean the Brotherhood out of these corridors. I don't want detentions. I don't want enforcement. I want freaking disinfection. Understand?"

Knox swallowed hard. "Yes, sir."

"Fine. We both know you're as stupid as a bag of hammers, so there's no reason for you to know anymore for now. Cut orders for the Militia. Use the drones with your IR shit. Blast them—napalm, white phosphorus, let the assholes use whatever they want. Clean the perimeter—that's the first goddamned step. You follow, Knox?"

Knox said, "Yes."

"Copy me on the orders. Now get the hell out of my sight."

Two hours later, the orders flashed onto the Director's work screen.

To: Corporate Militia, First Division; Counter Terror Command
From: Office of the DDSJ
Re: Uncontrolled Brotherhood Activity—Militia Response Required
Date: September 30, 2049

The Director has identified a significant threat of terrorism-related activity in the "Iron Triangle" area of sector H (see map). The Director has authorized the use of IR Drones equipped with anti-personnel incendiary munitions. This is a Priority One counter-insurgency operation. Militia units are authorized to fire upon and destroy all Brotherhood cells operating in the designated zones. The decontamination can begin at the command officers' discretion within 5 days of the date of this order.

57
DRONES

Emma wondered which was worse: delirium, fever, and blood loss, or being well and having people insist that you still needed to rest. She played the wounded bird long enough. Her strength had returned. It was time to fly. Doc shared her impatience. He wanted to run hard across the night once more. She was twenty-four-years-old. She would go to her father and tell him she was leaving for Ithaca. He would not deny her his blessing.

There was news that Ned Wolff was not well. Drew Collins had seen him a week before. Ned had lost weight and had a bad cough. As expected, Caleb insisted his daughter wasn't fully healed and pleaded with her to take more time. They lingered over the last meal then sat outside as evening crept across the Shire. The earth breathed and they found pleasure in the sound.

"You know," Caleb ventured, "I'll bet Virgil could get a peak at Ned's GRID records. Could save you a trip over."

"Dad," Emma laughed, "like you would trust the Digital Doctor."

Caleb smiled faintly. "You know, you're all I have left...."

The daughter reached out and touched her father's hand. Venus hung low in the western sky with Jupiter just above her. High overhead, Emma knew without looking, was Saturn, the old man of the sky.

"It's time," she said.

"I know." Her father held her and looked into her dark hazel eyes. They were her mother's eyes. He kissed her gently on the forehead. "I love you, Emma."

"I love you, Dad."

Caleb reluctantly loosed his grip. Emma donned her riding cloak, shouldered her rucksack, and walked down to the Turnpike looking back, once, to wave goodbye.

She trotted along the road, heading west. It felt good to run, to be free, to be perched, as all living souls must be, between the warm damp earth and the stars sparkling high above.

She heard Doc coming up from behind her, fast. He was at full stride, offended that she had started without him, eager to join her. When he caught up with her, he circled, snorting and stamping in the way that she found so endearing and everyone else found so terrifying. "OK, let's go, Doc." Emma leapt onto his back and they were off, a dark star crashing through the night.

At midnight on the second day of her ride she approached a camp of Brotherhood. She circled carefully, looking for signs of a watch. There was none. She hopped to the ground and crept closer. Doc followed at a distance. She entered the camp, walked directly to the main tent, and pulled back the flap. Inside, a score of wounded men lay on the ground, the women and children doing their best to tend to them. Serena pale with exhaustion. "Thank God you're here." Jerry was one of the few men able to be up and around. The three of them huddled together.

"A week ago, I don't know, maybe a hundred miles north of here," Jerry explained, "we hit a convoy and they had Militia—hidden—not showing like they usually do. They come out and start shooting rubber bullets close range, and then they beat the men."

Emma nodded.

Serena picked up the story. "Jerry, he's lucky. Took a rubber bullet to the side of the head and it knocked him out. They thought he was dead so they didn't beat him." Jerry, he had the "raccoon eyes" sign that usually indicated the presence of a skull fracture.

Emma rolled up her sleeves and set to work. By three in the morning it was time for a break. She stepped outside eager to feel the cool of the night air. Jerry and Serena joined her.

"Ned Wolff's sick. I've got to see him."

The world was breaking apart.

Jerry nodded. "You should go. Not much more you can do here."

Serena asked, "You will stop here on the way back—won't you?"

Emma agreed, "I will."

"One more thing," Jerry turned to face Emma. "The Militia—I guess it was Militia—closed the hole in the fence. Put up stainless steel. We had to go up north, about a half a mile, made a new opening there."

Emma nodded in the starlight.

Serena said, "Jerry you should ride out there with Emma, show her where it is."

"Whistle up that devil horse of yours and I'll get my bike." He kissed Serena. "I'll be right back, hon."

"I love you."

"Love you, too."

Doc followed the noisy smoke belching motorcycle at a sullen distance. The path was craggy, uneven, and littered with downed branches. It was rough going with a bike and a horse, and Emma marveled that the battered Brotherhood had made the passage.

"The opening's here and it's just the same on the other side. Just head south along the creek and you can pick up the old path from there."

"Thanks, Jerry. I'll be back soon." Doc began to prance and paw the earth.

"Hey, your ride wants to get going," Jerry said.

"No," Emma said. "Something's wrong. Kill the engine."

A deep, unnatural thrum reached them from a great distance. It was the sound of machines, powerful machines moving fast. They were coming down from the north.

Jerry spat, "Drones."

Emma closed her eyes and listened.

"They're robots, robot helicopters. The Militia uses them for surveillance. They've got night vision. We've got to get out of here." He kick started the bike's engine and they retreated into the bosom of the forest. Moments later, a pair of drones roared past only a hundred feet off the ground.

Jerry waited for them to fly past the Brotherhood's camp. Instead, they stopped, circled over the hiding place, hesitated for an instant, and then opened fire.

Dozens of incendiary shells slammed into the camp. The resulting fireball cast shadows in the night.

Jerry screamed, jumped on the bike's kick-start, and sped toward the camp. Doc and Emma kept pace behind him. The attack ended as quickly as it had started. The Drones retreated to a higher altitude, circled twice, then continued south along 81.

The heat was intense. The Brotherhood's vehicles had been reduced to blasted hulks. The tent, which had sheltered the Brotherhood, was reduced to ashes along with everyone inside. Jerry found Serena lying on the ground just outside of the entrance. She lay face down in the mud. He rolled her over. He begged her to answer him—but she did not move. Emma knelt beside him and laid her fingers on the place in the neck where the pulse should be. There was no pulse.

Jerry staggered to his feet, wailing for Max and Will. Emma bent down and felt for breath. There was no breath.

Out of the night Max's small voice asked, "Daddy? Daddy?"

The twins edged out from behind a boulder. Jerry ran to them, knelt down, and held them. Max began to wail. "Mommy told us to run. We ran like

Mommy said. We didn't make this fire, Daddy. Honest we didn't." Little Will nodded affirming his brother's plea.

"I know. I know you didn't. Bad men did this, not you."

Max caught sight of his mother and called out to her. The twins broke free from their father's grasp and ran to her side. Their mother's unseeing eyes frightened them, so Emma closed them gently with her fingers. She had closed the eyes of so many.

She looked up at Jerry. "We have to go. Now. They'll be back. They'll want to inspect their kill."

Jerry could not speak.

Emma stood and made the piercing whistle that meant *Doc, I need you*.

The stallion, eyes wide, braved the choking smoke, picking his way through the wreckage until he stood at Emma's side.

"Serena," Jerry mouthed the name of his beloved.

"Serena's dead, Jerry, but we are still alive. She'd want us to go."

Already the sound of a Militia convoy could be heard in the distance.

Emma leapt onto Doc's back.

"Give me Max." Jerry handed the wailing boy to Emma.

"Put Will behind me and then you get on." Jerry numbly did what he was told. Doc understood that it was time to go and found his way out of the ruined camp and into the forest.

The sound of trucks fast approaching was soon joined by the dull thudding of the Drones. Emma urged Doc on, and he responded. They climbed up along the Post Rider's trail, switching back and forth across the wooded face of the hillside. Emma caught glimpses of the camp, now far below. It was bathed in the light of Militia vehicles.

The drones—eager, angry, probing—arrived on the scene. Orders were no survivors.

"They'll be on us soon. Just leave me. Take the boys."

"No," Emma said. "The drones, they see heat, right?"

Jerry grunted, "Uh huh."

"Hold on." Emma wheeled Doc and they cut into a thicket and from there to a stand of hemlock that had grown up along a small stream. Emma climbed down from the stallion's back. She helped the boys down and then gave a hand to Jerry. A shallow pool of water reflected broken shards of moonlight.

"You three stay here, beside this stream. If the Drones get close, you get into the water, all the way in. Tell me you'll do what I say."

Jerry nodded.

"Stay here—right here. We'll be back for you."

Emma leapt onto Doc's back and the stallion reared. He was eager to run.

The Drones searched the valley floor but when they found nothing, their attention was directed to the hillside. They crisscrossed each other's paths like a pair of demented ravens.

Emma waited in a clearing just below the ridgeline. They stood in the open. Waiting.

A drone whooshed overhead, wheeled high in the sky, and returned for another look. Emma and Doc plunged into the thick of the forest. The other drone swung around in front of Emma and fired a shell into the forest. Above them, the crown of a maple exploded into flames.

In the Valley, the Militia's men raised a cheer. Doc took advantage of a well-worn deer path and they hurtled along its course toward the opening of a stony gorge. A second shot roared overhead, smashing into a ledge on their right.

Another hundred yards took them into the gorge. The drones followed in hot pursuit. The stallion lengthened his stride. The machines closed the distance between them.

Emma whispered, "Now, Doc." In the next instant, one ton of muscle, heart, and bone stopped, turned, and set out at a gallop back toward the opening of the gorge.

To the Drones' remote operators, it seemed as if the horse and its rider had vanished. They rechecked the IR readings, but the target was gone. Seconds were lost in the confusion, and now the walls of the gorge rose steeply in front of the machines, forming a narrow, stony prison.

The Drones' remote controllers pulled up—hard. The first banked left and smashed into the cliff. The second turned right, cleared the lip of the gorge, then struck a stand of oak and exploded into a ball of fire.

Doc and Emma retreated into the forest and caught their wind.

Far below, the operators reported to the Captain, "Both machines lost sir. Horse and rider. I don't know, they just disappeared. Maybe we got them, maybe they got away."

"Bullshit," the Captain answered. "File this: Targets eliminated, two Drones lost due to mechanical failure."

"Yes, sir."

The officer peered down at the remains of Serena Vazquez. "Bag this body, Corporal. It's evidence. Leave the rest. We're out of here."

Two days later, Doc and his riders approached Haleigh and Hannah's cottage.

"It's OK," Emma assured them. "My Aunties live here. They'll take care of you. You'll be safe here." The kitchen door swung open and Jerry, Max, and Will walked into their new lives as people of the Shire.

58
THE SNARE

Knox fidgeted outside of the Director's office. "He's in a state," Samantha murmured. Knox nodded in agreement. She rolled her eyes, "Obsessed I'd say."

"Oh, I don't know…" Knox was careful with Samantha. It would be just like the old bastard to put her up to testing his loyalty.

"Times are hard," he added.

The Director was on the phone interrogating a terrified database administrator in the health records section a dozen bureaucratic levels below him. "You're sure Wolff's records were properly locked and it was a hacker who got to them?" The man told the Director he was sure. "How long ago?"

"About three this morning."

"You moron! I told you to call me as soon as you had news. Jesus! Six hours?"

"I'm sorry, I…I didn't want to wake you."

The Director snapped, "You got a trace, right?"

"Couldn't. It was a crazy spoof. I've never seen anything like it. Trail went cold instantly."

Eron Wallace smiled. The bastards will know Ned is bad off—been zeroed out—finished. They'll try to help him.

"Anything else, sir?"

"No," he tapped the disconnect and buzzed Samantha. "Send the turd in."

The Director leaned back, slipped his left hand into his jacket pocket, and pulled out a thin, gold, brushed titanium cigarette case. He lit the cigarette, smoothly, expertly.

Knox gave his report. "The perimeter control operation you requested is complete, sir. One Brotherhood encampment was identified—and destroyed."

"Mmm hmm. Good. Survivors? Prisoners?" What he meant but didn't say was, "Witnesses?"

"The captain says there were none."

"Jesus Christ, Knox, you actually did something right."

The praise wounded him. He did a good job of facilitating the mass murder of innocents. He was supposed to feel proud but felt sick instead.

The Director leaned over the map on his desk. "I have reason to believe, Knox, good reason to believe, that the source of this infection is here." The Director's finger tapped a point on the map that was, apparently, the middle of nowhere.

Knox was sure the old man was losing his mind. "There?" He cleared his throat. "There, sir? Pardon me but there doesn't seem to be a 'there' there, sir."

"Oh, I know. I know there's nothing on the map, but there are people there. Evil, twisted bastards there." Flecks of saliva dotted the map.

"OK," Knox agreed, "but I don't—I can't—see how a band of destitute dead-enders could be behind it—behind all..." He struggled to find the word... and failed. "All of it."

The Director tapped his foot rhythmically. Nervous energy poured out of the man. Something was driving him, lashing him, punishing him.

Knox saw the bags under the eyes. The gorged, overfed appearance somehow left him gaunt. Haunted. Empty.

Knox knew there was much more to this than he was being told. He was a pawn. The Director would sacrifice him when the time came, he was sure of it. The time had come to put survival ahead of loyalty.

This realization passed across the face of John Knox, but the Director was staring at the map, his eyes boring into the past, into the Shire.

Knox intruded, "Anything else, sir?"

Eron looked up distractedly. "Stay close by, Knox. We may, we may be going on an expedition soon. We'll finish this, once and for all."

The Director never went anywhere. Ever.

"I'm going to issue the orders from here on out. I believe the bastards will soon be in our hands."

"So, I'll just..." Knox spoke cautiously. "I'll just standby."

Knox left the office without receiving the customary insult. Something strange and secret was happening and all he could do was wait.

59
NED WOLFF

The children of Bill and Jude Thomas gathered around their parents' old wooden table, bellies full, hearts heavy. Emma had returned to the Shire with the survivors of the GRID attack on the Brotherhood. The attack also meant that she had been unable to reach Ned Wolff. Virgil had accessed their old friend's medical records on the GRID. He was sick and had been zeroed-out. Virgil changed the "medical futility" designation on Ned's records, but every change was reversed seconds later.

Emma was insisting she should be the one to ride to Ithaca. Her victory over the Drones had led her into a deep faith in her own immortality—which worried them all.

It was agreed that the brothers would make the ride. They'd leave at nightfall.

"Who'll tell Emma?" Zach asked.

"We will," Hannah answered.

"Alright then," Caleb said. "We'll join up in Bywater, at dusk."

The Director stayed late in his office, savoring the moment. The city gleamed outside his window but he did not notice it. The movie that was running through his mind was far more appealing. The past, which for so long had been dead to him, was alive again. The bastards would get a taste of his justice. The whole goddamned Shire would tremble before him. He hadn't asked for this—he would have been content to let them all rot—but they hadn't known their place. They dared to crawl out from under the rock where he left them. Eron Wallace grunted as he raised his vast bulk to a standing position. He ran his hands over the delicate nanofiber fabric of his suit. Even after all these years, the touch of it still pleased him.

He pressed his private elevator's 'up' button. His sister would be a widow soon. Val and his mother would have no choice but to return to the city with him when it was over. The thought made him smile. It would be like the old days, in Chicago, before the Fall. The Director stepped into the waiting elevator cab, turned, and watched the doors slide noiselessly closed. He would sleep well.

In the depth of the night, hoof beats thundered against cold earth. Three riders bent low over their mounts, their boots dug deep into the stirrups, their riding cloaks fluttering and snapping behind them. Ahead of them, the moon's last quarter slipped quietly into the western sky. Ned Wolff needed them, and they were on their way.

60

RETURN TO THE SHIRE

The call came early, but it did not wake the Director. He lay in bed, awake, eyes staring, without seeing, into the darkness. His mind buzzed with excitement. The phone chirped, and he tapped the connect. "Have you got them?"

"No, sir. Not yet. But we have confirmation they entered the Cornell Demo during the night."

The Director grunted.

The voice in the earpiece faltered.

"Ah, the youngest one, Caleb Thomas, obtained four vials of Ticarcillin—illegally."

"And Wolff?"

"They are holed up at his place. No sign of the old man."

"When are you going to take them?"

"We brought an extraction team up from District Nine last night. They'll be in position before dawn."

"Good. I want them taken alive."

"Yes, sir."

"Alert Knox and have him prepare the broadcast convoy. We'll meet you at the rendezvous point."

"Yes, sir."

The Director tapped the disconnect and closed his eyes. The bastards had screwed with him—had disrespected the GRID. They deserved everything that was going to happen to them. He lingered over faded memories of his mother and sister, it would be good to see them, good to show them what real power and wealth looked like. He opened his eyes. The dawn's early light crept silently along his bedroom wall. He watched it grow in strength and relished its triumph over darkness.

The Militia formed a perimeter around Ned Wolff's house. They knew nothing of stealth, and the people inside were well aware of their presence and their intentions. Food and antibiotics had done Ned a world of good. He was stronger, but still very sick. It was double pneumonia, a nasty bug—Klebsiella, Caleb thought, though he couldn't be sure. The brothers gathered in Ned's room. It was time to say goodbye.

"Don't worry about me, boys, my time is done. You know it, I know it."

"Aww, come on, Ned," Caleb answered. "You're going to beat this thing."

The old man smiled weakly.

A harsh metallic voice broke the predawn stillness. "This is the Corporate Militia Anti-Terrorist Strike Force. We have you surrounded. Lay down your weapons and come out with your hands up."

Zach shifted his weight. "Ned, we need to get going. If we don't, they'll blow the house."

"You are only wanted for questioning, and if you come peacefully, you will not be injured."

"Go on, boys. I'll be fine."

They all knew it was a lie, but it was a good lie, a loving lie.

"Let's go," Virgil said. Each brother in turn took Ned's hand in his and said his farewell. Then they shuffled to the front door.

Zach answered the bullhorn, "We are coming out. Don't shoot."

The chrome and plastic voice warned, "Lay down your weapons and keep your hands up!"

Virgil grumbled, "They know we don't have any damn weapons. He's just showing off."

They stepped onto the front porch, hands raised, and faced a score of black-clad Corporate Militia crouched behind vehicles and bullet-proof shields. Half a dozen commandos fell on them with nightsticks and fury. The world went dark.

When Zach came to, he was hooded, cuffed, and chained to a floor bolt in the back of a Militia pickup truck. His head ached, but he could feel and move his arms and legs. The truck's engine was at idle and the sun felt strong. It was likely noon or later. Virgil stirred next to him.

"Damn," he said.

Caleb groaned as he woke. "You guys OK?" Zach asked.

"OK? Uggh," Virgil grunted.

"I'm alright, Zach," Caleb said. "Nothing broken. Sore head, though."

"Shut up!" A rifle butt slammed against the truck's side panel rattling it like a drum. "No talking."

The driver's side door slammed shut, the engine roared, and the truck lurched forward.

All around them, men called orders as the convoy set out on the long journey to The Shire.

The soldiers made camp alongside the Turnpike, between Bag's End and Summer Hill. The hoods were pulled off the prisoners and each was shoved roughly into a separate cage. The people of the Shire watched but remained unseen. As soon as the identity of the prisoners was discovered, the word went out to find Emma Thomas.

Within the hour, Emma and Doc skirted the east edge of the Militia's camp. She hid inside a thick stand of hemlock and studied the camp and its men carefully. Her gaze found the cages that held her father and uncles. An hour later she heard a second convoy making the long uphill pull out of Bywater. The sentry guards waved the vehicles, a sleek collection of carbon black motor coaches and tractors trailers, directly into the interior of the compound. It was as if the GRID itself, wearing a uniform of armored chrome and fear, had arrived in the Shire.

Emma watched as her father and uncles were marched under guard to the largest of the vehicles. They emerged twenty minutes later and were returned to their pens.

Emma whistled for Doc. Together, they made their way toward the Long House. The Council was waiting for her. Inside the circle of Elders, Emma reviewed advantages and disadvantages of the site the Militia had chosen, the flimsy nature of the barrier they had erected, and the general demeanor of the men who were guarding the Thomas brothers. Her report came to an abrupt end when a young man barged into the Long House. "The man from the big black bus—the man they call 'the Director'—he's asking for, he wants to see Kianna Wallace and Val Thomas. He says they have to come, right away."

PART IV

61

THE SIGN OF THE POST RIDER

The autumn sun was already riding low when Emma and Doc approached the main gate of the compound. She addressed the sentries in a tone that was neither fearful nor defiant. "I have come," she said, "to answer the summons of the man in the bus."

The guards hesitated. "We were told there would be two."

"There is only one."

They escorted Emma to the gleaming black motor coach perched along the south edge of the camp. A slatted metal awning sheltered the vehicle's main entrance. Beside the door stood an armed guard. Inside the vehicle's main compartment, the walls were covered by flickering flat panel screens. The air was cold as death. Hidden speakers issued a jumble of overlapping voices. The guard urged her toward the rear of the vehicle. He thumbed a lock then pushed her into the cramped inner sanctum. There, a fat man, his bulk extended well beyond the chair's margins, sat facing away from her. He grunted intermittently. Finally, "No more screw-ups, Donald—do you understand me? This is the last time." The phone call finished, he turned slowly toward his visitor. He reached absent-mindedly for his cigarette case, opened it and removed a cigarette, studying Emma as he did so.

She spoke first, "Are you the one they call the 'Director?'"

He exhaled a lungful of dry, blue smoke and answered, "I am."

Emma wanted to be sure. "You are? You're the Director of the GRID program, 'The Trial?'"

"I am the Director of the Department of Security and Justice." He paused, giving the young woman an opportunity to express her astonishment at being in the presence of the Director of the DSJ himself. He waited but Emma's stubborn silence soured his mood. "You'd better have a good reason for disturbing me. I sent for Val and Kianna Wallace—not some errand girl."

Emma watched him, watched how he shaped his lips, how he moved his eyes, how he held himself. She knew his name. Without emotion, she said, "Val and Kianna are dead."

"Dead?" he answered weakly.

"Kianna died, after a bad fall, ten years ago this winter. Val died this spring. Cancer."

"Did you...did you know them?" He could not stop himself from asking.

"Of course I knew them," Emma answered evenly. "Val was my mother, and Kianna my grandmother. You are Eron Wallace, my uncle. You ran away from the Shire the day I was born."

A heaving grief threatened to overwhelm him. He had never imagined that they'd be gone. Even in his distress he was aware of Knox's presence. He could not show weakness in front of his Deputy. Instead, Eron lashed out, answering Emma with a wicked laugh and news of his own that was sure to wound.

"So very sorry, my dear little niece, but it seems your father and uncles are very bad men. Murderers, in fact. The three of them killed poor old Ned Wolff, killed him in cold blood. I am going to put them on trial for their crimes right here live, tomorrow night. Three-hundred million people will watch those bastards pay for what they've done." He paused then asked with pretended concern, "Did you come to pay your last respects?"

Emma kept her balance. "They loved, we all loved Ned Wolff. You know that. They went to Ithaca to help him."

Eron snorted. The girl was helpless, naïve, pathetic. She was just like the rest of them. No surprise. He leaned lazily back in his high-backed chair and tipped the ash from his cigarette. "Unfortunately for them, the time has come for justice to be served."

A movement in the shadows caught Emma's eye. They were not alone. A tall thin man stood watching, his back against the wall. His pale clean-shaven face would have been more revealing if it had been carved from a block of wood. He held his arms folded across his chest.

The Director noticed Emma's gaze had found his assistant.

"That's Knox. He'll be handling logistics. I'll be supervising the script. Perhaps, if you're nice to him, Knox will get you tickets to the show."

"I didn't come for tickets. I want my family back."

"Well, little Emma, we all want things we cannot have." The Director remembered the day he received the glorious news of his ascension into the GRID's DSJ Academy. He decided to tell her the real story of that day. While Eron rambled, Knox stepped out of the shadows and stood directly behind his superior, as if to demonstrate, in a physical way, his intense loyalty to the man. He stared hard at Emma. The Director rehearsed his many grievances against the Shire and its people. The grudges warmed him and he looked away from the girl, turning his gaze instead upon a point an infinite distance beyond the ceiling of the bus.

Emma was free to return the assistant's gaze. He glanced down. It was a silent message. She was to look at his hands. She watched as Knox slowly and deliberately made the sign known to all Post Riders: *Off.*

Off the GRID.

The Director demanded Emma's full attention. "So you would have to agree that this treason was really a crime against you as well. You were denied the opportunity to have a real life. Instead you rotted away on this stinking hilltop. You have my sympathy, Emma."

She swallowed hard and said, half-smiling, "Go on, uh, Uncle Eron."

He was pleased to continue. "Yes, as I was saying." He went on to offer his niece a colorful review of the enemies he had vanquished, the many nefarious plots he had unraveled.

Again, Emma turned her attention to Knox. The Director's voice rose as he described the riots that had nearly destroyed San Diego.

Knox made the sign, *Later.* Emma blinked twice and the message was acknowledged.

Gradually, the Director came back around to the case of the Thomas brothers. "I suppose even you can see how it is both my duty and the cause of the greater good that force me to put them on trial. After all, those who spare the wicked injure the good. My hands are tied." He held out his wrists as if they were joined with invisible manacles.

Emma smiled weakly, "Yes, Uncle Eron. I understand. I am sorry I bothered you. I'll go now."

"Well that's a good girl. None of this is really your fault, remember that. We can't choose our parents, after all."

Nor can parents choose their children, she thought, but did not speak the words.

"Would you like to see the, ahh...Trial?"

"No, Uncle, there is no need for that. I'll go now."

The Director turned away from her and brought a bank of hungry flickering screens to life.

"Knox," he barked, "show my niece to the door."

The two stepped out of the bus and into the fading twilight.

"I'll walk you to the main gate," Knox said.

When they were out of earshot, Knox hissed, "When? Where?"

Emma kept her gaze down. "The base of the falls, at midnight."

Knox grunted his assent.

They parted company.

Later, Emma briefed the Council of Elders. She told them about the man named Knox. He seemed to be at odds with the Director and knew the signs of the Underground. He wanted to meet her later. They would take the risk of trusting him, but she would not be left alone. The people of the Shire would be there too, watching but unseen, ready to act if Emma needed them.

62
THE FALLS

When the 23:00 security brief was in the Director's hands, Knox announced he was going out to scout locations. "I want something really special, for the executions. I know how much it means to you."

"This is business as usual, Knox," the Director snapped.

"Of course, sir," Knox agreed.

The Director suppressed a smile. "Take an armed guard. It's dark and... people, you can't trust them."

Knox shuffled his feet. "Sir," he said, "it's just like you said, these people are completely untrustworthy. I'm nothing to them of course, but you...you are the Director. I worry that they might try something against you because, you know, because of the history. I couldn't live with myself if something happened and I had drawn down your perimeter guard."

The Director rubbed his unshaven chin. "Mmm hmm. Go ahead, but watch yourself. I've got enough on my plate without having to deal with another one of your messes."

"Yes, sir."

Knox was let through the gate and stepped out onto the Turnpike. It was a little less than an hour until his rendezvous, and all he knew was that the falls lay to the west. He snapped the flashlight off and looked up. The moon soared high and mighty above his head, its pearly light cast a stubby shadow at his feet. High clouds scudded across the sky blotting stars at irregular and changing intervals then draping across the moon as if they were vaporous scarves. His eyes adjusted to the darkness, and he realized he didn't need the flashlight. A soft breeze rustled the trees—gone as soon as it announced its presence. Knox swung the rucksack off his back and stashed the light. He wondered if this was how Post Riders saw the night, how they heard, smelled, and felt the world around them. He felt alone, alone and wonderfully free. Not sure which way was west but eager to be just as decisive as he imagined Post Riders to be, he turned right and began to walk down the middle of the road. The sound of whispered words stopped him. The voice belonged to an older person, he could tell that much. He turned slowly through 360-degrees, straining to find the source of the sound. "Show yourself," Knox demanded in his most authoritative voice.

"Turn around. The falls lie to the west. She is already there waiting for you. You better hurry."

Knox's wounded pride made him lie, "I was testing you. I was tricking you into revealing yourself." There was a slight rustle and the voice went silent. A brisk thirty-minute walk brought him to the edge of a brook. Here another unseen voice, a young man's, directed him onto a narrow footpath that switched back and forth until it delivered him to the floor of a gorge. A woman, hidden in a shadow, told him to leave his pack and wade upstream in the cold ankle-deep water. "She waits for you there."

Only the faintest glimmer of the moonlight penetrated the depth of the gorge. The stone underfoot was slick with algae so Knox's progress was slow. At the base of the falls, the white water seemed possessed of its own luminosity. Knox looked more closely and saw that a moonbeam had found a slender opening and lent its light to the falling water.

Emma spoke, "Come forward."

Knox did as he was told.

She watched him. He was different, so different from the people of the Shire. She could not help but compare him to the young men she grew up with. They were open, unguarded, and unafraid. Their directness, which could be appealing, also made them seem plain, even simple. This man was wary, mysterious. He had secrets.

"You did well, Knox."

"I had help."

Emma stepped into the light.

"We all have help, Knox."

"Call me John—he calls me Knox."

"All right, John." Emma did not smile but her face was warm, inviting.

"You've ridden post, John?"

Knox blushed, but the moonlight did not betray him. "No, but I know the Post Riders and the Elders much better than you think."

Emma did not want to press the question. "My father and uncles are your prisoners, but they have done nothing wrong."

"The Director hates them. I don't know why."

Emma stepped closer to him. "What are we to do?"

This blunt question was offered without hesitation or evident anxiety. Knox was surprised. He had imagined there would be tears. He imagined her begging for his help. In his excitement he even supposed that he would be able to hold her in his arms as he told her his plan. The disappointment ran deep. It wasn't too late. He could have her arrested. He had the authority but, somehow, he lacked the will.

Emma continued. "You say you understand the Underground. You know its signs so you must know," Emma hesitated. "The world is changing."

Knox closed his eyes. He let the mist of the falls wash his face, just as the high clouds kissed the moon's. This was real. The water, the light, the woman. It was all real. The brothers must be freed and he, alone among all men, knew how to free them.

He opened his eyes—blue in the light of day but gray now. "I will help you, but it will be dangerous and it may not work. There are no guarantees."

"Nothing is ever certain," she answered. "Now tell me your plan."

63
THE SCRIPT

The Director hunched over his notes. The cast meeting was an hour away and he needed to be prepared. This had to be perfect. When the outline was complete he read it out loud, just for the pleasure it gave him.

Theme: Justice Served! Cold-hearted killers poison an old man leaving him to die a horrible death.
Emphasis on <u>Pain</u> and <u>Suffering</u>.
Treason: He had been a friend, but they <u>turned</u> <u>on</u> <u>him</u>!!!
<u>Good</u> <u>man</u> so they killed him
Plot point: They are <u>cowards.</u>
Afraid to face the <u>truth.</u>
But we *are* the <u>truth</u>.
After conviction: Slow death by poison (If they repent <u>fully</u> <u>on</u> <u>camera</u> may offer hanging.)
Note: Changes must be cleared by me personally.
Defense Council need shots of you weeping with sympathy for the victim.
This is <u>Best of Year</u> material. VL bonuses are riding on this!

The meeting proceeded according to the Director's carefully crafted plan. The players were big stars, but they would never forget that Eron Wallace was their star maker. When it was the Deputy Director's turn to speak, Knox said, "Out late last night, scouting locations. Some great stuff, really different. Anyway, I was thinking, we should do the trial in the courtroom as usual—best control that way—and tease the penalty as something really special, never before seen, et cetera. Really get the Xenos going."

"So what have you got?" The Director rumbled.

"Well," Knox plunged ahead. "They've got this crazy circle thing called a labyrinth. It's something out of ancient Greece, I think."

Eron remembered the labyrinth but acted as if this was news to him. "Go ahead."

"Well we put the convicts in the center and shoot them with dart guns, like the animals they are. Then we stand at the edge with an antidote. If they can crawl out, they get a..." Knox held up his fingers and made scare quotes, "...pardon."

They all laughed.

Eron Wallace loved it. "Very visual, very dramatic, very final. Nice." Knox was finally coming around, showing some spine. Good.

Knox pushed farther. "The only problem is with the light and sound. They're going to be a bitch. We'll need to capture every detail so it'll take four cameras." The Deputy flushed red with fearful excitement. "I wonder if we could shoot the trial hard and fast—wham, bang—with just two cameras. Straight up with a lot of punch." John Knox paused and took a deep breath, "And to top it off, it would be amazing, simply amazing, if the Director would take the controls and do the show from the command center—just like in the old days."

The Judge chimed in, "Oh my God, Knox is right. People would go crazy to see the Wallace style again."

The prosecutor agreed, "Never been the same since the day he was promoted."

Knox turned to the Director. "It would free me and a crew to make the execution scene perfect, absolutely perfect. Would you, please, sir?"

Eron rocked back in his chair and made a temple with his fingers. A circle of expectant faces surrounded him.

"Goddamn it, I'm in!"

64
RIGHT SIDE UP

The prisoners were granted a meeting with family to 'finalize outstanding personal matters.' The room was, of course, under full audio and video surveillance, and any useful material would be edited into the broadcast. As soon as Emma entered, Caleb signed that they were being watched. After a tearful round of greetings, Emma gave the men the latest news from the Shire. When she finished, she made the sign, *Upside-down*.

Caleb understood. His daughter was inviting him to play a game from her childhood. The only rule was that the players had to say the opposite of what they meant. It was harder than it seemed.

He shook his head and said, "I don't understand."

"Uncle Eron is an honest man, and the only thing he wants is justice. All of his men are loyal to him, every single one."

This gave them hope.

"He's convinced me that you really did kill Ned Wolff and that you deserve to be punished."

Virgil balled his fists but did not speak.

"My advice, and Uncle Eron knows all about this, is that you accept your fate and don't even think about bringing up things from the past. This is all about what you did to Ned Wolff. You should be polite, do what you are told, and don't embarrass the Shire."

Again Caleb shook his head. "Emma, you can't tell us what to do or how to act. And Eron..."

"Uncle Eron is a very busy man, and he probably won't have time to watch the trial. It is very important that you do not disturb him."

"So, then, no distractions."

Emma's eyes rimmed with tears. "You have no hope." She signaled for the guard and choked out her final statement. "I hate you. I hate you all for what you have done. I hope," she swallowed hard. "I hope I never see you again."

Virgil closed his eyes. "Emma, you are the greatest disappointment of my life. I can't believe what you've said to me and your uncles, and I am deeply disappointed that you have not lifted a finger to help us."

Emma turned her back on them. Then she was gone.

In the control booth Eron Wallace whooped with glee. The utter truth contained within the exchange between Emma and the prisoners made his heart sing. They were fools. Even innocent little Emma could see now that he lifted the scales from her eyes. Justice might have been delayed, but it would not be denied.

65
ACTION

E ron settled into the Director's chair and slipped the earbuds into place. Music swelled and the "Security and Justice" logo splashed across the screen. Then came the voice—his voice—a voice that was a trusted friend to hundreds of millions of people. "We live in dangerous times. Evil doers are among us—threatening our way of life, but fear not. We bring you Security through Justice." Then came the tease, "Cruel murderers on the loose. An old man tortured to death in his own home. Now these deviants are on trial for their own pathetic lives. Get your voting devices ready. Opening arguments after these messages." Eron barked commands at the crew. It was just like the old days.

The VL screen faded to black. Knox shuddered then flipped the switch. In an instant, the audio-visual stream from the courtroom was disconnected from the satellite feed and the output from Knox's camera set-up on the labyrinth took its place. Emma stepped forward on cue and took her place in the pool of angelic light Knox had prepared for her. Her light brown skin, her long hair, and her fine white flaxen robe seemed to glow. She was magnificently alive, lean and strong, confident and smart.

She was beauty come to life, and John Knox loved her.

Emma stood at the center, while an audience of 300 million people fixed its attention upon her. It was up to her to save the lives of her father and uncles and, Knox knew, her own life and his as well. She looked at the camera with the blinking red light.

I am Emma Jane Thomas, daughter of Caleb, niece of Zachary and Virgil. (She made the sign, Post Rider.*) I stand before you now and declare that these good men are innocent of the charges made against them...*

The Director panned the courtroom. It was a fake, a theatrical set his men had constructed in a single day. Patterned after the courtroom sets used in the movies and television programs of the 20th century, the judge sat on a dais with the witness box below and to his left. Attorneys for the defense and prosecution faced him from their respective tables. Behind them, the gallery was crammed with soldiers dressed in civilian clothes. State of the art lighting and Eron's skillful direction combined to bring it all to life for those who watched the proceedings on their GRID screens.

Close up—District Attorney: "Your honor, I rise to declare that these three men are among the sickest, most depraved, most cruel fiends ever produced by any human society. While they do spring from a race of vagabonds and resisters, such misfortune cannot be used to excuse or forgive..."

Hold for a beat...Camera three.

"Murder by poison."

Well-rehearsed uproar issued from the costumed gallery. The judge hammered the sounding block with his gavel.

"Order! Order in the court! I will have order!"

Bang!

Bang!

Bang!

Perfect, Eron thought.

I will speak of the world as it truly is and of the power that would deprive innocent men of their lives...(Emma made the sign, Remain hidden.*)*

"I call Zachary Thomas as witness—for the prosecution."

"I object! Objection your honor, objection! The Prosecution cannot ask my client to testify against himself."

Sneering, "Counsel, if your client (voice drips with disdain) is as 'innocent' as you claim, he will have nothing to fear."

Turning to defendant, "You don't have to do this! You have a right (raises arm and shakes fist) to remain silent!"

Defendant is undeterred. "The truth is burning inside of me. I am going to testify for the prosecution and you (pointing at Defense Council) can't stop me."

Eron leaned close to his screen.

"Defendant Zachary Thomas, I think you will find that I am a fair man, a man of truth, really. All I want is the truth, the whole truth, and nothing but the truth."

"I understand."

Zach Thomas took the stand.

"Tell us about your youth. Isn't it true, you spring from a strange race?"

Camera two.

"I was born before the Fall and my parents had, um, many bizarre beliefs."

"For example?" The prosecutor inquired.

Zach shrugged, "They told me that they'd traveled to a hidden part of the world, a place they called Kallimos. All I know is that I grew up here, in the middle of a wasteland. We didn't...we didn't have electricity or even... television."

Crowd gasps. Gavel bangs. Order is restored.

"You may continue your questioning counselor." The judge's voice was warm and sweet, like syrup.

The Prosecutor took a deep breath. "Your taste for cruelty, it showed itself early in life?"

"Objection!"

"Overruled!"

The Master Herdsman gritted his teeth. "I have been cruel to animals. I have even forced others to bear the consequences of my own cruelty."

"And one of those you persecuted went on to become a great and powerful man. Isn't that so?"

"Yes."

"You're sorry now, aren't you?"

Zach grunted.

"You brutally abused children and helpless animals, you reveled in sadism, and never felt a single moment of remorse until now, until the DSJ brought you to justice."

"Objection!"

"Overruled."

Cut to prosecutor. Speaking directly into camera, "And that was just the beginning, the seed of spiteful vengeance grew, year after year. It led, as I will show, to murder—the murder of Ned Wolff!"

Sometimes it can be hard to know the truth. Haven't we all suspected, at one time or another, that forces far greater than ourselves have conspired to deceive us, have spun a web of falsehood around us? Today will be different.

Today, a simple woman stands before you and asks but one thing of you. Will you trust your own eyes and ears, will you rely on your own common sense as you wrestle with the terrible question of guilt and innocence? (Emma let silence fill the air then made the sign, Need your help.) *My father and my uncles are men of caring, men who have risked their lives to help others. These men have been friends of Ned Wolff their whole lives. This is a man they loved like a brother.*

Caleb was on the stand and in the oleaginous hands of the actor who played the Attorney for the Defense.

"Much has been made of the difficulties posed by your background. Rightly so, I'd say, but isn't it true you were often quite ill when you were younger?"

Caleb studied the plywood courtroom ceiling, recalled Emma's instructions, and did his best to play his part. "There is something more, a great sin that I feel I must confess to."

The Defense Attorney pushed on, "Well, at any rate, we have established chronic illness as a mitigating condition..."

"No!" Caleb roared the word. Camera three zoomed in.

It was such a pleasure, Eron thought, to watch them as they faced the truth, under his control, with no hope of escape. He was doing his best work ever. By the hundreds of millions, people bore witness to personal revenge and professional triumph merged into a single unassailable masterpiece.

Caleb beckoned the camera closer. "When I was sick, I would, I would travel...to other Demos. I would sneak into them at night and I would infect the healthy people who lived there. I did this many, many times."

This time the court erupted in a genuine, spontaneous storm of outrage. The man was a devil, all three of them were. Real evil had been revealed, and would soon be extinguished.

Eron had known that the murder charge, while justified as a means to an end, was false. Now the fool had released him from even the faintest twinge of regret. His eyes darted to the tracking screen where early votes of guilt or innocence would already be piling up. The screen was dark. He cursed. The crew chief would pay for his mistake, later. No matter, long experience told him that the conviction tally would be going through the roof. He turned back to the main bank of screens. The fools were killing themselves. The thought made him smile.

Calling Virgil to the stand would let him highlight the murder itself. Whispered instructions soon brought this about. Unfortunately, the middle brother proved to be a balky, sullen witness. His mumbled monosyllabic answers started to drag the pace. "Smith," Eron hissed to the prosecutor, "go after the bastard, punch it up. Let's get some energy going."

Smith wheeled on Virgil and began to mock his seemingly calm demeanor.

"So this is what a cold-blooded murderer looks like," he raged. "On trial, for your life, and you don't give a damn."

"Objection!"

"Overruled!"

Smith bore in on Virgil, taunting, attacking, twisting his words and even his gestures. The Prosecutor approached the witness box, taking care to offer camera one a profile of his best side. Eron grunted appreciatively, Smith was a pro's pro.

Spittle showered Virgil as Smith raged. "Isn't it true you obtained the poison that killed Ned Wolff?" He glowered. "No! Shut up, shut the hell up! I don't want you to answer you stinking sack of filth. The truth means..."

Virgil uncoiled. He grabbed Smith by the throat and plowed his fist into the side of Smith's face. The fragile bones of the Prosecuter's face gave way beneath Virgil's fist. Smith crumpled. A stun gun hit Virgil in the chest, and he followed his victim to the floor. Virgil's brothers vaulted the defense table and tackled the actor who played the bailiff.

A gallery-clearing brawl ensued.

Eron was on his feet, shrieking orders. "Cuff those bastards and drag their asses to the cooler, now! Franklin! Franklin, listen to me! Smith is totally screwed up. You've got to do the wrap. We've got 5:14 til credits, knock it out of the park or you'll be answering to me directly! I want order in my court. Now! Put camera one on Franklin and isolate his mic. Ready. In five, four..."

John Knox held up five fingers. She had five minutes left. Five minutes to save their lives. She acknowledged him with a nod.

The Thomas Brothers have been falsely accused of murder. Now the time has come to right that wrong. You have the power to save their lives. (She made the signs, Tribes of Eden, *then,* Giving thanks.*) Where are their accusers? Why have they failed to stand and deliver even the faintest shred of proof? They do not show their faces because they dare not. I stand before you knowing that if you take time, if you talk to each other, if you listen...then you will vote to free these men.*

Five, four, three, two, one...fade to black. John Knox flipped the switch that transferred the feed back to the GRID. Up came images of the old republic's Supreme Court building and the sonorous voice of the Director.

"The DSJ needs your help. We have just presented you with the truth as we know it. Now it is time to return your verdict. Remember, the red button on your controller means guilty as charged, while the green button means not guilty. Good night and good luck."

Knox staggered backward and slumped into a folding canvas chair. His phone buzzed ominously behind his ear, as he had known it would. He tapped the connect and awaited his fate, their fate.

66
CONVICTION

The direct line from the Chairman's office flashed red on Eron's screen. It was rare, extremely rare, for the Chairman himself to call with congratulations. He tapped the link. "Yes, sir!"

The weight of the words pressed down on him, crushing him as if they were stones piled atop his chest. When it was over, a well-worn habit made him tap the disconnect. He'd been zeroed out. The gleaming metal cocoon in which he sat, its shimmering liquid crystal light, the sweet babble of disembodied voices, the rich flood of detailed information was no longer his. He pulled himself heavily to his feet and looked down at his great vast belly, so rich, so fat. Even now, he registered a flicker of satisfaction. The smoked windows, backed by the night, made themselves into mirrors, let him see himself as he had been. There, in the glass, a rich and powerful man stared back at him. He heard Knox's transport roar into the compound. He heard him barking orders at the men, then nothing. Knox stormed onto the bus, swept past the former director, and plunged into the private office in the rear. Slowly, he understood that Knox had taken his place. He wondered when the fool had turned on him. He hadn't seen it coming, then again neither had Director Peterson when the young Eron Wallace had taken him down.

The steel and chrome were now more prison than haven. He was unpleasantly aware of its mechanically dried, warmed, and filtered air. He needed to get out. At the compartment door, he punched the control. It opened slowly and outside air rushed in, damp and cool. He liked the feeling. It was different. He was different. Everything was different. A cold drizzle peppered the metal awning overhead. He stepped down onto a corrugated retractable metal step, then lowered himself awkwardly down to the ground. The sentry was no longer at his post. He did not bother to wonder where he had gone. The man reached back and slammed the door shut. The deep metallic thunk pleased him. He would miss that sound. For the first time in at least a dozen years, maybe more, he was alone outdoors, in the night.

Emma had watched Knox answer the call, saw him freeze with fear and then flush with excitement. When it was finished, the Deputy Director jumped into a vehicle and headed west up the Turnpike, toward the Militia's camp.

Emma sprinted into the forest and whistled for Doc. Knox had betrayed Eron Wallace; would he turn on her as well? Thick wet clouds rolled in from the western sky and with them came a light cold rain. She and Doc followed Knox keeping off the Turnpike. When they arrived at the compound, she found the main entrance standing open and unguarded. The men huddled close to their machines, uncertain.

Emma jumped down. "Doc, stay close."

She drew her hood down over her face, slid her hands into her sleeves, and disappeared into the night. The men never suspected her presence as she passed through the center of the camp and came up on the south side of the black bus. She heard Knox shouting orders. His voice tingled with the thrill of newly acquired power. She saw him approach the bus, watched him pace anxiously to and fro. He pulled hard on the latch and disappeared inside.

Emma waited.

A quarter of an hour later, the door opened, spilling light and sound into the night. Eron lumbered down the steps and slammed the door behind him. He lit a cigarette and smoked it with pleasure. When he was finished, he flicked the butt away. Overhead, the wind rattled branches already bare. The sound drew his attention. He looked in her direction; he suspected that he was being watched. Then he turned away from her, walked out from under the awning, and disappeared into the night.

When he was gone, Emma went to see Knox. Inside the bus the main compartment buzzed with digital life, but Knox was in back, sitting in the Director's chair, talking on the Director's phone. She pushed the door open and Knox swiveled to face her. He held his forefinger to his lips and motioned for her to sit down. She remained standing.

"Put as many men on it as you need."

Emma closed her eyes and listened to cold drops splatter against the metal roof.

Knox tapped off. The words tumbled from his mouth, "Looks like you've got your revenge against the old man. He's finished, zeroed out."

She ignored the comment. "I'm here for my father and uncles."

Knox made a show of shuffling the reports on his desk. He expected her to feel the way he felt. Together, they risked everything, absolutely everything. He looked up into her face, so beautiful, so distant. Emma Thomas, he reminded himself, had faced death many times. The act no longer thrilled her. Straining for a more official tone he said, "I am the new Director, effective immediately." Knox paused, waiting for her congratulations. None came. He cleared his throat. "The prisoners are being processed for release. Please try to be patient."

She studied him, worked to understand what he was thinking and feeling. "Patience is something I have plenty of..."

He offered her a seat again, this time as a friend. She slid into the chair across from him. She could tell that there was something pressing on him, something he needed to get out.

"What I am about to tell you is highly classified."

"Are you sure you can trust me?" Emma asked.

"I'm sure."

"You are right."

"The GRID is a complicated thing. Nobody really understands it, not anymore. What we do know is that all of its many billions of parts depend entirely on less than a hundred communications satellites. Those satellites are woven together like a net. They work together. But now," Knox dropped his voice to a hushed whisper, "they are starting to fail."

"Nothing lasts forever."

"We can't replace them anymore. So as they fail, the GRID fails." He looked at her as if he had just uttered a ghastly truth.

Emma shrugged. "The Elders know this."

John Knox conceded, "Yes, of course. Do they understand what we must do in the face of this crisis?"

"They do."

Knox smiled broadly. "I was hoping the Tribes would see the value of a partnership between us."

Emma shook her head. "The Elders considered this many years ago. The answer is no."

"But they remember the Fall. They can't possibly wish for the chaos, the disease, the fighting to return. Together, the GRID and the Tribes can stop it from happening again."

"I'm sorry."

The Director's face flushed with emotion. "I've been reading posts for years. I understand the Tribes, what you believe, how you think. Not less than an hour ago I risked my very life for the Underground."

"And that chair."

The truth of what she said stung, but he checked his anger, "Because I am sitting in this chair, I have the authority to offer the Eden Underground a partnership, a full partnership with the GRID. We must cooperate to prevent another Fall."

"John," Emma leaned close. "The Elders anticipated your offer."

"The world needs action. I mean, I know the stories of Kallimos and I love them, just the way you do, but stories can't save us now. The Tribes have the right ideas, but they have no power. None!"

"Those stories saved my family, right here, tonight."

"Yes, but..."

She spoke softly. "The Underground reached you, even though you were in the DSJ's inner sanctum. It changed you." Emma made the sign, *Friend*.

A woozy flood of tenderness swept over him. She was so beautiful, so wild and free. He loved her. He didn't want to argue with her.

Instead, he asked, "How does it end?"

"The Elders say that the GRID will fray like a cloak worn too long. As it unravels, the Tribes of Eden will take its place. We will not fight the GRID, we will not even challenge it. We will simply welcome the people it has abandoned."

Again, he decided to gamble. "I think I'm in love with you." He looked away and whispered, "Tonight doesn't have to be the end, you know. It could be a beginning, too." He brightened as he said this, for this was his heart's desire.

Emma refused to meet his gaze. "No."

"Is there someone else?"

"No."

"Then why not?"

She smiled and took his hands into hers, "The last two days, they seem like a lifetime. All that we've done—together—all of it makes it seem like we could be together, but we can't."

"Why not?"

"If I came with you, there would be questions about what happened tonight. If you came to live here in the Shire, the GRID would call you a traitor. It would find you and destroy you...and us."

The logic made a bitter gall, but she was right. John Knox swallowed hard and relented. "What can I do for you, for the Underground?"

Emma stood and leaned against the doorframe. She was deep in thought, but Knox focused on the way her form was outlined by the shifting light of the screens in the main control room. He got up from his chair and came around the desk. He stood close to her and she welcomed him, put her arms around him.

"We must stay underground until the time comes. You can help."

"How?"

"Chase the Post Riders. Harass them. Make sure they ride at night and hide during the day. Catch them when you can, but don't hurt them. Give them VL penalties and let them go."

John shook his head. "That's not helping."

"Yes, it is."

"You want me to play games with the Post Riders, with the Underground?"

She smiled at him and he felt warm.

"Alright," he agreed. "But what about us? When will I see you again?"

Emma held him close. "You are the new Director. The Underground needs you there."

The buzz of the radio broke a solemn silence.

"The prisoners are prepared for release, sir."

He let go of Emma, reached across the desk, and pressed the mic button, "Bring them to my vehicle."

"Yes, sir."

Emma reached out for him, pulled him to her. She buried her face against his neck, letting her tears fall upon his nanofiber shirt. She looked into his face and wanted to record every feature in her memory. They kissed, slowly, carefully, with a passion that can be felt only by those who know they will never kiss again. Emma let go of John Knox and slowly, gently drew away from his embrace. "They're waiting for me."

He watched her leave but could not say goodbye.

67

THE PEACEMAKER
Summer, 2052

The windows of the old house were opened halfway, admitting a cool breeze along with the early morning's sunshine. The curtains puffed gently as if they, too, found pleasure in the moment. Emma sat in her favorite ladder back chair in front of the tall fall front desk that had stood in the house for more than sixty years. She rose at dawn because she wanted time with her journal before the demands of the day arrived in full. She scanned the flowing script that filled the page, felt satisfied, and then let her attention drift upward. Ceiling beams, strong and silent, ran overhead. They were sawn, planed, and lifted into position nearly seventy years before. Above her was the room in which she was born. Now it was her bedroom. Her grandparents had left the house to her. She'd lost them during the hard winter following the uncles' trial. Influenza. Her grandfather had always called it "the old man's friend".

The morning would bring her 27th birthday. Her family and her friends would celebrate together on Summer Hill's Green. Emma placed her pen in its holder. The Eden Underground had been born in this house, too, on the very day she was born.

There was, she felt, peace in the world. John Knox had kept his word. Militia no longer prowled the night. The GRID no longer hunted the Post Riders. We have our world, she thought, and they have theirs. She screwed the cap onto the ink bottle. It was new, and very good. She'd be sure to tell the Master how much she liked it when she saw her at the Midsummer Feast.

There was a knock at the door.

"Coming!" Emma returned her leather-bound journal to its place on the shelf, nestled among her grandfather's books. When she opened the door she found Claudia Jones, Post Rider of Cazenovia, on her porch, standing in the light of day.

Emma gasped.

The young woman fell into her arms and sobbed wordlessly. Emma held her, whispered gentle reassurance into her ear. When the Rider regained her strength, Emma led her unexpected guest into the kitchen, sat her down at the table, and set about making a fire for tea.

The rhythm soothed Claudia's shattered nerves. "Cody Brooks sent me. I went to the Aunties, like I always do. I told them what happened."

Emma nodded patiently and busied herself with fire and water.

"The Aunties told me to come here, in the light of day, to you." She mumbled the last half of the statement, nervous about confessing so boldly to a breach of tradition.

Emma answered softly, "You were right to come. The Aunties know best."

Confident that she was forgiven, she examined her surroundings. This was the home of Emma Thomas, the witch, the wonder, the dark rider of the night. This was the house that Bill and Jude Thomas had built upon their return from Kallimos. Emma rustled in the pantry picking through the apple bin, looking for the best. She was eager to hear the crux of Claudia's message but did not want her guest to feel rushed.

In a casual voice she asked, "How is our friend Cody Brooks?"

"Cody is good. Yes, he is fine, and he sends his best wishes." Emma laid her table with fruit, bread, and cheese and sat down next to Claudia. The young woman ate hungrily then braced herself for the task of delivering the terrible news. "Two days ago, the Bishop announced that Cazenovia, that we, all of us, had been zeroed out. He said it was a mistake, a terrible mistake, told us he would file a protest. The GRID went down that afternoon." The young woman quivered with fear. Emma understood why. The convoys would not return. Without fuel for the generators there would be no power, no water, no heat. The few who managed to survive til winter would freeze to death. Claudia seemed about to cry, but did not. Now Emma knew, now Emma would help; now there was hope.

"Did the Bishop say anything else?"

Claudia shook her head no.

"Is he afraid?"

"I think he is scared like all of us. I don't think he knows what to do."

"I'm sure he doesn't," Emma answered. "What does Cody think?"

"He said the Elders had seen this coming and preparations had been made. He asked for me to come to the Shire to ask the Tribes for help." Claudia's eyes brightened. "I've been here many times, more than anyone else."

Emma smiled.

"The Aunties, what do they say?"

"Not much," now it was Claudia's turn to smile. "You know how they are."

The knowingness felt good to them both so they savored it. "Haleigh said it was time for the Midwife to go to work, said she was going fishing and told me to find this house."

As night fell, the Aunties followed their niece into the dooryard. Haleigh spoke for both sisters, "My dear child, you are the Peacemaker of old, returned to us. Do as you think best."

Emma did not look back.

The road west out of Bywater ran alongside Mad Brook to a point just below Rexford Falls where it turned south and dropped down onto the valley floor. Emma walked alone, enjoying the solitude, confident Doc would soon be at her side. He joined her just as she reached the low ground, snorting and prancing, eager to be on their way. She reached up to him, wrapped her arms around his rippled neck, fussed with his tousled mane. "Not yet, old friend. I need to feel the earth beneath my feet."

When they reached the eastern bank of the Chenango River, Emma stood at the water's edge and watched the moonlight dance on the rippling water. When it was time, she swung up onto Doc's back. The stallion splashed through the ford's hock-deep water. On the far side, Emma nudged Doc north. He understood and gathered his strength in full. They raced for Cazenovia.

It was still dark when they drew near to the Demo. She left Doc in a creekside meadow where he could graze and still be within earshot of the south gate. Emma trotted along the Post Riders' footpath. It wound through the forest then delivered her to a hiding place where she could watch the gate without being seen. She closed her eyes and listened; the only sounds were those of the forest night. The people were at rest.

Ebony, deep purple, bands of mauve, crimson, and then rose. The eastern sky glowed pink when Emma heard the day shift report for duty. She came to the edge of the forest and studied the sentries who stood just fifty yards from her. Their words were muffled, but she recognized the tone. The men were anxious but hopeful. It would be another hour before the people inside the Demo were up and moving. The sentries stood stubbornly at their posts, peering down route 20, willing a convoy to appear. The light grew stronger. The men shared an intense, huddled conversation then retreated into the guardhouse. Emma guessed, correctly, that they were trying to reactivate their GRID terminal. She stepped out of the forest, walked calmly up to the chain link gate, lifted her hood, pulled its brim low, and waited.

"What the hell?" A faceless, black-robed witch stood just outside the gate. This was magic, dark magic. Emma drew in a sharp hissing breath and commanded them, "I've come for the Bishop. Go and tell him the Witch of the Night is here." The guards jerked backward, jaws slack. "Do not anger me or it'll go the worse for both of you. Now do as you're told." Emma slowly raised her left arm and the two sentries turned and ran, yelping for the Bishop as they fled.

When they were gone, she scaled the metal gate. From there, she catwalked to the hinge post and leapt onto the sentry's abandoned platform. The sun was already warming the morning air. She pulled the hood back and shook her long brown hair down onto her shoulders. In front of her, she watched the news of her appearance spread across Cazenovia like a wind-driven fire.

The men burst into the Bishop's house and found him at his breakfast table. Expecting good news, he threw his napkin down and whooped, "It's the convoy! The convoy is here!"

The men, still out of breath, doubled over and clutched their knees. The youngest caught his wind. "Your Eminence, she's here. She's here!" He pointed in the general direction of the gate as if that would make his meaning clear.

"Who's here?" The Bishop demanded.

The older one answered, "It's the Witch of the Night! She's at the south gate. She's come back. She says she's come back for you, your Eminence."

The cleric smashed his fist against the tabletop, his full round face and domed bald head both flushed red with anger— and fear. "You damn fools, arrest her!"

"Begging your pardon, sir," the younger one responded, "but she told us to come and get you."

Eyes bulging, the Bishop sputtered, "Told you? Told you? Damn it, she can't tell you to do anything!"

The sound of people moving and the babble of their excited anxious voices intruded on them. The sounds wrenched the Bishop's gut. The devil spawn was already working her evil on his people, sowing chaos where there was peace and order. Control had to be re-established, no matter the cost. He snatched his Bishop's stole from its hook and stormed out of the house trailed reluctantly by the guardsmen. This time she would not escape.

Hundreds of people already milled near the south gate by the time the Bishop arrived. Emma stood at the sentry's post, watching, waiting. The Bishop called for Kenny-Boy. The Captain of the Watch, along with his henchmen, took their places at his side. The men cleared a path through the crowd, machetes held high. At the foot of the gate, the Bishop turned to Kenny-Boy, "Arrest that damned witch." The Captain of the Watch looked up at the figure who towered above him.

He began tentatively, "You there! Come down. You are under arrest."

The answer came with a laugh, but it was not the high, mirthless laugh the people expected—that they were taught to expect. The sound was warm, loving, full of compassion. She answered, "Step aside. I've come to speak with the Bishop."

Kenny-Boy raised his voice. "You will come down and submit to the authority of the GRID and the Bishop." He menaced her with his blade but, notably, did not step forward.

"Kenny-Boy, how would you feel if I told all these people what happened the last time you challenged me?" The Captain of the Watch remembered how he dropped his sword, pissed his pants. He blushed and stepped aside.

The Bishop stood unprotected before Emma but she spoke over him, addressing the people directly. "I know that you've been zeroed out. The convoys have stopped coming. Your generators are burning the last of the fuel. There will be no more."

The Bishop found his tongue. "Be gone wicked witch! We will not be polluted by your lies. We don't want your sin, your filth." He expected the people to cheer him, the way they had the night he nearly captured her, but they did not stir. Incensed by this disloyalty, he raged, "You are a stranger and God knows we have no need of strangers here!"

Emma unhooked her riding cloak. The sun was climbing higher in the sky and the full heat of the day was coming on. She dropped the cloak at her side. She stood alone before the people, her skin shining like gold in the sunshine. She wore a close fitting tunic embroidered with the pattern favored by the people of West Farthing. Her leggings were tan, well-worn and plunged down a pair of laced calf-high riding moccasins. "This man claims that I am a stranger, but some here call me friend." Emma pointed to Kaitlin Saxon. "Who healed you when you came down with milk fever, after your son Nicholas was born?" The young woman swallowed hard. All eyes were on her. She looked up at Emma and answered honestly, "You did. You took care of me." Emma scanned the crowd. "Peter Drogge, when your son broke his leg and the digital doctor said nothing could be done, who set the bones?"

"You did." The boy, now about eight-years-old, called to her, "You should see how fast I can run now, Emma!"

The Bishop sputtered. These people, his people, had trafficked in sin, terrible sin. "Hear me you stranger-loving wretches. You will burn, burn in an everlasting lake of fire!"

Emma answered him, her voice loud, clear, and loving. "The Bishop offers you fear, fear and hate, but I ask you: Will fear feed your children? Will obedience keep you warm when winter comes? I am a daughter of the Tribes of Eden. We have food, we have tools, we have knowledge. We have always lived off the GRID, even since before the Fall. We offer you peace and friendship."

A pained wail erupted from the Bishop. "Noooo! She tempts falsely, these are lies, filthy lies." He turned to face the people, the mask of his certainty pulled rudely aside by his ferocious hate. He beseeched them. "Believe! People, believe in the GRID! The GRID cares for you, the GRID protects you. I beg you, do not lose hope."

"How will you feed the children, Bishop? How will you clothe them? How will you keep them warm and safe?"

The people cried out to Emma, "Who are you? How do you know us? Did the GRID send you? Where do you come from?"

Emma felt the world shift on its axis; felt the rush of a new life enter into her being. She raised her arms to quiet the crowd. "I am Emma Thomas. I am a child of the Tribes of Eden...I am the Peacemaker. I have come to welcome you into my family." She swung gracefully down from the watchtower landing lightly on the ground inside the Demo.

By mid-afternoon, the Bishop had grudgingly ceded authority to Cody Brooks and a Council of Elders. Emma invited Kenny-Boy to return to the Shire with her so that he could verify the claims she had made. He conferred with the Bishop, then agreed to join her. In the early evening, a crowd accompanied them to the south gate. They watched in anxious silence as they left beyond the Demo's wall and disappeared into the forest.

Emma could feel Doc nearby, out of sight, watching. An hour later they topped a rise, and the stallion let her glimpse him passing noiselessly among the trees. The light of day began to fade, and Emma announced her intention to make camp.

Kenny-Boy crouched low over his rucksack. "You didn't really think you'd get away with this, did you, you goddamned witch?" He withdrew the blade he had hidden inside the bag. "The Bishop and I agree. You deserve to die for what you've done. When I get back, I'll kill off that prune-faced traitor Brooks, too."

"Kenny-Boy, you don't want to do this," Emma pleaded.

"Oh, yes. Oh, yes, by God, I do. I promised the Bishop, swore to him I wouldn't let you get away this time."

"Put the knife down Kenny-Boy. Put it down and I'll protect you." She could already feel the thudding of the earth through her moccasin's thin leather soles. She begged, "Please, Kenny-Boy. It's not too late."

The Captain of the Watch snarled, "Bullshit! I'm sending you straight to Hell, you goddamned witch."

Kenny-Boy charged, blade raised high. Emma dove to the ground and rolled away. Two-thousand pounds of furious horseflesh plowed into Kenny-Boy, slamming him against the earth. The machete tumbled noiselessly to the forest floor. The stallion wheeled, eager to finish his work. Emma stood, putting herself between him and Kenny-Boy.

"No, Doc!" The stallion snorted and circled but held his ground. Emma turned her attention to the wounded man. His nose spurted bright red blood. Several ribs were broken, but he could move his arms and legs. He would live. She bent down low over Kenny-Boy and pinched his broken nose with her fingers, staunching the flow of blood. Her face inches from his she whispered, "If you ever try to hurt me again, Doc will find you, and he will kill you. No matter how far or how fast you run. Do you understand me?"

Kenny-Boy nodded stiffly. "I do. I do understand. I—I'm sorry."

Emma ruffed his muddy hair. Then she went to Doc. She whispered to him and he turned and trotted into the forest. Emma found Kenny-Boy's weapon. This was the blade that had twice nearly killed her. She walked to the bank of the stream and flung it into its depth. The episode concluded, she set to work making a fire.

Two days and thirty painful miles later, the two stepped into the Aunties' garden. Haleigh approached Kenny-Boy. He was dirty, his clothes ragged and torn, his face a mask of pain. Without speaking, she put her arms around him. The former Captain of the Watch leaned against her and grieved without limit. When he was done, Haleigh pulled a kerchief from her apron pocket and wiped his face, cleaning away the blood, dirt, and tears.

The Peacemaker said, "Aunt Haleigh, Aunt Hannah, this is Kenneth of Cazenovia. He is a good man."

345

Hannah laid her hands upon his shoulders, looked deep into his eyes, and said, "Kenneth, you are welcome here."

The Director of the GRID's Department of Security and Justice looked out the window of his office and let his eyes rest upon the city. It remained the greatest city in the world. Its lights still burned bright. The decay that was eating at the edge of the GRID had yet to touch its center.

The world's most powerful engine for stability, safety, and satisfaction was crumbling. At first, the losses had been rationalized as a matter of "right-sizing". Rural Demos at dead-ends of long supply chains were zeroed out. It was logical, and the choices were made voluntarily as part of a larger strategic vision. The Chairman called it 'pruning' in the belief that the cuts would lead to healthy new growth.

But there was no growth.

Now the time had come to make the hard choices.

The Director refocused his eyes on the pane of glass in front of which he stood. His once pale blonde hair was now mostly gray; his face bore the lines that came with unrelenting worry, fear, and loneliness.

The Chairman had called him directly and demanded a position on what was now called "the contraction issue". It was due by morning. The Director turned away from the window, clasped his hands behind his back, and began to pace. It had been so simple in the early days. The Chairman had backed Knox's pilot program in the rural northeast and it had gone well. The zeroed out Demos simply disappeared and were never heard from again. No blowback.

Now the dynamics were changing; instead of abandoned Demos—cold, hungry, and afraid—at its frontier, the GRID now faced the Tribes of Eden.

The Chairman said that he could feel them out there, in the dark distance, could feel the weight of their presence. Fear was the coin of the GRID's realm, and the old man was afraid. The Tribes haunted his sleep, swarmed through his dreams. It was not enough that the Tribes of Eden had never attacked the GRID, had never even approached the GRID. Perversely, it was their mystery and their disturbing passivity that provoked fear among the powerful.

Pressure was building for pre-emptive war against the Tribes. The Militia was eager to launch a series of attacks since doing so would bolster its claim to resources. The proposed strikes on "non-GRID population centers" were designed to sound clean and surgical.

Knox knew better.

People, innocent people, were going to suffer. The times demanded human sacrifices—there was no other way. The fear, like an invasive cancer, had spread too far. He dropped heavily into his chair and asked the workstation to display the most recent draft. His eyes flew across the text.

The office of the Chairman is correct to identify the growth and increasing coordination of non-GRID activities outside of the sphere of GRID action as an issue requiring a timely and effective response.

The Director rubbed his eyes. He hated the stilted sound of GRID-speak. The antiseptic syntax always obscured the dirty business at hand. The words themselves were lies.

Knox would be gracious to the Militia, though no one would be fooled. The senior officer's corps hated him for putting them back on a leash.

General Sampson has noted, correctly, tribal targets are 'soft' targets. Eden has no weapons, no ability to produce weapons, no military organization of any kind. I agree with the General. Operations directed against the Tribes could be concluded swiftly and with maximum lethality. The risk of losses on our side ranges from negligible to zero.

Though he was alone, Knox grinned with anticipation. Every trap needed...bait.

The concern of the DSJ lies with the after-action consequences. It must be noted that General Sampson is descended from people who now live in the heart of the Eden Tribal area.

Sampson was a thug whose mysterious background had long been the source of rumors. The Chairman would fret over the prospect of a General with potentially divided loyalties. Evidence would be demanded. The DSJ would forward faked transcripts.

All hell would break loose.

Knox snapped the trap shut.

Our Department's Special Operations Unit has been tracking a conspiracy which we believe may include General Sampson and members of his staff. Based on available evidence, I am forced to conclude that General Sampson and his co-conspirator's true plan is to use the proposed attacks against Eden to arouse and then arm the Tribes. Senior figures in the Militia see them as potential allies in a treasonous plot against the integrity of the GRID. Therefore, I am recommending that offensive Militia operations against the Tribes of Eden be delayed until such time as this conspiracy can be fully investigated.

There would be war, bloody war, but it would be between the DSJ and the Militia. If the DSJ prevailed, Knox knew, the Tribes would remain untouched.

The Director sighed heavily, and said, "Send report to Chairman." He looked at the antique digital clock on his desk. It read 02:30. Knox stood, returned to the window, and searched the darkness beyond the city. She was out there. He knew her legend well. She was the Peacemaker. She was the mother of the many tribes, the woman who rode across the night whenever the GRID withdrew.

He closed his eyes and tried to recall her scent. He still loved her—loved her more than ever. Turning away from the window, he walked to the elevator. He punched the button. The doors opened instantly, ready to whisk him to his penthouse apartment and its lonely bed.

69
GONE
2067

The waning moon was nearly down when the sound of hoof beats woke Emma from a deep sleep.

She tensed and listened hard. Something was wrong with Doc. She slipped on her robe and hurried downstairs and out the back door.

The stallion, black as night, stood at the edge of the clearing waiting for her. Emma listened again. His breathing was ragged, irregular. He was sick. She ran to him. Before she had closed half of the distance between them, Doc turned clumsily and hobbled in retreat. The fading moonlight exposed the deep gashes that raked his flanks and hindquarters. Emma sniffed the air. The wounds were infected. The stallion was weak with fever.

She stopped and spoke to him, "Doc, please." He chuffed softly, the sound as pure and sweet as any baby's coo. "Doc, I can help you. Let me help you." When she stepped forward again, the horse retreated to the edge of the forest. A cloud scudded across the moon, dimming its light.

"Please, Doc," she pleaded.

He watched her, felt her presence, drank in her scent.

Gradually, Emma understood he had come to say goodbye. She clasped a hand to her mouth and stifled a wail of grief. Then her body doubled, wracked by sobs she could not control. She staggered, but did not fall. She needed to be strong, for him. Grief could come later. Emma stood and looked her oldest friend in the eye. Doc returned her gaze. He was in pain. It was time for him to go.

She knew he saw her pain, too.

Emma put her hands together in the manner of a child at prayer and made a deep, slow bow, in honor of her dearest companion.

Nostrils flaring, eyes wide with effort, he shook his mane, the way Emma loved so much. Then he bent his great muscled neck and lowered his head before Emma, acknowledging her as the one creature that had earned his trust and his love. He spoke wordlessly, "I love you Emma. I have always loved you, more than life itself."

It was done.

He turned stiffly away from her and disappeared into the dense night of the forest, beyond the reach even of the moonlight. Emma quickened her senses and heard the fall of his hooves on the warm black earth. The sound, which she knew as well as the beating of her own heart, faded then disappeared into the night.

E mma decided it was easiest to leave the front door standing open. The house was full of the women and the girls she loved, family and friends all. They were gathered to help her celebrate. Sadie, Chloe, and Chloe's girls, now grown, were out on the Green raising the tent where the party would be held after. Tatiana of Cazenovia, a Master Brewer, swept into the kitchen. She married Kenneth in '59 and they made love and beer together ever since. Her oldest daughter carried a cask of the family's best on her shoulder. "Emma, old friend, where should Nina put this?"

The wooden trestle table was already piled high with food and drink. "It'll have to go on the back patio, not that it'll last very long."

Tatiana eyed the crowd affectionately. "A thirsty bunch, I'd say. My favorite kind of people." She hugged Emma. "I'm so happy for you."

The women ate and drank, laughed and cried, sang and danced. Together, they waited for the Moon.

Haleigh and Hannah stood together in the center of the labyrinth. At moonrise, Haleigh's frayed voice asked, "Who among us is ready to become a Crone?"

"I am."

"Come forward."

Emma walked into the center and took her place beside them. She looked up into the darkening sky and found the pale yellow light of Saturn high overhead. The planet stood in the very spot it had occupied on the day she was born. Once every 19 years, three times in all, it had returned there. This was her fifty-seventh birthday. She lowered her gaze. Around her, ordered according to their ages, stood a circle of women and girls. Each held an unlit candle. When the Strawberry Moon climbed high enough to cast a shadow, Haleigh faced Emma and asked, "Who are you?"

"I am Emma of the Shire, the daughter of Val, the granddaughter of Jude and Kianna. I am a healer, a Post Rider, a lover, a midwife, an artist, and a teller of stories. I am both the daughter of and the mother of the Tribes of Eden. I am the one people call the Peacemaker."

Hannah lit the candle of the youngest among them. The girl, just four-years-old, solemnly turned and lit the candle held by a girl to her left. Soon, a dozen tender faces glowed with reflected light. Emma thought of her childhood. She remembered growing up, wild and free, racing barefoot across meadows heavy with morning dew.

When the light came to the young women, she remembered the world as it was when she was their age. Beyond the Shire, the GRID's Demos teemed with fear, hate, and ignorance. The jagged edge of that hate had nearly killed her.

The flame passed to the mothers, women in the thickest part of life. It was the time of making, the time of love and sacrifice. She thought of the men she had known and loved. They married other women, started families of their own. Motherhood was a joy she would never taste.

Then came the young Crones. These were the women she knew since childhood. She looked into their faces and saw her own. The wrinkles, etched by time, the lines of worry and laughter, those were hers as well. The knowledge that their lives were already more than halfway lived, they shared that too. Lit from above by the light of the moon and from below by a candle, they were beautiful, and so was she.

Finally, the flame passed to the Old Crones. She admired them. Admired their poise, the graceful way they draped the mantle of age across their shoulders. They were what she might still become. When the candle held by the oldest Crone was alight, the circle was complete.

It was Hannah's turn to speak. "A Crone understands that she must give before she can receive the gifts of age. Are you prepared for this exchange?"

"I am."

Hannah escorted her niece to the eastern most point of the circle. "Your limbs once did your bidding without hesitation. Your face was smooth and unblemished and you knew little of life's worries or cares. Are you willing to set your youth aside?"

"I am."

"I offer you Elderhood in return. Know that your mind and body are just as they should be. You are as you should be. The Crone finds new beauty in age. It is a loveliness that the maiden cannot know. Honor this beauty, and it will honor you."

Hannah walked slowly to the south of the circle. "Once you held within you the potential for bringing forth new life. Now your wise blood flows no more. Are you willing to surrender the dream of making new life?"

Emma laid her hand upon her womb, ready, at last, to leave its aching emptiness behind. She said, "I am."

"Then age shall bring you the gift of understanding. Your wisdom, your patience, and your counsel will allow you to guide the young of many mothers."

Hannah found the circle's northern edge. "For too long, you've taken the promise of good health for granted. Are you ready to accept weakness and frailty when they come into your life?"

"I am."

"In time, and if fortune favors you, you will enrich the lives of others by allowing them to care for you. I offer you the blessing of knowing how to receive that care gracefully."

Hannah brought Emma to the western most point of the circle. "During your youth you clung to the belief that you were immortal. Are you ready now to surrender that illusion?"

"I am."

"Accepting that death will come gives depth to life. As a Crone you will have so much less to fear. I give you the freedom to speak and write and do as you think best."

They returned to the center of the circle and Haleigh said, "In the company of these women in the place on this night, you begin a new journey. You are, my dear sweet Emma, a Crone of the Tribes of Eden."

Their candles raised high, the women came forward to congratulate the Shire's youngest Crone.

NEWS FROM CHARLESTON
One Year Later

Emma left Bywater and headed east, staff in hand, along the Turnpike's long gentle climb up to Frogmorton. The Council of Elders would meet at the Long House during the afternoon. She wanted to be there, as a Crone and an Elder of the Tribes, she needed to be there. She had plenty of time, and the spring sunshine felt good on her skin. She walked alone, content with her unexpected solitude. Just above the watering troughs that marked the midpoint of the climb, an unfamiliar voice disturbed the stillness. She stopped, turned, and faced the man who called to her.

He was young, not more than thirty. His hair, a tangled mess of strawberry blonde, fell down onto his shoulders. She was taller than him, but not by much. He wore a fine jacket over a collared blue shirt. The tailored trousers were light brown. The material was exotic. Cotton.

He repeated himself, "Pardon me, Ma'am."

She welcomed him with a smile. The accent was unfamiliar. He had come far. She glanced down and saw that he fiddled nervously with the sheet of yellowed paper he held in his hands. It was a map.

Emma rested her staff against her shoulder. "What can I do for you?"

"Ma'am. My name is Edward L. Newburn and I hail from the great port city of Charleston." Emma did not recognize the name. "It's south, pretty far south," he explained. She nodded, encouraging him to continue. "Ma'am. I come in search of a place people called the Shire."

"This is the Shire."

"Hot damn!" he whooped. Then, remembering his manners, struggled to reassert an attitude of polite reserve. "I was sent, I've come all this way at the request of Charleston's Council of Elders. I carry a message from them, a message for the Elders of the Shire."

"Edward Newburn, you are in luck. The Council will meet this very afternoon. Better yet, I am on my way there now. You can walk with me, if you like."

This unexpected good fortune delighted him. "Yes, Ma'am, it would be an honor."

When they arrived at the Long House, Emma showed him to the visitor's bench perched along the south wall and promised that he would be called upon when the time came. She took her usual place, next to her father. The meeting was called to order and, after the agenda was completed, Emma introduced their unexpected guest. "He comes to us with a message," she concluded.

Edward L. Newburn rose to speak. "I am a son of the Tribes of Eden. I hail from a great city far to the south of here, on the coast of the shining sea. Sailing ships come and go from its docks each and every day of the year."

The Elders listened closely. This was interesting news.

"For the past two years, Captains of some of these ships have returned home telling of a strange occurrence. They report sailing into the sight of land where their charts say there should be no land. When they approach," he hesitated, not sure how the next bit of information would be received, "it vanishes." Emma was not the only one who gasped. "The Captains have consulted the Council of Elders and these incidents have been discussed at length." He paused again, now confident the Council would hear him out. "The Elders believe this land may be Kallimos itself. They believe the land can only be glimpsed because it's waiting."

A Crone asked, "Edward, what do the Elders think Kallimos is waiting for?"

"They believe Kallimos seeks the one people call the 'Peacemaker' and will show itself only to her. I come in search of her, to ask her to return to Charleston with me, to ask her if she will sail for Kallimos."

Emma Thomas' right hand clutched the gold band hung from the chain around her neck. She felt the gaze of every person in the room.

72
TWO OLD WOMEN

The north wind came to Kallimos bringing with it the tang of air—sharp, cool, and clear. Two old women felt it move across the land and decided it was a good day to climb up into the Summer Hills. They left their homes in the village and wound their way along the ridge that ran up and into the high ground. They stopped often to rest, recover their breath, nurture their hope. When they reached the summit, the sun was bent low behind them. It cast their shadows, long and thin, onto a rocky ledge.

The oldest swayed with the breeze, took it into her lungs, let it become part of her. "Can you feel her?"

The younger Crone watched the gray sea sparkle as the sun touched the distant horizon. She nodded.

"Yes. Soon, she will be here."

JOIN THE EDEN UNDERGROUND AT
WWW.EDENUNDERGROUND.COM

ABOUT THE AUTHOR

WILLIAM H. THOMAS was born in Tioga County, New York, and is the author of five previous books and two plays. Thomas' most recent book, *What Are Old People For?* draws on sources as diverse as evolutionary biology, Shakespearean sonnets, and Greek philosophy to make the case that elders belong in the heart of society.

After graduating from Harvard Medical School, Thomas spent 18 years living "off-the-grid" on a wind- and solar-powered organic farm in upstate New York. The prequel to this novel, *In the Arms of Elders*, tells the fictional autobiographical story of the Thomas' journey to the land of Kallimos and the origins of The Eden Alternative.

A visionary and internationally renowned expert on aging, Thomas is an Ashoka Fellow and winner of the Heinz Award for the Human Condition. In partnership with his wife, Judith Meyers-Thomas, he created The Eden Alternative and The Green House Project, both models to revolutionize nursing home care.

Thomas is a geriatrician, musician, professor, and public speaker. He now resides in Ithaca, New York, with his wife, three sons, and two daughters.

ABOUT THE EDEN ALTERNATIVE

THE EDEN ALTERNATIVE is a global non-profit seeking to remake the experience of aging around the world. Founded in 1991 by William and Judith Thomas, its core mission is dedicated to eliminating the plagues of loneliness, helplessness, and boredom that make life intolerable in most of today's long-term care facilities.

The Eden Alternative shows how companionship, the opportunity to give meaningful care to other living things, and the variety and spontaneity that mark an enlivened environment can succeed where pills and therapies often fail. Places that have adopted The Eden Alternative are typically filled with plants and animals, and are regularly visited by children.

Studies show that implementation of The Eden Alternative is a powerful tool for improving quality of life and quality of care for those living in nursing homes. Also, in homes that have adopted Eden as an organization-wide philosophy, there is often improved staff satisfaction and retention and significant decreases in the overuse of medications and restraints. Most importantly, Elders, supported by their caregivers, can once again direct their own daily lives.

WWW.EDENALT.ORG

A Word About the Materials Used in This Book

It was very important to the author, the publisher, and the production team to be as environmentally responsible as possible producing this book.

We chose to use Malloy, in Ann Arbor, Michigan, to print and bind this book based on their high level of commitment to environmental sustainability.

Malloy:
- Has a Zero Landfill status
- is FSC and SFI Chain-of-Custody certified
- uses vegetable- and water-based inks
- supports conservation efforts such as the Nature Conservancy's *Plant a Billion Trees* program.

www.malloy.com/environmental-commitment

The paper used in this book is 55# Rolland Enviro 100 Book Natural by Cascades Fine Papers Group, located in Saint-Jérôme, Quebec.

Cascades Rolland Enviro 100 paper:
- contains FSC certified 100% post-consumer fiber
- is certified EcoLogo and Processed Chlorine Free (PCF)
- is manufactured using biogas energy

For every short ton of this paper used*, compared to its virgin (0% recycled content) equivalent, these valuable resources were saved:
- 17 trees
- 16,546 gallons of water
- 5,437 lbs of greenhouse gases
- 2,092 lbs of solid waste

*this print run used roughly 6,000 lbs of paper, which equals 3 short tons

www.cascades.com